PAPARAZZI SUMMER

Eric Zeidler began cranking out a "quantity over quality" experiment as part of National Novel Writing Month in 2004. The result, a listing Tower of Babel, was compared by one reader to a brass band with too many instruments. Zeidler cut whole chapters and passages, trimming it down to one-third its original length. The manuscript still lacked cohesion, and Zeidler abandoned it as a failure. In 2011, after a serious illness and lengthy convalescence, he honed and chiseled the structure one last time.

By Eric Zeidler

1979
(edited by Jane Soslowski)

Life and Death in the Stone Age

The Truths That Won't Stop

In preparation:

Red Cell Ghosts: Collected Stories and Fragments

Strange Holiday

Shingle Springs (A Story of First Love)

ERIC ZEIDLER

PAPARAZZI SUMMER

TSEKH POETOV
An Imprint of Mad Tom *Publishers*

First published in the USA 2014 by
Tsekh Poetov
an imprint of Mad Tom Publishers
30 Miller Avenue
Dallas, Texas 75206
audumlasvyataya@aol.com

Cover photograph by Eric Zeidler

Printed and bound in USA by
Lulu.com
ISBN pbk. 978-0-578-15004-8

CONTENTS

ACKNOWLEDGMENTS

The author would like to recognise and thank the following individuals, all of whom in one way or another contributed to the finished manuscript: Patrick LoBrutto, Allison Low, Heidi Lamb, Victoria Scott, Ann Ralston, Susannah Benedetti, Christopher Andrews, Rita Schmig, and Andre Anthony.

I stared at the headline:

FERD BAGS HIMSELF A PLUMP JUICY DUCK!

The duck in question (Blussian) was far from 'juicy' in my subjective opinion. Rich she certainly was, and that counted for a lot—at least to Ferdinand, my debt-ridden father. But above and beyond all other considerations, she still made the Tabloids.

A pair of bewigged footmen flung the doors open, and Ferdinand himself strode gracefully into the room. He was a middle-aged Siamese, with velvety ears and a coal-black, sleek muzzle. His blue eyes can be striking. I always find myself looking away when he makes one of his dramatic entrances. The contradiction—between what he looks like, and what he actually *is*—is too painful, otherwise.

"Good evening, Children," he meowed.

I looked down at my unfashionable shoes. They needed polishing. I could hear the chair creaking slightly as he seated himself at the head of the table and asked the butler, Matthias, to bring him a generous helping of baked sturgeon.

Annie couldn't contain herself any longer:

"Did you have something you wanted to tell us?"

"I reckon you've seen that sorry gaggle of frustrated journalists camped outside. I'm sorry. They only grow more persistent if you try to avoid them."

"So why are they here?" she demanded.

Her fangs gleamed in the wattage of the overly bright chandelier.

"Can I go upstairs and talk to Blussian now?" Maria unexpectedly demanded in that snuffling, congested-sounding voice of hers.

"Blussian?" our father, thrown off balance, mechanically repeated the name.

"She's upstairs?" Annie gasped in a choking voice.

Her own large blue eyes (which everyone always goes into raptures over, gushing on and on about how she inherited them from her 'illustrious' father) were positively flashing, like gem stones from which the candlelight was striking millions of microscopic but spine-tingling sparks.

Ferdinand must've felt them. Or maybe he was just unusually discomfited. In our family, discomfiture takes the place of embarrassment.

"Uh, Maria, sweetheart—"

"I know she's upstairs."

"Now what makes you think that?" he forced a smile from g-d knows where. And believe it or not, it actually wavered for a moment before solidifying on that surprisingly adaptable, friendly-looking mug (that a thousand tabloids have celebrated).

"I can see through walls and doors."

"Now Maria, sweetheart," he sighed expansively, "Sugar Plum, Dear Little Sprite—we've discussed this a number of times, haven't we?"

She nodded.

"And you've sat in Dr Ginzburg's office and so much as told me, to my face, that all this talk, about seeing through solid objects, was merely a stunt—an understandable one, mind—I know I've been a rotten father, but all that's going to change, I promise you—I know it's a shock, reading all that blather in the tabloids, but, kids, just give her a chance, please?"

"I told you that because Dr Ginzburg, before you joined us, explained that I damn well *better* say that—I was looking you straight in the eyes, and seeing nothing but eye-sockets; there was nothing but a *skull*—"

"That's enough," he yowled, the smile vanishing.

(It was my turn to smile: his countenance *did* suddenly look rather skull-like, and haggard.)

"May I please go upstairs and see her?"

"Depends what you want to see her about."

"Bloody Fangs of Mother Bast," Annie blasphemed, "So she *is* up there. Sounds like Maria knows her stuff. Maybe this X-ray vision could be marketed somehow; you're certainly gonna need the income—the Lady Blussian has damned expensive tastes, from what I read in the papers."

"When did she get here?" I tried to make myself heard, "You better not have let her go in my room."

"Maria, Honey," he persisted, having got down on his knees beside her chair, staring with those empty skull-like sockets into the scared, searching eyes of his daughter, "I want you to tell me something. What, exactly, do you plan on discussing with Blussian? Cause if it's any of this—this psycho-babble—"

"He's afraid she's gonna say something compromising," Annie guffawed, slamming her fist down on the table-cloth, "He's afraid Blussian might have second thoughts—"

"IF YOU DON'T SHUT YOUR MOUTH I'LL SLAP IT SHUT!" the Cat screeched, whirling round, nearly upsetting empty chairs as he bounded across to where Annie sat, arms crossed, defiantly staring him down.

For what seemed an eternity (except that it didn't last long enough), my father and sister faced each other, breathing hard. Annie was always his Little Darling, the pampered favourite; *I* was always the bookworm, the oddball, the freak. Even when Annie broke the rules, he always contrived somehow to whitewash what had happened, exalting the misconduct, gilding the transgression as though it were something prodigiously fresh and clever, which we dullards, the rest of his children, could never hope to achieve.

Last summer she'd pulled all the stops. There was a club called "Teach Me to Put My Fat Lips Together and Scream" (better known as "The Perforated Eardrum"). Annie made it famous. She placed it on the map, so to speak. Suddenly she was getting her picture on page 34, page 17—right before the end of the summer she'd even made it to Page One, once or twice (she was photogenic—especially when getting arrested).

Our Mother, Jane, fought only for me and Douglas. Isn't that strange? Five children, and the custody fight bypasses three of the five. She must've known how that would look to the

Court—and even worse, to the tabloids. Her solicitor tried to force me to take the stand. I refused. I wasn't going to say which one I wanted to live with. Maybe I didn't want to live with either of them. Maybe I wanted them to stay together so I could go on living with both of them. Even now, I'm not quite sure what I wanted (or want).

I confided as much to my friend Marc. Believe it or not, I actually did have one friend. And unlike Annie's boys (some of whom happen to be friendly, on the side, as a by-product), this one—mine—was a friend who just happened, also, to be, at the same time, a boy.

But I'm getting ahead of myself.

At last, flexing his jaw muscles, our father backed down, unable to continue returning his little virago's charged gaze. To my surprise, Annie didn't savour her victory. She got up from the table, kicked her chair over, and strode out of the room.

We could hear her stomping up the stairs. Her heels struck against the marble with a loud cracking sound. It was like a series of cap-guns going off.

Ferdinand wiped his mouth, rang the little silver bell, and instructed Matthias to clear the table. He then said:

"I'm sorry for all the fireworks and turbulence to which you kids have been subjected for so long. I really am. You can believe me, or not. I've been a pretty ghastly parent, but at least I'm honest about it. You have to give me that much. And here's a nice tidbit for that little diary of yours, Sylvia: I do it because I can't help it. I'm a pathetic, miserable poltroon, but at least I'm not a hypocrite, or a sadist. I'm suffering from what's called an addictive personality. I'm seeing a new shrink, Dr Polhemus, a Great Dane. He charges the highest fees in the world, so I'd say he's no slouch. How much he charges, never mind. He's damned expensive, let's just leave it at that. And he ran a battery of tests, gave me a complete physical, examined me for hours and hours, probing forgotten memories, fears, aspirations. He tells me I'm a gambler, a sex addict, an alcoholic—when I was growing up, they didn't have labels for these terrible weaknesses."

His eyes were actually filling with tears.

"All they had was blame. Blame, and hatefulness. But now we have labels. Label something, and you're half on the road to licking it—"

"Specially if it's a good lick of Cocaine, right, Dad?" I shouted at the top of my voice.

"You can go right on punishing me, Sylvia—for the fact that I'm addicted, to pleasure—pleasure can be a mighty slippery thing, especially for a tired sad little kid like yourself, who's never known any—who's never had the guts to go after any."

"Why do we always wind up at each other's throats?" I tried to make my voice as hoarse and quavering as I could. It was of course a manoeuvre, trying to flush him out into the open, so he'd lower his guard. I'd got some good hard hurtful jabs in, in the past, by seeming to sit there all alone in the dust, tired and vulnerable.

Blussian must've given my Dad a new lease on life. He straightened his collar, facing the looking-glass over the mantel. Then he adjusted his cufflinks, re-knotted his cravat, admired his long black sleek muscular tail lashing between his elegant coattails, and with a flourish paused at the double doors. He never could resist the proverbial parting shot.

"I'll tell Blussian you wanted to speak with her, Maria. She'll be touched. We're traveling to the French Riviera for the next fortnight, at least. Blussian has quite a bit of prime real-estate tucked away down there. We'd like to have it appraised, and do some partying, on the side. Read the papers," he gave a half snort. "Vicarious fun can be almost as good as the real thing—actually, that's not true; I'm just trying to cheer you girls up. It's *not* as good. It's like one-twentieth as good. Take it from a connoisseur. But that one-twentieth of a slice of venison, that smidgeon of gristle, that piddling breadcrumb— when you're starving, it sure can taste good."

With that, he broke into a loud roaring guffaw. Pleased with himself, he staggered out through the double doors. The footmen, exchanging inscrutable glances, closed them with a soft click.

My best friend Helen shewed me the tabloids every morning before school. She smuggled them into the house in her frayed rucksack which none of the domestics would've even thought to inspect. Our father, you see, had issued stern instructions that his children were to be kept from reading the newspapers, or watching television. Impossible task. The damn television was blaring from every shop window; the tabloids with their lurid screaming headlines were everywhere, spilling out across the pavement—from every newsstand—like some stinking catch-of-the-day.

I think the servants wouldn't have enforced this embargo too strictly in any case; they were tired, and demoralised. The shenanigans of the past decade, played out behind closed doors but always just under their quivering noses, would've been enough to sap the moral strength of a Heracles.

On the way to school the next morning I got a splitsecond glimpse of my secret 'boy-friend' Marc peering from the window of his armour-plated limousine. My heart of course began hammering like a small animal trying to escape the cage of my chest, and I felt a surge of warmth shooting down to the tips of my toes.

A mechanised detachment of paparazzi materialised from out of nowhere, cameras going off, bulbs popping, minicams jostling one another. I strained all the harder for just one more glimpse, a flash of gold fur. He was one of those adolescent Lions, still half cub half untested adult, his burnished mane catching and imprisoning the sunlight, giving it back to mortal sight refined, like a kaleidoscope separating the dazzle into blurry oranges, glowing greens, cool dripping purple-reds.

Not that his golden fur, and green eyes, and long lashes, and big floppy paws that scarcely knew their own strength weren't also indescribably beautiful. But in the rough-and-tumble of slavering paparazzi and snarling bodyguards each justifying the others' existence—amidst the flurry and crush of ungainly limbs and waving cameras—the sunbeams danced and flashed round a blazing halo which kept disclosing itself in splitsecond flashes and winkings of Morse code (the way a flake of micah winks on a hillside of worthless shale, reaching out to the geologist from miles and miles across an impassable valley). Abruptly the object of all this scrambling and shoving got swallowed up at the entrance to the East Annex of the school building, and the metal doors slammed in the very snouts of the jostling paparazzi and parasites.

"Coming to the assembly?" he whispered towards the end of our first-period class (Rhetoric, taught by Silenus).

"The assembly?" I stupidly frowned.

"Here's a flyer," he chuckled.

The piece of paper he thrust at me was mimeographed with the words in boldface: JUST SAY NO.

"What's it about?" I asked.

The bell had sounded, and a river of yelping, gibbering kids had begun pouring from the classrooms, bearing us along towards the auditorium.

"It's about the dangers of turning your back on chastity," he grinned, "and taking those first steps along the primrose path leading to adolescent fornication."

He was so beautiful, I couldn't stand it.

"Which of course you and I, being moral teenagers, both completely abjure."

I couldn't take my eyes off him. His fur was so golden. The grace of his fluid movements had me stumbling along in a daze. I always felt so stupid in Marc's presence. I wondered what it was made him seek me out, day after day.

The assembly was so offensive, I could scarcely endure it. This idiot painted pony who introduced himself as Nigel was bemoaning the effects of having fornicated—more times than he could count.

8

"I was seventeen and a half," he tried to sound tearful, but the effect his nasal, braying monotone produced was one of inescapable boredom. There were long pauses and painful interludes during which he blew his nose, stamped on the floorboards, and even played with the microphone, adjusting and endlessly readjusting it with clumsy hooves that rapped against the podium, to catcalls of indescribable obscenity (which I shrink from transcribing). The most frequent admonition was for the Ruminant to lower his trousers and give us a demonstration with some willing accomplice from the ranks of the faculty as to why it had taken him till the ripe age of seventeen—when most of my depraved classmates had become quite 'jaded' by the onset of pubescence (some even earlier).

"I remember this filly from our 4-H club," he whickered listlessly, his inexpressive eyes failing to reflect even the weakest glimmer of life. "She was…I don't remember her name, but she was my best friend. I mean, she was…like…like, a friend, y'know. Someone…like…I could talk to."

"*Scandalous*," Marc whispered in my ear startling the hell out of me—I thought he'd sat down at the very end of the back row, beside the fire-exit. That had always been his favourite perch to sit out these ridiculous and insulting assemblies. Now, however, he'd moved up to the row behind me, and was leaning forward to whisper. I hoped this demonstration of intimacy wouldn't compromise him. (Already a number of my persecutors were nudging one another, and pointing.)

"Added to which, this Nigel doesn't seem very bright."

"No, he doesn't," I whispered back, hoping that his brazen indiscretion in so publicly switching seats would be forgotten amidst the 'entertainment' taking place on the stage.

"One night, she stayed over, in the barn, to help me clean out the hay. I felt funny. I felt all…like…warm, inside. Like…like I wan'ed—"

"To f—?" someone shouted, provoking a storm of appreciative laughter.

"You got it," the Horse nodded, ignoring the jeers and catcalls. "So when I started taking off my clothes, she, like…asked me what I was doing, and I said, I don't know, but…well…one thing led to another…and purdy soon—"

"You were f—ing!" several voices cried out in unison.

In response, the Administration flipped its lid, so to speak, sending Hall Monitors wading amongst us, armed with staves and colour-coordinated, remote-controlled restraining devices.

"I'm leaving," I whispered in total disgust.

"Let's go," Marcus whispered back, his warm Lion's breath raising gooseflesh beneath the sensitive fur of my slender neck and angular skull.

"Oh," I hesitated, glancing round at all the faces eagerly watching us, "Maybe…"

"Maybe we…shouldn't, she said, an' I said—"

"Let's f—!" several of the brats sitting just two rows up predictably shouted.

By the time the troublemakers had been silenced, Marcus, on reflecting, had discreetly decided that, yes, perhaps we shouldn't. His 'lapse' might be taken note of, and even discussed (within the Government—not that I would've minded, but Marc always hated being discussed—by anyone—least of all government Ministries—I think he was afraid of the Emperor finding out—or, even worse, his harpy of a Mother, Diane de Poictiers, royal concubine to several previous monarchs).

"So finally, like…we ended up doing it." He blew his nose. "An' she didn't even like it, that much."

Constant interjections and monstrously obscene catcalls kept sounding from every corner of the darkened hall. I was praying that the Headmaster, Gorm, would have the sense to put us out of our misery by terminating this joke of an assembly; I just wanted to crawl off to the nearest alcove, and catch up in my diary—Marc's indiscretion in whispering at such close quarters had been both alarming, and—terribly exciting.

"So then, I met this Zebra, who was kind of…a slut."

10

That was it. I couldn't take any more. Rising to my feet, I began scuttling down the row of seats, to a groundswell of gleeful whispers. Some sadists at the very end of the row tried to obstruct my progress. One of their number, a Pug, *bit* me in passing—I simply had to shake him loose and keep going (that evening I found that his stinking teeth had left a deep bruise).

Marcus was right behind me. We reached the foyer together. A Hall Monitor instantly accosted us. Before she could demand anything, Marc forestalled her with a quiver of those sensuous lips. The nondescript, cringing Marsupial formed quite a contrast to the splendid young Beast regally staring her down. With an imperious gesture, the Prince Imperial (he was third, or fourth, in line for the Succession) caused the drab little stooge to give way.

"C'mon," he whispered, his yellowish fangs softly clicking against his lower incisors: "I know a place where we can talk—no one should be able to find us there, but steady on—I say, Sylvia—"

My heart fluttered; his pronouncing *My Name* made it feel like the entire world had gone mad.

"They saw us leave together," I panted, conflicting impulses and emotions wrenching me to the roots of my being.

"Bugger them," he snarled with genuine passion of the sort that it's impossible to fabricate, "I'm so sick of this place—this joke of a school."

"So am I, Marc," I dared breathe his name.

He led me into a sort of glorified broom closet, locked the door, and then turned to face me. I tried to stare at his huge, bottomless eyes, without falling into them.

"Did this morning's assembly have any direct, *personal* relevance for you?" he pointedly asked me.

The unexpectedness of his question took me aback.

"I'm afraid I don't really know what you mean."

"For instance," he frowned, his delicate eyebrows becoming momentarily furrowed (according him an irresistibly boyish persona), "Have you ever—"

11

"I'm going to be late for a tryst with my lover," I shouted, astonishing myself, as I fumbled for my books.

"Sylvia, what's wrong?"

"Is that all you wanted?" I gasped, my chest heaving (and yet my eyes were perfectly dry), "To ravage me? Deflower the only virgin left in this g-dforsaken cesspool, and then brag to your rich, aristocratic friends about it?"

"Is *that* what you think of me?" he softly demanded.

Oh my g-d. What had I just said?

"Not necessarily, Marcus," my voice quavered, "It just came out—I'm insecure—I'm sorry—please forgive me?"

"I don't have many friends," he murmured as if to himself. "And the few I've managed to get close to always wind up disappointing me. I always get hurt."

"So do I," I softly whimpered, inching towards him.

"Maybe it's better not to have friends."

"You can't live in isolation," I whispered, "It doesn't work. Believe me. I know."

"How do you know?"

"Because my life was completely empty, before I met you," I swallowed a sob, staring at the filthy tiles between our feet. "And I know now that I can't go back to living that way."

"I think an animal can get used to just about anything."

"Getting used to something doesn't mean it's the right way to live."

"What is the 'right way' to live?"

"Have you ever…" I tried to bite down on my tongue, but the rebellious words defiantly came forth of their own brazen accord: "you know, been with a girl?"

He shook his head.

I mean, he shook his head: *Yes*.

He *had* been.

It felt like a knife was methodically going at right angles, making cutlets of the little bit of me that was still breathing.

"It was last spring," he grimaced, "This chambermaid; I don't know what came over me—"

12

"You don't have to tell me the details," I nearly shouted, covering my mouth in horror, staring across at his half angry, half vulnerable face.

"Did you think I was going to?"

"No, but I'd like to hear them. Or better yet..."

"Better...yet?" he shook his head in bewilderment scrunching up his beautiful eyes.

"I—can't—"

It felt like I was choking. The room spun around.

"*Sylvia*," I heard his enchanting adolescent voice roar.

The Young Lion that roared.

The room was spinning faster and faster. The last thing I remembered was his beautiful face coming closer and closer.

An explosion of laughter woke me. Loud drunken laughter. The kind of laughter that betokened my father on one of his wild drinking binges, the house full of riffraff.

"Lie still, dear," Goody Thorpe, my Nursemaid, applied a warm compress to my fevered brow. Her large watery brown eyes expressed everything: I was back home. My father was 'entertaining.' A loud, scatterbrained arpeggio of discombobulated giggling indicated that his new 'wife' (the term stuck in my throat) was obviously lolling down there, on one of the sofas, as well.

Watching me closely, Goody Thorpe skillfully handed me a plastic bucket just in time. As the tidal wave of nausea whelmed my senses, clutching and sucking at my very essence, I could well imagine the pitying look of steadfast but slightly bargain-basement compassion with which she bent over me, caressing and petting, her muscular white wing (for she was a large Hen) brushing my ears down flat against my skull and then brushing, or caressing, them again as her wing passed back the other way and they sprang upright again.

"Poor Sylvia," she whispered, "Poor little Duck."

That's what she often called me as I was growing up: Poor Little Duck.

But guess what: an actual, real life DUCK was downstairs. A duck to fuck. A fuckable potluck duck, a huckster's clucking buckshot-riddled, cuckold-producing, lucky, *lucky* fuck-duck, for fuddy-duddies like my Puckish *muck* of a fucking 'father' so stuck on himself it makes me want to puke even though I just puked my guts out.

"That is," she stammered, realising her faux pas, "I mean…"

"Never mind."

"I expect you'll be wanting to know what happened, having swooned—and in the company of a young Lion—ehh," she coughed, "a young *Imperial* Lion, and *unchaperoned*."

"Yes, well," I clicked my teeth as loudly as I could, "Perhaps then you could be so good as to tell me the news. You know, the gossip. The hot gossip concerning a baseborn Tabby found in close proximity—potentially sexual proximity—"

"It's alright, Love," she clucked soothingly, "The doctors performed an examination…"

"An 'examination' you say."

This was getting worse and worse. Beyond any nightmare.

Another drunken roar of laughter from downstairs caused my stomach to lurch, followed almost immediately by a sharp staccato knock on the door. Before I was able to say Come in (or *don't* come in), the slimiest, most despicable of all my father's creatures stood lounging—*inside* my room—twirling his oily Weasel's whiskers, and grinning.

"Mistress Sil-vyah," he smirked.

"Judd," I spat.

"Mind if I smoke?"

"State your business, and get the hell out of my room."

Goody Thorpe found it impossible to keep quiet any longer: "How *dare* you come in here—I'd like to know what you think you're about."

"Conveying a message. From the Master of the house," he smirked. "Your employer, as well as mine. Any objections?"

"Get *out*," the Hen fairly screeched, flying at him in a passion. She outweighed the vicious little weasel by a ratio of more than three to one; he gave ground steadily—till she'd chased him over the threshold, and out of my room. I lustily applauded for all I was worth.

"The Master," he snarled from the safety of the corridor, "instructed me to summon Miss Syl to come downstairs for the entertainment of his guests as well as the edification of his new *bride*." He winked offensively. "And Sweet Seti on a stinking stake—she is one hot little number. I'd sell my mother to the jackals for half an hour with a high-class hooker like that one."

I burst out laughing. It was nervous, hysterical laughter.

"Well then, Judd," I regained control of myself, "We mustn't keep the Master waiting. And this high-class hooker sounds interesting."

"That's one word fer it," he led the way (three or four paces in front of me) towards the big marble staircase that anchored the townhouse.

As my paw slid down the smooth—almost slippery—oaken bannister, the cacophonous laughter from the ground floor increased in volume. Zithers and lutes were braying dissonantly. I smiled contemptuously at the realisation that Ferdinand had actually shelled out for some 'live music'—rather than simply shoving a CD into the decaying hi-fi system (which despite its faulty wiring could still shake the rafters).

"Dearheart," he called as soon as his watery eyes had focused on my silhouette (with its incipient curvature of the spine) etched against the light streaming in from the brightly lit dining room.

Dearheart happens to be the pet name he used to call me back when I adored him, and he reciprocated (or at least kept up the pretence), ages ago.

"Is this the little Brainiac, as dahling Anas-tahsee-ah calls her?" an undeniably toothsome Duck drawled, the curves and lineaments of her person bedazzling the eye.

"Dearheart," he drunkenly repeated himself, "I'd like to present you to our royal guests—"

A duet of soft laughter some 120 degrees to my left caused me to wheel round—the most beautiful creature I'd ever seen in my life was reclining with regal voluptuousness (as only Lionesses can) on the best antique divan in the house; I could only take my eyes off her for an instant—to glance nervously at this somehow perverse-looking Lion with cunning slitted green eyes which glistened provocatively; he was attractive, but something about him caused me quickly to glance back at the

16

Lioness (besides, she was simply too magnetic to look away from for long).

"Sylvia," she murmured, "Marc speaks of you with genuine respect and compassion, which coming from Dear Marcus, as we all know, amounts to something quite priceless indeed."

At the mention of *Marc*, I felt as though the jig was up. Swaying on my feet, I heard the Lion say:

"Respect? Does he always 'respect' little spinsters like Seel-vee-ah? I hope he at least used protection."

The curvaceous Duck, Blussian, erupted into a predictable fit of monotonous quacking laughter. The Lion winked, and she blushed. I turned to stalk out of the room, but everything (including my balance) had treacherously started to tilt. I willed myself not to fall down—in front of such scum.

"And here, in this humblest of habitations," I heard my father declaiming as if from a great distance, "we find ourselves cringing before Her Imperial Highness, the Princess Delilah."

So *this* was the famed Delilah: daughter to the Emperor, and larger-than-life shipwreck to hundreds (if not thousands) of aristocratic but over-ambitious bachelors, every one of them hoping against hope…

"Sylvia? Hon?" he prompted.

"Excuse me?" I squawked hating the sound of my pusillanimous voice, "You said something, Ferdinand?"

"You haven't genuflected yet, before the Grand Duke and the Princess—one *always* performs an act of obeisance, in the presence of Royalty."

"Don't you mean, rather, an act of abasement?" the Lion, Nero, gave a thin-lipped and not very comfortable smile.

This Nero had already become something of a celebrity in his own right, even in some of the highbrow periodicals (like the *Chalice*). For one thing, he was a notorious pander, procuring all manner of whores and degraded transsexual 'creatures' for the fleeting enjoyment of the younger members of the Imperial Family. Fortunately Marcus (to my knowledge) was *not* among

17

them—and furthermore, speaking of dear Marc, he absolutely detested his degenerate cousin. Why waste ink on the more degraded, unnatural practices this Profligate was whispered to prize most unabashedly, having become an adept in all the baser conjunctions and alloys of passion?

"Perhaps she's a radical, one of these revolutionists," he sneered. "Tell us, Sylvia," his pronunciation of my name somehow made me feel tainted, "Do you believe in the abolition of the Monarchy? Have you joined the so-called People's Will? Assisted in the recruiting of terrorist cells, perchance? Or maybe you've decided to don a shroud and become one of the so-called Dark People—"

"Stop it, Nero," Delilah surprised me, "Your lack of originality is becoming conspicuous, once again."

Even more surprising, the jaded sensualist visibly coloured, flashing *me*—instead of the Princess Delilah—a look of concentrated malice that made my flesh crawl.

"Anyway," she continued, "We've got to adjourn, presently, to our respective (and separate) bedrooms. I came here to tell you what I had to say. You now know my reasons for giving in to blackmail, and marrying this degraded piece of filth."

Nero's tail began to lash back and forth. His eyes gave off a devilish glow, but it was the creature's *mouth* that sickened me the most: its elasticity, the suppleness of its myriad interconnecting little muscles—the way the slavering lips squigglingly bunched up and changed shape.

"I think Sylvia had best leave the room," Ferdinand meowed in a frightened voice. I noticed that even Blussian was no longer smiling.

"No, she needs to hear this," Delilah drawled in that extravagant voice of hers, "Any friend of Marcus—"

"Yes, but she *seduced* him," Nero lashed out, "employed her feminine wiles, and not to put too fine a point on it, fucked His Grace as many times as she could—"

"That's—a—lie," I gasped (probably turning white as a sheet). I was going to call it a monstrous lie, but my voice was

18

only good for a few words before my throat closed in on itself. To my astonishment Delilah swept over to where I was swaying and took me in her arms—instinctively I buried my face against the warm, scented fur of a Lioness in the height of her charisma and seeming invincibility.

"Of course it's a lie," she soothed.

"I have my sources," he gave an oily smirk, "And the medical exam to which they subjected her clearly established that her no-longer-virginal person was just bursting with a young Lion's discharge—"

"Watch your tongue!" my father exploded—probably more for the benefit of his new bride, or to keep from offending Delilah.

"Tell your daughter to watch her libido," he reponsded, "Unless she wants the forensic evidence to be used against her in court—"

"That's enough," Ferdinand sounded surprisingly convincing.

"One word to His Celestial Majesty—"

"I happen to know for a fact that the medical exam turned up no such thing," Delilah practically yawned, "and without direct evidence, my Father would sooner turn His displeasure—"

"How do you know there were no such results?" Nero angrily growled, "My own network of informants—"

"Invented what they thought you wanted to hear—as usual," the Lioness laughed. "You're even more of a master, my dear, at the fine art of sadism (as I've had occasion to learn, to my personal cost) than all the smears and character assassinations on which your reputation so deservedly rests—"

"How did you find out the results?" he demanded.

"Marcus told me. He also assured me that nothing took place."

"Still randy, and ready for more, I've no doubt—"

"Take no notice of my *husband*," she pretended to whisper, but with such stentorian amplification that everyone else in the room could hear every syllable, which made me feel like some sort of stage prop—rather than a distressed young Tabby needing comfort and solace.

"He's a bastard," she smiled, "with his own patented mixture of innuendo and brazen falsehood garnished here and there with bits of bleeding 'fact' sprinkled in for good measure, the confection served up steaming and raw to the tabloids (he has a controlling interest in both the *Sun* and the *Carcass*)—I was just explaining to your father, who last week asked me to marry him—"

Several people cried out: Ferdinand in outrage and mortification, myself in disgust, and the one such news most concerned (at least to my way of thinking), Blussian herself, in a loud groundswell of half jaggedly dissonant, half arpeggio-like, quacking laughter—which put Ferdinand (and Nero, as well, by the look of him) completely out of countenance. Whereupon Delilah joined in.

"Bravo, my Dear," she trilled her R's affectedly, "I salute you for being almost of my own calibre; the two of us are well matched—these poor poltroons," indicating Ferdinand and Nero, "should furnish us with a veritable smorgasbord of nonstop entertainment."

"I still don't see why you have to let this brat cheapen the evening," Nero sulked, "to the extent of demanding that her father have her summoned from upstairs, interrupting her masturbation festival—poor Marcus. I almost feel sorry for the idealistic, naive little wanker—"

"One more off-colour remark of that sort," Ferdinand hissed, his tail actually bushed out, his ears flat against his skull—

"Save it, Ferd," he pretended to snigger (though I noticed that he backed away several paces, his green eyes shifting uneasily from my father to Delilah, and back again).

"This farce of a marriage," Delilah continued, stroking my white fur (I'm afraid I began purring—it'd been so long since anyone had caressed me that way), "has of course *not* been consummated—"

20

"You treacherous little slag," Nero began—

Delilah flung me to the floor, bounding across to where the blackguard was turning to run—her roar shook the rafters.

"INSULT OTHERS AS YOU PLEASE," she snarled, baring her sharp fangs (she looked almost like some primeval Sabre-tooth'd Cat)—

"I'm—sorry—Delilah—please—"

"Address me henceforward as Your Grace," she let go of him, "Now find your way to one of the guest-rooms; I'm sure this place has hundreds of them."

"Well, not exactly hundreds," Ferdinand fussed nervously with his cravat, standing equidistant between Delilah and the scrumptious Duck lolling over on the divan by the window. I picked myself up from the floor, preparing to slink out of the room—

"Look at Sylvia trying so hard to make herself invisible," the Lioness smiled, shewing the tips of her teeth. "If only the rest of your children were similarly self-effacing; I had an interesting exchange with *darling Anastasia* this afternoon—"

"What did she say about me?" Ferdinand ejaculated, precipitating a peal of laugher from both Delilah, and Blussian. I almost felt a split-second twinge of compassion for the decaying voluptuary (he *was* my father, after all).

"First let's dispense with dear Sylvia," she placed a lean paw (the steel tendons of which were like coiled springs, bursting with force) on my knobby shoulder. "We haven't yet had *her* version of …what happened, this afternoon."

So I told them. I'm afraid I gave a highly selective account, omitting a number of my pathetic and self-revelatory little outbursts, and lapses. But isn't that the nature of the beast: trying to cast yourself in the least damaging light possible, at the expense of those around you, dragging them down, smearing their feathers with petrol? Not that I did much smearing; I mainly skipped over things.

My father's jaw became slack with disapproval and, regrettably, anger. His own social standing was so bloody important to him, so colossally all-encompassing—never mind that his daughter—flesh of his flesh—was in a jam of her own, and a tight one, at that.

"Don't you remember my having explained, time and again," he erupted towards the end of my self-justification, "that the Imperial Family—"

"Save it, Fernando," Delilah cut him off.

"I love it when you call me *Fernando*—"

"And does Blussian feel the same way?" she flared her sensitive nostrils.

We all glanced over to the divan simultaneously. But the Countess' graceful head had slipped down against the colourful plumage of her unruffled breast. She was snoring, ever so softly.

"A good idea, for all of us," my father meowed. "We have to be at the aeroport by nine o'clock sharp."

"But you still haven't explained all of this to poor little confused Sylvia," the Lioness licked her chops, her delicate earrings jingling as the large sandpapery tongue curled and snaked its way in and out between her incisors and fangs. "You're not being a very conscientious parent, Fer-nan-do."

"I love it when you call me Fernando," he arched his back, Tomcat-fashion.

"You know, Blussian's *still* your bride," I couldn't help but point out (even at the cost of defending such a hedonistic, empty-headed, self-centred creature), "Your *new* bride, wedded just a few hours ago—"

"Yes, well," he began—

"Not to make too big a deal of your predictable, run-of-the-mill infidelity—"

"Some things you're too young to understand," he steamrolled right over my moralistic little objections. "The fact that this enchanting Lioness gracing our drawing-room happens to be irresistible—"

"Sylvia's right," the 'enchanting' Lioness snuffed the candle-flame of his rising libido, "This is quite unseemly, to say the least. With your bride lying over there, dead drunk—"

22

"You're right," he shrugged, "Her behaviour *has* been unseemly—"

"It's *your* behaviour, Fer-di-nand," she nailed him, "to which I allude."

All the remaining wind went out of his sails. I could've laughed out loud, if it weren't for the slightly sneering glint lurking in Delilah's predatory, but sapphire-like, eyes.

"Of course," her tone became caressingly warm and velvety, "She might, getting back to what we were discussing earlier, be just the right medicine for him. Stranger things have happened."

For a splitsecond I actually believed that she was somehow referring to *me* (vis-à-vis Marc). I probably would've come to my senses, even if my father hadn't hastened to say, "And Nero doesn't exactly strike me as the type of Lion to disregard the voluptuous person of a Duck worth at least 75 million roubles, into the bargain."

"Yes," Delilah smiled, scarcely trying to extricate herself from my father's elastic embrace. "Into the bargain."

"And what a bargain," he indistinctly mumbled, burying his drunken face in the golden, aromatic fur of her bosom (she was wearing a rather low-cut dress, which in my opinion shewed far too much cleavage—if, indeed, a Lionness could be said to *have* cleavage)…

I'd seen enough. As I glided noiselessly out of the room I glanced at the footmen, ranged like statues along the far wall. Their eyes flickered in the dying embers of the fireplace. Blussian continued softly snoring, a drunken quack every so often punctuating the emptiness of her torpid slumber. Casting a glance over my shoulder, I saw my father attempting to unfasten one of the Lioness' satin shoulder-straps. As I hurried up the marble stairs, I tried not to listen to the mumbled gurglings and slurring of his lust-sotted voice.

23

"I can't believe so many of those vermin are following us,"
I exclaimed, more to myself than anyone else.

We'd been cruising along the M1 toward Heathrow for
what seemed an eternity, a pack of Paparazzi on motor-scooters
and leaning from the windows of souped-up Astras and Jags
making the trip a living hell—a Ferrari zoomed up alongside the
passenger window, a snaggletooth'd Norwegian Rat (the kind
that used to carry Bubonic plague—now he was carrying a
Nikon) snapping away for all he was worth—I buried my face in
the cigarette-smelling upholstery of the backseat.

We were divided between two automobiles. Nero,
Delilah, Ferdinand, and the Heifer Judith (Delilah's Lady-in-
Waiting) were comfortably speeding along in Nero's armoured
limousine (with the tinted, bulletproof windows). The rest of us
had had to pile into the family Daimler—there was plenty of
room: Annie, with consummate timing, had apparently run away
from home again (it was the fourth time since the Divorce).

"I wish *you* were the one that'd climbed out of her
bedroom window at three in the morning," Maria snufflingly
whispered, "Even Annie's a bed of roses, compared to someone
like *you*."

"Grow up," I tried to sound nonchalant.

We were crossing one of the unused runways in the back
of the aeroport. Long before I'd finished counting all the security
vehicles with their flashingr blue lights, we abruptly accelerated
into a sort of hangar. Up ahead I could just make out the two
Lions and my father being hustled through a side door. Not
surprisingly, most of the paparazzi were swarming after them,
pouring through a series of what looked like storm drains—very
fitting for the Rats, Mice, Weasels, Ferrets, Jackals and
occasional Hyenas that made up their profession. I was hoping
either to be spared the ordeal of having to run the gauntlet of their
intrusive, slavering prurience, or else (and this feeling was new to

me), I wondered what it must be like to find oneself the object of all that collective frenzy and jostling. Instead, a mangy worn-out looking coterie of second-stringers and understudies (chewed up and spit out by the seething cauldron known as Fleet Street) assailed us, but with scarcely any enthusiasm or drive. They were just going through the motions, trying to cadge a squib of text in the very back of the Afternoon Edition—most of them weren't even bothering to photograph any of us but the curvaceous, giggling Duck ushering sweet Douglas and darling Maria towards the refuge up ahead—leaving *me* to stumble along as best I could, behind them, gritting my teeth.

A wild impulse came over me to give the clustered microphones and tape-recorders something red-hot:

I'm in love. His name's Marc—and I think he loves me.

"You stupid little chit," I hissed aloud, to myself.

"*Silvyah* said something," a moth-eaten Hyena called across to the others of his tribe, shambling closer, pressing his verminous person practically in my face.

Judd materialised from out of nowhere, pulling me by the wrist towards the side-door and shoving me through.

"Let go of me," I meowed at the top of my voice, but the brute held me fast. We were in a sort of lounge, complete with expensive hors-d'oeuvres arranged enticingly on a sideboard, with mixed drinks and black rum.

"Where are the rest of my family?" I demanded.

"At the press conference," he cocked his head towards a door on the opposite side of the room.

"What about Maria and Douglas?" I shouted (the walls were probably soundproof but I actually caught myself wishing they weren't). "What've you done with them, you skulking dishonest caitiff?"

He gave my arm a sharp twist before explaining that my younger brother and sister were both *at* the press conference.

"They get to go, and I don't?" my eyes filled with tears.

"I have my instructions," the bastard smirked sanctimoniously.

"What's that supposed to mean?"

"It means you're a complete psycho," he brought his stinking face right up against my own, "a total and complete liability—"

"That's a gross oversimplification," I sulked.

"Plus let's face it: you crack lenses all over the place," he burst out laughing, so pleased with himself that for an instant he relaxed his grip on my arm. That was all I needed. Scratching his face, I twisted free—and made for the door. Flicking the latch just in time, I propelled myself like a cannonball into the midst of the press conference. Hundreds of cameras and microphones swiveled to record the disturbance; I glimpsed Nero, Delilah, Blussian and my father whirling round in various combinations of anger, astonishment, amusement, disdain—it sounded like Nero had been saying something; his mouth twisted in an ugly grimace of hatred. I heard Blussian giggling for all she was worth. My father, his mouth hanging open, just stood there, paralysed, frozen.

Only Delilah seemed completely in command of the situation. She beckoned, an enigmatic smile uncovering the tips of her teeth. As I reached the bank of microphones, Nero toatally lost it, kicking and swiping at me with his unsheathed (but manicured) claws. The cameras went crazy, filming me flinching but standing my ground—as several of Delilah's operatives subdued the raging Lion, actually dragging him off to the side. I felt a surge of adrenaline rocketing through my fibres, catapulting me into a lunar trajectory of hot burning excitement intertwined with sadistic euphoria—I'd managed to 'crash' their carefully choreographed little press conference, after all.

"My daughter, Sylvia, has psychological problems," I could hear Ferdinand trying to put the best 'spin' on the turn things had taken.

"What sort of psychological problems?"

"Was she institutionalised?"

"Is she zonked out of her head?"

26

"My good friend, Ferdinand," Delilah's cool, mesmerising voice reasserted itself, "happens to have brought his two *youngest* children, Maria and Douglas, because they already love their new Stepmother, to an almost unhealthy degree."

"We sure do—can I have some more jaw-breakers?" Dougie screeched beginning to jump up and down. No one had thought to bring his assortment of toys—well now they were gonna see, first-hand, the true meaning of *Hyperactivity*.

"Will someone shut that brat up?" Nero couldn't contain himself.

The paparazzi went wild with questions and shouted comments. In the meantime, Douglas was being whisked over to his nurse, Popova, for some sort of mysterious injection (probably Thorazine).

"Does he always act like that?"

"Do you have to send him to a special school?"

"Is he not quite right in the head?"

"My sources tell me he isn't the first of your kids to be involuntarily committed—"

"Is he under the care of a qualified child psychiatrist?"

"Does he light fires, and wet the bed?"

"D'ya think he's retarded?"

Waiting for someone—anyone—to tell these filth-mongering bastards to pick on someone their own size, I actually caught myself feeling protective—towards *Douglas*. Bear in mind that this was the most insufferable, manipulative *brat* I'd ever known in my life. And yet now I wanted to scoop him up and take the poor thing far away from all these innuendos and smear-tactics. After all, he was just a little Kitten, still chasing balls of yarn and pouncing on stuffed mice. He also happened to be my little brother. And no one else seemed to give a rat's ass— *Ferdinand* (his nominal father) was too busy ogling Delilah and darting angry glances at Nero.

"He's not retarded," I tried unsuccessfully to project my voice, "He just suffers from A.D.D.—and he may be dyslexic;

my stupid father's never had him—never had *any* of us—
tested—for anything."

My voice trailed off. Delilah was staring at me, a
forbidding look on her face. I quite literally lost my voice. My
larynx contracted, shunting off all further sound as I tremulously
gulped (and probably blenched for good measure).

Suddenly the sound of Blussian's giggly quacking caused
a look of unguarded—almost naked—jealousy to contort her
otherwise classically beautiful features. From out of nowhere the
surprisingly wily duck had seen an opening—and seized control
of the press conference (or at least managed, however fleetingly,
to make herself the momentary focus of all that concentrated,
corrosively voyeuristic excitement).

The paparazzi of course were lapping it up:
"Blussian! Oy, Blussian! Over here, for the camera!"
"What's it like, being married to Ferdinand?"
"Did you make him sign a prenuptial agreement?"
"Has the marriage been consummated?"
"Is ol' Ferdinand still any good in the sack?"
"Did he lie about his age? My sources maintain that
he did."

She simply threw back her sloping skull with its bird-of-
paradise plumage, and laughed riotously. The seasoned hacks
and filth-mongers joined in. It made me sick. I glowered across
at my father. There he was, scowling at his new wife, perhaps
regretting the way things had worked out—it was plain as the
hangover he was nursing that he was quite simply *besotted* with
Delilah—he obviously cherished the notion that She, whilst
clearly not besotted herself, might nonetheless have at least
considered a marriage proposal—if only that slimy scheming
Nero hadn't beaten him at his own game.

"What's wrong, Sylvia?" someone shouted.

Heart thumping against my ribs, I wiped the sneer off my
face, but it was probably too late—several hundred cameras had
swiveled, clicking, whirring and blinding me.

"C'mon, Syl, why the look that could curdle milk?"

28

"I enjoy cracking lenses," I gritted my teeth, jerking away from Judd who, it seemed, had sidled up from behind.

"D'you resent Ferdinand's being such a rotten parent, not to mention all the alcoholism, the neglect and so forth?"

"Do yer hate Blussian as much as yer Dad?"

"How do you feel about this new marriage?"

"Why *didn't* you testify at yer parents' divorce?"

"Yer mum told us in a recent interview that Ferdinand just loves Annie—she's clearly his favourite—"

"Are those tears we can see welling up in yer eyes?"

"Throw the floodgates open—"

"C'mon Syl, you can trust *us*."

"Say something—once you get the first word out, it'll start gushing till you can't stop it, like a good stinging long piss—"

I could scarcely breathe at this point, clawing at the air—swiping at the nervous lackeys hovering round me waiting for their chance to bundle me off someplace out of sight—sweeping me, like I'd been swept all my life, under the suffocating, proverbial carpet.

"Are you crying 'cause of *Marcus*?"

"Did you get to Third Base with 'im?"

"Admit it: you got 'im all hot, and then fucked his brains out."

"Stop it," I panted.

"Were you a virgin?"

"Was Marc a Virgin?"

"How would you rate Marc as a lover, technically speaking?"

"Is Marc 'well endowed' for a Lion?"

"What positions does he like?"

"How long does he last?"

"Does he roar when he climaxes?"

Long sinuous paws which were delicate (but with an underlying strength that began seeping into my shoulderblades, keeping me—in the nick of time—from crumpling to the ground)

29

took hold of me, the sharp claws digging into my shoulders with stabs of pain that gave me *something*—something *else*—*anything* else—to grab hold of. Looking down at my big feet as they shuffled one after the other, I could hear Delilah, as she steered me back to the lounge, calling out to the slavering vermin:

"If you had any shame, you'd examine the way you've reduced this poor child to a gibbering wreck As for Anastasia being the favourite, that's crap. Ferdinand has always loved Sylvia—and why not, she's brilliant. As for the ridiculous rumours concerning an act of fornication between Sylvia and my Cousin, the Prince Imperial, well," she gave a curt laugh, "just look at this child. Does she strike you as being a midnight temptress, a seductive, lilac-tinged slut?"

"Sluts come in all flavours, and fucking happens round the clock, every day of the year."

"In that case," she took hold of the doorknob, skillfully propping me against the door itself, bracing me with her slender but muscular thigh, "you'd best go after it, ay? You can all go fuck yourselves."

Hustling me inside, she slammed the door behind us, conducting me over to a chair in the corner. A number of servants, bodyguards, and assorted hangers-on were helping themselves to the hors-d'oeuvres; they jumped backwards in alarm. One of them dropped a silver tablespoon, loaded with caviar. At the same instant the door flew open admitting Nero followed by the Heifer Judith, and peering nervously from behind her curvaceous collarbone, my father's black velvety face with the large, soulful blue eyes, tapering ears tilted back ever so slightly, his thick spray of whiskers quivering, twitching, intent.

"That was just beautiful," Nero quaked and stomped in his rage, "I hope you're all happy. This brat has completed fucked us over, but *good.*"

"In what way has she 'fucked us over' as I believe you so elegantly phrased it?" Delilah arched her eyebrows. "Those questions and rumours are going to be seething regardless—why not address them head on? Try and put an advantageous complexion on things—make a positive, out of a negative?"

"Spare us, Delilah dear," he slammed his fist down upsetting several cups of champagne, "Just because you've started facing the paparazzi and giving press conferences—"

"I think she's done a damn brilliant job," Ferdinand raised his voice from behind Judith (whose hooves, I noticed, were firmly planted far enough apart to block anyone from coming into the room).

"Thank you, Ferdinand," Delilah smiled one of those ravishing smiles. "Though I'm afraid you're exaggerating. All the same, even if not 'brilliant' I do believe I've managed to hold my own, shall we say?"

"Beginner's luck," the Lion spat, then snarled a profanity as black caviar splatted against one of his boots; he'd stepped on the spoon.

"Yes, well," Ferdinand cleared his throat, "Couldn't we discuss this on the comfort of the Lear Jet, without all these hordes of eavedropping servants and such?"

"Give me just a few minutes, alone, with *Sylvia*," she commanded in a peremptory voice.

"We don't have time for this," Nero growled.

"Leave us."

She simply turned her back on the lot of them. In scurrying through the door, the servants carried the volubly cursing and snarling Lion on the tide of their irresistibly fearful obedience. In a flash Delilah had jumped up and bolted the door from the inside. Signing for me to remain silent, she quickly, deftly, checked all the objects in the room for hidden microphones. Apparently satisfied, she turned round to face me.

Something in her face turned my entrails to ice.

"That was stupid," she informed me. "That whole performance. Haven't you learned by now that one *never answers* them? Not unless you have an agenda of your own, with points and items for general public consumption."

31

I still couldn't speak. Gulping and swallowing, I dipped into the last reserves (praying they hadn't run dry).

"Poor Sylvia," she shook her regal head, exquisite jade earrings clinking ever so softly. "I realise you were, quite simply, short-circuited. Flummoxed. Out of your league. At first, when you were beginning to do all that damage and I had to step in—I was going to have this private chat regardless (I feel we haven't properly laid our cards down on the table, just the two of us)—but at first, I was almost resolved not to pass his message along. I see you know *whose* message we're talking about. Here, drink this; we can't have you fainting."

His message—my eardrums fluttered and the room spun around. The sweet-tasting but tart-edged stuff she proffered me slid down my throat, going straight to my head but getting there too late—those words *His message* had already lobbed me veering and zigzagging into the stratosphere. From the vantage point of which I glanced down at myself: a pale white insignificant Tabby being coddled—perhaps cozened—by a carnivourously resplendent, treacherously beautiful, overpowering Lioness.

"Marcus chatted with me over a secure phone line this morning. He's very upset."

The euphoria came crashing down in shards and fragments. My eyes filling with tears, I opened my mouth. Taking hold of my upper lip (her sharp claws pierced my sensitive skin) she gently but inexorably closed it again. I was surprised not to smell any perfume, just a dry sage-like essence (and possibly a far-off ghost-like suspicion of broome).

"Says it was his fault," she continued—

It was my fault, I tried to speak, but her paw was still clamped over my mouth.

"I apologise for having perhaps half doubted your truthfulness. Not that it matters to me whether the two of you fuck yourselves numb."

I winced.

"Just be discreet, and don't get caught. He's not the one who'll pay the price: *you* will. Remember that."

She took her hand away from my mouth—which flew open with babbling words to the effect that we never in our wildest dreams could have harboured the slightest inclination or predisposition towards the fleetingest whiff of carnal desire… (But then, could I really and truly look myself in the face and swear by Marc's precious lifesblood that the *thought* had in fact never once crossed the threshold—)

"So," she handed me a scrap of paper, "Memorise that. It's the secret number to his private cell phone—which *cannot* be monitored by the Security organs, or more importantly, the goddam paparazzi." She absentmindedly splayed the pads of her left paw, her eyebrows coming together. "Remember, Sylvia, this is *your* arse in the sling. Be careful. I say that as a friend."

"We weren't up to *any* sort of—"

"I can tell just how head-over-heels you are for the little brat," she gave a malignant chuckle that smacked of both condescension and ridicule. "I say that with genuine fondness."

"For me, or for Marc?"

"Oho, so it's *Marc*," she chortled. "Not even Marcus, but Marc…"

"Please don't make fun of me," I fought back tears, "or what I mean to say is, you can make fun of me all you want (everyone else does, after all), but please don't make fun of my friendship with—your Cousin."

"*Marc* somehow sounds more convincing; it makes your face light up—oh cool it, Sylvia! I'm not 'making fun' of you or Marcus or anyone else. This is too serious for laughter. My cousin picked a fine time for some innocent-seeming or perhaps not-so-innocent intrigue—and with an inferior branch of the Nobility—Ferdinand's not even a Viscount, much less a Peer of the Realm—it complicates my own little project, and I'm sure mine complicates his (and yours)—we'll have to help one another as best we can—ever heard of 'damage control'?"

"I think so," I nodded.

33

"If I can play this just right, I should be able to manipulate the paparazzi and the tabloids, to get round my Father—he'd never accept my Young Lion."

"So it's a Lion, then."

"I stick with my own kind."

"I don't understand," I hesitated, my face turning hot, "I *heard* you and—and my—father, last night—"

"Shall we add voyeurism to your list of accomplishments?" she gave an ugly laugh, "Sylvia Romanoff, peeping through keyholes—"

"I haven't peeped through any keyholes," I defended myself, "I ran up the stairs to shut out the sound of," I gulped, "those awful, disgusting *noises...*"

"Then you didn't see how it ended," her detached, matter-of-fact voice made me feel like some kind of prurient sicko. "He was dead drunk, Sylvia. I let him paw me a bit, before extricating myself. The last thing he probably remembers was fumbling with the shoulder-straps; they're custom-made with a little hidden catch—which only *my* claws possess the trick of unclasping—"

"I saw that part of it—I mean, his fumbling—"

"But you obviously *didn't* see me push him off me; he fell sprawling onto the floor like a sack of potatoes. I readjusted my bodice, and left him lying there, snoring just a few paces across the floor from his equally stupourous wife. The domestics doubtless carried them up to the master bedroom soon after."

"But," I gesticulated helplessly, "you had to submit to his slobbery kisses, his inept gropings—"

"All in a day's work," she shrugged , the cool, supercilious smile never leaving her face, never wavering.

"If you really *love* this young Lion, doesn't that bother you?"

"*Well of course it bothers me,*" she roared causing me to duck my head down between my shoulders, "But I want more than a quick roll in the hay with this beautiful strapping youngster; I want to make a life with him."

"You've—you've actually—"

34

I guess the look on my face, and the catch in my voice, made it pretty obvious what I was trying to ask.

"*Constantly*," she gave a dreamy smile, and licked her lips. "You've no idea how wonderful it can be, if you're really in love. His silky mane, his sensuous pawpads—"

"Please tell me it isn't—"

She burst out laughing. I hated her for being able to read my mind so easily—and for lots of other reasons as well.

"You can relax, my dear, it's not Marc. I don't go for kids. Nor incest, particularly. Though it certainly would've helped if my Beloved were distantly related, some fourth cousin once removed—as it stands, he not only doesn't belong to the Imperial Family; he doesn't even have a drop of Royal blood in his veins. That's where the political difficulties come into the picture. My Father would hit the ceiling, perhaps even have my young Lion arrested (or worse)—if we were discovered, at this stage of the game."

She'd stopped pacing and was now looking wistful, staring off into space.

"But isn't it awfully hard to keep something like that secret?" I couldn't help asking, "constantly scrutinised, your every movement and gesture—"

"Difficult, but not impossible."

She turned to face me:

"You have to learn how to manage it, Sylvia. Or you can kiss Marc goodbye."

"But I don't know how," I started blubbing once again.

"Then you'd best learn, and fast."

With that she drained the glass of iced coffee she'd been toying with, and slammed it down on the table.

"Are—are you *sure* it's not Marc?" I found myself yammering in her ear, having dashed over to the Lioness and literally hooked my claws in her *priceless* dress—it was studded with seed pearls and large glimmering stones that looked like opals. I'm no good at describing clothes; all I can say is that the sleeves were nice and wide, and gave plenty of traction.

"His name begins with the letter D," she vehemently whispered, unlatching the door. "Just like mine. Okay, Sylvia? You dig? You gonna go freaking out on me?"

There was a touch of restrained menace animating her powerful voice.

She flung the door open, to a sudden cacophony of shouted exclamations and reporters springing to their feet, flashbulbs already going off, all over the place. I quickly scanned the scene: Nero, Ferdinand, and Blussian (lolling on his elbow) were standing over by the portable boarding steps, a flight attendant waiting for them by the open hatch leading into the aircraft. Delilah, mobbed by servants and State Security personnel, bounded over to join them.

"So long, kiddos. Be good," my father shouted—

"Daddy, please! Take us with you!" Maria somehow projected her voice (but with a strange woodenness, as if reciting on cue), grabbing Douglas by the wrist, and scampering— unimpeded—the cameras rolling and clicking—over to Ferdinand, who went white as a sheet (from surprise, from anger?)—

"*Of course you can come with us*," Delilah announced, her regal voice echoing through all the crannies and corners of the immense, vermin-infested hangar; "Judith, take them to the observation deck, in the back of the plane."

I didn't know whether to cry or laugh—I was sure Delilah had her Machiavellian reasons—perhaps it would tie down and occupy Blussian. And since Nero *hated* children—I almost smiled (midst the tears welling up, making everything blurry-edged and surreal).

"Take her back inside," Judd materialised from out of nowhere, "Before she fucks up the Grand Exit."

"Can I at least watch my family board the plane?"

But it was too late. The hatch-door had swung shut, and the gleaming luxury jet, like some huge malformed buzzard, was already taking off, with a smooth, booming *whoosh*—that made everything vibrate. The glasses and dishes (as they hustled me

36

into the lounge) were still tinkling and clinking—I stared at the glass Delilah had slammed down. Its ice-cubes were melting.

When we finally pulled into the driveway, I spied Goody Thorpe standing over by the servants' entrance. As we screeched to a halt, she waddled over to the cardoor as fast as she could.

"I saw it all on television," she clucked, stroking my fur. "Poor Sylvia—come upstairs for a nice relaxing warm bath."

"Don't have time," I dashed inside as though trying to outrun my feelings, "I have to get ready for school."

"Wait a moment," she clucked, hurrying after me as I bounded up the stairs.

"You need to write me an excuse, for being late to class— where's a clean pinafore?"

"I don't think you should go there to-day."

"School happens to be all I have left," I snarled "I wonder if Helen—"

"They won't let you in."

Her words brought me up short.

"Your Da explained it to me last night. The school folk, the Headmaster and that lot, don't want, what do you call it, publicity? Any student caught speaking to the press—"

"But if I stay home I'll lose a whole day. I didn't really speak to the press—"

"It's on *television*," she insisted with a touch of pigheaded obstinacy. "You can see for yourself. It's pre-empted all the normal daytime soaps and game shews. You *shouldn't* have let them get yer back up like that…"

Pushing past her, I switched on the TV:

"AND SO, TO RECAP—"

I hated their lack of originality: always recycling the *same* worn-out phrases.

"FOR THOSE WHO'VE JUST TUNED IN, HEATHROW THIS MORNING WAS A SCENE OF ABSOLUTE PANDEMONIUM; IN A HANGAR OFF-LIMITS TO THE PUBLIC HER SERENE HIGHNESS, THE IMPERIAL

PRINCESS (AND GRAND DUCHESS OF LICHTENSTEIN), GRANTED THIS NETWORK AN ALL BUT UNHEARD-OF EXCLUSIVE."

"That domineering *Lioness*," Goody Thorpe clucked dismissively, "thinks she's so irresistible. I'm glad she and all them fine folk have finally cleared off to greener pastures—waiting on that Heifer she brought along was no bed of roses—she *is* pretty, though…"

"The Lady Judith?"

"Delilah. The Princess."

I was forced to agree. Delilah *did* look almost as breathtaking on television as face to face in 'Real Life.' Blussian and Nero seemed to pale in comparison. My father, predictably, came across as this twinkling-eyed, roguishly incorrigible 'scoundrel' of the type women seem to adore (for some incomprehensible reason).

Taking it in from the vantage point of spectator as opposed to participant, I found myself marveling at the way the Camera *subverted* things. At the same time I had to take my hat off to Delilah; she parried and circumnavigated the brazen rapid-fire questions so skillfully that it almost seemed as if she had nothing to hide. I noticed that the strings of shouted-out questions sounded rather 'different' when broadcast on television—the repulsively smutty, obscene quality that had so nauseated and paralysed me in person came across, now, on the other end, as merely 'daring' or even somehow clearing the air. Those like myself who ducked the questions for whatever reason (often simply because they were fired off so rapidly—there was no way a respondent could sandwich in monosyllabic replies) were cast in the role of slippery squirming prevaricators.

Delilah, in contrast, skillfully sized up their garbage-bag of insinuations, fighting fire with fire, sneering or laughing at pronouncements she judged as beneath contempt, answering difficult questions with pointed, barbed questions of her own, ticking them off as she went down the list. Of course it helped that her faithful heifer, Judith, was standing there, notebook in hand, taking it all down word for word (and prompting her Mistress point by point). I could have used a Judith of my own.

Thus far, the 'feed' this station was broadcasting hadn't featured *me* in the slightest—I'd scarcely appeared for more than an instant or so, at the edge of the screen.

"I thought you said *I* was on television," I couldn't help sulking out loud.

"Count your blessings," she said in a flat tone of voice, reaching for the remote control—which I yanked from her grasp, accidentally muting the sound.

"I thought you said they got my back up."

"They *already* broadcast the bit where you have your little kerfuffle—with them Rats and Weasels and such."

"You mean we missed it?" I tried not to sound disappointed. "They're not gonna shew it again?"

"How should I know?" the White Hen ruffled her feathers, "It wasn't exactly a quality performance. Besides, they seem to be concentrating on that tin-plated Lioness."

"I know I'm not as interesting to the average working-class viewer—"

"Let's switch this off now."

"So why wasn't it a quality performace? What'd I do wrong?"

"I'm turning this off."

"Was I somehow not sparklingly sophisticated enough?"

"I do wish you hadn't said those things about the Prince Imperial," she shook her head agitatedly, "He's such a handsome young lad."

I felt the colour draining from my face.

"I'm sorry," she let go of the remote, "I shouldn't have said anything."

"What did they make it sound like I'd said?"

"Oh, you know how it is; I expect you didn't know what you were saying," she looked away evasively.

"Did they try to make it sound like—"

"How *ever* could you tell them what he looked like—without his clothes on—"

"But I never… I *never*…"

"Oh Sylvia, dearheart," she tried to embrace me, "It's like you were trying to imply that you'd slept with him. Didn't you realise how it was coming across?"

"I didn't say *anything*," I wheezed, "It was all in their obscene, ugly *questions*."

"So you didn't sleep with him?"

Her mixture of prurience with childlike gullibility made it difficult at first to register what I was seeing, on the screen—

"Oh my g-d. The Divorce."

There it was—that awful courtroom, my Mother taking the stand, the cameras focusing on us children, zeroing in—I'd never seen this before, struggling with the remote to get the sound back—Goody Thorpe, as though possessed, was trying to wrench the damn thing out of my grasp.

"Let go."

"Oh, Sylvia, please—"

"HER NAME IS SYLVIA ROMANOFF, SHE'S ONLY 15, AND THIS ISN'T THE FIRST TIME SHE'S BEEN SOMETHING OF AN EMBARRASSMENT TO THE FAMILY…"

"THAT'S RIGHT, BRIENNE. HER MOTHER, THE FORMER HEIRESS, JANE SEYMOUR, WAS DISCOVERED IN A RATHER FLAGRANTLY COMPROMISING POSITION, AS IT WERE, WITH THE WELL KNOWN GIGOLO, FREDERICK RATCLIFFE, WHICH UNDERSTANDABLY HURT FERDINAND'S FEELINGS…"

They were *laughing*—about the Divorce.

Goody Thorpe finally pried it loose from my claws, and switched the wretched thing off. I tried to yank it out of her grasp.

"Let go of it," she wheezed.

"I *have* to hear what they're saying about me—"

One of us, in jabbing at buttons, flicked the broadcast back on:

"WHY DID YOUR BOARD OF TRUSTEES DECIDE TO GIVE SYLVIA THE OL' HEAVE-HO SO TO SPEAK? HASN'T THE POOR KID SUFFERED ENOUGH?"

"The Headmaster," I gasped.

For there he was, large as life, on the screen:

"LIKE I SAID BEFORE," his pendulous jowls were *so* repuslive (he was one of those stub-tailed, almost inbred-looking Boxers, practically bursting at the seams with sanctimonious humbug), "AS A SOCIALLY HARMFUL ELEMENT—"

Goody Thorpe yanked the plug from its outlet. The screen went blank with a soft crinkling noise.

"So the upshot is: I've been *kicked out of school.*"

My faithful Nurse (after making me swallow some valerian drops) must have tiptoed out of the room. I lay there, face down on the bed. My name was Sylvia Romanoff, I was a 15-year-old white Tabby that'd been kicked out of school, my father was an alcoholic, and worst of all I lusted for a member of the Imperial Family. I kept trying to picture Marc's beautiful face—but instead kept imagining the two of us locked in a broom-closet awkwardly ripping our clothes off. Suddenly, in place of that angelic Lion's face I was staring into the grinning mug of a (naked) Hyena. The door flew open. Everyone was laughing, and taking pictures—the click and whir of innumerable cameras subsumed the faculty of hearing. Looking up at the night sky, the stars and constellations were gone—cameras and microphones twinkled in every direction, shimmering to the far horizon and back.

vi.

"Wake up," my friend Helen shook me, "We've got to get moving."

"I had the most awful dream—"

"Here, put this on. We're going to pay a visit to your father's accountant."

"What's so important about some stupid accountant?"

I hated to admit it, but the valerian drops Goody Thorpe was always going on about had, for once, done the trick: I felt well enough to take a second look at my problems, perhaps even grapple with them. So I'd been kicked out of school—it wasn't the end of the world (though I have to say, my head ached, my temples were throbbing, and I felt slightly feverish).

"I spoke with the Ministry of Education, regarding a private tutour," Helen sounded even more pleased with herself than usual. "They said that if your father could come up with a lump sum, they'd pull some strings and jump you to the head of the waiting list (which contains *thousands* of starry-eyed, idealistic young would-be Scholars, mostly from the middle classes, but brilliant)—"

"Wait a minute," I massaged my swollen eye-sockets, "This is all happening too fast."

"They made it crystal clear that you can forget about going back to the Tenishev or any other accredited school—"

"What do you mean by saying, *they'd pull some strings?*"

"A private tutour, though astronomically expensive—"

"I refuse to receive any special privileges, or have the rules bent, if that's what you're getting at."

"But Sylvia," something in her voice brought me up short, "Both of us—all our relations and friends—everyone we know— we've been receiving special considerations and favours—getting ahead of everyone else—since before we were born—"

"But not deliberately. Not like *this.*"

"My mother sent round her own private car. It's waiting downstairs," she tugged at my sleeve.

"I'm not doing this if they jump me ahead of anyone else—"

"Didn't the Headmaster 'bend the rules' the *other* way, in having you kicked out like a piece of refuse?"

She saw that her words had scored a direct hit; I quickly looked away, staring down at the counterpane.

"Did you know that they ripped open your locker, with a pair of bolt-cutters? Left it standing wide open for all the scum to rifle through, at their leisure?"

"I didn't need to know that," my voice became icy. "You needn't have told me. I consider it a gratuitous act of sadism—the most insidious, deep-rooted, subconsciously self-perpetuating—"

"I'm sorry Sylvia," she grabbed me by the shoulders, "I don't know why I said it—maybe to try and make you mad enough to buck up and fight back for a change."

"Instead it just makes me want to curl up and die."

"The car's waiting outside. Mother needs it for a late-afternoon social engagement—can we please talk about this on the way to see Fleckenham? London traffic—"

"Who the hell's Flecknum?"

"Your father's business manager, among other things. Arlova gave me his address."

"Oh."

The muscles round my mouth tightened.

"It figures that Arlova would be the person you spoke with."

"When are you going to forgive Snoopus for being a flesh and blood animal," she demanded, "with needs just like those of any other animal?"

Helen had been every bit as shocked and disillusioned as I was, back when we first found out that Arlova was more than just a 'confidential secretary.' In fact, she was Snoopus' *Mistress*. It still pains me to write that word, even now.

"Muldoon! Muldoon! Muldoon!" Helen skipped over to the idling Daimler, precipitating herself into the driver's compartment (leaving me all alone amongst the upholstered grey seatcushions with their armrests and silver ashtrays and velvet tassles for releasing the diaphanous grey curtains embroidered with what I vaguely remembered to be the Bronte escutcheon). Fortunately she remembered to lower the soundproof partition.

"We need to take Sylvia to 30 Chancery Lane," she excitedly chirped, "So, Muldoon, can you take us? D'you know where it is?"

"I reckon we can find it, one way or another," the big chocolate Labrador grinned, eyes twinkling, as we barreled out through the gate.

"How far to Chancery Lane?" Helen wanted to know.

"We're hitting mid-afternoon traffic," he shrugged, "Could be another five to ten minutes."

"I'm climbing into the back," Helen announced, propelling her head and shoulders across the partition.

"I wish you wouldn't do that, Miss Helen."

"Why not, Mr Muldoon?" she impishly taunted as I helped her wriggle and squirm into the backseat.

"It's not a Ladylike way to behave, Mistress. You know that. You've been punished—"

"But *you* won't tell on me," she fluttered her eyelashes. "Not this time, at least?"

Watching the poor Labrador (from a sort of instinctive affinity), I saw that he visibly blushed (even under all that brown fur).

"Have I ever been the means of your getting in trouble?"

"Of course not, my *sweet* Muldoon," she prattled. "In fact, you've taken the blame for my mischief, whenever you could."

Her mouth was opening, to say something else, but then closed on itself, with a soft clicking of teeth. I glanced across from the fidgeting young schoolgirl to the silent Labrador.

45

"What's wrong?" she teased me. "Surely you don't disapprove."

"How could *I* disapprove, after all the things the paparazzi have said about me?"

"Don't let's talk about it," her smile vanished.

"Listen, Helen," I switched gears, "Remember that time last summer when we attended the political demonstration across from the Winter Palace, in Senate Square?"

"The demonstration for the repeal of the Poor Laws? Of course."

"It didn't change anything."

"Change frightens people," she observed judiciously. "It can take a long time."

"Or never come at all. Everyone was so euphoric when Cleopatra ascended the Throne—remember how excited our parents were? The dawn of a new era. The Universal Rights of Animalkind."

"I guess our parents were too optimistic."

"First Cleopatra gets poisoned. But no worries: after the dark night of reaction under Henry, and then the hundred-day reign of terror under that syphilitic degenerate mass-murderer, Alexis—"

"Agrippa came to power, and set things to rights."

"Yes, the Emperor, Germanicus Agrippa," I sneered, "grieving husband of the slain Cleopatra, with their lovely Passion Flower of a daughter, Delilah—"

"I don't know that you should be talking this way," she nervously activated the soundproof partition.

"Listen to this," I scarcely recognised my own voice, "I had a nice long chat with *Delilah* herself—at the aeroport, this morning. Bast, was it really only a few, finite hours ago? It feels like a lifetime."

"Delilah," she looked towards the thick panel of glass sealing us off from Muldoon, "may be a trifle decadent," (she lowered her voice) "but she's inherited her Father's intellect; Snoopus used to tell us how brilliant she was, remember?"

46

"I've seen for myself. But don't you think it was *too bad* of her Father—rotten, you might even say—cowardly—"

"Sylvia," she sounded genuinely frightened, "Please—"

"To turn the clock back on all Cleo's reforms?"

"Henry and his perverted whelp Alexis had blown those reforms to smithereens—and destroyed the social fabric in the process," her eyes flashed. "He's still putting the pieces back together—it'll take years to undo all the damage they caused—"

"I still can't help juxtaposing—"

"Have a little faith," she intoned (like the secret Evangelist I sometimes teased her for being—I once or twice even told her she should swathe herself in a chador and go live with the Dark People), "or if not faith, at least patience."

"He *could've* repealed the Poor Laws right off the bat—his beloved *Wife* did after just three weeks on the Throne."

"You shouldn't speak that way even in private," she gripped me by the wrist. "I'm serious. They arrest people for that kind of thing."

"I know. That's one of the reasons I'm so disillusioned."

"Well anyway, we protested, remember?"

"And scattered when the paparazzi started arriving. Tens of thousands of working-class demonstrators—not a single reporter. But as soon as their network of informants tipped them off that a coterie of the so called *Golden Youth* had shewed up in solidarity with the poor—"

"We hid under an ice-cream stand," Helen giggled, "bribed the vendor, but realised he was one of their informants when we saw him take out a mobile phone—"

"So we scrambled onto a passing double-decker bus, just in time."

We both giggled, leaning against each other.

"I should've stayed, Helen," I suddenly became serious. "Stayed, and faced the music."

"Faced the music?"

"The paparazzi," I clenched and retracted my claws, "*We* should start using them the way they so shamelessly use and exploit *us*, 24 hours a day."

"*Use* the paparazzi?" she shook her head. "That's like trying to bite a Cobra."

"Is it? Is that what it's like?" I couldn't believe the sneer that had crept into my voice. "You can press the button now and lower that soundproof glass. I'm through talking sedition."

"All these years we've been best friends," her face was unreadable. "Suddenly it's like you've turned into a complete stranger."

"Because I want to pay them back for what they did to me?"

"Looks to me like you want to beat them at their own game."

"What's wrong with that?" I demanded.

"It's a filthy game, with marked cards and crooked dice. Money seems to be the only object—"

"Or notoriety."

"Since when did you, the introvert, get so interested in *notoriety* of all things?"

"Since I learned that the Midas Touch of a celebrity doesn't just have to destroy—it can also protect, and preserve."

She shook her head: "You're turning into someone I don't even know."

Muldoon dropped us off and then circled to find a parking spot. Chancery Lane was bustling with crowds of harried-looking stenographers, messengers, and sallow-faced clerks. None of them gave me a second glance. (So much for being on television.)

Number 30 had seen better days. Its caryatids above the front doorway were soot-blackened, and the windows, extending upwards four or five storeys, were grimed and streaked with pollution. There was no reception desk or information kiosk inside. We'd been hoping to find some sort of floor-by-floor register but instead came across the foulest graffiti imaginable (some of it so explicitly graphic that we caught each other trying to steal closer glances—before we both, with exclamations of righteous indignation, gave up and began searching for someone who perhaps could give us directions).

Helen plucked up her courage to ask the concierge.

"Number 4-G. Now bugger off, I've got me own problems."

Our climb up the stairs left us panting for breath. I can't remember which of us knocked on the door.

There was no answer. Helen took it upon herself to push the door open. Scurrying in as it closed behind us, we found ourselves in a sort of waiting room, or antechamber, deserted of course. The magazines were without exception three or four years old, and covered with dust. Two of the doors at the far end were shut. The third door was ajar, and a languid, tired-sounding voice was yammering, on the other side, as if in slow motion.

Seizing the initiative, I boldly traversed the chamber and, gritting my teeth, softly knocked.

"He'll never hear *that*," Helen scornfully whispered.

"I suppose *you* could've done it loud enough to raise the dead," I shot back. "Why don't you give us a demonstration?"

Instead of knocking she pushed the door open. Horrified, I could only seize hold of her sweater, and found myself peering over her shoulder at a large bob-tailed Black Manx. Placing a shapely black paw (loaded with rings—mainly of the agate and bloodstone variety) over the telephone receiver, he gave us a quick, disinterested glance, and dismissed us with the words, "Not interested."

"I beg your pardon?" Helen strove to retain some semblance of dignity (though we were both visibly trembling with mortification).

"If you're selling something, I'm not interested—speak English? *Comprende?*"

I was stricken dumb as a plank, but Helen it seemed was made of sterner stuff: "This is the Lady Sylvia Romanoff, daughter of your Employer, if I be not mistaken."

"Call ya back, Bernie."

He slammed down the receiver.

We braced ourselves, waiting for the flood of apologies, excuses, groveling paroxysms of self-flagellation.

"I thought she looked familiar," he almost yawned in our faces. "Come to think of it, they've been flashing her mug all over the place, even on some of the half-decent channels."

Helen, it seemed, was now also stricken dumb. I watched the muscles of her jaw quivering, as she strove to gain control of herself.

"And who might *you* be, Miss Whitey?"

The absolute cheek. I was so glad he was addressing his insolent remarks to poor Helen. With an effort she finally mastered herself:

"Helen Brontë," she replied in crisp, measured syllables.

"Are you jealous of your friend Sylvia?"

"Jealous?" she frowned.

"That she's been on television."

"I hope I shall always try to avoid *that* sort of," she priggishly paused for emphasis, "publicity."

He threw his head back and laughed.

50

"A right pair of young Nuns."

Unamused, Helen cut to the chase: "Are you by any chance Mr Fleckenham, Comptroller to Ferdinand Romanoff's household?"

"Or in plainer language, his accountant?" I couldn't help clarifying (just to be sure).

"Never heard of him," he frowned, shaking his head.

"Oh, but…" I tried to keep my voice from quavering, "They said his offices were located at 30 Chancery Lane…"

"*Offices*, no less," he burst out laughing. "Your pardon, m'dears. Couldn't resist, though I see now it was inappropriate. And how can Elias Fleckenham be of service to such *dignified* young Ladies on this fine afternoon?"

"It's not so fine for some of us," Helen licked her lips, "Thanks to a piece of slander appearing in the tabloids—and on television—your Employer's daughter has been kicked out of school."

Mr Fleckenham threw his head back and laughed.

Seemingly undaunted, she pressed full steam ahead: "The Ministry of Education are arranging to find her a private tutour, but we need at least 20,000 pounds sterling, preferably in cash—"

The blackguard burst out laughing again. But this time the laugh was more surprised, and less fluid.

"I can see from your expressions of naïve outrage," he smiled, "that you're serious—that you're actually *not* joking."

"Unlike you, it would seem."

"Oh, believe me," he leaned forward propping his elbows on the desk, "Where it's a question of 20,000 pounds, I seldom joke. And I'm deadly serious when I say there's not that much in your father's checking and savings accounts put together."

"That's impossible," Helen challenged him, the hackles of her fur actually standing up (which I'd never seen happen before).

"They seemed to think it a fairly trifling amount," I ventured, drawing closer to Helen.

"Who are *they*?" he wanted to know.

"The Ministry of Education."

"They need a refresher course. The market these days has been incredibly volatile; interest rates are going up—"

"My father lives like an oriental satrap," I began—

"Whatever that is," he chuckled.

"What Sylvia's trying to say," Helen began, but I wasn't just 'trying' to say it; I was determined to do so, in spite of Helen's and Mr Fleckenham's continued interruptions:

"It's hard to believe that someone with a 23-room townhouse in London, a picturesque villa in Capri—"

"It's already been sold," he shook his head, with a smile. "A piece of prime, seaside real estate—"

"And he couldn't spare 20,000?"

"The entire sum was *drained* just yesterday, to pay off two of his most pressing debts. Ever heard of *liquidity*, by any chance?"

We both shook our heads. (If Helen, at that precise moment, had trotted out some precocious definition, I swear I should have fastened my teeth in her throat.)

"Well neither does your father, it seems," he was beginning to pace back and forth, becoming more and more agitated, "I work miracles, and look at this office—I haven't even got a bleeding secretary—I'm about to give notice—have to answer my own telephone, write my own correspondence—no instructions whatsoever, except to send *plenty* of cash—sell off property, stock, whatever it takes—to keep a *steady* infusion of cash gushing his way—to Capri, the Riviera—he faxes his constantly changing itineraries on practically an *hourly* basis— and what thanks do *I* get? I *share* my so-called support staff (basically accountants-in-training) with two other offices—and I even have to make my own goddam fucking *coffee*—twice a day—every morning," he gasped for breath, "and every goddam afternoon…"

Panting, his sides heaving up and down, the Black Cat just stood there. I saw that he was suddenly embarrassed— staring down at the carpet, he glided noiselessly back over to his desk, and sat down behind it. He probably wanted nothing so much as to rid himself of our troublesome presence—I *had* to try and get him to help us.

"I can't think why Ferdinand doesn't sufficiently value your services," I began—

"I'm afraid you're gonna have to skedaddle," he coughed. "I'm working against a four o'clock deadline."

"Ferdinand really is the most incorrigible bastard," I tried again, my eyes halfway welling up with tears (which surprised me). "I ought to know—I've grown up slighted, swept aside, and left as garbage, to rot…"

"Look, I'm sorry, okay?" he hesitated, standing by the door. "Your thirst for knowledge is truly commendable. Maybe you can enroll in one of the polytechnics—some of 'em have some pretty generous financial-aid programmes."

"Now look here," Helen raised her voice—

"Helen, please," I moaned, "I'm tired, and hurting all over—can we please just go home?"

"Although on second thought," he conducted us through the antechamber, and paused at the entrance, "Seeing as you'll pop up in the registry as one of Ferdinand's brats, I'm afraid you should probably err on the *pessimistic* side of the balance sheet. Translation: don't expect shite."

I hated Ferdinand. That was all I could think about for the first part of the ride—from our house to the edge of the unsavoury district in which Jane resided. Then, as the indicators of urban blight began to worsen, closing in round the rickshaw, whose driver, a young Sloth, clearly felt a bit apprehensive for his personal safety (I couldn't blame him), my resentment expanded to include *her* as well. For the hundredth time I asked myself: why did my mother have to live in a slum?

It was almost twenty-four hours since the farce with Helen and my father's accountant. I'd made a beeline straight to my miserable little bedroom, and popped a pawful of transquilisers—hoping I'd never wake up again (before nervously checking the label to make sure I hadn't 'really' taken an overdose).

"This is as far as I go," my driver abruptly skidded to a clumsy halt, almost throwing me from the conveyance, to the chuckling and whispered obscenities of some 'toughs' hanging out at the streetcorner.

"Three Sovereigns," he demanded.

"That's absurd," I exclaimed. "The fare should be—"

"OK gimme whatever," he wheezed, "I thought you looked like such a proper young Lay-dee of quality, not some kinky thrillseeker out for an afternoon of slumming—and a skinflint, it seems."

"Oy! C'mere then," one of the streetkids shouted. The poor Sloth took off so fast, the rickshaw almost lifted up off the ground. My coins got spilled all over the pavement. Cursing to myself, I set off as fast as I could. The gang of thugs paused to gather up the loose change, which gave me a headstart at least.

Jane lived right next to the Projects. I couldn't go there after dark. Even in broad daylight, bad things frequently happened (like to-day, for instance). I could hear my pursuers getting steadily closer. Not daring to look over my shoulder, I tried accelerating my pace, though my breath was already coming in ragged gasps, and I had a stitch in my side. Jane's building, half the rooms taken over by squatters, most of the windows broken, loomed straight ahead—but would I get there in time?

"Oy, stop!" someone shouted.

"Leave her alone," a husky newcomer's voice caused me to peel into the homestretch, giving it everything I could, on the point of collapse. It sounded like an altercation of some sort were happening some twenty paces behind me; I was sorry if my Good Samaritan were paying the price for what amounted, in this neighbourhood, to an overdeveloped civic conscience—I was too busy gasping for breath, just inside the ponderous metal doors, to give it much thought.

The lift, of course, wasn't working. I had to go up the stairs, all sixteen flights. Some of the steps were sticky, and others stank. Twice I gingerly skirted some derelict, passed out on the landing.

At last, reaching Number 8C, I stood there for a moment, trying to regain my composure, smoothing back my lank, lifeless fur, squaring my shoulders.

Resolutely, I pressed the buzzer, and waited.

The door flew open so fast I actually jumped backwards—instinctively.

And there she was. My Mother. The persecuted animal who gave birth to me, was there when I took my first step, mewed my first word—the animal who raised me, always there when my father was out screwing and gambling and getting smashed—ground down to a husk of what she might have become under different circumstances—robbed of her potential— robbed of the Best Years of her Life.

And for what? Ungrateful, squalling brats like myself. Sure, she could be vindictive and spiteful. But then, who isn't (these days)? And what the slow, poisonous accumulation of insults and treachery—being made the butt of jokes and gleeful, whispered speculation—what it must've done to the poor thing's sagging, all too vulnerable spirit! She kept it bottled up inside, a ticking timebomb (which I longed to defuse).

Even now, after all the stinging recriminations and put-downs flung back and forth during previous visits, my eyes filled with tears. Before me slouched a true *Hero*. (Not a heroine—our chauvinistic society tries to *denigrate* women with equivocal terms like poetess, huntress, adultress—it makes me sick to my stomach.)

"Sylvia. What a surprise."

She knows the effect it always has on me to see her for the first time after a long absence—I didn't even try to conceal the conflicting emotions. Instead, I practically flaunted them, standing there ramrod-straight in juxtaposition to the insidious awfulness of her own terrible posture. (I think she does it on purpose—even exaggerates it—for some inexplicable reason.)

"I haven't seen you in so long now, Mother," I managed, my voice rebellious and husky.

She shrugged, leaning against the doorway. I noted, with a shiver of disgust, that underneath the bathrobe she either had nothing on, or was wearing her trademark negligee. The team of sleazy lawyers my father hired for the divorce proceedings held up her collection of negligee for public ridicule—the tabloids went crazy. I just couldn't understand why she insisted on making herself look so incontrovertibly *cheap*. She never went around half-dressed back in the sunny days of my childhood.

She's a middle-aged Lioness, of average height, her eyes brown, her fur a tawny, dun-coloured shade of brown, like bricks of mud left to bake in the sun. I used to think her the most beautiful creature on earth, what with the lynx-like, tufted ears, the polished whiskers, the manicured, retractable claws. She never used to wear jewelry, seldom even painted her eyes—she once slapped Annie for sneaking into the boudoir and pilfering some of her makeup.

"Lost in thought?" Jane brought me back to the here and now. "Or zonked out of your gourd on a pinch of toe-tapping, fur-zapping Junk? They sell it just down the street."

56

I felt like whirling round and storming back down the stairs. Her acidic laughter didn't help. Why did she always have to bait me this way?

"Sorry, love. Since I started getting stabbed in the back, I'm afraid my sense of humour—"

"Ever heard the term *perscecution complex*?"

I couldn't help it. The words had *forced* themselves out of my mouth.

"Let's not fight," she gave a manifestly insincere smile. "Why don't ya come on in? I haven't seen you in ages. So nice of you to give in to what passes for a conscience, and come visit the old drudge, subjecting yourself to my insufferable company."

There. I'd done it. I'd actually endured a string of her barbs without bristling (outwardly at least). I took a deep breath.

"You know how much I love you, Mother. I wish you wouldn't say things like that. It hurts me."

"I didn't know anything *could* hurt one of *his* children."

"I'm your child as well," my eyes filled with tears.

"I know, I'm sorry, don't mind me, it's been the most Hellish day," she embraced me. "Let's have a nice, steaming pot of tea, and catch up on things."

"If only you knew," I sniveled, clinging to her for dear life, "How much I love you, need you—"

"There, there," she clumsily chucked me under the chin, having tried to dry my tears but simply ended up smearing them all over the sensitive white fur covering my sculpted cheekbones.

"Let's not stand here, on the landing," I managed.

"Afraid the neighbours might be watching, through their nifty little peepholes which give a fish-eye perspective?"

"Let's go inside," I suggested, preceding her.

She slammed the door behind me, double-locking it, sliding the deadbolt home and then securing the chain for good measure.

After the Divorce, my Mother went on the dole. She applied for food stamps and aid to families with dependent children, pocketed the allowances for our school lunch fund, and

57

even tried to sign up for Meals on Wheels, despite the fact that she was able-bodied and young. It felt as if she were practically *wallowing* in a morass of very public (and self-conscious) degradation. My anger and mortification had to go somewhere: Ferdinand was never around. The first time I came to this flat (provided by the local Council—my Mum wound up in *subsidised* housing) we kicked off a series of explosive, head-butting rows.

"Mother, *please* leave this disgusting place," I remember having tearfully begged her.

By way of reply she simply laughed in my face.

And from there it was strictly downhill all the way; her Council flat was filthier and more disorganised every time I had the misfortune to visit—it was like Jane didn't even *want* to take care of herself. Stealing glances at the slovenly squalour in which we found ourselves, I noticed a torn chemise, some hose, and a housecoat crumpled in a heap on the floor. A brassiere was hanging from the back of the *only* chair, currently placed at the "breakfast table" where she took all her meals. Cigarette butts in a dish (she didn't even use an ashtray!) were smudged and tainted with lipstick—a coffee cup bearing several concentric rings of stainage was decorated along the rim with more of these signature smears of bright crimson... (I detest and abhor "lipstick" forever and ever.)

I could feel her watching me. To defuse the mounting tension, I carefully picked my way across the cluttered living space (she lived in a "bed-sit" which means the bedroom and sitting-room doubled as one) till reaching the window I just stood there, gazing out across the dilapidated rooftops and housing projects of the slums of East London.

"You take your tea with milk, isn't that right?"

"With cream, just like I always did—as you very well remember," I tried, not very successfully, to keep my voice on an even keel.

"Let's not fight, Sylvia sweetheart; you visit me so seldom as it is."

"If you'd stop eternally harping about it," I ground my teeth, "the sad fact that I don't tend to visit that often might become less of a fact..."

"I think perhaps we'd best sip our respective beverages in silence. Did they ever teach you that old adage in school: Silence is golden?"

"*I've been kicked out of School*," I shouted. "Don't you watch the News any longer? You used to be a regular television *junkie*."

Oh, great. I could see she was fuming. Why do I always let my mouth run away with my good sense (what little there is of it) till I'm facing my Mother's tightly compressed lips all alone, just me and those quivering lip-muscles? (She could crunch a broom-handle in two, just with her lips.)

"I'm sorry, Mother," I hung my head and tried to look penitent.

"Remember when Annie used to insult me?"

"Don't compare me to *her*."

"Your Dad used to just throw his head back, and laugh."

"But *I* didn't, Mother," I could feel the tears welling up again. "Remember what *I* used to do?"

"I've got myself a Special Someone," she smirked.

I could feel my stomach turning over, in revulsion. Immediately after the Divorce, Jane had taken a new lover (I mean, someone different from that Alaskan Husky, Frederick Ratcliffe, who never should have responded to her persistent—and all too public—advances); this new lover was one of her solicitors. The paparazzi went crazy; she made the Front Page. And the demeaning thing (to me at least) was that she hadn't even gone after the Lead Attorney; she chose one of the assistants, who never even spoke in Court. After that, she took another, and another, and then some. It was like she was trying to make up for lost time. Each headline stabbed me, right in the heart. Eventually the tabloids lost interest—but the less they printed about her antics, the more outrageous they became. Every time a squib appeared, buried somewhere in the back of one of the Fleet Street rags, describing some drunken orgiastic scene or incident committed in flagrant, open breach of Society's mores, it felt like a flaming spear vivisecting my insides. I feverishly imagined the other kids at school gathering the sizzling embers of what the tabloids had spouted (wearing gloves of course) and loading them into a dumptruck, which they backed over to where I was struggling, held down by others of their kind, my mouth prised open, the back of the lorry tipping its redhot load down my supersensitive throat, acrid smoke pouring from every orifice, the stench so extreme that even my tormentors had to turn their heads and retch, letting go of me, so that I could scamper home and crawl upstairs to curl up under the bed, howling and sobbing, as my sister Annie threw her head back and laughed. At least, that's what it felt like—every time my Mother committed an additional act of fornication, embarking on another fling. Perhaps I should've hated her, but strangely I didn't—or at least I suppressed the surging waves and churning ripples of hatred—after all, it was *Ferdinand's* fault.

"I feel like vomiting," I weakly managed.

"A Special Someone," my Mother raised her voice, "who wouldn't tolerate the abuse to which you delight, it seems, in subjecting me."

"To which I delight?" I gasped, turning pale under my white fur.

"You just said you needed to vomit."

"I was talking about Ferdinand," I burst into tears.

"A likely story."

"Oh, Mother, please—"

"The loo happens to be over there, through that doorway—I thought you needed to urp," she taunted me.

"*Ferdinand* makes me feel like urping," I wailed.

"Well it looks like the attack must've faded away," she coldly observed. "When you were little, the vomit, by now, would've been all over the place."

"Mother, can we start over?" I said as calmly as I could, breathing deeply, flicking the tears from eyes that were doubtless redrimmed and swollen.

"Start over?"

"I mean, can we pretend that I just arrived? I'm sorry. I didn't mean to insult anyone, least of all you."

"Well, I mean to say, what's the point? Shouldn't you be going pretty soon now?"

"But I just got here," I miraculously managed to keep from bursting into tears all over again, but my heart was beginning to throb painfully. I sat down on the one chair without being invited to do so.

"If my Special Young Bloke gets here," she smirked, "you may not *approve*. And more to the point, the feeling may be mutual, from *his* point of view."

"Why do you have to be this way?" I expelled the words in a compressed jet of sibilant breath.

"Because *you* have to be the way *you're* acting, from the word go, the instant you stepped through that doorway—makes me so glad to be living alone."

"How! How am I acting?" I squawked, the tears oozing down my cheeks like viscous rivulets of blood and hot gore.

"*Judging* me!" she exploded. "Just like that fucking Court two summers ago! Just like your father, and sisters, and the fucking tabloids—"

"Mother, please don't use words like that—"

"You see," she shouted, her own tears washing away all the repulsive, thick makeup, "You're doing it right now—the way I speak, the way I look, the way I live, the way I fuck blokes who love me the way you never could—"

"I'm leaving," I tonelessly mumbled the words, my limbs twisted, etched in stone, paralysed.

"Good. I don't think Brandon would exactly approve."

"Brandon?"

"Don't you dare mock his name," she shouted, wiping the tears away and cursing under her breath.

"I'm sorry," I sprang to my feet, "Let's fix him something nice to eat, shall we? Please?"

I didn't dare turn my head to look at her.

"Please, may I fix him something? What would he like?"

"The fridge is empty. He went shopping. Drink your tea—it's probably cold by now."

"I'll drink it," I tried to slurp without sounding too coarse, just so she'd know how grateful I was for that awful-tasting cup of slop with its milk which'd gone bad. I couldn't finish it. I knew the milk, which was way past its date of expiration, would make me violently ill.

"Listen, Mother," I cleared my throat, "There's something I need to tell you."

"You're pregnant," she made it sound more like a statement of incontrovertible fact than an honest question with room for negation.

"You *have* to be—"

"Joking," she grinned like a crocodile. "You never *could* take a joke."

"You're right," I tried to make it sound like I was chuckling under my breath, "but what I've got to tell you is no laughing matter."

"So it's a good thing we laughed, ahead of time," she sat down in the chair.

I leaned against her, and to my inexpressible joy she began stroking my fur, the way I remembered from earliest childhood. I began loudly purring.

"There's a dear," she murmured. "No more insults for your poor old downtrodden Mum."

"I'd rather jump out that window and break my ungrateful neck."

"Don't even joke about something like that," she soothingly whispered. "You've got your whole life ahead of you—unlike me. If anyone should be thinking about it—dashing their brains out on the pavement below—"

"Can we talk about something else?"

"I'd rather talk about killing myself. Something nice and gory—lots of blood for the tabloid photographers. That's the only way to get *their* attention—once they've dropped you—once you're *stale* news. Used goods, as they say."

"Mother, listen—"

"I'd like to strap a bomb to my hoop skirt, crash one of his little Press Conferences, and time it just right: blow myself to bits all over him—leave him standing there, gaping."

"I'd rather you planted the bomb on *him*," I vehemently intoned.

"But that would ruin all the fun," she sneered in that unbalanced tone of voice that I'd started noticing shortly before the Divorce.

"Mother, it's Ferdinand I want to talk about."

"Don't ever pronounce that name in my hearing!" she screamed.

"I—I'm sorry," I half sobbed, "I should have known better."

She was moaning, her torso writhing like a snake, chest and shoulders making the cardtable sag.

"He's gone away, again," I forced myself to persevere with what I wanted to say: "He and his floozies, his tarts, and his whores. The same thing as last time. A junket. He's visiting the Côte d'Azur, then flying on to Vienna, spending rivers of cash all over the place—"

"Must be nice," she whimpered (so I knew she was listening).

"Mummy," I reverted to my little-girl voice, practically mewing like a kitten, "If I tell you something about Dad, something important, will you listen?"

"Depends what it is."

"It's something you can *use*," I whispered the last word leaning forward till my lips were practically touching her ear. "Something that could change everything."

"I don't see how," she said. "That fucking judge set the alimony payments in stone—one of his close, close chums—the fucking tabloids of course didn't report *that* particular little tidbit—guess it wasn't *tasty* enough…"

"I thought they did report it," I scratched my head. "I could check my old clippings, but—"

"Always has to have the last word," she lashed out. "Keeps clippings of everything, the way a buzzard holds onto bits of decaying flesh—"

"Mother, please."

"Good people," she declaimed histrionically, "I'd like to introduce you to my loving daughter, Sylvia. She goes round pretending to be the most *devoted* daughter on the whole face of the earth—"

I could've hit back, hard. I could've made some pointed rejoinders, especially regarding the effects of protracted Alcoholism on the speech centers, but that would just fan the flames (stoked as they were by a half-empty flask of cherry-flavoured brandy, sitting there on the edge of the table), so I bit my tongue, and instead of shouting at the top of my voice, simply raised it slightly (or perhaps more than slightly):

"We visited his accountant yesterday—wanna hear about his finances?"

That brought her up short. Her mouth half open (like the half-empty bottle wafting its turpentine-like fumes in my direction), she just sat there.

I started to pace.

"Helen helped me find it. Disgusting little place, over by Chancery Lane."

"So, get to the point—how much does he have?"

"His finances have run dry; he's having to liquidate assets all over the place, selling stuff right and left—"

She gave a loud cackle of glee, pounding the table and stamping her foot. The bottle of sherry or brandy or whatever it was jiggled slightly, the stuff inside sloshing precariously.

"The bastard," she yelped. "The fucking bastard!"

I winced. "It's about time, that's all I can say."

"And this morning most of the servants had—*vanished*."

64

(I was telling the truth: I'd slept like a dead thing till almost noon—Goody Thorpe never came in to wake me. Downstairs I'd had to fix myself a sandwich; it took me over five minutes to find the bread-knife. I was seemingly *alone* in that palatial mansion with its twenty-five rooms. I did find a note from Goody Thorpe—she was having to 'moonlight' at a second job; the note went on and on about having to provide for those ungrateful nephews or grandchildren or whatever they were—I wished she'd gone on and on about *me*—even a few words would have been such a great comfort.)

"They just…vanished," I stupidly repeated the word.

"Sounds like something out of the Arabian Nights: *Hocus Pocus*," she threw her head back and laughed.

"For your information there's nothing funny about it," I tried to keep from raising my voice, "He hasn't paid them in weeks—they've threatened to decamp en masse—"

"*Decamp en masse*," she slapped her thigh, giggling and chortling; there were tears in her eyes.

"The point is: we're completely unsupervised. He took Maria and little Dougie, the brat—"

"Douglas is not a brat," she choked on her laughter. "How dare you talk about him that way—you've always hated him, just because I *divide* my love between the two of you. Undivided, unconditional love—it's All or Nothing, with *you*."

"What *should* it be?" my voice quavered.

"So the servants have…disbanded? What was that word you used? You can be frightfully funny, at times."

"I told you: it's not funny," I insisted, hating the sound of my voice. "The point is, we're completely unsupervised, no adult in the house, no one to look after us, prepare and serve meals, bathe us, dress us—"

"You're breaking my heart."

My eyes welled up with tears, but from anger just as much as from hurt. I guess the boundaries, between emotions like anger and anguish, can jiggle and quiver, fading in and out of focus, moving back and forth. What a counterpane of quilted scraps we stitch together, and swathe ourselves in—I guess being 'in love' means sharing a single counterpane with somebody else. Although, these days, the boundary between love and 'fucking' seems to have got awfully hard to *discern* (for some people).

"Do you think anyone serves *me* breakfast in bed?" she whined. "Your father never did. Maybe it's a good thing you're learning how to look after yourself for a change. No one else is going to."

"The point, Mother Dear," I gritted my teeth, "is that it's bloody illegal. We're still minors, or at least I am."

"I don't follow," she squinted.

"Get a lawyer over there, document it, and you could conceivably regain custody—of all bloody five of us..."

The successive expressions flitting across my Mother's wasted countenance brought me up short.

"Five kids would be quite a handful," she muttered as if talking to herself, but quite distinctly, and loud enough to reach every corner of the disheveled room. "Not to mention the upkeep...the bills..."

"Well," I took the plunge, "Me at least. You could get *me* back."

"It's not that I don't want you back, Sylvia, sweetheart—"

"I can't believe I'm hearing this—"

"But I'm—I'm seeing a bloke now—"

"You already told me."

"He doesn't fancy kids, underfoot."

"Well," everything was blurring as the shimmering tears drowned my vision, "could you, like, testify," I swallowed a sob, "to get us taken from *him*, at least—even foster care—the social services—would be—less—awful," my throat closed on itself.

I stood there making snuffling sniveling sounds.

"Lawyers cost money."

"What about the *royalties*?" I somehow managed. "You can't pretend the sales have dried up."

Shortly after the Divorce she cranked out an exclusive tell-all, covering what it was like to be married to Ferdinand

66

Romanoff. She had it ghost-written of course. It was called *Cat Got Your Tongue? Reminiscences of a Professional Drudge* and was a runaway bestseller for at least 3 or 4 weeks. Our father decided that two could play at that game. He wanted a slice of the financial pie. So he hired a Black Norwegian Rat named Serenghetti to pen his own kiss-and-tell 'spin' on things. Except it never got published. A number of High Society movers and shakers joined forces and filed a motion, to prevent lots of juicy secrets from haemorrhaging into the public domain. A restraining order was issued, and there went those hefty royalties he was already borrowing money against.

Cat Got Your Tongue? in the meantime devastated me. It was such a hurtful pastiche of half-truths and distortions. Like, she claimed that I was manifesting tendencies towards Lesbianism—she actually had the *hurtfulness* to claim that she once caught me in bed with Maria! Nothing of the sort ever happened—or ever could have happened.

I guess the more improbable the wild stories and red-hot allegations, the better she and her committee of ghost-writers hoped it would sell. They were all charter members of the paparazzi. Big black and brown Rats. Vermin.

"You wouldn't believe what a huge percentage of the take they demanded. My co-authors, I mean."

"I know who you mean."

"And you wouldn't believe how fast I went through what was left."

"You're right. I wouldn't believe it."

"Well you'll just have to not believe it then."

"Could I see the cheque-stubs?" some perverse force was egging me on, "I know you still have them."

"You bloody well *cannot*," she exploded. "Forgive me for not realising you'd been hired by the Tax office, to do their audits this year."

These ugly irruptions of raw, unbridled temper were becoming increasingly frequent. Before the Divorce, she never even used to *frown*, much less raise her voice. Annie claimed she was just bottling it up, inside.

"Mother," I tried to stand on my dignity, "I can't pretend to be a psychiatrist—"

"Because you're so busy impersonating a Tax Assessor— I hope you brought a search warrant."

"Mother, please—"

"How dare you pry into the details of my personal life."

"How do I dare?" I shot back, "because I'm your *daughter*, in case you'd forgotten."

"How could I forget? You never *let* me forget."

"What's that supposed to mean?"

"Whatever you want it to mean—look, Sylvia, what did you want, Love? My new bloke, Brandenburg, is due back here around mid-afternoon. He's a rare good catch, but not partial to *kinder*—he just might take it into his head to use you for kindling wood!"

Her laughter had grown coarse. Then again, she never used to laugh at all, so maybe it was still a net gain.

I *should have* inclined my head slightly, and taken my leave.

Instead:

"You *did* hear me, earlier, when I said I was kicked out of school?"

"I heard—something."

She made a vague gesture.

"Your ex-husband's accountant said there's no money to send me anywhere else. I may have to drop out of school."

Waiting to see what she'd have to say in response to *that* little bombshell—

"Well I expect you'll land on your feet. Kids these days usually do. Look at Branden, for instance."

"Branden's a *kid*?"

Something in my voice caused her to whirl round, the veins standing out in her neck.

"There's nothing wrong with a mature woman having sex every now and then with a goodlooking teenager."

"I've got to go now," I gathered my things.

With a languid sigh she collapsed on the bed, lifting her hindlimbs like they weren't even part of her body—anything for her slothful, supremely *physical* comforts (as she sipped her alcoholic beverage with a loud, obscene squelch).

"You'll never see me again," I sobbed, turning in my tracks, my hand on the doorknob, "My father's throwing me out on the street—I'll probably die of venereal disease, or syphilis— after being gang-raped."

"Syphilis *is* VD," she burst out cackling. "It's a wonder your Dad never brought it home; I would've expected him to infect me with everything out there. I guess he has a grain of intelligence after all, and uses precautions..."

She was just lying there, like some shellfish, or primitive organism. So maybe I didn't want to come live with her, in this slum. But it still would've been nice for the One Person who gave birth to you to act, like, halfway interested—or even act like she halfway enjoyed your company from time to time—or even wheedlingly to take the notion of your coming to live with her under consideration, however briefly, with whatever obvious insincerity—but I guess that would've taken too much emotional energy away from her boozing, and cradle-robbing.

She'd never sunk this low before.

"Mother," I sniveled, "Is your mind functioning on a coherent level? Or has the alcohol made you dead-drunk at 2 o'clock in the afternoon?"

"You sound just like your father."

"I *want* to run down the stairs, out the door and to the tube stop, but you see, Mother, there's this gang of scum who pelted me with filth (verbal and otherwise) all the way over here—"

"They're harmless. Their bark is worse than their bite."

"Oh, so you know these individuals," I furiously dabbed at my eyes, "Is Brandenberg, by any chance, one of their number?"

"Of course not—"

"In that case, may I please wait for him to get here, so he can walk me to the tube stop?"

"Oh no you don't," she sat up in bed, scattering several cushions and a wadded-up comforter, "I *won't* have you two fucking."

The shock was—it was like having a shotgun-blast tear your leg off—you didn't even feel it; you just felt the spray of warm blood, and fell sideways, thinking someone had punched you—terrifically, terrifically hard.

"I—I would *never*—"

(Just *shut up*, a little voice was yapping like a furious Pomeranian inside my stunned, frozen brain; just *get out,* crawl, run, walk—just GET OUT…)

"I know *you* wouldn't," she slurred her words, "You're probably still a virgin—don't ever tell *him* that."

"You're right: we shouldn't ever meet. I'm going. If I get murdered, maybe that's the best solution, all round."

"Oh please," she made a dismissive clucking sound.

Then, seeing that I really was leaving, she wrenched herself off the bed.

"Hang on," she shouted, "Let me find my flip-flops and house-coat."

(I blushed at the negligee she was wearing, and the complete immodesty with which she flung off some—and swathed herself in other—garments, in front of me.)

"C'mon, we'll get you to the nearest tube-stop," she jauntily announced, taking me by the hand, and threading our way down the stairs, circumventing the numerous bits of flotsam and animal detritus seemingly washed onto the steps after one hell of a storm.

Inwardly marveling at her steady pace, her upright gait free of any weaving or staggering, I cursed myself for wanting to cradle my head against her shoulder. It was like I was seven years old again, and she was Mummy: tall, strong, indestructible.

But sure enough, those thugs were still out there; I instantly spotted them, brazenly lounging hither and yon, as we emerged from the tenement. And of course they spotted us, lurching into motion, paralleling us, pacing us.

"Oh," her lip curled, "That mangy lot. Cyrus' lot. They shan't give *us* any trouble."

"But Mother, they're stalking us…"

"Sylvia!" the situation seemed to give her fresh energy, "Buck up, I said!"

Suddenly her face and bearing imperceptibly softened. So did her tone of voice:

"I should've been just as petrified, in your shoes," she whispered. "I was scared and helpless, just like *you*, when I first moved here. *He* offered me some Hush money—I wouldn't touch it. His creatures tried to get me to reconsider, said there were no strings attached, it just looked bad for his ex-wife to be on the skids."

We rounded a corner. I couldn't see the thugs any longer. Either they'd got tired of stalking us, or else had switched into high gear, and were doing it for real now, keeping completely out of sight.

"He didn't realise I had to *find* myself. Sometimes you can only do that by bottoming out—you can't wade across a stream till your feet find the bottom, right?"

"That doesn't make any sense."

(I thought I could make out the tube-stop, just up ahead.)

"I used to be a good mother, didn't I?" she plaintively beseeched, taking hold of my sleeve. "You can be honest."

"I thought you were the Best Mother in the whole world."

"Your brothers and sisters wouldn't agree, I'm afraid."

"Sod them."

"Stop it Sylvia. Don't talk that way. Just because I gave up, I won't have you doing so."

"Mother—"

"He ruined everything!" she screeched loud enough for the vagrants and tramps lounging round to nudge one another, "still thinks it all revolves around his personal pleasure. The world can go down in flames, so long as he's able to use it to light his Hashish pipe—I may be broken in pieces, the wreck of a person, but at least—at least—"

Her eyes filled with tears.

"Here's the tube-station. Now piss off home. And don't talk to strangers."

When I got home and locked myself in my room, I found six roubles in my coat-pocket. Taking leave of my Mum, turning away to cross through the barrier (and hide the tears in my eyes), I'd felt her thrust something into my pocket. She'd reached in so deftly and skillfully, her practiced claws limber and supple, applying the perfect touch to the operation, I had to suppress an involuntary shudder—it felt like a *pickpocketing* in reverse, like we were in a film going backwards—they'd pressed the Rewind button for the scene where the naïve young pseudo-intellectual gets ripped off—by the middle-aged, decaying Alcoholic.

"*You're* the pickpocket," I softly snarled at myself, "Judging your own Mother. And here you're not fit even to lick the soles of her flip-flops—"

A soft knock at the door made me jump. I quickly wiped the tears from my face, took a deep breath, and opened the door to find myself face to face with literally the last person on earth I wanted to see—my sister Annie, that familiar half-sardonic, half-quizzical look on her face, her beautiful sapphire-like eyes dancing with mischievous laughter.

"Thanks a lot for bailing on us yesterday," I exploded, "Where the hell have you been?"

"I dunno. Drinking and whoring." Those stunning blue eyes of hers did look a trifle bloodshot. "What can I say? My own bed just doesn't seem to have that great an attraction for me—ever since Dad brought a duck into his!"

"Well now it looks like he's angling to replace the duck—"

"With a Lioness?"

She twirled her whiskers (exactly the way our father twirled his—she was a chip off the old block, whether she was willing to admit it or not). I tried to return her cool insolent gaze, but wound up looking down at the floor.

"So what happened?" uninvited, she swept into the room. "You went to see Jane, right? I mean, I know that's where you went."

"Look, Annie, I don't mean to be insulting, but could you get the hell out of my room?"

She threw her head back and laughed. Some people have a knack for crying on cue. Annie could giggle—for hours on end. Her laughter could be infectious as hell. Maybe she really was able to find comedy in all situations. Even this one.

"I'm feeling kind of depressed right now," I fought back the urge to burst out laughing, myself, "Our Mother lives in complete poverty, abandoned by everyone—"

"*Poverty?*" she incredulously chuckled, her voice heavy with sarcasm. "Listen to this—"

She produced a folded-up newspaper clipping.

"Never mind the headline; it'll give you apoplexy. Let's cut straight to the good stuff: 'Poor Jane, our favourite drudge and charity case, was seen splashing about in high style this past weekend, squired about on the muscular arm of that energetic young Meme and frustrated fortune-hunter, Brandenberg Tisch, aka Randy Brandy for his amourous exploits with the Marquise de Frotteuse-Ganaille. But why, our readers might ask, would Brandy waste his valuable time on a washed-up, self-described Drudge notorious for the squawking, breast-beating performance she gave in Divorce Court two years ago, the three-hour duration of which was productive perhaps of more dozing than sniffles, and the operative, boiled-down, key idea of which might best be encapsulated in the two words: Poor Me! Her recent bestseller notwithstanding (which my colleage, Addie the Muskrat, savaged in his incisive book review column), Poor Jane would have us believe that she lives in absolute squalour, with scarcely a kopeck to spare for a nice sustaining pot of cabbage-stew with some chutney. But Randy Brandy, it seems, was more perspicacious than the rest of us—just check out the diamond bracelet she's wearing in the illustration captioned Exhibit A: notice the solid-gold cigarette case Brandy's brandishing at our intrepid photographer (Blackie the Rat). A professional jeweler employed in Eddie's Pawnshop signed an affidavit attesting to the worth of that cigarette case as being *not less* than 500 Roubles (and possibly all the way up to *fifteen hundred*, depending on various 'tricks of the trade' which our source was not at liberty to elucidate further)'—"

"Did anyone stop to think that maybe the scum she's going out with is the one dropping all this filthy cash all over the place?" I interrupted her impassioned delivery.

"You should write for the tabloids—three sentences farther down, that's exactly the phrase he uses: dropping wads of cash down the cheeping throats of all the little chicks and hangers-on of the fabled Disco circuit between Finsbury Park and the Palais-Royale! Maybe not *exactly* the wording, but close…"

"So this is all just a big joke, as far as you're concerned—"

"It's not a joke," her blue eyes, which a moment before had been dancing, flashed dangerously. "It's part of the reason our lives have been fucked. And you're wrong about Brandenburg or whatever his name is being the source of the largesse—the article goes on to analyse his net worth—they've got informants coming out the wazoo through all the government ministries, and that includes the Tax office. Listen to this: before taking up with Poor Jane, young Tisch was over 1600 Roubles in debt, from gambling, mainly—so get this: almost from the first night of his current fling with our Mum—"

"This really doesn't interest me—"

"His debts have all been, mysteriously, paid off. He's been running up *astronomical* fresh debts: golden trinkets and knick-knacks (the wages of sin?), expensive tailor-made outfits, his fake coat-of-arms embroidered with genuine pearls—"

"I get the picture, okay? You really don't need to go into all these sordid particulars."

She placed a velvety paw on my shoulder: "I'm not doing this because I'm a sadist (or at least, not a complete sadist); you really need to know how much our sainted mother has squirreled away in the bank—"

"*This* is how much," I gave a strangled sob, digging into my pockets and producing the crinkled, rainbow-coloured notes, a Five and a One.

"Sylvia? You're hyperventilating. That Nurse of yours, Goody Thorpe—I can run down the street to that new hotel, the Omni—isn't that where she's gone? Can you *speak* for Bastsake?"

"Aren't you going to tell me how much 'Jane' (as you disrespectfully call her) has squirreled away in the bank? No doubt it's some secret account it took all the ferrets and paparazzi longer than usual to sniff out, with their prying proboscises, and quivering nostrils?"

"Your own are quivering—I'm going for Goody Thorpe."

"Wait," I commanded in a piercing tone. Remarkably, Annie was brought to heel, and stopped in her tracks.

"She gave me *this*," I squeezed and clenched the crumpled notes till the tendons of my arm hurt. "It really is what she has in the bank, even if she doesn't know it. It's called Love. It's all she has. It's all any of us have. And this is what happens to it—"

I struck a match, and the beautiful, wavering flame was like pure Spirit, counteracting—consuming—all the filth, and muck—

"Stop it, Sylvia!" she shouted, diving forward, grappling with me, shrieking and cursing as she stamped on the bits of flame that the burning money had scattered all over the carpet. I lay back, exhausted.

"I'm going with you, to-night."

I announced it casually, as if to myself.

"What did you say?"

"I said I'm tagging along with you and your folk—your thuggish Neanderthals—when you go out to-night like you go out every night, drinking and whoring. Just try and stop me."

"What makes you think I'm even setting foot outside my own bedroom—even getting out of my fucking bed, for that matter?"

"Oh you'll set foot outside your bedroom alright," I shivered as if in an ague, my face contorted, babbling like some sort of demented soothsayer, "Just try and resist your own self-destructive, primitive urges. We none of us can, you know. The disease takes over, consuming us. Till there's nothing left."

"This is quite a surprise—"

"Good. I'm tired of being a predictable, self-effacing little nothing. Like Maria and Helen."

I tried to start laughing. Only mine somehow didn't sound convincing, the way hers always did.

"Sylvia?" her voice silenced the last moribund cacklings. "You and I need to bury our differences. Delilah's using Ferdinand. I don't know why yet, but I can tell that she is. And speaking of family members being used, the tabloids claim she took *you* under her wing, at the aeroport."

"Oh," I squirmed uncomfortably. "I think that's slightly exaggerated."

"Tell you what," her manner changed abruptly. "I think I'll be charitable. You *can* tag along with me. I'm going clubbing to-night, after all."

On account of the house being largely deserted, we were able to sneak downstairs (as the clock struck twelve) instead of having to climb through the bedroom window—that was the first piece of good news. Then when we locked the side door behind us and quietly glided over to where Ramses was standing under a tree in the dark, I breathed a huge sigh of relief on seeing that he was all alone—there were no *other* young lads.

Ramses, of course, was bad enough on his own. I've always hated him. He's a perfect example of *Egoism*. Yes, he's a member of the Royal Family, but only on his mother's side, and so far down the totem pole (in terms of the Succession) that even some of the palace *footmen*, well known for their devastating wit, have poked fun at the insufferable little twit (there's no risk in their doing so—he's far too stupid—he even joins in the laughter—thinks it couldn't possibly mean *he's* the one being laughed at).

He calls himself *Ramasses* in a tone of voice perhaps meant to be sonourous. Poor thing. I could almost feel sorry for a mincing, strutting popinjay existing on the remote fringes of power, pathetically snapping up the crumbs of Imperial privilege and pomp (never grasping the difference between pomp and pomposity), posturing as though he were Second or Third in the line of the mouthwateringly stupendous, inconceivable Succession.

He's always been mortally jealous of Marcus—and for that reason alone: Fourth versus something like fortieth. Never mind the fact that Marcus happens to be beautiful as an Archangel (Ramses has a sort of bland, debauched handsomeness, though it's beginning to look a trifle 'worn out' round the edges); never mind Marcus' scintillating charisma, his intellect, his principles (all Ramses cares about is enjoying his next act of depraved fornication—and then his next meal—and finally his next hit of Methamphetamine, or Acid, or whatever he's currently using to destroy his brain-cells); never mind Marcus' subtle appreciation for irony, innuendo, finesse—he loves to attend all the avant-garde plays being produced in those basements along the Griboyedov Canal—he used to tell me about them, every morning between Poetics and Rhetoric (after me, he was top of the class in both subjects); never mind his smouldering sensuality, the way his luminous green eyes coalesce with flakes and slivers of glittering gold, like bits of micah sprinkled all through the Antipodes—the Loadstars—of his constellation-like eyes. Next to him, Ramasses was a degraded, pitiable creature—and yet, Ramses was jealous of my Beloved's genealogical promixity to the epicentre of power. A mere accident of birth. And that's all the sot cared about.

He used to persecute both me and Helen—he was very inventive. And my loving sister, Annie, connived right along with him to dish out the abuse. This must not be glossed over. I was glad that Annie seemed to have turned over a new leaf, but my guard was still up—and would be for some time.

"Remember how you helped him smear that indelible paint all over my face—"

"That was kidstuff, now shut up—he'll hear us."

We stepped boldly forth from the shadows; in addition to the black hose, the embarrassing miniskirt that looked like it was made of some sort of shimmering, metallic stuff, and the platform heels on which I was precariously teetering, Annie had insisted that I don a wig and dark glasses (we'd both equipped ourselves with these accessories for the brief moment of greatest vulnerability—crossing the pavement from the automobile to the special V.I.P. entrance). Probably she was curious to see whether her 'date' would recognise me—I was sure he would, given our shared history. Blood enemies have an almost chemical aversion towards one another.

"Cool," the little bastard enthused. "You di'nt tell me I was gunnah git t' have a chick on each arm."

"Typical," my sister's lip curled in derision. "You're so wasted, you don't even know who this is."

"Duz id madder?" he gave a repulsive grin. "Long as she n' me speak the lang-wijj of luv…"

"She and I," I icily corrected the sot.

His eyes widened. I think my clipped, precise voice was beginning to register. Annie, predictably, burst out laughing.

"Ohh, ohh wow," he promptly took a step backwards. "It's—it's her. The Psycho-Dyke-Bookworm. Ohh, wow. She almost, like, could pass…"

"Ramses got tricked by *Sylvia Romanoff*," my sister unhelpfully jeered, capering round the both of us, giggling and pointing (from me to him, and back again.)

"That is, like, so wrong," he wrinkled his nose.

"Why?" Annie waved a claw in his face, "Cause it made a complete and total fool out of you?"

"Cause stuff like that's not s'posed to happen," he seemed to be getting angry. "I mean, what if you pulled this little stunt on one of the other lads—like Brantislav—who might actually, like, fall for it—"

"*You* fell for it, hook line and sinker."

"No I didn't."

"Oh, please."

"I-*didn't*-fall-fer-it-Annie!" he gritted his teeth. "I was jus' goin' along, to build up the punch-line. I mean, d'ya really think something like *that*"—he gestured in my direction—"could actually fool a member of the Imperial Family?"

"Ask me no questions, I tell you no lies," her intonation went up a notch.

"What's that s'posed to mean?" he demanded.

"Think about it, I'm sure you'll figure it out."

"Careful, Annie," an ugly tone had crept into his voice, "I might just choose not to overlook this little joke—"

"It's not a joke," I could tell she was getting impatient. Gone was the mischievous glee. She'd never exactly liked Ramses; she made use of him, and that was that. I suppose, in his own way, he reciprocated.

"OK, a stunt? Pretty impressive, but we're, like,

wasting time."

"Sorry to tell you but there's been a slight change of plan," she sneered. "Call it a sisterly obligation."

"What are you talking about?" the little bastard reminded me of nothing so much as a yapping Chihuahua. The fact that he was (technically speaking) a young Lion was, like, *so wrong*, to use his own words.

"She's tagging along, just to the Danceteria—"

"You've gotta be kidding me—"

"Oh please, Ramses—for once, just, grow up."

"I am not," he sounded like he was beginning to hyperventilate, "repeat, not going anywhere with that Psycho Bookworm Dyke."

"Hey watch it," her intonation went up another notch, "that's my sister you're talking about."

"Get real," he spat. "You've treated her just like the rest of us treat the little weirdo dyke—anyone who wants to be part of the Scene, mix with the In-Crowd, had fucking well *better* treat *that*—her and her kind, I mean—the way we've always done."

"What a fantastic justifi-ca-tion," she sneered.

"Look, why the hell are you suddenly pretending to care whether your so-called sister lives or drops dead?"

"Because she's my sister. And because I need to expiate the sins I've committed."

"I don't know what this psycho-babble crap happens to be, but we're wasting time. You coming, or not?"

"Not without my sister."

"I don't believe this," he almost seemed more scared than angry. "What's the matter with you, Annie? You've never acted this way before."

"Perhaps Marcus Agrippa—"

The effect was instantaneous: both Ramses and I visibly winced. But for different reasons.

"Don't ever mention that name!" Ramses took the words right out of my mouth. "She loused things up, but good—you should be around the Winter Palace these days—talk about a hornet's nest, and for what? Cause this precious sister of yours—this Psycho—this Nympho-Dyke—tried to seduce—actually tried to fuck my fucking Cousin, tried to fucking take advantage of his being fucked up—"

"That's not true," Annie defended me, her eyes blazing.

"Probably timed it, to try and get 'erself knocked up."

The crackling combustion dancing and flickering from my sister's wide-open eyes was beginning now to shoot sparks and little bits of incendiary venom—the way a spitting Cobra ratchets up the toxicity. I could see that Ramses was scared.

"My sister may be a basket-case, but she's not some manipulative slut."

"I say she is," he somehow managed to keep his quavering voice from squeaking all over the place—he clearly didn't want to back down. I'd seen this particular type of confrontation resolve itself again and again back at school. It always ended the same way: a brief scuffle, and then the weaker belligerent was flying headlong, tail tucked neatly between his or her scampering legs.

"Take it back this instant," she bared her incisors, "or you know what'll happen."

He gulped, and began edging away.

Quick as a flash Annie had him on the ground, straddling his chest. It happened faster than the eye was able to follow, faster than a snake striking. Ramses began sniveling.

"I'm sorry, Annie. Really I am."

"Take it back," she softly murmured, picking up a sharp stone.

"For Bast's sake let him go," I heard my horrified voice ineffectually wheedling.

"I take it back."

"Are you fit to lick the soles of Sylvia's meanest pair of slippers?"

"No I'm not fit."

"And now Sylvia, the so-called slut, pleads for me to let you go. Like I said, she's not a slut; she's a Basket Case."

She climbed off of him. Rolling awkwardly, scrabbling in the dirt, he quickly righted himself, scampered to the gate and screeched:

"Slut!"

"Hurry up and get the hell out of here—before I do more than just throw you down on the ground," my sister screeched back in a voice rich with contempt, taking a step towards the unfortunate carnivore—who squealed like a slit pig and took off in the dark as fast as his four legs could pelt.

"Can't believe I actually liked that baggage, once upon a time," she softly spat out the words.

"Oh, Annie," I stammered, bewildered.

"Relax. It's over now. Wonder whom I should summon, instead."

"But can't we go—alone?"

She threw her head back and laughed. Though I'm sure my whining voice had sounded pathetic, I bristled just the same. Sensing this, she uncharacteristically took hold of my shoulders, exerting a pressure that was almost painful, then beginning to caress them with her supple, chocolaty pawpads.

"Unless we want to be taken for dykes—sometimes I play that particular angle, but to-night—"

"Whatever," I tried not to sulk. "Go ahead and choose another conscript from your veritable army of lads."

"If only I could just swallow my pride and ring Stephen," she closed her eyes at the thought, "Mmmm… *Stephen*. Puts me in the mood for a shag."

"Do you think we could possibly minimise the references to 'shagging' and fucking and sex—"

"Look, you asked to tag along," she exploded. "Begged me in fact."

"It's just," I shrugged helplessly, "Do we have to go on and on about shagging, and fucking?"

"You don't like it, go stand out of earshot."

It felt like we were slipping back into the old, adversarial paradigm. Casting about for some way to reverse the inevitable-seeming deterioration, I forced myself to ask something more or less out of character: "If you crave Stephen von Oxenburg so much, why not simply invite him to come over? I'm sure he'd be pleased as punch to strut about at the Clubs wearing *you* on his sleeve."

"You wanna know why not?" she took a deep breath, "I'll tell you why not—Stephen used to be the love of my life."

Why was I standing here listening to my sister rhapsodise about a bloke I absolutely detested? Granted, he wasn't as loathsome as Ramses. That's something, I guess.

"I remember the night we first met. I was twelve years old. He was eleven."

"This seems kind of personal," I observed in my typical mealy-mouthed voice, "Maybe we don't need to discuss your most intimate secrets—"

"He'd never properly slept with anyone before he met me. I taught him—so many things..."

She looked up at the stars. I wondered if she saw what I saw: a few scattered pinpoints of light flickering against the backdrop of all London's accumulated fog and pollution.

"I just can't believe he'd ever seriously take up with someone else," Annie meowed, "especially a cunt like *Yvette*. Not just 'take up with' in the sense of going steady—they're practically engaged."

I'd never seen her like this.

"Yvette?" I timidly prompted, "What's her last name—"

"Tverskaya!" she fairly shouted. "You know, *Yvette*."

Oh. *That* Yvette. My nose wrinkled.

"I may not be any great prize," she yowled as if to herself, "but at least I'm not a glorified prostitute—"

"Annie," I took a deep breath preparing to do something that was out of my 'comfort zone.' "You're a thousand times sexier than Yvette Tverskaya."

"You don't need to try and cheer me up—"

"You know I'd never do that," my own vehemence took me half by surprise. "This is Sylvia, the Basket Case, talking.

Remember me, Sylvia? My obtuse, bookish honesty? Flattery happens to be abhorrent to my intrinsic value system—when I say something, it's what I truly believe."

"Well thanks for your vote of confidence," she flashed me a quick, probing glance.

"Surely you understand the reason he's with a vapid nonentity like Yvette Tverskaya?"

"I guess he's turned on by nonentities."

"*Ferdinand* happens to be the reason," I tried to keep my voice under control, "He's guilty of pulling the proverbial rug out from under us—liquidated all his assets, to play house with his two Heiresses, Delilah and Blussian..."

Her silence goaded me.

"Don't you realise the extent to which we've suddenly become socially *leprous*? Even *you* it seems (which has never happened before). We suddenly have no money, no connexions, no 'juice'—I hate that expression, but for once it seems apt."

"Maybe if I confronted Stephen, face to face..."

"How much, offhand, would you say Yvette's worth? Twenty-five millions? Forty-five? Her family happen to own most of the bloody Ural Mountains—with all their iron, platinum, manganese—steel mills, mining concerns... Eighty-five? We're talking Pounds sterling, of course."

With no warning she embraced me. Teetering on the cinderblock-platforms, I nearly fell over.

"Brilliant," she intoned, rapidly punching a sequence into the cell phone.

"Please don't ring Stephen—"

"I'm phoning a dependable limousine service; we're going alone," she smiled as I clapped and carefully (mindful of the cinderblocks) attempted to jump up and down.

The driver they sent (his name was Melor; he was a big muscular Meme with tufts of curly red hair) happened to be friends with Annie; the two of them were already flirting as we pulled out of the driveway and through the front gate.

Feeling not just tired but now depressed (as well), I stared out the window. At first we seemed to be stuck in lots of bumper-to-bumper traffic as we made our way down Shaftesbury Avenue. The theatres must have just let out; crowds of revelers, tourists, insomniacs, homeless vagabonds (hawking the usual sort or merchandise: contraceptives, drugs, stolen jewelry) and various other creatures of the night were crossing in front of us, threading their way through the idling traffic, ignoring the din of horns blaring every time the lights changed.

A ram with serrated-looking horns and tortoise-shell spectacles, wearing a tweed leisure-suit, was trying to unfurl an umbrella (it was starting to drizzle). I watched a mangy Hyena seemingly stumble against him, apologise in a guttural, drunken-sounding voice, and then take off rapidly, his sprightly nimbleness in direct contrast to the pretended inebriation of a moment ago. A distinguished-looking Chocolate Labrador was shepherding two teenage girls who looked like they might have been about my age towards a cab-stand; all three of them clutching playbills, laughing and bantering. I could almost hear what they were saying, but not quite. A police siren that'd been getting louder and louder at last obliterated everything else: I clamped my paws over my ears and shut my eyes for a bit.

"Look at the fucking shrouded psychos," the hatred in Melor's voice caused me to sit bolt upright and peer out the window at a bizarre mob of hooded, chanting figures (apparently of every conceivable species).

"The Dark People," Annie rolled down the window.

"Please don't," I ineffectually pleaded.

"I just want to hear that crazy gibberish they spout; what's wrong with that?" she defended herself. "You seldom even see 'em, most of the time—must be close to that Festival of theirs; they come out of the woodwork thick as cockroaches—"

"Seething white maggots!" the Meme shouted at the top of his voice (causing me to scrunch down as far as I could), "Scuttle back to your rotting turds and stop stinking up public streets!"

Appreciative thuggish laughter sounded from all sides, along with taunts and catcalls from various bystanders. The sound of breaking glass—a beerbottle thrown at the pavement—caused me, feeling an unexpected camaraderie with the scapegoats and pariahs (being one, myself, after all), to pray with every fibre of my being:

Please protect us. Please make them stop.

We were moving again. I opened my eyes; the flashing neon signs and advertisements were rapidly giving way to drab office buildings with darkened windows. Only a few pedestrians were hurrying home (or to the nearest pub) after a hard day at the office. Some were carrying umbrellas. Others strode along in the rain. I watched a studious young Antelope wrapping three or four books in a plastic sack that had seen better days.

I couldn't get the Dark People out of my mind. The thought struck me: Do *I* elicit as much sick hatred in strangers driving past, as I make my way home after school? Correction: in the *past*, when I *used to* make my way home from school.

What was left for me now? Should I join those shrouded Fanatics? I, too, had had beerbottles thrown at me, and been spat on, and shriveled in the cross-hairs of corrosive group *hate*.

"Annie?" I interrupted her ongoing flirtation with Melor (my voice sounded hoarse), "Which club would have the most paparazzi to-night?"

"Depends on what *kind* of paparazzi you're talking about," the big Meme sagely observed.

"I hadn't realised their classification comprised various subdivisions."

"Don't mind Sylvia," my sister gave an infuriating little chuckle, "She reads too many books."

"Is there any way you could slow down?" I was clutching the armrest, "I don't want to get car-sick."

"Keep your fur on—or in this case, yer wig," she rudely sneered (to make Melor laugh), "We're nearly there."

With a sickening swerve, we accelerated. He skillfully (shewing off for Annie, I'm sure) drove us past some bottle-banks, down a ramp, and into a sort of subterranean garage.

"Here we are," he announced.

"I'm feeling sick to my stomach," I tried not to sound scared.

"Relax," Annie patted me on the shoulder, "The Danceteria's just round the corner. Unlimited Freakout and The Funhouse are on down the block."

She must've been able to read the dismay in my face.

"Look, Love, you wanted to go where the paparazzi are camped out? Well these are the latest clubs—believe me, this is where they're all hanging—upside down, like a covey of bloodsucking bats."

"Maybe I should wait in the car," I mumbled, despising myself.

"If you're scared," Melor twisted his bulk round to peer through the divide, "Perhaps I could come along, as a guard of sorts. Used to be a bouncer at Hot City before the Lumumbas turned it into a shooting gallery—all the junkies used to go there; they'd come from as far away as Chalk Farm—one of 'em got cut into pieces—"

"That's not what she's scared of," my sister knew just where to twist the knife, "She's scared of *herself*—of the things that're starting to stir and simmer, inside."

"I'll stay here. I can probably sleep on the cushions."

"Shut up and get your wig fixed with those hairpins."

"If she doesn't want to go—"

88

"You can tag as *my* bodyguard, how's that? Acceptable?"

The poor fool looked too happy to speak.

"Wait outside for a minute."

He precipitously got out of the car, locking the front door behind him.

"You're really not coming, after all this botheration and whining?"

"I'm sorry; you must think me a fool."

"What I think is my own business," she fixed me with one of her penetrating looks. I glanced down at the black leather skirt I was wearing.

"Have a nice catnap," she sneered.

"You're going on, then?"

"You didn't think *I* was going to lie down here, and waste the rest of the night?"

"Of course not. I'm just…"

"Expected me to try and talk you into coming with us?" she laughed. "I'm not surprised. I knew you'd flake out. This New You seems damn'd impressive at first gasp, but it can't really go the *distance*, now can it?"

"No, I suppose it can't."

"Have a lovely sleep," she smirked, shutting the door.

I watched her and the hulking Meme (who was built like a tank) begin shambling towards the stone steps. A strange stabbing sensation jolted me into a rapidfire sequence of actions: adjusting the blonde wig, putting on the dark glasses, checking my handbag for some spare cash in case of emergency—I flung open the door and nearly broke my neck in stepping onto the pavement (swaying on the cinderblocks), barely able to make anything out but the overhanging electric lightbulbs.

"You forgot to lock the goddam cardoor," Annie's voice savagely whispered, as I heard the door slam shut just behind me.

She took me by the wrist, guiding me across the smooth concrete. Other people were also heading for the exit; I could make out their indistinct shapes all around us. The steps were tricky; Melor had to help guide me as well.

"Yer friend blind?" someone tittered.

"Let it go," the Meme forcefully whispered.

He was obviously well acquainted with Annie's volatile temper.

"I know," she surprised me with the level-headedness of her response, "We've got to get inside, first."

We emerged from the garage into a dense throng of jostling, tight-packed animals illuminated by all the sizzling neon displays flashing rapidfire nonstop animation. At least it had stopped raining.

"What street is this?" I whispered.

"Goodge," her warm breath tickled the soft fur inside my pointed ears, "The older clubs are over on The Spurl, and Neskuchny."

"We should've driven up in the Limo," Melor cursed softly, pushing us through the complaining youngsters like an icebreaker forcing its choppy but inevitable path.

"La-di-dahhh," someone sneered.

"Oy, watch it!" a young lad, coked out of his skull, blustered for a moment, before cooler heads restrained his youthful impetuosity. I could see through the murk of the shades that he was a mere slip of a thing, compared with the muscular compactness, the overarching bulk, of our driver. I was sandwiched between Melor and Annie, the weakest link in the chain. Whispered remarks, questions, challenges, barbs continued to pelt us from all sides at once.

"Nearly there," he muttered. "Steady. Almost..."

"Who's the Doorman?" Annie wanted to know.

"Looks like...Belvedere."

"Oh barf. It would be Belly-up Belvedere."

"Oy! Where'd ye think yer goin' then? We've been here in queue—d'yer see the queue, mate?"

"They think they're quality, they do."

"Back off," the Meme threatened, "I'll break your sodding little nose. Want to try me? C'mon, I'd love to give demonstrations, no charge."

90

The crowd backed off sufficiently to give us a small sac of empty space, like an air-bubble within the bloodstream; Melor seized the opportunity to press forward, shoving the last few hedonists right and left, like a spray of chaff in the wind.

"You better be on the Guest List," a large wheezing Kangaroo interposed himself in front of the garish red velvet door. I assumed he was Belvedere. Melor leaned forward, whispered something, and the Kangaroo responded with a string of whispered oaths and imprecations, the sense of which somehow escaped me.

"I'm all she needs tonight," the Meme insisted. "She's only staying for a few minutes. And this is just her sister—never been in public before."

Another, lengthier, exchange, and then Melor leaned in front of me and I heard him whispering something to Annie—the only word I could catch was *Stephen*.

"I don't give a shite," she exploded—

"Get 'er inside, now!" the Kangaroo choked on his words, "Before she rips off that disguise and causes a riot. I can't *believe* you brought her here, *tonight* of all nights..."

Several flunkeys opened a side door I hadn't noticed, and hustled the three of us into warm, smokey darkness. The door clicked shut behind us, and the noise of the slavering, gibbering mob outside was completely sealed off—the walls must have been soundproof.

I nearly fell over.

"Take your fucking shades off," Annie reached over and rudely snatched them from the bridge of my nose.

I blinked as my eyes accustomed themselves to the warm, smoke-filled gloom. There was a thudding sort of music coming up through the floor and making your very bones tingle and vibrate. The lights were dim, unevenly spaced, giving off weird cone-shaped emanations of flickering electricity masquerading as brightness.

"Take 'er to the VIP lounge," a voice barked.

"Is she here?" Annie wanted to know.

"Let's go to the Lounge," Melor whispered, "We can see everything, and everyone, from there."

"OK, but you're not keeping me in the bloody Lounge."

Her voice was making me nervous.

"Why the fuck did you have to suggest this!" Melor belted out the words like a prize-fighter swinging his fists. To my astonishment, I realised he was speaking to *me*.

xii.

As soon as we were comfortably ensconced at one of the corner tables with a perfect view of the dance-floor, Annie started making trouble. I knew it was coming—just not the form it would take.

She ripped off the blonde wig. I noticed that all the other tables had quieted down; our own was the focus of an almost breathless expectancy.

"You keep your bloody hands to yourself," I heard her sneering voice slicing and slashing at poor Melor. Their disagreement was rapidly spiraling out of control. She jumped up, spilling her drink.

"Just wait for like five minutes," he pleaded.

"Like hell I will—keep an eye on *Sylvia*; she looks like she's about to pass out."

She slouched swanking her way across the Lounge, to the unisex powder room. You could see hundreds of pairs of glazed eyeballs rotating, following her every step. Melor barged in behind her. I was left all alone. And sure enough, in the next instant a sort of bartender type (he was a Wildebeest with bloodshot brown eyes) shambled over and handed me a folded-up napkin.

"From an admirer," he whispered.

Wonderful. I'd come here to make a splash; instead I was being propositioned by some sleazy Lothario. Gulping, I unfolded the missive and scanned the following words blocked out in capital letters (in the cheap blue ink of a ballpoint pen):

Sylvia—
I've seen your sister when she gets this way; you'd better do something, before all Hell breaks loose!

There was no signature. I took a deep breath, trying to keep my feelings in check. *Who* could've recognised someone as

93

insignificant and relatively unphotographed as myself? It scared me. Almost as much as Annie being out of control. Minutes must have slipped past. Time has a way of becoming elastic, when contorted by certain types of overpowering stress. And behold: a Vision clothed in the earthly clay of my sister's all too corruptible flesh glided forth from the restroom. I didn't know what she'd done to herself—perhaps nothing physical (she didn't seem to be wearing any additional makeup) but for all that, she was *breathtaking*. Her burning eyes (no longer recognisable, even to me) were smouldering in their sockets; her being *exuded* a raw, almost frighteningly intense sexuality (like a chemically induced chain reaction in danger of spiraling out of control).

Everyone seemed to have been holding their breath, and now—noiselessly—gave vent to a collective, dizzying sigh—which vibrated down through your spine and turned your thighbones into twin tuning-forks aligned at cross-purposes, jamming the frequencies of rational thought.

She was standing as if mesmerised, looking across at the dance-floor. I already knew exactly what she was seeing: as soon as we'd sat down at our table I'd instantly noticed Stephen von Oxenburg and Yvette Tverskaya swiveling about on the dance-floor—I've always despised them both, so why watch them trying to turn everyone on? Except Annie was now hogging all the attention—I could see heads turning, and limbs pointing up towards our vantage point. I felt queasy, feverish.

Another folded-up napkin was placed on the table:

You'd better do something, fast!

How could I tell whomever-it-was that I hadn't the power? That I was literally paralysed, exerting all my concentration to avoid throwing up?

I risked glancing over at the dance-floor. They were threading their way to the bar. The next thudding song had begun, but Yvette, dimpling her little nose, was heading, flanked by two guards, over to the VIP lounge.

"*Please make Annie somehow let her go past, unscathed,*"
I silently offered up a prayer to the Cat Goddess, Bast.

But Annie was no longer there. It took me a moment to
locate where she was in the crowd—a small air-bubble, round
which the throngs were mobbing and packing themselves,
disclosed her, with Melor, going right up to Stephen.

She was saying something. Yvette, it seemed, had
disappeared into the powder room. Stephen's lips were moving,
and then Annie's. Something electric was starting to implode,
from all sides. Even before Stephen lurched forward, lunging,
throwing himself on my sister, the flashbulbs had already started
going off. As the two of them began a sort of grinding, overly
sexualised writhing—against each other, on the dance-floor—I
could see what looked like hundreds of rats and ferrets taking out
cameras, cell-phones, other pieces of electronic equipment—
there were vermin all over the place—coming out of the
woodwork—how the hell had they got here that fast, or had they
been here the whole time lurking in all the darkest corners?

The flashbulbs and strobe lights from hundreds of
cameras were flashing from every which way.

"*You've got to do something!*" a voice somehow shouted
its way into my consciousness. "Don't your family have any
reserves or back-up waiting in the wings—didn't you bring any
bodyguards?"

Too much was happening at once: Yvette came out of the
loo and stood there for a moment, more cameras going off in our
direction; for an instant it was all I could do to keep from leaping
in front of them. Turning, I found myself face to face with a large
black Rat, his beady eyes glinting in the dim light.

"*It's too late,*" he shouted into my ear.

Sure enough, Annie had picked up a beer bottle—as her
rival charged her, she brought it down with a demonic flourish,
cracking open Yvette's silly little head.

Everything had gone wild already. It simply got worse.
The screams and melee blotted out the thudding music. I could
see Melor slugging Yvette's entourage, taking fearful punishment

himself—Annie was being forcibly hustled out the side-door; 7 or 8 bouncers were struggling with her as cameras continued popping and going off, making the puddle of blood flash and glitter as it sluggishly seeped round Yvette's chalky face, staining her platinum tresses—

I heard someone screaming the word *doctor* and then, as news of Annie's little scuffle reached the mob outside, shouts and catcalls merged into this vast, throbbing roar that made the walls shake—it sounded like tens of thousands of animals, going berserk.

In the distance the seesaw bleating of police sirens was gradually getting louder.

"The fliques'll be here any minute," the Rat squeaked, "Put your shades back on—hurry."

"I can't see," I sobbed, "It's the Apocalypse."

"No it's not; it's just London on a Saturday night. C'mon," he squeezed my shoulder, guiding me through a swirling melee of noise and flashes and jostling, "If we can make it as far as my Jag down the street, I'll take you straight home."

"Home," I gasped.

The word flashed through my mind, in blocked-out capital letters.

"Sure you can't give me just one little *hint*? You know, concerning the lucky sod she's knocking off, right under her Dad's static-electricity-reinforced whiskers? We all know you know."

My g-d. Just what, exactly, had I been yammering to a Fleet Street reporter? This broke all my previous records—for abject stupidity. I mean, here we were comfortably idling just half a stone's throw from the front door to my house. Insidious flashbacks kept derailing my train of logical thinking: again and again I re-experienced leaving the club, staggering through a veritable Bedlam—police on horseback were charging the crowds, driving them back, recklessly swinging truncheons. For a split-second I'd glimpsed the flashing lights of an ambulance, as we careened (in the Rat's elegantly streamlined—but utilitarian—vehicle) towards a police checkpoint or roadblock or whatever it was.

He'd fished a laminated ID-badge from out of his jacket, and the thuggish constable had waved him through, practically snapping to attention.

The buildings and squares and monuments gliding past (from the window on the passenger's side) didn't make any sense—I scarcely knew what they were. The Rat had told me I was hyperventilating; he said to breathe deeply.

For a long time I concentrated on my breathing (and hung onto the act of doing so the way a person who's never learned to swim clings to driftwood).

And talked my fool head off?

Or was he simply planting the idea in my head, so as to panic me into laying my cards on the table?

Could it be that the large sleek Norwegian Black Rat with the discerning beady black eyes and the sharp versatile front teeth honestly hadn't recognised Stephen? I found it hard to believe.

Perhaps if I could hazard a throw of the dice—to make him lay *his* cards on the table—

"We all know I'm not as deep in Her counsels as you seem to think."

"Whose counsels are we talking about?"

"Hers. The person you asked me about."

"And her name is?"

"Names can be dangerous. How do I know you're not secretly tape-recording this conversation?"

"You're absolutely right. I could be."

"But you *aren't*, right?" I gulped, "I mean, that wouldn't be very sporting."

"Life isn't very sporting."

I was becoming warm and drowsy again. I *couldn't* let my guard slip—

"We're talking about Stephen von Oxenburg. There. Can I get out of the car now?"

His eyes imperceptibly widened. Or perhaps it was just my imagination.

"Go ahead," he flashed me a sophisticated, half-crooked smile. "The door's not locked. I hope you didn't think it was."

"So what about Stephen?" I recklessly demanded. "Do you like him?"

"Do you?"

"I can't stand him."

So what if he printed what I was blabbering? It was the simple unvarnished truth.

"And she?" he caught me off guard.

"You won't get me to say anything against my sister. I'm sorry."

"Your *sister*?" he sounded incredulous. "But we were talking about the Princess Delilah."

It felt like I'd been slugged in the gut.

"You were telling me all about when she took you into that room, at the Aeroport. Did it surprise you, the things she was saying?"

"*What* things?"

Somehow, I unaccountably knew, deep down, in the marrow of my still inexperienced bones, that even I never would've been so daft as to run off at the mouth concerning *Delilah*.

I forced myself to return his steady, unblinking gaze.

"You win," he finally released his pent-up breath, stressing the first of the two words with a sort of topheavy signification. He winked for good measure. Despite the palpable release of tension between us, I warily held myself in readiness— for the next probe, the next feint.

To my surprise he burst out laughing. Even more surprising, I found it difficult to keep a straight face as the Rat continued, in a partly fervid, partly cynical, tone of voice:

"You thought I was trying to get your defences down, lull your vigilance, that sort of thing. Yes, I'm an investigative reporter—if you suddenly wanted to start feeding me a story, I'm ready and willing. But I gave you the lift home for a completely different reason: I like you. It's as simple as that."

My face must've betrayed something in spite of itself.

"Don't look so horrified," he burst out laughing again. "I didn't mean it like *that*. I simply mean, I like you, as a person. You seem far too nice for the sort of company you've been keeping of late."

I managed to keep my mouth shut (but the ridiculous pleasure must've shown in my face).

"I don't think anyone really *understands* you."

"You can say that again."

Another laugh brought me back down to earth.

"So how could a grubby, flea-infested Rat hope to do so? I *don't* understand you, or anyone else. But there's something— something about you—that's special."

"Oh," I tried to wipe the smile off my face.

"Here's my card. Give me a ring anytime you need a friendly ear—or a flea-bitten shoulder to cry on."

"I will," I said.

And I meant it.

"You can ring the competition, with any hot revelations."

We both laughed. Gathering my things, I climbed out of his sportscar.

"No, seriously. I'm called Tosk."

"Tosk," I repeated, smiling.

"Oh, and Sylvia?"

I stopped, turning back towards the window on the driver's side (which he'd rolled down).

"G-d keep and protect you, Dear Heart."

"Aye but which g-d?" I wanted to know. "Ours, after all, is a polytheistic society."

He grinned (or was it a grimace?) before driving off.

My first thought, on waking up the next morning, was a stab of sudden remembrance combined with icy adrenaline: *what in the world could've happened to Annie?*

I'd seen her being dragged kicking and fighting through one of the side entrances. The roar from outside certainly hadn't boded well. All of a sudden, I felt sick to my stomach. What had I been thinking? Was it my fault we'd even gone there (as Melor crassly insinuated)? Had Annie even made it home yet?

Slipping into the first mismatched assortment of clothes I could get my hands on, I tiptoed through the outer chamber where Goody Thorpe always slept (my tiptoeing must have been an automatic reflex). Hurrying down the corridor, I had to stop for a moment at the bend, where it turned the corner, collecting my thoughts, catching my breath.

Creeping forward, like an assassin, I pushed open the door. Unlocked: a bad sign. Summoning all my courage and strength of will, I rushed through the antechamber and flung open the door to my sister's bedchamber—

Empty.

The bed had never been slept in.

Her boudoir with all its clothes and floor-to-ceiling mirrors was similarly undisturbed. Every room in the large suite was utterly devoid of life—or even the tiniest signs of life. I didn't want to think about what this might mean.

Torn apart by the mob?

Trampled by the mounted police?

Perhaps even now some jaded coroner were flipping through a special directory—smearing it with his greasy hooves—in looking up the unlisted number for His Excellency, Mr Ferdinand Romanoff.

Of the few servants still presumably on the premises, none could be expected to answer the ill-omened jangling of a telephone-call—at this time of the morning. As I descended the main staircase, however, the mouthwatering smell of cooking caused me to quicken my pace. I expected to catch one of the cooks frying himself a quick bite to eat but instead found myself throwing my arms round Goody Thorpe, burying my face in the white feathers of her muscular wing.

"I'm gone for just one day," she gently but firmly disengaged me, "and look what happens: the whole place is at sixes and sevens."

She handed me a plate of steaming porridge. I hadn't realised I was so famished; sitting down at the breakfast table, I began ravenously bolting it down—I half expected her to rebuke me for such 'unladylike' deportment, but her mind obviously was on other things.

"Just because I have to take a job down the street, cause your Da doesn't know, or care, what happens to anyone else—including his own family—if it weren't for my Maggie's poor fatherless angels, I certainly wouldn't be scrubbing floors in some damn hotel—what I'm trying to say is, long as they pay me (at time and a half), I'll still be here, to take care of you—evenings, and nights, and first thing in the mornings."

"We'll scrape the money together somehow," I stammered turning red in the face.

"Hurry up and eat your brekker—I've got to be back at the Omni by 7 o'clock at the latest."

She glanced out the kitchen window at the Moon's wasted sickle hanging low in the sky.

"And another thing—"

I squared my shoulders; her tone of voice warned me tp expect something unpleasant.

"I wonder what in the world you girls could have been *thinking*!"

"Do you know something about Annie—"

"I mean seriously. For once even I'm speechless—"

"You don't sound that speechless to me—"

"It's been the talk of the morning news programmes and panel discussions—I haven't had the courage yet to look at *The Carcass*."

"By *it* I suppose you mean—"

"Your antics. At that dancehall or whatever it was. Even for Miss Annie—what they say happened was just—beyond the pale of civilised, polite society—but *you*—I never thought I'd live to see the day that a charge of mine *ruins* herself!"

"Just what the hell are you talking about?" I spluttered.

"Don't take my word for it."

She walked over and flipped on the TV.

"Wish I could offer some words of wisdom," she clucked, "but I've got to get going. Can't be late for my second day on the job."

"That's right, never let me live it down," I shouted right as the phone started ringing.

Sweet Bast, here it is—the Coroner, I thought to myself. My knees turned to jelly; I grasped the edge of the kitchen table.

"Come quick, Love, it's your Father," she cupped the receiver with an arthritic wing. "I'll turn the sound down..."

She hastened over to the blaring TV—I gestured for her to 'mute' the thing but not switch it off. Now (as I took the receiver) I was able to focus on the nauseating film footage of Annie being hauled into a police van, in the midst of a riot.

Slamming the door behind her, Goody Thorpe pelted across the courtyard and through the front gate. A feeling of desolation swept over me. I could hear my father's querulous, petulant voice even with the receiver held at arm's length. I brought it up to my ear:

"—certainly aren't going to be pretty—"

"Father—"

"So there you are *finally*—you *finally* deign to accept an International person to person phonecall—"

"What do you want?"

I heard a sharp intake of breath. My tone (it seemed) had brought him up short.

"Look, Love, I've been under a veritable mountain of stress—"

"I should have thought going on honeymoon with a still-desirable Heiress worth a cool three million a year—"

"She's not worth nearly that much—believe me, the reports of her wealth have been grossly exaggerated—"

"Is *that* the sort of 'stress' you've been unhorsed by, in the rough-n'-tumble financial tiltyard?" I tried to keep my voice sardonic, but steady.

"Little brat," he started to wheeze, "you've never loved me—never in the slightest—"

"That's not true," I shot back, "I *have* loved you. Probably more than you deserved."

"Is that the reason you *destroyed* me this morning?"

"Please try to stay calm, father."

"Calm! *Calm* she tells me!"

I heard a chorus of giggling.

"Who's there with you?" I demanded.

"My wife of course. Do you find it extraordinary that I should be in the same room as my legally wedded *wife*?" he for some reason broke into a loud peal of put-on sounding laughter.

"Is that *Delilah's* voice?" I demanded.

"Never you mind," he choked on his mirth, "It's none of your business—not after the way you and Annie crucified me last night. And this morning—oh yes—the martyrdom's only beginning—"

"Martyrdom?"

"Yes, martyrdom!" he practically caterwauled. "It's a Page One story—your loving sister's in gaol, waiting to be hauled before a Magistrate—"

"Oh g-d," I felt sick to my stomach.

"The pundits all say she'll be lucky to get off with just Mayhem, as opposed to Hooliganism, Felonious Assault—she has a prior rapsheet you know—this isn't going to be pretty—"

"Isn't there anything we can do?" I practically wailed into the receiver.

104

"And worst of all," he sobbed, "Yvette Tverskaya's father who's *already* rich as Croesus—owns half the steel-mills this side of the bloody Dee—happens to be suing not Annie, but *me*."

"What can we do to help her?" I shouted, my heart beginning to race.

"Will you forget Annie for half a nanosecond—"

"No I won't *forget* her!" I screamed. "Nor Jane, your ex-Wife. You're good at forgetting people—"

"Have you seen the News yet?"

My heart congealed painfully.

"A certain Imperial whelp, of no consequence ever before, used the Press Office to issue a statement. Can you guess the whelp's name?"

Ramses. So that's why the television at this instant was featuring an old Beaver in a powdered wig standing at a lectern in front of the Imperial coat of arms, speaking into more microphones than I'd ever seen in my life.

"Just what," I gulped, "what is this—this statement—"

"He says *you* suborned Annie to try and persuade him to entice Marcus Agrippa to sneak out of the Louvre. He further deposes that you loudly bragged about drugging Marcus' school lunch and committing a sort of date rape on the innocent, hitherto *virginal* young Prince of the Blood—that furthermore you were attempting to blackmail the same: unless he (Marcus) continued fornicating—satisfying your voracious appetite for premarital sex—you threatened *not* to terminate your nefariously engineered pregnancy, giving birth to whatever it was (Lion, Cat, even Human), and going public with the whole filthy business! When he—"

"No, father, no more—"

"When he indignantly refused, advising you to procure yourself an abortion, you vengefully instigated a fight at the Danceteria, playing on your sister's jealousy, working her into a frenzy before unleashing her on poor defenceless Yvette— according to Ramses, everyone knows that Marc finds the ravishing young heiress—we're talking about Yvette Tverskaya—

sublimely irresistible—I'm giving you a direct quote—his exact words, verbatim—"

"He does not," my voice quavered.

"Aha," the Cat pounced (like the skilled Mouser one still sometimes half-glimpsed from under the blurry-edged lineaments of a drunk, wasted life), "Could there, perhaps, be a smidgeon of truth—"

"The only truth is that he *cannot stand* that repulsive, yapping bitch—she started the fight, not Annie—Marcus never once acted like—I know it's not true."

I burst into tears.

"Is that all you care about?" he twisted the knife.

"Father," I sobbed, "I can't even begin to try and put into words—"

"Good, then don't," he sneered. "Listen for a change. This has totally compromised me—"

"You selfish bastard!" I screamed.

"Oh. Of course. You don't fully understand yet," he caused me to grind my teeth in helpless rage. "The News hasn't hit the tabloids yet. We thought it best to try and keep our little secret," he gave a drunken hiccup of a giggle, "for a few extra days if possible—our last days of Peace and Quiet..."

His voice had become nauseatingly self-satisfied. A feeling of dread almost, but not quite, trumped the nausea.

"Let me call your Stepmother to the phone."

I could practically feel him licking his chops.

"Wait," I shouted into the mouthpiece, "I've got to get in touch with your solicitor—to try and help *Annie*—remember *her*?"

"Remember *me*?" a voice I did indeed remember enquired in that cool, commanding timbre which made people seemingly want to fall all over themselves in obeying—and pleasing— *Delilah*, Goddess incarnate—my father had hit the sodding jackpot at the end of the Rainbow.

"He married *you*?" the words tumbled out before I could stop them.

She laughed ravishingly. It raised gooseflesh, which tingled up and down my malnourished arms.

Suddenly I was falling all over myself to try and explain: "My father said that *Ramses* has been promulgating—"

"Don't worry about it."

"But he published the most awful, repulsive things imaginable."

I hated my quavering voice.

"*Sylvia*," hers lashed me like an elegant riding-crop held over a flame till it was flickering with white-hot incandescence, "*Listen* to me: I *said* don't worry: Ramses has next to *nothing* in the way of credibility—no one gives a flying fuck (at least in the Court circles that count)—there'll be some sniggering, some raised eyebrows, and then in just a few days (or weeks) the ripples from this little tempest in a teapot will have been completely forgotten."

How could she be so complacent about the whole thing? I certainly harboured no illusions regarding my own relative unimportance—I knew I counted for far less than Ramses, in terms of credibility or anything else. But even so, couldn't something like this conceivably torpedo (or at least compromise) this stupid *marriage*—which was bound to make her the laughingstock of her precious Court circles—

"How could you marry a wretch like my father?" I heard myself meowing into the phone, "I thought you said you loved—"

"*Shut the hell up this instant!*" she roared, hurting my ears, "We don't know who's listening in—apart from Ferdinand, my new *husband*."

The mockery was unmistakable. Ferdinand, it seemed, had picked up on it as well. I heard him softly whining, remonstrating, in that voice I sometimes felt would follow me to the grave and beyond.

"Leave us," she peremptorily commanded the sot.

"I don't see why I should have to be excluded—"

"Because Sylvia and I have things to discuss."

"What possible business could you have with *Sylvia*?" he sounded incredulous (which made me smile, in spite of myself).

Delilah must have thrown a breakable object; I heard the sound of something smashing in the background, punctuated by a yelp on my father's part—of pain mixed with fear.

"Escort him to the antechamber."

It must be nice, I mused, having slaves and bodyguards to obey your every command, no matter how whimsical, absurd or transparent. Not that having my father thrown out of the room was anything other than sensible, and—I was sure—long overdue.

She picked the phone up again:

"Now we can talk for a bit. Your father's upset, to put it mildly, because this little caper of yours is going to make the Privy Council much less inclined to ratify his own little scam— we've taken the blood tests and signed the prenuptial agreements in all their repetitive legalistic boilerplate—he gets nothing financially, and, it goes without saying, absolutely no Sex—not even a hand-job,"—I winced—"never mind that he claims he had himself sterilised after the birth of his fifth whelp—I can't afford to take any chances regarding so explosive an issue as the Imperial Succession—*my* neck could wind up on the block. Besides," she gave a little laugh, "he doesn't turn me on in the slightest."

Then why...

"Of course, I can appreciate *his* point of view—all this time scheming, struggling and manoeuvring hundreds of factors and variables—and now, this farce of a marriage is finally almost within his palsied grasp (pending the public announcement)— when suddenly, WHAM!" she chuckled sadistically, "This whole Page One scandal involving not just one daughter this time—"

"But what's *your* point of view?" I probed, brazenly, like one of the paparazzi. I imagined my Rat's whiskers twitching.

"Clever girl," she sounded like she was smiling (I fancied I could feel the sharp tips of her half-exposed teeth, coming through the receiver).

"So he's already chucked Blussian, then."

"It's actually the other way round, or would have been," the Lioness yawned, "She skimmed all the rest of Ferdinand's assets, and now my jilted ex-husband Nero's paying the price for his vulnerability to public opinion—she demanded tens of millions of zloty—it'll be marketed to the paparazzi as a double marriage; everyone saves face, and Blussian's now *loaded*."

"Wasn't she quote-unquote loaded before?"

"Not like she is now," Delilah mirthlessly chuckled.

"What about *Annie*?" I suddenly felt in no mood to play games.

"I thought I told you—"

"I'm sick to death of being told not to worry."

My paw flew to my mouth.

"Look, Love," she sounded impatient, "It's in the Crown's interest to see that no charges are preferred, all down the line. You dig? The Lord Advocate knows what to do. That's all I can say, beyond the fact that Ramses overreached himself—he'll live to regret stirring this up. Anyway," she cleared her throat, "Annie should be on her way home from Newgate right now, as we speak."

"How can you be so sure?"

"You worry too much."

"She's my *sister* for Bastsake," I exploded.

"You think she'd do all this for *you*?" her voice socked me in the gut, "if the shoe were on the other foot?"

"Yes," I answered without the slightest hesitation, "Maybe not before, but I know she would, now. This family of ours is finally coming together, like the sides of a wound coming together and healing—from the inside out, organically—both collectively, and for the individual constituent members—like the bits of protoplasm within a unicellular—indivisible—organism."

She burst out laughing.

"Speaking of the patched-together 'organism' in question," she gasped for breath, "two of those very bits of protoplasm you were going on about (one of them's a

Ritalin-case, the other—Thorazine?)—in short, Douglas and Maria—I'm sending them back by a special Government courier; they should be on your doorstep the day after to-morrow."

"But *we* can't take them," I stammered in confusion, "Most of the servants have sought employment elsewhere—I think they got tired of not being paid."

"Maybe they'll decide to come back."

"No they won't—I mean—with all due respect—"

"I *know* they will. Trust me."

Well what could I say?

"Oh, and Sylvia—I saved the best bit for last."

Her voice, which was already focused, came into a sort of super, sharp-edged intensity like the lens in a gigantic telescope, concentrating the light-rays—when we were younger, Annie used to take a magnifying glass and pinpoint the sunlight on a scrap of paper till it caught fire, shriveling in a mantle of flame.

"I've taken the liberty of setting you up an appointment with the Ministry of Education—"

"But that's no good," I had the cheek to interrupt her, "I mean, with all due respect to Your Highness, seeing as Blussian skimmed the last of my father's reserves—not that he ever would've given me a blessed farthing—"

"Nonetheless I think you should go," she said. "Two o'clock. The Ministry."

"Even though I can't afford—"

"*You need to go*," she imbued each word with its own calibrated, percussive punch: "Promise me you'll go."

"But what's the point?" I stubbornly forced myself to speak the words in a breathless torrent, "I mean, there's no money. And what school's going to accept Sylvia Romanoff with this latest—"

"You really must learn to *connect* things," she seemed to be controlling herself, just barely, "and see the big picture for a change. If I say, do something, THERE'S USUALLY A DAMN GOOD REASON!" she roared.

I nodded my idiotic head up and down, till I remembered to speak:

"Yes, Your Imperial Highness."

"You never know," her voice became honey'd and cloying, "Your luck might finally be fixing to take a turn for the better."

Flinging clothes all over the bed, I tried to concentrate my
scattered thoughts on the simple task of getting ready for my little
trip to the Ministry of Education. Who could fathom what Delilah
had up her sleeve? I might be walking into a trap. Even so, what
else could I do?

My plan had been to walk to the tube-stop, board the
Koltsovaya, transfer to the Northern Line, and get off at the Place
de Grève, which was only a stone's throw from the Ministry with
its sinister battlements and netting over the entrances to catch
those who jumped—*desperate* graduate students (all too often
specialising in Engineering or Calculus) whose meager stipends
were liable to be cut off for no reason.

Right as I was heading out the door, a large black Packard
pulled up at the gate. I felt a rush of adrenaline. After all, things
were seldom (these days) what they seemed. The automobile
could very well contain armed assassins or would-be malefactors
of some stamp or another. Perhaps, at best, they'd got turned
around and needed directions. Then again, it *could* be a carload
of slavering paparazzi—

I licked my lips (and actually caught myself salivating).
"Sylvia?"

Well this *was* a surprise. From inside the automobile
Arlova (of all people) beckoned impatiently. I awkwardly
vaulted up onto the running board, stooped down, ducked
through the open door, and precipitated myself downwards and
forward—simultaneously—such that my angular pelvis came into
contact with the cushioned backseat—at the exact instant the
stupid driver accelerated, throwing me against Arlova's durable,
if somewhat plumpish, physique.

She pursed her lips. Her face made a grimace. I picked
up my notebook, checked that my satchel with its pencase was

still slung over my shoulder (I refuse to start carrying a rucksack, like all the other little boys and girls), and adjusted my skirt.

"Git 'er to shoot the friggin' door," the driver, a Porcupine, grumbled.

"It seems the light's blinking," her mellifluent voice filled the cramped interior of the big shiny black motorcar. "Perhaps you could try to crack the door open, just the slightest bit, and then slam it—a bit harder?"

I understood Annie. I actually understood her rebelliousness, the twin pools of limpid fire that her eyes sometimes became. I, myself, had never liked Arlova that much. My sister on the other hand had always detested the baggage— absolutely detested her—and I'd never known why. Till now, perhaps? Or was I just being contrary?

"Sylvia," her voice made me jump. "You're not listening, Dear."

"This isn't the way to the Ministry—"

"As I was *just* explaining, the plans have changed."

Delilah had changed them. I was beginning to feel more and more like a puppet. Or a piece on a chessboard, but which piece, and which colour?

"It's not often that I get to be the bearer of good news," she licked her lips—

"Why is that, d'you suppose?"

"I beg your pardon?"

(She also didn't like being interrupted.)

"It sounds like you're more used to delivering bad news, than good—"

"Sylvia, this is important," her voice lost its artificiality, becoming more blunt, "We need to concentrate on the business at hand—it's not far to the Point."

Harmony Point. So we were going to see Snoopus. My heart began to beat faster. It had been almost two years now. Snoopus Brown (almost no one remembered that he still had a surname), the legendary, towering symbol of Enlightenment, Tolerance, the Universal Rights of Animalkind—of species not only coexisting side by side without violence, mass rapes and pogroms, but actually integrating, helping one another, combining to forge something truly titanic—the legendary pioneer of Education in the true sense of the word—tutour to four of the last five Emperors—already, by the time Helen and I had started going to school, was so old, and so fat, that he could no longer effectively teach. He simply didn't possess the stamina. His two deputies, Yekaterina Alekseyevna Arlova and Michael Faraday Sheop, did most of the teaching. We tried to idolise them (since we idolised Snoopus); it didn't quite work. On the rare occasions when Snoopus was carried in on a litter and, sipping frequently from a medicinal-looking container, undertook to conduct the day's lesson, we *knew* we disliked them. How could one avoid disliking the paltry substitutes fobbed off in place of the riveting, consciousness-expanding lectures Snoopus himself was able to weave like a spell?

Helen of course defended her. After all, Arlova was a Meme, one of that persecuted species Snoopus surrounded himself with (except for Michael Sheop, a woolly-fleeced Ram). She was also the only female in the entire teaching faculty (which appealed to our burgeoning feminism). But alas, most of all, she was Snoopus' mistress.

I detest that word, *mistress*. For a long time both of us (Helen and I) tried to deny that it was even true. Annie took vindictive glee rubbing our noses in the filth and muck of its incontrovertible status as fact. The tabloids supplied a vast cesspool, or reservoir, of innuendo dressed up as proof—except for once the orgy of character assassination actually turned out to be, more or less, 'on target' (give or take a few stray allegations that went wide of the mark). The damning procession of evidence had a cumulative, avalanche-like effect. I remember the day that I finally gave way and accepted it. Helen and I had the most terrific row, and stopped speaking to each other for about a month. Only afterwards did I discover that Helen had already known, and simply pretended to be arguing that where there's smoke there's *not* always fire.

And yet, perhaps the buxom temptress, the doe-eyed pedagogue, Arlova, indirectly prolonged the Great Snoopus' life—perhaps it was more than just 'sex'? Perhaps he genuinely depended on, and, almost, loved her. I can't ever believe that Snoopus really and truly—unreservedly—loves Arlova. She's simply too calculating. Too complacent. Too common.

Ironically when Snoopus, under political pressure, dissolved Harmony House (the old school we used to attend, in the Halcyon days), and we were all parceled out to various posh reformatories (as Helen and I contemptuously termed them), I realised how good we'd had it, under Arlova. At least she tried to emulate Snoopus.

She'd plucked her eyebrows, I noticed. Thank Bast she didn't still pencil them on. She'd stopped using rouge, but now she painted her eyes. (Or had she always done so? I couldn't remember.) She definitely had always been a large-boned, fleshed-out sort of Meme, with curves and padding—which always made me phantasise about which position she and Snoopus—I shuddered, and forced myself to concentrate on what she was saying.

"He's *not* in the best of health I'm afraid. We've tried to keep it out of the tabloids to the best of our ability, but his health *has* been failing for the past four or five months."

You sound calm about it, I wanted to shout.

"Go easy on him, Sylvia."

"What do you think I'm going to say?"

"Ask him for something, what else?"

"If that's your opinion of me—"

"Early this morning he got a special phonecall on the Rotator connecting him straight to the Louvre. That's all I know. He wouldn't tell me anything about it. I was hoping *you* might."

"Citizen," I cleared my throat, "I was expelled from school for something I never did. And now I'm trying to find a new school, or a tutour at least, but I don't have any money. That's all I know, or care about. And since no one's going to

115

teach a single verb or gerund—without that I shove a wad of cold hard cash in their face—it looks like I'm fucked."

"*Sylvia,*" her voice would have slapped me, had it possessed a physical hand.

At the same instant the Porcupine driving us gave a loud cackle.

"Yes?" I sullenly replied, gritting my teeth.

"I'm not accustomed to language like that. If you're doing it for effect, my advice is—"

"Well I'm not," I exploded unable to stop myself, "so you can shove your bloody advice where the sun doesn't shine."

The driver burst into a loud, appreciative-sounding guffaw. Unable to face Snoopus' *Mistress* (of whom, even now, I was rather afraid), I turned my face to the window. The rest of the relatively short drive unfolded in silence.

They ushered me straight into that study I remembered so well, with its sagging wall-to-wall shelves, its heaps of musty books shoved every which way all over the place, its rickety (but still comfortable) armchairs upholstered with their cracked leather out of which the stuffing was beginning to come in places, and somehow, most of all, the millions of glittering dust motes suspended in the thick, motionless air with its sweet smell of tobacco, coffee, and ink.

Snoopus, swathed in a voluminous dressing-gown of purple velvet, was reclining in his favourite armchair, bathed in sunlight, a capacious tray heaped with papers, books and mugs of coffee girdling his bulk. His spectacles flashed as he turned his massive skull towards me, fixing me with his watery brown dog's-eyes, large as saucers, and wise beyond comprehension.

"My dear Child," his shockingly enfeebled voice brought a lump to my throat.

I rushed over, dropped down on my knees, and began to snivel as his rubbery pawpads caressed my white fur, but with a tentativeness, as though his thoughts were elsewhere.

"It's been such a long time," his cracked voice rumbled, gathering strength.

"I'm such a disgusting, ungrateful sow-bug," my sobs somehow sounded uncouth—against the backdrop of the room's accumulated antiquity, like a huge hourglass measuring infinity one grain at a time.

"There, there," he chuckled, beginning to stroke my fur a bit less absentmindedly, "We've had our *distractions*, you and I, both…"

"Yes, we have," I managed.

"This business with the damned Rats and their terrible *lies*," his voice began to find itself, increasing in resonance, "has grieved me ever so much."

I opened my mouth, but he forestalled me by lifting his paw. Only Snoopus could ever lift his paw that way, soliciting our undivided attention, holding the entire class spellbound.

"I don't watch the so-called News, you know—nor read the mass-circulation Dailies—I didn't know till this morning—no one told me"—his tone sharpened (could this be a swipe at Arlova?)—"else I should have offered to undertake your Education myself."

Words failed me. I had to gulp several times before I could speak.

"This nonsense about charging people *money*," his nostrils flared contemptuously, "for something as necessary to living and breathing as Education has always distressed me; the word *tuition* should be stricken from our collective vocabulary—I don't care how many new schools Arlova managed to open since taking over the accounting department—"

I suddenly remembered something with a sort of white-hot intensity:

"But Snoopus—excuse me—"

I'd startled him.

"Are we quite alone, d'you think?"

"You mean," he chuckled, "could Arlova be eavesdropping."

"Well could she?"

He blinked, making me feel ashamed—till the thing I'd remembered overrode even my shame:

"I don't care if she is—"

"To my knowledge," he emphatically pronounced the three words, "we find ourselves, at this moment, having a private, Arlova-free conversation."

Something in the Dog's tone of voice would've tugged at my heartstrings on any other occasion—I realised that he was on the point of confiding in me—about Arlova, about the decrepitude of old age, with all its indignities and limitations—and it was heartbreaking—only—so was my own life—

"Listen, Snoopus," the most horrific suspicion had just illuminated everything—momentarily—like a bolt of lighting, "What about *Marcus*—have they saddled you with *his* education?" my voice was giving out. "Well *have* they?" I squawked.

Mercifully, Snoopus cleared his throat, opened his mouth, and began speaking:

"In fact, I *have* undertaken his Education as well, but only from one to four o'clock every day. I'm sure the time could be found—"

"It's between one and four *right now*," I went scarlet with shame. "So *that's* what she meant about my so-called luck taking a so-called turn for the better—is he here? *Tell me!*" I shouted, *almost* shaking—assaulting—the corpulent Octagenarian.

But the coarse, ringing shout was assaultive enough on its own. My paw flew to my lips, as I sagged forward on the edge of the chair, my head swimming. I dimly perceived my beloved Teacher impatiently waving a crowd of servants and bodyguards out of the room. So someone *had* been listening—well it wasn't Snoopus' fault. Besides, a disruptive, gut-wrenching scream would've alarmed anyone—not just those like Arlova who were either listening at the keyhole, or wanted to listen.

Arlova—speak of the devil. She was gesticulating, refusing to leave the room. Someone (at first I thought it was Snoopus) had laid me down on the sofa, arranged the pillows, and drawn a musty coverlet up to my chin. At length I perceived that all the noise had died down. Snoopus fretfully supervised a couple of servants, one of whom was pouring out the strong, black coffee he loved, whilst the other strong young Meme lad (they were both Memes, of course) was moving his master's favourite armchair (just as decrepit as the old Dog himself), carrying it over to the sofa, so that we could converse softly, intimately. Or at least such was my hope.

And sure enough, the two Memes withdrew. Snoopus deposited his vast bulk into the creaking chair with a wheezing sigh of relief. Leaning towards me, he proferred a cup of aromatic Espresso. It was piping hot and burned my gums, along with the sensitive membrane of my oesophagus, but I managed to sip the stuff, concentrating every fibre of my being on the fact that Marcus, a classmate of mine, a young Lion to whom, for whatever reason, I'd become fatefully attached, might possibly just happen to be in one of the adjoining classrooms, separated from my raging desire by everyday walls and doors—that *was* a 'good' thing, right?

I *wanted* him, with every fibre of my being, correct?

Or had I puffed him up into something he wasn't?

"I think too much, Snoopus," I confessed with a rueful shake of the head.

"A failing to which all scholars are liable," he smiled, squeezing my delicate catspaw within both of his, which were swollen, ravaged by degenerative arthritis—Arlova didn't seem to know how to bandage them properly, I disapprovingly noted.

"In answer to your impetuous question of a few minutes ago," he shifted his bulk, "His Grace, young Marcus, missed his regularly scheduled lessons to-day; his private Chamberlain informed me that the poor child happens to be indisposed—"

"Is it serious?" I remembered just in time to keep my voice under control.

"Just a twinge of splenetic depression—we used to call it spleen back when I was a youngster," his large unwinking brown eyes seemed to be worming their way through all the layers of artifice, between my soul and his.

"I mean, what a tragedy for the Nation," I stammered, "For the Imperial Succession—were anything serious—to befall," I gasped for breath, "such—such a reputedly praiseworthy young—"

My throat had closed on itself, leaving "Lion" buried alive.

"Your solicitous outburst," the unwinking brown eyes were expanding, filling the universe, "leads me inevitably to the reluctant supposition—"

120

"Snoopus," I clasped his big arthritic paw between my delicate youthful ones, "Can you tell me anything about him? Does he seem in good spirits?"

The question clearly made him uncomfortable.

"Young Agrippa," he cleared his throat, then sipped some coffee, leaning back in his armchair, "happens to be a sensitive Animal. These scandalous rumours—"

I flinched.

"The Klieg lights of concentrated, tabloid-driven, blindingly intense—"

"He's too beautiful, too sensitive—"

"Like *all* youngsters, on the cusp between childhood and adolescence, he finds himself simultaneously repelled and attracted—"

"By—"

"By all the *attention* concentrated on the trembling shoulders of a Fourteen-year-old," he beat me to the punch, "the *enormity* of finding himself on the tip of millions upon millions of salivating, half-loquacious, half-slavering tongues. I expect *you've* been undergoing much the same experience, these past few days?"

I wasn't going to let him change the subject that easily.

"Tell me, Snoopus—does he ever—"

"I'm afraid—"

"*Does-he-ever-talk-about-me?*"

There.

I'd said it.

I'd got the words out.

"My poor child," Snoopus wheezingly, snufflingly coughed, "I'm afraid I can't answer that particular question."

"Why not?"

"I've been advised—not to answer—such questions."

"Advised by *Marc*? Oh, Snoopus, please tell me."

His expressive brown eyes scrunched almost all the way shut. He was frowning, staring up at the ceiling.

"Can't we talk about—about what sort of a scholar he is?" I gasped for breath, "At which Subject does Marcus excel? Has he been getting high marks? You can tell me, Snoopus—please, give me *something.*"

I heard his breath release itself in a wheezing, worldweary sigh—which meant: he was going to try and give me some sort of answer. I stayed perfectly still, staring down at my knees.

"I've only had the privilege of instructing His Imperial Highness beginning yesterday—"

I shuddered, closing my eyes, imagining the sun-kindled tawny fur, the large dreamy golden-green eyes—the intent look of concentration he got when I was saying something. And to think He was *here*. Less than twenty-four hours ago.

"Which doesn't make for a very reliable evaluation," he coughed. "We spent most of the afternoon administering diagnostic tests—"

"So how did he do on the tests—I know you can't tell me the Scores—but—he *is* brilliant, yes? At least *intelligent?*"

"Young Agrippa is highly intelligent," the Minister of Education smiled, as I felt myself blushing to high heaven, irradiating a mixture of pride, desire, and embarrassment.

The door opened; we unexpectedly found ourselves peering at the ugly mug of a creature (I think it was some sort of Razourback, or perhaps a tusked Peccary) who could be nothing in all the wide world so much—so inescapably—as a State Security operative.

"Not finished *yet?*" the Intruder had the nerve cynically to demand, in a bored-sounding voice.

Snoopus looked around for his spectacles. I handed them to him.

"Well, yes," he cleared his throat, beginning to reach for his cup of coffee, then changing his mind, "I mean, No." He coughed. "Not just yet. My dear Sylvia—"

"This is a private discussion we're having," I coldly informed the rogue. "Now please get out, and shut the door behind you."

"Fine," he shrugged, perhaps trying to smirk. "You can get back to fucking each other's brains out, for all I care—I get paid by the hour."

The scoundrel closed the door just forcefully enough to keep from slamming it. Poor Snoopus, who was clearly discombobulated by this most intrusive interruption, started violently, and then began coughing. I poured him a fresh cup of coffee, adjusted his lap-rug, and rearranged some of the cushions between his sloping shoulders and the rickety back of the chair.

"I'm so sorry," I began, "for being the indirect cause—"

"Listen, Sylvia," he cut me off, "we need to settle this. I'm not feeling very well," he raised a paw forestalling any further interruptions on my part. "So here's what we'll do: you can start coming to the Gatehouse for lessons with Michael Sheop—he's taking a sabbatical from his administration of the Academy's graduate and post-doctoral courses. As I'm sure you realise, your new teacher's a pedagogical genius—runs the whole Ministry on my behalf, on days when"—he grimaced—"my age indisposes me."

"But—"

He raised his paw:

"Your expenses have all been paid, in advance. Three-quarters of a million pounds sterling."

"But who—"

"I don't concern myself with *that* question, and neither should you. For your own safety."

"My own safety?" I gulped. "Then you must have an idea who's behind this whole thing. Arlova said you took a phonecall this morning—"

"She should never have told you that."

"With whom did you speak?" (I almost said, Who did you speak with?—dangling a preposition truly *was* unthinkable, in Snoopus' rarefied presence.)

He simply shook his head, his eyes crinkling painfully shut, a frown creasing his massive, ponderous brow.

"Why can't I have my lessons with you and—and Marcus?" I demanded.

"Be content for Bastsake with what *they're* letting you have as it is," he unexpectedly hissed the words in a shrill, sibilant whisper.

"*What* exactly are *they* letting me have, as it is?"

"There's nothing to say you can't take your breaks over in the Refectory, or the Garden. And if the Prince Imperial happens to be taking a stroll, stretching his cramped, adolescent limbs, at that same moment—"

"Oh, Snoopus!" I hugged him. "Ohhh! Oh, thank you," I burst into tears.

When I got home I found a letter from Annie—she'd eloped with
Stephen von Oxenburg. Bast knows where they were by the time
I read the letter. It was of course dripping with venomous outrage
concerning our father's marriage to the Princess Delilah—most
of the imprecations and epithets with which she filled the margins
were quite obscene—but also hilarious. I was finally beginning to
'understand' Anastasia—and appreciate the unique facets to her
peppery character. It made me (almost) sorry that she'd run away
again. Because this time I somehow had an inkling that the
situation was different. More serious. I had a feeling that we
wouldn't be seeing her again—at least for quite some time. I
hoped I was wrong.

The next morning of course was sheer torture, creeping at a
snail's pace by fits and starts—grinding to a *standstill* when I
started gnashing my teeth. It felt like the clock hand would never
get to 11.45 as I paced in circles, having long ago gathered my
books and put the finishing touches on my lackluster appearance.
    I'd of course phoned Arlova first thing. She said they'd
send a car round to collect me at fifteen minutes to twelve.
    Picking out the clothes to wear, taking a bath, brushing
my fur and whiskers—it took longer than usual, but not long
enough to bridge the yawning emptiness between now and the
time (at half past eleven) when I could finally troop down to the
front gate. For now I tried to kill time with an article on semiotics
but kept reading the same sentence over and over again, till the
words stopped making sense. My eyes must have glazed over.
    "Whatcha doin'?" an earsplittingly shrill voice caused me
to drop my book on the floor.
    The Divorce 'did something' to my brother Dougie.
I mean, it did a number on all of us, but especially in his case.
Maybe because he's the youngest. Insufferable pest, hyperactive
brat, manipulative little pathological liar. It's embarrassing to

125

confess, but quite truthfully I couldn't stand him. Even now I'm not quite sure if it was jealousy (for the way Jane and Goody Thorpe both treated him like he was King of the Universe), or perhaps something more twisted. I suppose, in retrospect, it was only natural for a Seven-year-old to be curious about an oddball sister staring over the edge of her book at the far wall, as if in a trance.

"How dare you set foot in my room—get out—this instant."

The look he flashed me was so loaded with petulant resentment, I had to bite down on a wild, erratic laugh and instead brought out the words, "It must have been fun—a regular funfest—a real barrel of laughs—flying to the bloody Cote d'Azûr on a luxury jet. I've never been on one, Dougie—did the pilot let you take the controls, did Blussian cram your face with lots of Ladyfingers and Chelsea buns?" my eyes filled with tears. "Did you ever think for one instant about those *left behind*?"

The story of my life: being Left Behind (which of course is a subset of being Left Out).

"I wish they *had* left me behind."

"Because you didn't get your way as often as you're used to getting it, back here? Could that be the reason?"

"Maria's right," his eyes glisteningly welled up with perfect dramatic timing, "You're mean."

Cut to the quick (for some reason), I jumped off the bed and stormed right past the brat without letting him see my own lackluster eyes (not blue and striking like his) unaccountably brimming with their own lackluster tears.

"Wait," he grabbed me by the tail.

"Keep your fucking grubby paws to yourself!" I yowled ready to scratch the hell out of him.

"In the Coat-Does-Your or whatever it is" he was obviously trying to keep from blubbing, "the servants *laughed* at me…"

You're breaking my heart, I thought to myself—and then remembered the way Jane had sneered those exact same words, just the day before yesterday.

"They held candy right in front of me, an' then jerked it away."

"They *what*?" my mouth fell open.

A wave of anger unexpectedly galvanised me.

"So when I scratched and bit, they *slapped* me," he sobbed, "and locked me in a dirty ol' broom-closet. They didn't let me out for the rest of the day."

I could only shake my head, an updraft of contending emotions making the room feel too hot. Suddenly a terrible suspicion dashed cold water on the embers of my righteously smouldering empathy—

"Did you make this up, Douglas?"

"You would say that," he sniveled.

I seized him by the wrist.

"Your supposedly 'harmless' fibs have been increasing in frequency—you've become addicted to lying and deceitfulness ever since the Divorce—why the hell should I believe you this time?"

"Cause this is diff'rent," he glared through his tears. "An' I don' care if you b'leeve me. You can go ask Maria—she doesn't have to believe me, she *knows*."

"Alright then," I sighed, feeling strangely chastened. "I'll believe you, for now. But if it's true, it's an outrage," I gritted my teeth. "Does Ferdinand know about this?"

"He never knows about anything."

"Or *cares*," I softly intoned under my breath.

"Yer right. He *doesn't* care."

My paw flew to my mouth: Douglas obviously had razour-sharp hearing.

"He doesn't care about anyone," he continued, "except that mean Lioness. She's only nice to me when all those Rats and Weasels are around, shouting things and taking pictures."

He could understand more than people realised.

"What do Ferdinand, and that Lioness, talk about?" I cautiously ventured, trying to sound casual.

"They yell at each other. He doesn't like her to talk on the phone. Her voice gets all mushy, on the phone. Ferdinand wants to do that icky thing grownups are always talking about, and trying to get each other to do. But she wants to get mushy, and then icky, with somebody else. It's some Lion she talks with on the phone in her room. She locks her door, and he pounds on it, but I was locked in the closet, and could hear through the wall."

"Do you know that Lion's *name*?" I whispered, "The one she wants to get icky with?"

"She said it all the time, but it was hard to remember. For me at least."

"C'mon, Dougie," I wanted to shake him, "I know you can remember. Concentrate. I promise I'll never be mean again, if you can tell me that Name."

"I thought maybe you weren't gonna be mean cause you *liked* me," his voice changed. "Not cause you *wanted* sump'n."

"If you tell me, Douglas, I can help all of us—those servants deserve to be punished, but I can't do anything—without that *Name*."

"You sound like a grownup."

The word *grownup* was the worst insult he knew.

"That's just because you're not *concentrating*," I idiotically intoned, "If you tell me that Name, I can help us both—isn't there anything you'd like me to *help* you with?"

"I want Mummy to come back," he said the words so softly I could barely hear them—maybe that's why they sliced their way to the inner core of my being.

"We can get ourselves in a position to make Ferdinand do whatever we want—just tell me the Name," I reached out and grasped his plump shoulder. "Remember those Rats and Weasels? They're like—Magicians. They can give us," I took a deep breath, "whatever we want…"

I pictured the Press Conference: thousands of teeming, salivating rodents hanging on my every word, cameras recording my every gesture, every twitch of my whiskers—as I toyed with the vermin, telling them riddles, dangling the *Name* the way those sadistic French chambermaids allegedly dangled their sugary treats in front of Dougie's quivering nostrils.

Practically swaying on my feet, I imagined the headlines, with their big black typeface in capital letters dominating the Front Page of the tabloids, day after day:

SYL PROMISES TO SPILL IN JUST 24 HOURS!

SYLVIA GIVES A FRESH HINT!

TRANSCRIPT OF SYLVIA'S LATEST PRESS CONFERENCE!

AN ANALYSIS OF SYLVIA'S WORD CHOICE AND IMAGERY…

A loud knock on the door made me jump.

"So how are ya gonna make Mummy come back?" he demanded.

"You have to tell me the Name."

"I jus' did," his lower lip jutted out, "You weren't even listening—no one ever listens to *me*."

"You told me the name that Lioness kept repeating?"

The knocking became more intrusive.

"Just a minute," I shouted, then lowered my voice: "So tell me right now—hurry! We don't have much time."

"I can't remember," he sulked.

"Oh, Douglas," I wanted to slap him—and almost did.

"Is that Sylvia?" a stranger's voice called from the other side of the door.

"I said to *wait*," I practically snarled.

"You were supposed to be down at the front gate—"

"Sweet Bast," I felt my insides contort before turning to jelly, "Are you from the Ministry of Education?"

"We used to be," the voice sneered, "before we turned into skellingtons, waiting."

"Dougie, listen," I pleaded, "I have to go on an errand—please don't tell anyone else about this, OK?"

"I think I'll tell Nurse," he flashed me a not very nice, ever so sly, smile. "Or maybe those Rats—"

I hauled off and slapped him—

"Oh my g-d," my paw flew to my mouth as he burst into tears.

"I'm so sorry, Dougie!" I tried to make myself heard above his caterwauling and earsplitting screams—you'd think he was being torn limb from limb—I screamed something back—from sheer frustration (it was one of the gutter profanities I'd heard the paparazzi bandying back and forth) and flung open the door. The Driver, a big flocculent-faced Porcupine, staggered several paces before righting himself—he'd had his ear to the paneled wood. His cunning, shifty-eyed expression was like the physical personification of my inner drives and perversions.

Dougie's tantrum was still echoing in my frazzled mind as we zoomed along in the big streamlined automobile towards Snoopus' compound. I couldn't believe how *inept* I was with other people—especially my own family. Now the little brat would never speak to me again, much less divulge the identity of Delilah's Young Lion. Douglas and Maria would form a United Front, closing ranks against the common enemy, the loathsome pariah—how did *I* always somehow wind up as the villain? No wonder Marc was probably gonna puke his guts out, the instant he clapped eyes on my unlovely person—after these past few days, with all the smear-jobs and slander.

"Want some Starbursts?" the Driver shoved something—a roll of candied lozenges—in my face. I just barely mastered a wave of nausea before managing, in a prim cold-sounding voice, to tell the wretch, "No thank you."

"Just tryin' to be friendly."

This doomed, illicit *passion* for Marcus (for what else, once the tinsel and polish had been scoured off, could I call it, beyond an almost chemical lust?) was clearly destined to be the death of me—*perhaps I could pull 'im down with me, swive his brains out on the way down—*

I gave myself a sharp ringing slap—right in the face—as hard as I could.

"'Ere now," the car swerved, "Are y' prone to fits, then—it looked like you fair wallop'd yourself."

"It's none of your business," I spoke as coldly and primly as I could.

"She really is a Psycho," he shook his head, "The Papers are right…"

Would Marcus think so?

Indeed, assuming he was even going to be there, what could a wallflower like me possibly say in the presence of those

Eyes with their Lodestones drawing the filings from my magnetised heart? What does a compromised young girl say to the towering Everything of all her pathetic little hopes and desires? I couldn't believe I hadn't composed a script in advance. Perhaps, at heart, I was wiser than I realised—scripts can be fatal (and they're always—*always*—dangerous)…

I wondered how I could even look him in the face after all the things the tabloids had printed—would I lose my voice, would it 'dry up' (which seemed to be happening more and more often)?

"Good day," I softly murmured in a sub-audible voice, "I shudder to think what nefarious calumnies, devious distortions, insidious innuendos…"

"Crazy as a Loon," the driver brazenly cackled.

Producing a small pane of silvered glass, I examined myself. The reality of what I saw almost reduced me to tears. Electronically lowering the back window, I flung the shard at a passing schoolbus—it shattered pleasingly against one of the tinted windows.

"None of that!" the Porcupine exploded, quickly locking all the controls and all the doors, with a series of beeps and clicks, "I drew a real fackin' winner, to-day."

He pressed a button, and the soundproof glass barrier electronically came between us, isolating me like some carrier of yellow fever or cholera.

Up ahead I glimpsed that famous graven image of the Fish god, Icthyus, glowering down with his carved fish-eyes at the densely packed traffic, and behind Him, rising at an angle, Dolphin street, which snaked its way up the eminence on which Snoopus had built his observatory and model school, Harmony Point. None of the Ruling Families would have been caught dead sending their jaded brats and precocious sex perverts here, for the simple reason that *Meme* children—among other assorted dregs of society—were admitted, on scholarship.

Here were the two gold-plated Dolphins that guarded the gate. My heart began hammering painfully as the surveillance camera swiveled and the gates opened; passing through them, we barreled into the courtyard.

Michael Sheop was standing there with a number of Meme acolytes, waiting for me—in fact he was pacing back and forth. I scrambled out of the motorcar quick as I could. He gestured for me to follow him. The Memes opened doors in front of us, and closed them behind us. At length we entered one of the smaller classrooms. The door was pushed shut behind us.

"Right," my new governor bleated, "I've been briefed on the particulars of your personal situation." He cleared his throat. "Let's turn to page 453 in the grammar text and do some warm-ups by conjugating all the irregular verbs we find in the following excerpt from Lao Tzu's famous poem on the abiding serenity of the Beatitudes, beginning with physical chastity..."

I tried concentrating. It was next to impossible. I kept seeing Marc's handsome face superimposed over the conjugations with which he was filling the blackboard. I answered by rote, faltering more and more often.

"Kindly translate the following sentence from Hindustani to Farsi—"

"Do you think we could—I'm sorry," his countenance had visibly darkened, "but do you think I could have a fifteen-minute, or even a five-minute, break? A breath of fresh air might—"

"I don't believe in frills," the Ram lifted a manicured hoof. "Simplicity!" he brought it down on the desk with a loud rapping sound. "The Ancients rightly prized Simplicity above all other principles. This custom of granting, and taking, 'breaks' as I believe some have called them—"

Baa, baa, baa—I was so *sick* of his pompous bleating.

"My bladder's about to burst," I unblushingly lied. "So I've got to make a quick trip to the Loo. On top of that, my sister Annie's run away for good this time, my brother Philip's in a Drug Treatment borstal, and my kid brother, Douglas, is rapidly turning into a pathological liar. I have to sort some things out in my head. I'm sorry if I'm tainting the simplicity of the Lesson Plan through the infiltration of frills."

He opened his mouth.

"I should be back soon," I added, jumping up and hurrying out of the room before he could say anything.

xix.

The Garden appeared to be deserted. I'd timed my little escape to coincide with the midmorning break (it seemed most of the teachers were still enamoured of 'frills'), but by now the last loiterers had drifted back into the quadrangle. Could this whole thing be an elaborate practical joke? Snoopus would never do such a thing—but Delilah might.

A stab of adrenaline—a young Lion flitted past, between clumps of lush foliage.

My knees wobbled, before knocking together. Everything was going dim—it felt like I was about to keel over. I had to take a series of deep breaths to anchor myself, before my vision cleared, and I regained control of my limbs.

Stationing myself at the intersection of the two main pathways traversing the garden in the semblance of a large figure-eight (Snoopus had explained that it symbolised Infinity), I looked down at the gravel. All the pebbles were of more or less the same dun-coloured, sandy hue. I knelt and began picking through them, one at a time. Here was a stone that was almost rosaceous, glistening with a quartz-like consistency—as far above its fellows in pulchritude as Marcus—

A shadow fell across the path, almost touching me. Pretending to scrutinise the piece of quartz, I continued stupidly to crouch there in the gravel, utterly paralysed—till the thought of what I must look like—squatting there before him, my ungainly haunches bunched up—caused me awkwardly to scramble to an upright standing position—but facing *away* from the young Deity (which was just as well, considering the state of my countenance).

"Forgive me, but—"

I whirled round and there I was: face to face with a complete stranger—a Lion, yes—but not Marcus.

135

"Wait," the handsome young look-alike grabbed me by the wrist (how could I ever have confused him with *Marc*)—

"Let go of me—"

"Please," he relaxed his grip stepping back several paces, "Don't run away."

Something in his voice made me hesitate.

"Who are you?" I managed, before a nervous tic reduced me to the level of caricature. To my surprise, no taunts were forthcoming. Instead, the young Lion said in a measured, almost pleasing baritone:

"Sorry if you were expecting Marcus."

My mouth actually came open—for a split-second it was my turn to grab *his* wrist, to steady myself.

"I'm a friend of his," he blithely continued, "He sent me over here to collect his assignments and class notes. Also, to tell Snoopus that he's feeling better; he'll definitely be here to-morrow."

This was too much, too surreal, to take in.

"Are you Sylvia?"

I nodded warily. At the same time a look of something bordering on anguish momentarily darkened the stranger's handsome young face. He managed to thrust it from his countenance, flashing me a bright, winsome smile.

"He talks about you every now and then—"

My body went rigid.

"I mean," he grinned, "more than every now and then."

"What does he say?" I somehow got the words out.

"I dunno," he scratched his head, "He told me you're one of the few people he really respects."

"What else?"

"Well," he maddeningly prevaricated, "Would you like me to take him a message? Then maybe he can tell you straight from the Horse's mouth, as it were."

"Can—can we sit down, for a moment?"

I was on the point of collapse. The gallant young Lion took me by the elbow and steered me over to the nearest bench—

I didn't sit down, but at least it was right there, in case of imminent swooning.

"You said you're a friend of Marcus?" I tried to smile, but the effect was probably closer to a grinning death mask.

"I've known him ever since my Father *forced* me to move into the Louvre."

"Forced you?"

"I probably shouldn't say that—"

"Why did he force you?"

(And who *is* your father? And who are *you* for that matter?)

"It's kind of a long story…"

The quasi-painful look darkened his face once again.

"Well never mind then, but tell me—is Marcus OK? You said he was sick."

"It's just a touch of Hay Fever."

"You're sure it isn't Bronchitis?" I couldn't help clucking like an over-anxious, compulsive Hen, "He had that last month."

"I remember, believe me—I had to help him catch up with all the homework he missed—"

"Excuse me," I couldn't help setting the record straight, "but *I* helped him with his homework."

"I guess we both did."

He *was* sad, it struck me. But without wearing it on his sleeve—with a dignity to his particularised, personal grief. Which I caught myself wishing I could somehow assuage—what was it about Lions and Lionesses that always made them seem larger than life?

I caught myself stealing glances: he was certainly handsome, ravishingly so (perhaps, objectively speaking, *almost* as goodlooking as Marc). And yet, his perfect looks did *nothing* for me. I could 'enjoy' drinking in his overpowering beauty without *being* overpowered, without paying the price. I'd have to admit, however, that I did find myself instinctively liking this mysterious young stranger—despite the all but certain probability that he was, in fact, a *spy* (planted by Delilah, her Father, or Bast knows what personage—perhaps he himself didn't know). Even so, there was something studious, forthright, in his gaze—that involuntarily awakened an answering sympathy. I looked away lest he 'read' me too easily.

But it was too late.

"Why do you keep staring at me?"

"Not for the reason I'm sure you're imagining," I blurted out before I could stop myself.

He flashed me a look of astonishment.

"I'm sorry—I didn't mean to be rude. But most of the kids where I used to go to school (before I got expelled by the goddam Headmaster) ridiculed and derogated my every gesture—my every hint, ghost or sketch of a gesture—I guess it's made me a trifle…embittered."

"I say," he generously changed the subject, "Did you want me to take a note back to Marcus?"

"Oh," I blushed in confusion, "Certainly. Let me write something—I'll try to be quick."

"Take all the time in the world," he smiled expansively. "Leave it to De to be right about everything, as usual. She said you'd be in the garden."

"De?" I frowned.

"You know. Delilah."

Sweet fucking Bast.

Infinities crystallised.

"You're Delilah's *Young Lion*."

There. It was out in the open.

"You mean…she didn't tell you about me—about us? You had to figure it out?"

The look on his face—how many times had I registered that exact same look, especially over the past few days and weeks making up this ridiculous *paparazzi summer* (as I'd taken to calling it)?

"Stop laughing at me."

"I'm not 'laughing' at anyone," I tried to explain, "I'm smiling because you remind me of myself, OK? My father—"

138

He winced.

"Well never mind about my stupid father! And I'm not smiling any more, see?"

The balance of power (between us) had shifted. At first he'd had the upper hand (or as Annie loved saying, he had me 'by the balls')—simply by dangling Marcus on a hook. Now I had him, by dangling Delilah.

"Don't worry," I couldn't restrain myself, "She doesn't love Ferdinand."

"How do you know?" he petulantly demanded.

"She told me."

I could feel the Power shifting, from him to me. The *addictiveness* of the feeling disconcerted me strongly (and perhaps gave me a handle towards understanding the 'predators' like Delilah, and Annie).

"She's using my father," I just couldn't stop, "as a means to an end. Just like she's using me."

"How is she allegedly 'using' you?" he demanded.

"I shouldn't have said all that—it's not safe," I inhaled, "*Please* don't repeat it. Just *believe* me," exhaling, "She really doesn't care a fig for my lout of a father. Believe me," I fixed him with my nearsighted eyes: "I know."

"I do believe you."

He smiled—and I could almost imagine his leaning forward to give me a (chaste) kiss on the forehead. His smile was electrifying—I could (almost) see why 'De' liked him so much.

"What's your name?" I was suddenly curious.

"I shouldn't tell you that," he grinned, "It's not safe."

"I know it starts with D."

"How do you know that?"

"Your Lady Fair told me; you should carve your initials on a treetrunk: D plus D equals Love."

He grinned irresistibly: "What about S plus M?"

I felt a twinge of discomfort.

"You mustn't tell anyone about us, OK?"

"Of course not," he took offence, "Just like you won't tell anyone that De loves Di and Di would die for his De."

"Die?"

"Diocletian," he whispered.

"Oh."

"Listen, you'd better scribble something—if you want me to carry a note back to the Louvre. I'm sorry to rush things, but I need to get going."

"He'll be here to-morrow, right?"

"I guess so," he frowned. 'I mean, yeah. To-morrow. Of course."

"So there's really no need for me to scribble a note."

"You think I'd read it or something?"

You honestly don't think Delilah's gonna have a peek at that note? I wanted to shout. But of course he didn't think so. He had so much to learn.

"I swear to Bast, that's not what I think," I assured him, "It just doesn't seem worth the effort, if you know what I mean."

"I think I do at that," he managed a crooked smile (which even in its crookedness dazzled me). "You'd make a good teacher," he added. "So long, Sylvia—do you mind if I call you by your Christian name? I don't mean to be disrespectful."

"Of course not. But I think I'll call you Diocletian, instead of Di."

"Only De calls me that—mostly when we're…"

He blushed.

"Thanks for offering to carry the note," I smiled.

And for being a breath of fresh air.

As he set off with a sauntering, purposeful stride, I could certainly see why 'De' was head over heels for him. Not that I, like her, was responding on an animalistic, physical level. To the contrary, a nobility of spirit filled him out, like wind stretching the elastic but unbreakable fabric of a ship's painted sail (or inspiration filling the equally supple canvas of a fame-hungry painter).

Foam flying from the ship's prow,
Fame spattering the razour-sharp plough
With loamy bits of itself...

Not that Diocletian was an Artist, Sail-maker, Blacksmith—or anything but a young adolescent in love.

I wondered if he could hold his own against the swim, or drift, of a Force (foot-candles per square inch?) such as *Delilah* personified? She obviously wanted to make herself look good by pulling everyone else down into the muck. And that included both Marcus and me—together, in the muck.

The operative word was *together*.

No headlines have ever sprung from the cold, virginal propriety of everyone minding their Ps and Qs separately, scrupulously. Headlines presuppose a hectic, feverish, *promiscuous* mushing together of not just everything and everyone under the sun, but specifically the mushing together of beautiful young Lions, and uptight, repressed White Cats with lifeless, lank fur. Delilah needed the muck. I wanted the Lion. Perhaps for once her needs, and my lusts, intersected.

That night my brother Philip tried to commit suicide. The so-called staff at that horrible place where he was incarcerated had lackadaisically fed him his meals, jotted down the most hair-raising nonsense in his private chart, and repeatedly given free rein to their slimier inclinations and weaknesses (in the form of long-lasting, extended, *indescribable* orgies).

No wonder the poor kid slashed his wrists in despair. They'd left him locked in a room with a blaring TV he couldn't turn off. (I would've done the same thing, watching Ferdinand holding his infernal press conferences.)

We got the news just as our father's plane was landing at Heathrow. I don't remember which of the vermin (except that it wasn't Tosk) gleefully shouted out the news as they filmed us. But I'm getting ahead of myself.

At five that morning I'd jumped out of bed, stretched, taken a long bath, and dried and brushed my lank fur almost lovingly (certainly painstakingly), thinking of the assignation to come. It was fixed for that afternoon, right? Diocletian had casually but unmistakably mentioned that Marcus expected to be back at Snoopus' the next day, for a resumption of his lessons. I planned to be there for a different kind of resumption.

Downstairs at the breakfast table I decided to ring Helen after sipping my scalding cup of tea down to the dregs. Goody Thorpe (all the servants were back, reimbursed by some mysterious—and unknown—paymaster) was sitting across from me, labouriously spoonfeeding her darling Douglas. He fixed me with his impudent, restless blue eyes. I had to remind myself that he was, technically speaking, still just an overgrown kitten. Marcus called him a *Bairn*. When I asked him what the word meant, he gave me one of his sly, irresistible smiles, and said he'd just learnt the word himself, from one of the servants, that morning. Hers (Bairn, that is) had died—of malnutrition, or rickets, or some such affliction.

His smiles, I reflected, were downright *celestial*. Giving off beams of light.

"Whatcha thinkin' about?" Dougie's shrill voice cut into the reverie.

"Leave me alone, you fat slug."

Perhaps I over-reacted, but no one can be as annoying as Douglas—especially at breakfast.

"What's a slug?" he petulantly demanded.

I opened my mouth, but Goody Thorpe clucked, "It's the same as sugar and spice and ev'rything nice. And fat ones," she lovingly pinched him producing a squeal of delight, "are even better, 'cause there's more for the rest of us to love."

I couldn't stand it.

"Can we cut the crap, Dougie? For a change of pace?"

A baying babble of voices rose from all sides, but I persevered:

"You *know* it means a snail without its shell—I've caught you squashing them on the back porch often enough. You're just being provocative with this *act* that you don't know things—"

"What's provocative?" the little imp brazenly provoked me some more.

Maria leaned towards him and whispered something, except I heard every snuffly syllable (as she no doubt intended):

"She was thinking about *Marcus*—don't let her change the subject—you know how *mean* she can be, but it's three-to-one, if we stick together."

"Who's Marcus?" I tried to sound disinvolved.

"The paper says you may be taken up for endangering the morals and contributing to the delinquency of a Minor—"

I felt myself turning pale. So many different fragments of thought were whirling about in my head:

He's only five or six months younger—
Does 'taken up' mean arrested—
How do you 'endanger' someone's Morals—

143

What if they come for me before I get to see him—
Don't cry in front of these slavering Jackals—
But not all of them were Jackals. I'd forgotten that
Goody Thorpe was *my* Nurse as well.

"Don't you worry, Dearheart," she began stroking my fur,
"That was an editorial from the likes of *The Daily Carcass*, and
they didn't say you were going to be taken up; they said as how
you *ought* to be taken up—considering some of their past
editorials, you're in mighty good company."

I clung gratefully to her mass of soft, aromatic feathers.

"And as for you lot," her tone hardened, "I've told you
not to bring that filth into the house."

"*You* read it," Maria whiningly remonstrated.

"Only because you children waste your lunch money—or
whatever kind of money—buying the filth."

"*You'd* buy it if we didn't," Dougie shrilled, his blue eyes
practically bulging from their sockets. (I hoped the servants were
keeping up with his 'meds'—in the past the correct dosages
hadn't always been ingested at the correct times, and the various
drug interactions had been disregarded—with rather unfortunate
consequences, as Ferdinand's Dream Team found out, during the
Divorce.)

"That's neither here nor there," she raised her voice. "I
don't want to find you reading, or repeating, this muck anymore."

"*Muck face*," my little brother shouted, and barreled out
of the room.

"You always take *her* side," Maria burst into tears, and
hobbled after him.

"I'd better go see to *them* now," she grumbled.

"Thank you, Nurse," I planted a heartfelt kiss on her
flexible, muscular wing.

"And as for *you*," she wheeled round to face me, "Some
would be of the opinion that this was completely your fault."

I felt the blood rushing to my face.

"Just because I *responded* to Marcus Agrippa when *he*
initiated a series of seemingly innocent conversations," my voice

tripped over itself as I swallowed, fighting back tears, "Anyway, he started it."

My paw flew to my mouth.

"I mean it's your fault that this whole squall, at the breakfast table, erupted in the first place."

"Oh, that."

I began scarfing down spoonfuls of porridge.

"I can't turn a blind eye to what you were babbling about a moment ago," she raised her voice. "You're in way over your head—"

"What's it like to have a gizzard?" I tried changing the subject. "Does it help you digest your food?"

"Getting back to what you thought I was talking about—"

"No!" I stamped my foot, spilling the porridge.

At that precise instant, the kitchen door flew open admitting *Judd* of all people—my father's chief pimp and procurer, his prop and crutch, the notorious 'shadow' who seldom if ever left his master's malodourous side—

"Is my *father* returned then, like an avenging prodigal, knife in hand, to slay all the suitors till the blood collects in puddles and trickling streams and raging rivers of gore?"

"Sounds to me like yer ripe for the Nut Hatch," he (prophetically) smirked.

"You didn't answer my question."

"Yer Dad's still in the air. He and the rest of 'is entourage," he lovingly moulded the word with his tongue, "including, of course, yer new *Stepmum*," his eyes smouldered expectantly, "should be landing, at Orly, in about an hour, or so."

"Well goodie gumdrops."

"He expects every member of the family not currently institutionalised to be waiting on the tarmac. That doesn't give us much time."

"I'll go round up the children," Goody Thorpe announced, and then made herself scarce.

"So Sylvia," the degenerate smirked, "Long time no see."

"I'm afraid I can't possibly—"

145

"Yer Dad's instructions—"

"Sod his instructions."

I was *determined* to 'stick to my guns' (to use one of Helen's favourite expressions). For once my father was *not* going to buffalo me, twisting my resolve like a moist blade of grass.

"His instructions contain a secret little clause," the pander intoned with malevolent glee, "sugarcoated just for *Sylvia.*"

"I don't want to hear it."

"Tell her, if she tries to dig her heels in and practise her newfound, love-besotted stubbornness—"

"What's that supposed to mean?"

"Tell her, if she says," he trotted out the most repulsive caricature of my voice, "*What's that s'posed to meeen*—"

Extending, retracting, extending my claws, I controlled myself only with the greatest effort.

"Tell her, if she gives herself any condescending airs, climbing onto the buttocks of that High Horse she's so fond of staring down at her betters from—"

"Quit dangling prepositions, and get on with it."

"So you can hurry off to Marcus, and try to convince him to dangle something besides prepositions?"

"*Get out,*" I screamed, "or better yet *I'll* split right now just like Annie—she had the right idea—"

"If yer not at the Aeroport to greet yer Dad for the paparazzi," his voice, reinforced with something cold and hard, transfixed me, "a certain telephone call to a certain Someone, an' *poof.* Yer castles in the sand go Bye-Bye. The Young Lion never shews up at Harmony Point this afternoon—or the day after that—leaving a certain White Tabby, embittered and spinsterish, to water Snoopus' rose-bushes with hours and hours of sobbing. You don't go to the Aeroport, it's a *done deal,* you dig?"

A pause ensued. Out of breath, he stood there wheezing as he cocked his malformed head to the side. Choking, the breakfast table blurring as I fought back tears, I managed to whisper that Annie had embarked on one of her sprees.

"He doesn't care about *her*—she's a lost cause," the gloating edge to his voice made me want to fly at the wretch. "But you," he chuckled, "you should feel *damn special*, m'dear."

Pursued by a smaller contingent of rats and weasels than last time, when we finally reached the cordoned-off tarmac I saw the reason: hundreds more (if not thousands) were converging round a newly landed Aeroplane like ants round a sticky piece of candy, still coated with saliva, that some careless child had spat on the pavement.

I was already feeling so utterly disconnected from the moorings of 'everyday life' that it was all I could do to force myself out of the Packard, stumbling along between Maria and Douglas, and then the vermin ambushed us with the news (about Philip), and everything turned kind of grotesque.

I wanted to feel something. I tried to think about Philip, but kept picturing Marc. All I could wrap my head around was the impending afternoon rendez-vous at Snoopus' compound, just hours away. I felt like a monster for putting my own selfish desires ahead of Philip's welfare—perhaps his very survival. (Never mind the fact that he and I had never been close, that Annie was his best friend in the world, that he and she had joined forces, ganging up, combining against me, *actively* persecuting me for much of my childhood.)

At the end of what felt like an eternity (my ankles and feet had gone numb), concentric ripples of anticipation began to jiggle back and forth, washing over the motley horde of reporters. A set of stairsteps was wheeled over, and behold: the door opened. Flashbulbs started going off like crazy as Delilah emerged, flanked by bodyguards and attendants. My father's reception, I noticed, was *visibly* less 'delirious' than that of his Bride—whereas his was simply kicked into high gear with lots of jostling and shouting, her own was truly, in every sense of the word, *Electric*.

After Nero and Blussian (with lots more jostling and shouting) had gracefully emerged from the back of the plane (and gone down their own, separate, flight of steps), the long-awaited Press Conference, at last, could begin.

The first few shafts (disguised as questions) were aimed, predictably enough, at Delilah: *How was your honeymoon? Did it measure up to your (doubtless gargantuan) expectations?* That sort of thing. And she didn't allow it to jar her cool collected thoroughbred stride by one jot. I'd seen it all before, though— why the hell did people get so worked up over *Press Conferences*?

Of course, if *I* were the focal point of the Conference, it might actually be worth watching, for once. I imagined the sort of precision fencing to which I could, with skill, elevate the proceedings:

> *Vermin: Are you in possession of cold, hard proof to the effect that Marcus Agrippa requites your admittedly tempestuous feelings?*
> *Sylvia: No one has ever asserted anything, one way or the other.*
> *Vermin: Was Judd correct then to use the term 'castles in the sand'?*
> *Sylvia: Of course he was correct, technically speaking. We all of us build Castles in the Sand every instant. I don't have* proof *that Marcus feels anything more than impassioned Friendship towards me—perhaps I am just building castles in the sand, at low tide, my mind addled from sunstroke...*

The fantasy had taken a depressing turn. I forced myself to begin listening to the actual press conference:

"My source reckons he lost a quart of blood; they had to fibrillate him in the ambulance, or he'd be one dead little Morphine addict—dead as a plank."

I winced, feeling sick to my stomach.

"Let me address that right now," Ferdinand extended a claw, jabbing it into the air for emphasis, "I've already spoken with my Solicitor, and not only are we seeking punitive damages in the amount of over 5 million Roubles," (how eagerly they were all taking it down, lapping it up) "but I'm seeing to it that a full investigation gets launched, and I won't rest till that scurvy, cost-cutting disgrace of a so-called clinic gets run out of town, and the premises padlocked—Bast only knows how many other kids, without Philip's connexions or social standing, have been ill served—possibly murdered—but I'll restrict myself to saying 'ill served' by such charlatinism, neglect, and rank sadism..."

He'd run out of breath. My father, it appeared, was getting too old to make speeches. Anyway, Delilah was the smouldering lynchpin holding the whole thing together—all the big sleek Black Rats—the Norwegian carriers of plague some 500 years ago (they bristled ferociously if called Plague Rats, maintaining that it was ruddy fleas carried the Plague—and every mammal has fleas, even the posh feline Aristos)—were ignoring Ferdinand and screaming, from all sides, at Delilah—taunting, baiting the Princess, to grace them all with another of her pithy (and sometimes unprintable—hence Front Page) observations.

Ferdinand was trying to elaborate on some of the sententious claptrap he'd already voided by the bladderful, but every one of them were continuing to harangue the overpoweringly charistmatic young Lioness—her Magnetism dominated the entire assemblage of seasoned, hardnosed, cynical 'Journalists' (as they liked, on occasion, to call themselves); I could feel my father's petty irritation beginning to border on the explosive, as with spastic gesticulations he tried to attract at least someone's attention from amongst the second-stringers and small fry, to the rear of the Horde.

"Ferdinand seems downright puckish," she pursed her lips playfully, "at the prospect of squeezing some ready cash from the drug-addicted udder of his eldest son, and Cash Cow."

150

The laughter was downright acidic—I could feel my own teeth grinding, as my father turned pale with what I recognised as extreme, repressed rage.

"*We could hold a free concert in Vondelpark,*" with a supreme effort he successfully projected his voice.

"Of whom would the line-up consist?"

"Could the public bring their own beer?"

"Of course," he tried to smile, his spiteful anger (so very much like my own) gnawing and biting at the grottoes of his self-control, "And why stop at beer? We want the crowd to be mellow. As for the line-up, I'm inviting my good friend, *Krabbb*—"

A squeal of excitement erupted at the mere mention of Noster Krabbb, lead singer for that legendary super-group, the Silver Scarabs (never mind that they'd broken up some time ago—and never mind that I'd *never* heard Ferdinand bandy the name round before)—

"Isn't that a bit irresponsible, in terms of public safety?" my friend Tosk for the first time fired off a question (and a surprisingly 'responsible' one, from my point of view), "I mean, remember that riot back when the Slit Pigs held their little be-in at Vondelpark—17 people knifed to death, over one hundred seriously injured…"

Ferdinand's mouth fell open; this was obviously some spur-of-the-moment whim he'd scarcely even considered before opening his big fat mouth—he *always* leapt before looking.

"Eh, well," he waved his arms frantically to try and stem new lines of questioning, "The Silver Scarabs are *not* the Slit Pigs—"

"You've actually *signed* the Silver Scarabs?" a Weasel I recognised as one of the diggers of dirt on the Rock Music circuit screeched half accusingly, half rapturously, "For their first Reunion in over five years?"

"The ink's not dry on the contract—I mean, there *is* no contract, yet—"

"Getting back to public safety," one of the Rats squeaked after Tosk had whispered something into his tufted, twitching ear, "Is this Free Concert gonna be at night, cause if so—"

"Have you hired security?"

"What about sanitation?"

"Can't you lot come up with anything more interesting to ask me about?" he grimaced, trying to keep from gulping in his palpable nervousness. "Here I've just married the most sizzling—"

"Did *Annie* know about it?" Tosk lobbed the question with a sort of curved, spinning punch.

"Know about *what*?" his irritation was shewing.

"About the way her brother Philip was being mistreated in that terrible place you're planning to sue into the ground, and prosecute for criminal negligence?"

"How in the Hell would *Annie* know about it?"

"So that's *not* the reason she ran away from home— *again*? Surely you knew—"

"*Did* you know?" voices chorused from all sides fast and furious.

"Well—of course I knew," he tried to chuckle, with disastrous results.

"What are you doing about it?"

His mouth fell open again.

"My sources reckon she's shacked up with Stephen von Oxenburg in one of the vans traveling with Lobotomania, that so-called freakshew and circus which keeps getting raided by the provincial police—they've currently gone to ground—"

"My sources," a Ferret with a hairlip who up till now hadn't got a word in edgewise pronounced his consonants perfectly, with a look of insane (but understandable) pride, "have 'em nailed down in that shanty-town south of Harper's Ferry—"

"Thanks a lot for publishing that little factoid," Ferdinand pounced. "Now they'll have to move on—in a hurry. And *of course* I've been in touch with Annie—she's my Daughter isn't she?"

"Your ex-wife Jane claims—"

"You can fuck Jane," he lost control of himself, "Most everyone else has! She's the most uncontrollable trollop—and liar into the bargain—I didn't forget to say *liar*, did I, perchance—can anyone here say 'liar' without dragging little Juanita's name into the frickin' conversation? Hey?"

He was literally dancing in his rage, the cameras and film canisters going into overdrive, shouts and imprecations of encouragement serving to goad the enraged Siamese with a sort of piquant redundancy.

"Stop it," I heard my own voice ineffectually wheedling, "I don't condone that sorry hypocrite making a fool of himself, but you're egging him on—"

"Like this?" Maria hissed, savagely elbowing me in the ribs.

I would've jabbed her right back, if my father hadn't been saying, at that exact moment: "As a matter of fact, I'm sending someone—Sylvia, probably—to try and make her see reason, entice the poor Prodigal to come limping home, to the gilded cage fashioned specially for her—and everyone's—comfort."

"He's totally lost it," I mouthed the words, crossing myself.

And of course half a dozen cameras filmed my extravagant little gesture.

"Speaking of Sylvia," Tosk shouted (freezing my blood), "There's been quite a bit of—in this reporter's opinion at least— inflated palaver swirling round the poor kid—in short, her good name's been besmirched, dragged through the mud—any comment whatsoever concerning your *other* daughter, *Sylvia?*"

The Universe, like distilled sap, oozed to a state of near microscopic motionlessness, all the concatenated, but sluggish, emotion on earth distortedly shining through a single pendulous, hanging, oozing droplet of amber viscousness (which may once have been blood oozing from a slit pig before it turned into a silver dung-beetle)—

"She's getting a crash course in real life," my father finally managed (I heard the words in slow motion).

Even Maria, for once, kept her fists and elbows on a tight leash, straining, like some scrawny, mistreated animal, on a leash of her own.

"And you, Delilah," one of Plague Rats was squeaking, "How does it feel to have bagged one of the so-called world's most eligible bachelors?"

"Sort of a letdown."

"How was yer wedding night?"

"I was too drunk to remember," she basked in her unassailable sophistication, "But I must've been there, presumably."

"Any chance yer pregnant—"

"*Of course not!*" her eyes flashed. "If my Father expresses the slightest *hint* of disapproval—even mild disappointment—at what I've done, I'll have this marriage annulled."

Half the cameras swiveled to record Ferdinand's reaction, zooming in with their viciously snubnosed, telefoto lenses; his face quivered but somehow, miraculously, kept from caving in on itself.

"And I would *never* disrespect my Beloved Father," she continued, "nor the Privy Council, by tampering with the Holy Succession. I will *not* be getting pregnant—ever—except by a Lion."

"Does that mean you haven't consummated the marriage—"

"What marriage?" she fluttered her lashes.

The hardbitten, verminous throng lapped it up, roaring with laughter and scattered applause. I could almost find it in me to feel sorry for Ferdinand—if his (and his pander's) gibes and threats concerning my feelings for Marcus weren't still ringing in the back of my mind, the bleeding terrain of which was lacerated and gouged thanks, largely, to his direct, traceable selfishness; perhaps my father didn't *mean* to be hateful—was that the reason I felt the stinging tears welling up on his pathetic behalf (or had I

154

simply inherited his selfishness—and was sniveling because I was tired, my feet hurt, and I longed to see Marc)?

"We're going straight to the Louvre, first thing, before even unpacking," her vehemence was strangely infectious; it made me want to go straight to Snoopus' compound—perhaps they could drop me, on the way to the Louvre. "I don't consider myself properly married—to anyone—without my dear Father's indispensable blessing."

The smattering of applause picked up momentum and volume, like a snowball approaching a sort of critical mass as it rolled down a steepening slope that had been cleared of impediments.

"I'm sorry, Father," she spoke to the cameras, directly, "I don't know—why—" her voice seemed to catch on what she skillfully passed off as a sob; her eyes were glistening—"I don't know what I was thinking—I just wanted your attention, your approval, your love," she ratcheted the emotion up another unbelievable notch: "I feel sorry for every *other* daughter on earth—I couldn't *imagine* not having *You* as my *Father—please say you forgive me*?"

A spellbound silence had seemingly enveloped and muffled everything under the sun.

"No more questions," her Chief of Staff, a large ginger Cat, rapped out in a metallic-sounding, decidedly uncatlike voice.

Amidst the ensuing cacophony (like a bottle that'd just been uncorked) of shouted questions, rapturous ejaculations, applause and overdone sobs, I somehow ploughed my way through the dispersing throng of paparazzi to find myself, improbably, at my *own* father's side. He was trembling as if in the toils of a feverish delirium, his teeth chattering so that I could barely understand the disjointed words: "Maybe, just maybe, He'll still give us His Blessing—He could, ya know. He might, y'know. Don't be in such a hurry to shovel the first spadeful of damp earth on *this* particular marriage—it's not over, till the wheel stops spinning, and the ball comes to rest."

"Annie's run away from home," I bluntly reminded him. "Philip just tried to kill himself. Dougie was locked in a closet and brutalised; I was kicked out of school, and now, through the mysterious intervention of some recondite Samaritan, I'll be starting private lessons with Michael Sheop, at the same time and place as my good friend, Marcus Agrippa. I think Delilah must've secretly—"

"*Delilah*," he gave a sort of stifled squawk, and took off running as fast as he could go (which wasn't all that fast) after his 'bride'—who was making a beeline for a waiting Limousine, her bodyguards clearing a wide swathe through the jostling, gibbering vermin (whose cameras and flashbulbs were still going off all over the place, recording—immortalising—a sort of Cubist pastiche of the fascinating Carnivore from every angle and point of the compass). She gracefully ducked down into the vehicle, the door was slammed shut, her entourage jumped into the other vehicles making up the Princess' motorcade, and escorted by a troop of mounted Coldstream Guards wearing spiked helmets and long flowing white horsehair plumes, the cavalcade sprang into motion, rapidly crossing the tarmac, disappearing between two hangars, and leaving Ferdinand panting, his chest heaving as though he couldn't breathe, falling to his knees on the pavement, surrounded by a mob of gleefully screeching jackals and paparazzi, closing in for the kill.

"Let's go," a voice whispered.

I flinched, whirling to find myself face to face with a rat. At first I didn't recognise Tosk.

"I'll drive you to the gates of Snoopus' compound," he took me by the arm, "Otherwise you'll never get there on time."

"Punctuality happens to be one of the few things I have left," I idiotically observed, quickly turning away from the spectacle of my father's being torn apart by the vermin.

"You make things too complicated," he was saying, as he skillfully navigated us through the early-afternoon traffic of central London.

"But my father obviously needs—"

"A crash course in real life?" he sardonically smiled.

I could feel the delicate mechanism of my needle-thin sympathies tilting sharply, once more, in the direction of my pathetically ravaged father, despite all his cumulative trespasses and hurtful jabs of petty malignancy.

"That isn't funny in the slightest," I coldly stared out the window.

"What, then?" I could feel him grinning across at the back of my head.

"Can we not talk about it?"

"Butterflies in yer stoomuck?"

"How did you know that I was going to meet Marcus Agrippa—who's your source in the Ministry of Education?"

"I have lots of sources."

"Arlova, wasn't it? Confirm or deny: was she the one tipped you off, concerning this rendez-vous with the Prince Imperial?"

He grinned giving nothing away.

"I'm serious," I tapped the glove-compartment, "Was Arlova your source?"

"What've you got against *her*?" he countered, "Are you jealous of her influence over Snoopus, her hold on the arthritic old codger's final, deteriorating bit of time before he checks out?"

"Checks out?" my mouth fell open. "You can't mean before he—*dies*? His health—"

"Has been on the wane, to put it diplomatically, for a month of Sundays—an' you know it, so stop acting devastated."

"I know he suffers from arthritis, angina—"

"And we won't make it out of the A's for another five minutes," he accelerated to shoot through an intersection whose light had flashed amber. "Look, Love," his tone became gentler (which of course put me on my guard), "Snoopus is old as the hills, and he's had a good life. Bast, he was a Household Name back when my Dad was cutting his Rat-teeth—he's gotta die sometime."

"But not yet," I insisted.

"You want 'im to educate your own kids?"

"I'd never bring Children into a world this treacherous and falsehearted," I tried to look him in the eye for emphasis, but wound up scrutinising the elegant glove-compartment (my earlier tapping seemed to have made a slight indentation; I should've retracted my claws).

"But all the same, don't ya think that's expecting a lot from his faltering old heart with its arhymthmias, blockages—his lips turn blue at the slightest exertion—"

"You seem to know quite a bit."

"It's my vocation to know pretty much everything, and find out the rest."

"From me?"

"What do *you* know?" he sounded dismissive.

"More than you think—"

Oh my g-d—I'm actually taking the bait.

"Such as?" he practically yawned.

"I'm afraid I couldn't possibly divulge the particulars."

"Good, cause I'd hate to call your bluff and lay it all out on the table—every one of your supposedly earth-shattering revelations—"

"Then why talk if it's a waste of breath?" I lost my temper, "Concentrate on the traffic—I'll stare out the window."

"But I love to hear the sound of your voice—"

"We can't always get what we love."

"You should know…"

158

"What's that supposed to mean?" I physically had to restrain myself from latching onto the sleek rodent with my razour-sharp claws and giving him some *deep* scratches to nurse—

"I'm only doing my job."

"What did you mean by saying, *'You should know'?*"

"Let's concentrate on staring out the window, just like you said."

"If your insinuating little probe had anything to do with Marcus Agrippa—"

"For Bastsake, can we please change the subject?"

"I don't care about him. I never liked him—*never*," I ran out of breath—

"Well that's too bad, then," he shrugged.

"How so?"

"It was damn clever of me to take that left turn back at Oxford Circus and swoosh down to the Embankment—"

"Why is that 'too bad' then?"

"The Princess' motorcade, with all them damn paparazzi, have probably gridlocked traffic all the way from the Louvre to as far as Shaftesbury Avenue—"

"WHY IS MY NOT LIKING HIM TOO BAD?" I screamed at the top of my lungs (knowing my sensitive throat would be ravaged for the rest of the day, but not giving a damn).

"Aie! Aie!" he clapped a paw to his left ear, precariously holding onto the steering wheel with the other one, "My ears'll never be the same."

"Then answer my question."

"Nothing could be worse than an outburst like that," he shook himself. "Here goes then: my sources have it on the most unimpeachable authority that the Prince Imperial does not, shall we say, reciprocate your disdain."

"I never said I disdained him. I'm just not trying to entice him to jump into bed with me, contrary to what *certain people* keep indefatigably insinuating—on the tely and in print—till they're blue in the face."

159

"I brought that up, at the Press Conference—"

"Sod the bloody press conference—are you saying he's in love with me?"

My heart was beating so fast, I could barely express the words on a conveyor belt of spastic exhalations of breath.

"I don't know about 'love.' He talks about you nonstop. Rages at himself for his self-described cowardice—"

"It's *my* fault, not his," I burst into tears, "Oh, hurry, Tosk. Please hurry."

"I'm doing the best I can. If it weren't for my little detour back there—"

"Yes, thank you," I wanted to kiss his cute beady little black eyes, but then we'd probably have a car-crash, and I'd never see Marcus again—or explain to him that it certainly wasn't *his* fault. I supposed it to be the 'fault' (or symptom) of the prepackaged, spoonfed, mass-marketed, lobotomised, electronic 'Information Age' imprisoning every one of us, but especially someone like Marcus: sensitive, delicate, noble and ennobling, but at the same time terribly vulnerable—he needed someone like me to take care of him.

"Was Delilah your source?" I interrupted whatever he was going on about.

His mouth opened, the lower jaw hanging for an instant.

"Trying to get me snuffed out?"

"No, Tosk," I leaned sidways resting my cheek against the tinted window, "That's not my objective."

"You *want* to believe it. You want it so badly, you can almost taste it," he smiled. "*I* can almost taste your practically being able to taste it. I play with people; I play them like the notes on a keyboard; that's part of my vocation—"

"Not a very praiseworthy vocation—"

"But necessary. You'll never know how indispensable to the continued functioning of modern society."

"Getting back to Marc's feelings—"

"I never said Love. He talks about you. Sometimes."

"Only sometimes?" my voice squawked in sudden despair.

"Often. Lots of the time. More than just sometimes—"

"You're playing with me," I spat, "just like you said."

"Well of course I am," he rapped out, "but not consciously—not deliberately. And I *do* care what happens to you, Sylvia—I *care* about you, which is damn rare for someone like me. That's why I'm serving you up the plain unvarnished truth, on a platter. Just don't ask where I got it from. Instead concentrate on the fact that yer splendid Young Lion obviously cares one hell of a lot—"

"The same as you," I tried not to sneer. "How sweet."

"*I'm* just a primitive Black Rat classifies Friendship as Caring, and Love as—well, Fucking..."

"So he doesn't 'love' me then," I marveled at the plasticity of my calm-sounding voice, "He just wants to be Friends."

"He never said anything about fucking, so how should I know," he slammed down on the steering wheel, blaring the hooter as we swerved round an outcropping of taxicabs, "I'd say, search your own feelings, when yer all alone, without someone like me pushing your buttons, and if you really wanted to do it"—I winced—"back when you were making friends with him, and if he seemed really, how shall I put this—not exactly slavering, and I won't say encouraging, but *responsive*—friendly in response to your friendship—and you really *wanted* it—I'd say *he* wanted it, too."

"But how can I be sure?" I whined, no longer caring— about the rat, the rat's vocation, or anything in the whole wide world, except Marc.

"That's just the rub," he smiled with seeming sympathy, accelerating through an intersection, "You can't."

To his credit, Tosk didn't say much for the rest of the drive. I didn't really care any longer what he wormed out of me (or much less, what they printed in the damn tabloids about it), but I still found myself wondering if my instinct—that here was a decent, if somewhat coarse, animal—could be trusted (knowing full well how devious and addicted to manipulating people he'd proved himself, again and again)?

The traffic was awful. I still don't know how he managed to get us from the aeroport to Snoopus' compound in less than an hour—it was just past two o'clock when he waved at the closed-circuit camera, and the electronic gates opened.

"Believe it or not," the rat clicked open the lock on the passenger door, "I wish you the best, Sylvia."

It always weirded me out (to adopt Annie's lingo) whenever someone addressed me by name.

"So don't lose my number," he half leaned out of his car, "You can ring me day or night—"

"Anything to help you get an Exclusive," I quipped, picturing Marcus waiting for me in the garden—perhaps he was watching us right now, peering from a dense fernbrake, a canopy of honeysuckle brushing against his deliciously aromatic, sun-gilded mane.

"You think *that's* what I was driving at?" the Rat's baritone lost its velvety contours, "You Aristos are all the same," he slammed the car-door so hard I jumped.

"Sylvia."

I recognised Arlova's characteristically fretful voice and turned round—Tosk peeled out of the courtyard, setting the guard-dogs and sentries on edge.

"What do you suppose *his* problem is?" I tried to make conversation (her tone boded ill).

"Perhaps you should ask that question of yourself, Sylvia," her lips pursed themselves till the network of tiny muscles quivered. "Snoopus *personally* intervened on your behalf—he, alone, when no one else would touch you with a ten-foot pole, went out on a limb so to speak—he went to a great deal of trouble and effort—*don't interrupt*—"

My mouth snapped automatically shut. I had to admit that amongst all her other faults, Arlova was an excellent schoolmarm (that's how she'd first come to Snoopus' attention, according to Helen), a practiced disciplinarian capable of controlling the unruliest classroom—I could almost see how I'd once admired her—*almost*.

"Has it crossed your mind yet that the entire Ministry has had to modify its internal workings, just to accommodate *you*?"

This time I kept my mouth open, and even began speaking, but she bulldozed right over me: "Your lesson with Professor Sheop—"

My paw flew to my mouth—I'd *completely* forgotten—

"Was slated to begin at twelve o'clock noon."

"My father forced me to go to the aeroport—"

"You could have sent us a message—"

"I know. I'm sorry—it was—"

"It was the least that might have been expected from a previously responsible, well-mannered young scholar."

"Please let me go apologise to Professor Sheop—"

"He left the premises 45 minutes ago."

"He left?"

"He's the Acting Minister of Education, Sylvia." (I hated the way she kept pronouncing my name, contrasting it with the way Tosk did so—it almost made me nostalgic for the beady-eyed rat.) "He has a myriad of other responsibilities besides waiting half the day for a White Tabby to traipse in when it finally strikes her fancy. What with Snoopus' health these days—"

"Just what *is* his medical condition?" I demanded. "As one of his favourite pupils, I have a right to be told."

"Stop pretending to be all concerned about Snoopus," she sneered. "We all know you have Other Things on your mind."

"What's that supposed to mean?" I demanded in a quavering voice.

"Well here's some more to think about: Professor Sheop entered a Zero in his gradebook—"

So *this* was what a Zero felt like—I'd never had one before.

"Please let me make up the lesson," I found myself pleading as if my life depended on it, "My father forced me—I wasn't allowed to make any phonecalls—it was beyond my control—"

"He told me, one more Goose-Egg," she savoured the words, "and he's speaking to Snoopus about it. He can't waste his valuable time."

"What's wrong with you, Arlova?" I somehow stopped floundering and found solid ground underfoot.

"Excuse me?" she raised her voice, but her gaze dropped the moment I looked her in the eye. I realised we were almost the same height—either I'd grown, or the Incorruptible Arlova had stooped slightly, perhaps under the crushing weight of her own relentless perfectionism.

"You used to be different, that's all."

"Different?"

"Back when you were teaching us."

"And so were *you*, believe it or not," she virtually shouted. "We expected great things from a student of such unbounded promise. But the Tree sometimes becomes stunted, when nipped down to the very roots by the frost—the Fruit never ripens, and the careful Gardener finds himself disappointed."

"My character was maligned; I was the victim of slander—"

"Helen said the same thing, *at first*—"

"I'm sure you and she have had some grand ol' talks," I could feel myself losing control, "watching me on television being dragged through the mire."

164

"I don't waste my time watching the tely."

"Well neither do I," the firm ground under my feet had once again turned to quicksand, "but getting back to what we were talking about, I was forced to be at that press conference—please let me make up the lesson, and un-do the zero."

"What's it like?" her voice unexpectedly softened, "Does it make you feel like—a Star?"

"What are you talking about?"

"All those cameras, those bright lights," it looked like she, too, was sinking, but into a different sort of quicksand. Poor Arlova. We intellectuals and wallflowers are singularly unequipped to resist the schizophrenic push-pull of the Bright Lights and Cameras.

I took off scurrying.

"I'm afraid he's not in the garden," her voice like a skillfully thrown hatchet came whistling through the air slicing into the back of my brain.

Turning. Forcing myself to confront what she'd said.

"Where then?"

"I think it's best that you went on home, for to-day. We could phone your driver; I'm sure he's still in the vicinity—"

"For the second time, where is the Prince Imperial?"

"It's not just your own neck," she lowered her voice, "Ever since Snoopus' health took a nosedive—"

"*You* don't seem too upset about it."

I couldn't believe how easy it suddenly was, striking below the belt, so to speak.

"I realise," she was practically grinding her teeth, "what with your own *hopeless* entanglement, that you've been under duress—"

"Tell me where he is, and I'll gladly take my duress—"

"Snoopus has enemies," she savagely whispered. "Not that Sheop consciously wants to undermine the animal who gave him everything he now has…"

"Sheop?" I frowned.

"He covets that little gold pin."

165

She'd definitely lost me. I opened my mouth—it was time to put my foot down, and demand to see Marcus.

"Oh. You don't understand. You wouldn't, of course—"

"Arlova—"

"It's the golden pin Snoopus wears in his frock, the one with the intertwined Serpents of Knowledge—it's his Badge of Office, as Minister of Education—"

"I need to see Marcus," I raised my voice, squaring my shoulders, forcing myself to stand upright instead of slouching stoop-shouldered, staring her in the face instead of looking down at the gravel.

"He's not here, you ill-mannered little brat," she totally lost it, "not in the garden, nor the peristyle, nor any of the classrooms, certainly not in Snoopus' private study—nowhere in this whole bloody compound, okay? He never shewed up for his lesson. You were late, and didn't call. He phoned ahead, to say he's still sick. Which is the more responsible student?"

"Oh, fuck you," I shouted, stamping up and down on the gravel, the little pebbles flying every which way.

"Snoopus teaches us that profanity—"

"Shall we see what Snoopus has to say about this whole conundrum: my being late, my using profanity, Marcus cutting class for the third day in a row? He's becoming quite the little juvenile delinquent, these days."

"Snoopus can't be disturbed," she grabbed me by the shoulders. There was genuine alarm in her voice.

So Marcus was here, after all. That lying whore of a Meme—hiding him with Snoopus—

"We had to give him Nitroglycerin during the night," she confessed as we struggled there, on the slippery, shifting gravel, "You can't just barge in, unannounced—it could kill him—"

"So announce me," I hissed, kicking and biting my larger, and normally stronger, antagonist.

"You selfish willful undisciplined self-indulgent little *brat*," she half screamed, half whispered—causing me to burst out laughing—my doing so must've distracted the hyperventilating Meme; she slipped on the gravel and fell flat on her arse.

I took off pelting fast as I could; I made it past the guards, who all knew me of course. Arlova must've been thoroughly winded—otherwise she would've called out to the guards.

Flinging the door open and barreling into Snoopus' private study—scanning every corner, every nook and cranny—

"What an unexpected surprise," Snoopus' voice did sound weaker than usual.

I was longing for that alloy of smelted Red Gold, that compound of sensitive whiskers, quivering nostrils, large floppy paws (that dwarfed my own), long muscular thick tufted tail, sinuous haunches, gigantic bottomless kaleidoscopic golden-green liquid eyes leavened and sprinkled with filings of micah, sparkling fragments of feldspar and quartz—those eyes glistening like fire-opals, polarised lode-stones magnetising my loins, my breasts, my erect, aching nipples—scanning the room yet again, I let my breath out in a long, wheezing, sibilant groan of absolute, agonised, self-compounding despair.

"Sylvia," Snoopus called out to me softly, "D'you know, for a moment—only a moment, mind—I thought you were Cleo. Excuse me, I meant to say the Empress, Cleopatra, may She rest in peace."

At that instant Arlova burst into the room. Marching over to where I was standing, she slapped me as hard as she could. Perhaps I deserved it, but Snoopus fairly exploded and began feebly cursing and shouting, the veins on his brow and neck palpitating. Arlova pleaded with the elderly Dog not to excite himself. I tried to explain that the whole thing was my fault, but amidst mixing drugs, ringing for various servants, and measuring dosages, she signaled for me to shut the hell up and go stand in the corner, which I did (of course)—whereupon something in Snoopus' face shriveled and caved in on itself, and suddenly he was whimpering for his Arlova to come over and kiss him on the cheek before giving him his next dose of the Hemlock (as he called it, winking ever so slightly).

I turned to face the darkest part of the room. His croaking, enfeebled voice went right through me, like a sharpened, but invisible, spear.

"I'm sorry," Arlova whispered in my ear. "For everything. Not just that stupid physical tussle—though I do apologise, for that as well."

"What's wrong with him?" I nodded towards the animal who had been more of a *father* to me than Ferdinand, locked in the prison of his shallow, two-dimensional pipedreams and fantasies, would ever know (or, indeed, care).

"He had a bad night, that's all. When he doesn't sleep, it fogs his mind. He's almost 97, remember."

"I should go now."

"You can find your way to the gate, I suppose?"

"Of course," I whispered (Snoopus was starting to snore).

"Sylvia?" she hesitated.

"Yes?"

"He thought you were Cleopatra," she whispered. "You should be flattered. He's never said that to me."

I must have walked for miles and miles. It was mid-afternoon, and the teeming throngs and bustling intensity of central London were just what I needed to escape from myself. Alas, you can never stay outside of yourself. Maybe that's what Philip was trying to achieve when he slashed his wrists—the idea was certainly more compelling to me than it ever had been in the past.

I decided—quite suddenly, but irrevocably—to dial the magic number Delilah had given me. It was finally time; I could feel it in my bones.

The first red telephone booth I stumbled upon was, predictably, occupied. I quickened my pace, a spring in my stride for the first time in ages.

Skirting the Haymarket, dodging drunks (all of whom reminded me of my father), accelerating round bibliophiles and eccentrics browsing in the bookstalls (the most pathetic of whom invariably reminded me, with a pang, of myself—as though life were swishing past all of us, but at different speeds and distances), I kept my eyes skinned for the next available booth. And behold: just as I spotted one directly in front of me, its door opened, and a portly Possum crept out. As I reached forward to grasp the handle, a talon materialised from out of nowhere, also gripping the door.

"I believe I was here first," a statuesque Kingfisher, his voice reeking of cheap beer, slurringly screeched.

"It seems to me we both staked our claim simultaneously," I coldly observed.

"What?" the malapert fellow squinted, his avian faculties clearly intoxicated. I resisted an impulse to slap his gaping, odiferous beak.

"I'll wait," I said with a thrill of disgust.

"Wait?"

"Are either of you planning to use this bloody phone—"

"Yes!" I shouted at the impudent Black Bear making ready to push past us both, "The Drunk here can go first. Then I'm using it. Then you can."

"Bugger off," he snorted, and slouched back into the teeming anonymity of every species under the sun scurrying, shambling, and slithering past.

"I'm not drunk—what's yer problem?"

"If you're not going first, then I shall," I gritted my teeth.

"You're the same age as my daughter Nell, but Lor' how lucky she is, not to be an uptight aristo."

I shoved my way into the phone booth, and slammed the door behind me. There was no lock, of course. I supposed that must be the way they were made, to prevent folk from passing out in them, and dying before anyone could break the thick glass. It had to be thick, for to block out the noise of the traffic and crowds. And you could die, fainting in an upright position—we'd learnt that in school.

"Here goes," I said, to steady myself.

The numbered buttons were laid out just the same as on 'private' telephones. I'd memorised the Magic Number, but produced the slip of paper just the same, so as to ensure absolute fidelity to the exact sequence, as jotted down by Delilah herself.

Before I could analyse what I was doing (and freeze up on myself), I began punching the sequence, and hearing the electronic pips which corresponded to their numerical registers.

Two things happened almost at the same time, both of them highly upsetting. A recorded voice from inside the infernal machine instructed me, please, to insert sixty-five kopecks—at the same instant someone began tapping, hard as they could, on the glass.

The goddam drunk of a Kingfisher. Scrabbling in my disorganised reticule for the spare change, I whirled round to confront the slimy bastard—only to find myself face to face with a large black Rat, his sleek (faintly brindled) fur glinting in the late-afternoon sunlight.

"Don't we reco'nise each other?" he pulled open the door.

170

"Tosk," I fairly sobbed with relief. "D'you have sixty-five kopecks?"

"That depends on whom yer telephoning," he grinned.

"Don't worry," I smiled (perhaps somewhat evasively), "It's not a rival tabloid."

"Who is it then?"

"Oh," I tried to sound nonchalant (since clearly this chance encounter had effectively torpedoed the phonecall), "It's—personal—I mean, private," I looked away from the rat, "I mean, I wish I could tell you."

"I'll be waiting just over there," he pointed towards his automobile, "in case you need a ride home."

"Are you some sort of private Limousine service?" I couldn't help flashing a smile. "I mean, you seem to be driving me everywhere, these days."

"Praps I'm in loov."

A filament of irritation bisected my consciousness, zigzagging as I found the cheek to slam down the receiver, storming out of the booth.

"Why don't ya go ahead and make yer bloody phonecall?" he jerked open the cardoor, jumped into the driver's seat, and started the engine.

"It's—*personal*," I let my voice become a trifle hard-edged. "I don't understand why you can't understand that."

"Like I said: perhaps I'm in love."

"Alright then," my annoyance brought me back down to earth, anchoring me, broaching fresh reserves of endurance. "I'll make the bloody phonecall. Go back to yer bloody vehicle. I don't need you eavesdropping."

He poured a stream of kopecks into my cupped paws, far more than I needed—they started spilling onto the pavement. With enviable speed and agility he retrieved every one of them. Carefully securing the door of the phone booth, I watched him as he walked away from me. He'd averted his face. Suddenly he flung all the coins into the gutter. I didn't see what happened next. Adrenaline was coursing through every fibre of my being as, turning my attention to the intimidating array of buttons, I carefully dialed that magic phone number.

I noticed, bursting in through the kitchen door, that none of the servants were about (maybe they'd all decamped again—I just wished they'd make up their minds, one way or the other).

He never answered. It just rang and rang.

Annie had the right idea (running away from this place); I started grabbing books and tossing them into a suitcase. It's hard to be practical about such things, especially when you're upset to begin with (then again, who ever ran away from home without being upset?). I tried to include bath salts, medicinal soap, my toothpaste for sensitive fangs—by the time I'd zipped up the suitcase, it was impossible to lift—I must've filled it with too many books.

My sister, of course, had her strapping young lad to shoulder the physical burdens. I couldn't picture Marc shouldering anything—plus he wasn't mine and probably never would be. I'd based this entire ridiculous passion on a series of undeniably intimate schoolyard conversations—but that's all they were: conversations. Not declarations, vows, or even insinuations; he'd remained slippery throughout—slippery, and ethically unassailable—it was all in my head.

I kicked the suitcase as hard as I could, and yelped in pain. Running away, it suddenly struck me, was wholly beyond my limited reserves of character. I needed to make myself Strong—and Demonic—like Annie. But how do you go about altering your fundamental character—and didn't the fault, in fact, reside not with me, but rather with my surroundings, the imperfect (to put it mildly) world into which I'd been born?

These questions made a mockery of my exhausted, even bankrupt, competence—I was ready to fly with teeth and claws at the next person unlucky enough to enter my sanctum.

That person just happened to be my younger sister, Maria. She'd knocked and, receiving no answer, pushed the door open, venturing bold as brass into the room. I fleetingly wondered what I must look like, hunched over the suitcase, books strewn all over the floor.

"You should come back at a more opportune time," I controlled myself.

"What sort of a beast," she rapped out the words as though she'd rehearsed her little speech three or four times, "could snarl at an Innocent, subjecting him to untold emotional anguish and pain?"

"Maybe *innocent* Dougie enjoys manipulating the people around him. Maybe he's learned to throw tantrums with such unerring finesse—"

"Just shut up," she stamped her foot (reminding me of myself for a sickening splitsecond), "Jane was right. I didn't believe her at first—"

"Come, come," I bared the tips of my teeth (imitating Delilah, since Maria had usurped my own cringing persona), "Let's not resort to cheapshots—and that was a very cheap shot."

"What if it happens to be true?"

"So, Jane's been talking about me—to you of all people?"

"You don't happen to have a monopoly on Jane's affections," she enunciated her words with a stilted precision. "She hated Philip and Annie since *he*'d got them sewed up in his own pocket, but she didn't love just you—Douglas and I were also part of the package."

"You know something, Maria?" I swept past her, got between her and the door, and locked it. "You make the whole Divorce, with all the twisted hatreds and rivalries that have destroyed this family—you make it all seem not tragic, but stale—even laughable. I can't think why the paparazzi went to the trouble of covering the whole maudlin tragicomedy—must not have been much else going on."

"Let me out, please?" she began predictably sniveling.

"Worst of all, you remind me of myself—"

"That's a laugh," the stoop-shouldered little thing surprised me, flaring up with an almost Annie-like passion: "Because *you* certainly don't remind me of myself any longer."

"Thanks for the compliment."

"I used to worship the ground you walked on," her eyes welled up with tears, "All our teachers told me to work hard, and if I were lucky, I might just achieve a portion of *Sylvia's* intellectual brilliance—"

"Life's more than just a classroom," I stammered, discomfited by her unexpected outburst, "and there's more to the business of growing up than simply"—words momentarily failed me—"than simply cultivating a passel of tired intellectualisms and scholastic little blue-ribbon accomplishments—it's just mental masturbation—"

She gave an affected little shriek, stopping her ears (exactly as I would have done—just a few weeks ago).

"You sound like Annie," she got the words out with difficulty, her thin wasted shoulders beginning to heave.

"Go flit back to Douglas," my voice quavered as I flung the door open. "Tell him I'm sorry; I'll go find him a sugary trifle, or some sort of confection from the corner bakery just down the street—"

"Sylvia," her voice lurched most disconcertingly, "I'm scared—"

"Of me?" I tried to smile, "for seeming like a carbon copy of Annie?"

I hoped she'd say *yes*—realising it with a sickly thrill of self-loathing.

"If Ferdinand kills himself, what's going to happen to *us*?" she burst into tears, "I'm not going to live with Jane—I'd rather die than go live with her—I'm sorry for bringing Jane into it—she slags you off constantly (just like she slags everyone off), and for once I tried to play that disgusting card—from disgusting jealousy, and emptiness—"

"Whoa! Slow down!" I grabbed her by the wrist (she didn't even flinch, which alarmed me still further), "What's this about Ferdinand offing himself? Has he said he was going to? Has something happened?"

"You mean you haven't heard the News?" she melodramatically whispered.

"Obviously not," I just barely kept my voice under control, "Let's sit down here, together, on the bed, and you can tell me all about it."

She started sniveling again. I handed her some 'paper towels,' which she refused, saying they would irritate her sensitive nostrils. At last, having ransacked my chest of drawers, I found some handkerchiefs which she consented to use (in the meantime, her snot had dripped all over the bedspread).

"So? Let's get on with it," I prodded as soon as she seemed halfway composed.

"The servants," she gulped, "were hearing lots of gossip. So everybody gathered in front of the television. All the afternoon sitcoms and soaps had been pre-empted—Her Royal Highness, Delilah," Maria gasped out the syllables, "had the marriage, between her and Ferdinand, annulled—by Imperial fiat—apparently that can be done, if the Privy Council, at the behest of the Emperor—"

"The Privy Council can dissolve anyone or anything," I sneered, "Quickest of all a nettlesome marriage—"

"—sends the Annulment," she was being pigheadedly passive-aggressive, "to the Council of Five Hundred, who ratify it before kicking it up to the College of Cardinals. We learned in class yesterday, incidentally, that what started out as the Witan, composed of Barons and Thegns, more recently known as the People's National Assembly, under Cleopatra the Blessed, happens now, under Agrippa, to be a bicameral legislature—"

"I used to do the same thing," I let my breath out, inhaled evenly, let it out nice and slow. "When 'real life' got too threatening or upsetting to deal with, I also used to hide behind dry dessicated bits of driftwood-like intellection."

176

"They say Delilah went straight to the Emperor and begged his forgiveness. She's formally engaged, now, to marry some young upstart that nobody's ever heard of."

"But at least it's a Lion," I sneered, "and I bet she found one whose name conveniently also begins with a D! So the fireworks and wedding cakes and specialty items being sold in all the novelty shops can feature the letter D, produced twice, intertwined in conjugal bliss—the smart shops on Bond Street can sell diamond broaches, with Cupid's arrows transecting, and joining, the two D's—except the arrows should be composed of rubies, don't you think?"

"Now *you're* doing it," she muttered as if to herself.

"Doing what?"

"Hiding. Behind a stream of meaningless blather."

"I'm sure it's not meaningless to the Royal Family," I suddenly felt my knees practically give way. "So it *was* Diocletian? Please tell me his name wasn't—something else—whatever else that might be—"

"It's not that Cub you're in love with, if that's what you're driving at."

I almost slapped her; she saw the blow coming, and flinched. Fortunately I managed to rein myself in.

"And I'm right," I managed, "about his being Diocletian?"

"That sounds like the name they kept spouting. It was difficult for them to pronounce, and they didn't have any pictures—except this group shot, where he was standing in the back. They'd circled him with a magic marker, and blown up the detail till you could hardly see anything, because of how pixellated the shot had become—but he did seem to be goodlooking—some of the servants kept sighing, and cooing."

"Did you sigh, and coo?"

She stared stubbornly straight ahead off into space. Just as I do, when I feel either patronised, or persecuted. I smiled in spite of myself. Things could be worse—I could be like Maria: awkward, stoop-shouldered, brooding and sullen, destined for an early spinsterhood—but then, so I had been—a carbon copy of all the things she was now (or was beginning to try and shed, like a chick struggling to break forth from the egg). Perhaps she'd surprise us all, as I'd surprised myself...

"So what about Ferdinand?" I prodded. "Did he threaten to kill himself?"

"They said he'd gone crying to Blussian, but she wouldn't have him back."

"How could she—she's married to Nero—"

"No she isn't—Blussian's applied to the Council of Five Hundred to have that marriage annulled as well—"

"For love of Ferdinand," I sneered, "how sweet—"

"For love of anything but," she scathingly cut me off, "Nero punched her in the face, it seems—gave her a black eye— she said it was because he failed to satisfy her voracious 'appetite'—she impugned his Leonine masculinity, but I think it was just for revenge, and so do the other servants—she was hitting back, hard."

"I'm totally lost—"

"She made him fork over several hundred million zlotys, for a settlement; she's using the capital to invest in some steel mills in Yorkshire, and some coalmines not far from the borderlands. Ferdinand got some kind of cash settlement as well—Delilah wouldn't say how much it was; she called it 'severance pay'."

"How charming."

"Even some of our servants laughed. She does have a certain charisma, you've got to admit."

"So how come I wasn't mobbed by a gang of paparazzi, coming through the side gate?" I demanded.

"Because they announced that Ferdinand had gone into seclusion—in the suite of rooms he keeps at the Ritz—that whole part of town, from the Rue de Rivoli to Charing Cross, is completely jam-packed with reporters."

"But wait a minute," I tried to marshal the swirling thoughts and questions, "Why did Blussian reject him?"

"She publicly announced that she's finished selling herself to the highest bidder—she's going to start bidding, with the money she makes from all these factories, on some young lads who are more to her taste: easy-going, sense of humour, goodlooking, and randy."

"I hope *they* can accommodate her 'voracious' appetite."

For the first time, Maria smiled—she even giggled, bashfully.

"Getting back to Ferdinand," I sighed, watching the smile wither away, "and the position in which we find ourselves, at this moment, vis-à-vis his shattered prospects—"

"That's the part I can't understand. Delilah explicitly said that he was holed up at that hotel, seeing no one—"

"What's hard to understand about that?"

"The fact that she lied. He's here—upstairs—right above us. This four-door Sedan drove up about thirty minutes ago, with tinted glass—the door opened—a big Saint-Bernard, supporting him, practically carried him up the stairs—told Goody Thorpe not to give him any booze, or at least not his usual Nightcap of Brandy laced with about four shots of Drambooie—he, the Dog, had administered a sedative—and with that he climbed back into the Sedan, which made its way inconspicuously out the gate, and melted back into the rush-hour traffic."

"You saw this happen?"

"Goody Thorpe told me about it. The servants are all clustered downstairs, round the television, gossiping, and trying to decide what to do."

"I know what to do," I surprised myself, swinging into action as though guided by some disembodied intelligence.

"Sylvia, wait!" she shrilled, ineffectually galumphing up the stairsteps behind me.

We both hesitated at the door to the Master Bedroom (which was closed, but not locked). Too many bad memories resided therein. Maria kept nervously fingering the hem of the smock she was wearing.

"Perhaps, we…shouldn't bother him," she melodramatically whispered.

"Grow up, sweetheart," my voice became harsh (which gave me the courage to knock).

Two things happened. First Maria flitted back down the stairs. At the same time it sounded like a muffled voice—from inside the bedroom—had tried to say something. I took the liberty of pushing the door open just a crack. It was so dark I couldn't see anything.

"Annie?"

I deliberately held my tongue.

"If you're not *Annie*," the voice petulantly exerted itself, "then bugger off."

"I don't know why I bothered."

"Sylvia?"

"I'm going, don't worry."

"Wait a minute—"

I closed the door and, Maria-like, began flitting downstairs, three steps at a time.

"*Sylvia*," the strangled cry brought me up short.

He'd dragged himself to the top of the stairs.

"I meant Sylvia, not Annie," he managed, clutching the banister for all he was worth.

The barefaced, cynical lie disgusted me to the very core of my being, but what choice did I have: he looked to be on the point of collapse.

"You should probably lie down," I coldly suggested.

He gave what was perhaps meant to be a helpless-looking shrug (but it didn't pull at my heartstrings) before lurching over to the big mahogany four-poster bed. I scanned the contents of his bedside table; there was nothing alcoholic nor even medicinal. Ferdinand fluffed the pillows before draping himself against them with an almost inaudible sigh.

"How much hard cash did your ex-bride slap down on the table?"

"Look, Sylvia," his voice would've sounded almost impatient if it weren't so *drained*, "we need to talk about Philip."

"Philip," I mechanically repeated.

"That sodding shrink of his wanted me to drag myself over there, in all this traffic and botheration—to-day of all days. Perhaps if things had worked out differently—you know what I'm talking about?"

I nodded, trying to imagine what Philip would look like, after slashing his wrists.

"I told that bloody doctor that it was simply impossible, that one of *their* lot would have to transport the invalid from his current bedlam to *this* enchanting nut-hatch—I reckon he'll find his new digs depressingly familiar. Like they say: if you see one asylum, you've seen 'em all."

"I'm sure Philip—"

"Of course, if *She* (and I'm not going to utter Her name, ever again)—"

"To hell with *Delilah*," I stamped my foot as he gave a low moan, "Your son Philip, whom you profess to love—you said so at the Press Conference—which is a sight more than you've ever professed concerning me, or Maria—"

"You're absolutely right," he waved his paws distractedly, "but can we talk about it *some other time?*"

"Of course, Father Dear," I gritted my teeth, "but what about Philip—do you *really* think he's well enough to come home?"

A burst of loud, invasive tapping on the bedroom door (as from the point of a sharpened walking-stick) made us both instinctively flinch. A moment later the door was flung open, and several strangers unceremoniously swept into the room.

"Identity: Ferdinand Romanoff," one of them, clearly of subordinate rank, informed his superior, an imperturbable-looking, yellow-eyed Lynx. "And this one, fidgeting nervously over by the side of the bed, is Sylvia Romanoff, fifteen years of age, the second daughter."

181

"Holy Bast," my father caused me to cringe in embarrassment, "Has it come to *this*, then! Is her Revenge so unslakeable?"

"Father, please," I began—

"Shut your mouth!" he screeched. "Don't you understand with whom we're dealing? These are the Secret Police—I'm done for! Holy, fucking Bast... I'm done. It's all over..."

"The Pure in Heart," I couldn't help myself, "have nothing to fear."

One of them sniggered. The Lynx whipped out a lorgnette, scrutinising me with an air of condescending detachment.

"I want it clearly understood—and recorded," Ferdinand began babbling wildly, "that this impertinent young white Cat here, though related to me in close degree, speaks *solely* for herself, and has nothing—whatsoever—to do with my own beliefs and values, political or otherwise—"

"That's right, Ferdinand," everything was becoming blurred as my eyes filled with tears, "I keep the Emperor's commandments; you spit and stamp and dance on them—I've seen you *mock* our Holy Father, the Emperor!"

"LIAR!" he screamed in a piercing, almost incoherent tone of white-lipped hysteria. I knew the foam would begin forming, in flecks—Annie was the true master, when it came to baiting our father. She used to attend Bear-baitings, and Meme-baitings, to pick up useful tips and sadistic little stratagems of pure inventiveness (for all their being so awful, and spiteful)—it was like our own father's being a beast somehow freed *us* from the Social Contract as well.

"She's a sodding little pathological liar," he raved, the flecks beginning to fall on the carpet, "always has been! Wants to fuck the fucking Prince Imperial—write that down in your little secret notepads and minutes—turn your recording devices way up, and you can pick up the sickly thumping of her black, scheming heart—I reckon she fancies she can hear the flies creeping up and down the windowpanes—*Sylvia?*"

I turned my countenance as slowly, and majestically, as I knew how, to face him.

"Don't pretend you're not listening," he began to tremble, "I know I haven't exactly played the role of the Dutiful Father—believe me, the actual Model Fathers are also just role-playing—we select or get handed a *script*, soon after birth. I wonder what *hers* was like—I mean *Sylvia*'s—"

"We know you meant Someone Else," I sneered, making him turn the colour of greyish-white cheese.

"Is she for real?" he pointed at me, then suddenly, for some reason, switched gears, "Look, Sylvia—sweetheart, sugarplum, apple-blossom—I realise I'm a cruel callous bastard sometimes—"

"Sometimes?" I shouted, against my own will.

"All the time, then," (his dilated eyes were jerking and rotating like those of a trapped Wildebeest, hemmed in by the pack) "but surely you must *also* admit that it's—hang it all, it's a species of *preemptive* Cruelty."

"Preemptive?" I shouted, stamping my foot.

"You, Sylvia," he foamed at the mouth, "can be cruel with the best of 'em—you're Delilah's little Understudy—she's trained you damn well—you've done the cunt proud!"

"Hear him!" I began, myself, to dribble flecks on the carpet, "He just called Her Royal Highness a word that I shan't cheapen myself by repeating."

We both, father and daughter, like exhausted fighters in the ring, fell back a few paces, heaving and panting.

"I gather there's been a slight misunderstanding," the Lynx bestirred himself at last.

"Yes?" I hastened to address myself to the State Security operative with as much dignity as I could muster (which, alas, wasn't much).

He pursed his furry lips before speaking.

"It's true that we happen to be from the Ministry of State Security—"

"Holy Bast," Ferdinand began yammering, clutching one of the mahogany posts for support. "Sweet fucking merciful Bast…"

"But we're here in a strictly 'unofficial' capacity."

"Are you saying my father's under arrest?" I took my courage in both hands. "Or just being questioned?"

"Neither," one of the subordinates whinnied (a big bay-coloured Stallion), "It's *you* we've come to collect, as a matter of fact."

Two things happened: the floor began to pitch back and forth under my feet, and my father started filling the room with the most repulsive cackling laughter I'd ever heard in my life.

"Let's get going," the Lynx took hold of me (I was listing and swaying), "And you!" he shouted across at my father, "Shut up or I *will* give you something to laugh about—in the Isolator, deep underground."

Like a malfunctioning bit of gadgetry having its plug yanked, his laughter switched off, in mid-giggle. I watched him from over my shoulder. He stood there, clutching the bedpost, waves of colour changing his face from mouldy cheese, to boiled lobster, and back again. Our eyes met for a splitsecond—the prick of contact was almost electrically painful.

"Sylvia?" he keened from behind us as they hustled me through the door, "I didn't mean it, okay?"

"It's okay dad, I know."

He followed us down the stairs and out the door, to the big black automobile waiting there in the drive, its motor idling and filling the air with poisonous exhaust. The servants were glued to all the windows along the ground floor, some of them covering their mouths, a few grinning excitedly. Goody Thorpe burst out from the kitchen door, leading Maria and Douglas (it looked almost like she might be dragging them) to say Goodbye (for the last time?)—

My eyes welled up with tears.

Ferdinand lollopped up to me, brandishing a wad of rainbow-hued currency, along with some candied lozenges, cough-drops, and various odds and ends (scooped up from the bedside table on the spur of the instant); he shoved it insistently towards us, till at last one of the officers placed it all in an evidence bag —and even made out a receipt.

"I think Philip's going to like it here," he excitedly yammered as they helped me into the automobile.

His relief at my—and not his—being the Sacrificial Lamb was almost physically palpable. I think even the Police operatives were somewhat disgusted (and it takes a lot to disgust a bloke in their line of work).

"We're converting one of the guestrooms," he cupped his paws round his mouth as the cardoor slammed shut. "and hiring medical staff. Don't worry about Philip, okay, honey?"

We drove slowly towards the gate.

"I'm just sorry you won't be here," he called after us, "to welcome him home."

I closed my eyes and leaned back against the seat-cushions.

Arrested, by the Secret Police.

Every time I told myself that things couldn't possibly get any worse…

I forced my lips to try and shape themselves into the semblance of a grim unyielding smile. *Indomitable*. That's what I needed to become—and fast.

"Where are you taking me?" I tried to sound tough.

"We'll be there in another block or so," the driver, a phlegmatic Otter, responded.

"You're being taken to one of our Safe Houses, to meet a friend," the Lynx explained, leaning sideways and lowering his voice (I wondered if he and the subordinates were somehow at loggerheads, or couldn't trust one another—all the Security Organs intrigue continuously to such an extent, it must become second nature).

"I don't have any friends."

We zoomed round a corner, through an archway, and into a cobbled courtyard of sorts. Towering facades of brick and masonry surrounded us on all four sides. Craning my neck, I could just make out a patch of overcast sky. It reminded me of a famous painting I'd once seen, of a group of convicts taking their exercise, walking in a tightly circumscribed space.

"It's just through this door," the Lynx beckoned.

The others, curiously enough, had remained in the vehicle, which was once again voiding its noxious fumes of exhaust.

I thought of Marc—I couldn't help myself. Intellectually I knew it was impossible, but the fantasy of his being somewhere close at hand, in this 'Safe House' or whatever it was—Royalty could command certain of the Secret Police, no? He *could be* standing there, watching us through the Judas, just the other side of the door—which the Lynx was now proceeding to unlock.

My heart was hammering so that I could scarcely breathe.

And there I was, standing all alone inside an unfurnished reception chamber—just planks of flooring, and stark unadorned walls. I could hear the Lynx relocking the door, and walking back towards the idling vehicle. A moment later, I heard them turning round, and then driving off.

"Sorry about all the cloak-and-dagger secrecy."

I turned eagerly towards the voice. There, standing framed in a doorway, was none other than—Tosk.

My heart shriveled.

"And I'm also sorry it couldn't have been someone else."

"What's that supposed to mean," I somehow squawked, fighting back tears.

"I know you were hoping to see Marcus Agrippa."

I stared down at the floorboards.

"Even if he knew how to find you (which he doesn't), they'd never let him compromise himself, by getting it on with a commoner."

"I'm not exactly a *commoner*," the anger helped anchor me.

"But do you happen, then, to belong to the Royal Family, Sylvia?" he shamelessly pressed. "Aye, there's the sticking point, the one, gigantic fly in the ointment."

"Have you enlisted with the Secret Police?" I practically spat. "A police informer. Even Fleet Street sounds better than that."

"C'mon. We're going to visit a friend."

"That's what the State Security bloke just said."

"D'you think he meant I was the 'friend'?" he sneered. "Although, Bast knows, I'd like to be a friend. Perhaps, even— well never mind. Milady here has her feather-brained head in the stars. So let's go then," he squeaked. "Yer *real* friends aren't the sort to be kept waiting... I said, let's *go*."

Seizing me by the wrist, he practically dragged me through several more unfurnished rooms. Opening a side door, he hustled me into a waiting Rickshaw, which sprang into dizzying motion almost as soon as he'd flung himself onto the narrow cushion beside me.

"I hope you'll pardon me, Tosk, for any offence I may have had occasion to give, just now," I mumbled (wondering if the Rat pomaded his fur), "But the shock of being arrested, and then finding out that I'm not, it seems, under arrest after all—"

"Think nothing of it," he gallantly took me by the hand, and planted a kiss on one of the pawpads (mine are all pink, whereas Annie's happen to be of an alluring German-chocolate consistency)—

"I would have gone on kissing your pawpads, and then your claws," he confessed, "except that I can see in your face exactly what you think of me—and my presumptuous feelings which if I can't control them, at least I can put under a lid."

"What are you trying to say," I glanced over at the Rodent, with his beady black eyes and twitching whiskers, "That you—love—me?"

"Now you know how Marc must feel—"

It was only after I'd slapped him as hard as I could that I realised what had happened. My paw flew to my mouth.

"Oh, Tosk, I'm so sorry—"

"Think nothing of it," he repeated, but in a slightly different tone of voice.

"You shouldn't provoke me by talking about—Marcus," I gulped. "So he really *doesn't* return my feelings, and you know this," I gulped again, "for a *fact*? Through your backdoor channels of information, as one of the paparazzi?"

"I don't have the slightest idea as to what his feelings might be, in regards to your person, your character, your past— who knows what anyone really and truly feels—least of all ourselves…"

"Then what possessed you to say such a thing?"

"Probabilities," he shot back. "Factoring in his psychological makeup, cross-referenced to the composite of your own makeup, and needs. We all know how sluggishly indolent his upbringing has rendered him—at least sexually speaking."

I almost slapped him again.

"He fucked his first prostitute, as nearly as we can tell, around the age of eleven. Entering puberty with the other privileged young profligates of the Golden Youth's vaunted Fast Set: fast cars, fast living, fast girls, and fast Sex—"

"Please be quiet," I begged him—

"He soon became addicted to a special sort of nightcap: when he was younger, his voluptuous mother, Diane de Poictiers (also known as the Heifer of Babylon), used to sing him lullabies—he's afraid of the dark, y'know. And so, after those chums of his arranged for that first concubine to service him, he began to require a different (a new sort of) 'lullaby'—"

"Stop it," I gasped, "I'll jump—"

"We're almost there. And I'm telling you this for your own good—he's been pampered from the moment he first drew breath and was handed off to the wetnurse. It's not his fault of course. Bast knows it isn't. But facts are facts: he was petted and cosseted, every need anticipated ahead of time (some say his own Mother arranged for that first concubine)—"

He caught my hand before I could slap him.

"He's a *remarkably* beautiful young chap—even prettier than a girl—he *knows* he's Goodlooking."

"Is that his fault?" I sniveled helplessly, seizing a hank of the Rodent's pomaded (or else simply very oily) black fur, and clinging helplessly to the leering sophisticate. Or maybe he wasn't leering. Perhaps he really did think he was serving my best interests, at heart. I look back and find myself completely undecided, ambivalent, *adrift* (even now).

"And here we are," he gently took my paws, unclasping them from the fistfuls of his own crinkled fur.

I looked at my surroundings and blinked in surprise.

189

We were behind the palace of Whitehall (where the Dowager Empress resided). Before us stretched a forecourt of pillared arcades and leaping fountains. Sentries kept back the gawking foot-traffic of everyday life. And there it was, looming before us in the gathering darkness: The Louvre, current residence of the Emperor and His Court, dominating everything around it in its palatial immensity.

"A word of advice: pacing doesn't help," Delilah informed me. "It sometimes even makes the time pass more slowly."

She was editing and signing documents before putting them into a dispatch box on the edge of her beautiful teakwood desk with its lacquer and enameled mother-of-pearl. Quite a crowd of couriers and heralds had apparently gathered just outside the double doors. (She'd given instructions that she was not, under any circumstances, to be disturbed.) Only two or three minutes ago she'd rung for Tosk of all people (the Rat seemed to be in her pay) and sent him off lickedy-split—to *Marcus'* chambers, with a Royal summons.

"What if he *refuses*?" I asked for the third or fourth time.

"Then he refuses," she spoke as if to a mental defective, "At least you'll *know*. Isn't knowledge—whatever the outcome— preferable to the tormenting pangs of uncertainty?"

"I used to think so," I started pacing faster than ever, "before I met Marcus."

"Look, Sylvia—you're making me nervous," she licked the tips of her teeth, "which distracts me—this *is* State business, you know."

I slunk over to one of the bookshelves and extracted a gilt-edged volume at random. As though 'State business' trumped any and all personal considerations. I wondered if it trumped *hers* just the same as everyone else's—but then, "personal concerns" and "State business" boiled down to exactly the same thing, in *her* family. Not that I wasn't brimming with eternal gratitude to Delilah for having brought me here, and then sent Tosk to go and fetch Marcus. She *could* be merciful, I realised—so long as it didn't conflict with her own selfish desires and objectives. A more selfish (or should I say, self-interested) Lioness I never met in my life.

"When he gets here and the two of you stand awkwardly facing each other," her stylus made a scratching sound as she annotated a document, "I'll leave the room for a bit."

"Would it surprise you if he *doesn't* respond to the Summons?"

"Of course not," she absentmindedly signed a Decree. "It could go either way. These past few days he's adamantly refused to venture forth, from his private apartments."

"But what does that *mean?*"

"Either that he likes you, but doesn't know what to do about it, or…"

"Or what?" I tried to contain myself—

"Or else, he's *really* fucked up in the head."

A staccato knock on the door brought my heart leaping like a bullfrog almost to the back of my throat.

"*Entrez*," the Emperor's Daughter commanded.

Tosk skittered into the room, salaamed deeply, and was given permission to speak.

"He says, and you'll never believe this—"

"He wouldn't come," I burst into tears, "I *knew* he wouldn't come—"

"Is that in fact what happened?" she gestured for me to be silent. "Did the Prince Imperial refuse my Summons?"

"This is the first time it's ever happened," the Rat sententiously squeaked. "At least, that I'm aware of."

"In that case," Delilah said in an ominous voice, "we'll go to see him."

"Oh please let's not do that," I begged her.

"I thought you loved him. This is your chance to see whether he's got your picture hanging over the head of his bed."

"We *can't* just barge in like that," I dashed the tears from my eyes, "I'd rather not see him again, ever, than trespass on the sanctity of his private apartments."

"You fascinate me," she smiled. "No, really. You do. To come from a family, a background, a *father*—"

"I disown him, utterly," I raised my voice.

192

"And what about Jane?"

"I disown them both," I coldly informed her, applying a damp handkerchief to my tear-ravaged cheeks.

"Then what's left, but—"

"Marc?" I challenged.

"I was going to say: what's left but to re-invent your identity?"

"Sounds lonelier than being with Marc."

"Then let's go pay the young narcissist a surprise visit. I bet we catch him staring at himself in the looking-glass. Or wanking off—"

"Stop it."

"Or having his way with a call-girl," she stood up, handing the dispatch box to a liveried footman.

"Is that the reason you don't want to surprise him?" she yawned. "Afraid of what you might discover?"

"I just don't believe in *violating* people. I'm sorry. Should I go home now?"

"Wait till I get back from my conclave with Marcus. I may be able to persuade him—"

"*I'm coming with you*," the strangled words made me sound like a loon.

"Why not cool your heels in this luxuriously furnished set of rooms? You could even lie down on my bed—it might lay the groundwork for a crash course in seduction."

But I only half-registered what she was saying. For there he was—more beautiful than the sun or the moon or the stars. Standing framed in the doorway, fidgeting, staring awkwardly at the floor, a study in contrasts: extreme alienation (to the point of emotional shutdown) against the outward sting (it actually came close to feeling like a physical *sting*) of how goodlooking he really was—I wanted to deny it, deface and mutilate his attractiveness—deny that he was somehow essential to my continued existence.

He was just a gawky adolescent, half Lion, half cub. His riveting greenish-golden eyes weren't even visible—he was

193

looking down at his feet, or maybe the polished marquetry of the glistening floorboards. His tawny Fur (which delighted me so) was just fur, like anyone else's. Delilah's was just as burnished, just as creamy, dappled with big mottled spots along the forbidden, half-concealed underbelly. His whiskers were no more luxuriant than my father's (and Ferdinand prided himself on his urbanely drooping whiskers). His burgeoning Mane was no more sun-kindled than that of the Emperor (though the latter contained streaks of iron-grey, and even a few strands hoary-white with a pronounced leaching of all colour whatsoever—indeed Nero's mane, if we're talking about manes now, was shot through with hanks and tresses of premature grey. Both Nero and the Emperor possessed 'striking' heads of hair, doubtless—but lacking the super-charged brilliancy of radiant shimmering practically dancing layers of fiery, magical richness, super-silky—though I'd never have the pleasure of running my paw through it). His tufted tail, emerging from the back of his smart sailor's suit, was just a supple, responsive, almost dun-coloured appendage—rather lifeless at the moment (versus all the times I'd seen it lashing, coiling, expressively undulating)…

It felt like an invisible talon of steel-hinged rapacity was constricting my heart.

"Aren't you going to say anything?" Delilah's voice rent the stillness.

"H-hallo, Marcus—"

"I meant him, not you."

Another silence descended.

"She came all this way, the very evening her own father gets eviscerated by all the rats and jackals and vermin—she throws her own family aside—"

"That's a lie," I somehow managed to squawk the words—aloud, presumably, because Marcus looked up with those kaleidoscopic bottomless eyes.

"Then you tell him why he needed to come here," she sneered. "You explain what was so important that his whole evening had to be turned upside down."

194

"S-stop it," his golden voice slopped over the rim of those trembling sensuous lips.

"I'll leave you two, to get better acquainted."

I heard the door softly click shut. She must've left the room. My head was swimming. All I could see was the young Lion, enclosed in a sort of halo of brightness.

I waited for him to say something. He was looking down at the floor again.

"She was lying," I managed. "She brought me here. I was arrested by State Security—her picked operatives." My voice had got going, and now took strength from its own momentum. "They drove me to a secret house, where I was given to one, Tosk. Also known as Ratatosk—a large black Norwegian Rat. She goes on about the vermin savaging my poor father—well she's in league with the vermin—they're some of her best friends on earth. Any savaging goes on, goes on at her urging. I don't understand why she brought me here—I guess to have some fun. I guess because she was bored this evening."

I'd started crying, which I think (in retrospect) worked against me.

"And I don't understand why she dragged Your Grace here, clearly against Your Grace's own will, and wishes. Clearly," I sobbed, "against…your own…wishes."

I risked a tear-laden glance. He'd opened his mouth—that gorgeous delicate mouth (made for love, made for slow passionate mind-bending kisses—not that I knew what a kiss even felt like—but looking at that mouth, fashioned for the bliss of slow hours, and nights, and summer madness—my blood coursed with its own answers)—his half-open mouth seemed on the brink of—at least a few syllables, perhaps?

I stared across the parquet floor at the beautifully carved mahogany legs of a table. Its surface was some sort of cream-coloured marble veined with streaks and whorls of a reddish calligraphy. Waiting for him to say or do something, I tried to remember the last time I'd had an *innocent* conversation—without trying to get something out of someone.

He was gone. In his place, Delilah (having reappeared from some hidden vantage point) regarded me with a strange, unreadable look on her face.

"I tried to help you," she said. "I really did. I never play with anyone but my enemies—and you'll never be one of them."

She jerked one of the gem-embroidered tassels, and a gong sounded. (Earlier it had been a different tassel, which made a clean, light-sounding jingle—in place of the gonging finality I now heard plunk somewhere close by.)

Someone took me by the shoulders and guided me towards a waiting Sedan chair. I realised, with a splitsecond impulse to scream with hysterical splitsecond laughter, that Tosk had once again been appointed Messenger of the Gods—this time to remove an empty husk of detritus—like a Squirrel about to bury some half-rotten pecan (or a Rat preparing to devour it).

The last thing I heard was Delilah's mellifluent voice:

"Buck up, Sylvia, I shouldn't take it to heart. He'll come round. Just give him some time."

As the swaying compartment made its way out into the draughty corridor, she exerted herself, and shouted, "My poor Cousin never *could* stand to see anything hurt."

For the next several days my mind was full of delusions; I must have had a fever.

I kept thinking Marc had found a way to sneak out of the Louvre, make his way across town in the dark of night, and locate the Ladder—the one my sister's steady stream of boyfriends made use of—I kept expecting to hear a soft tap on the windowpane—when it didn't happen, I'd scream for Goody Thorpe to leave the room—I lied, and told her that I was burning up, and to please open the window. She reluctantly did so. Shivering in the freezing night air, I watched for his face to appear, thought I saw it, leaned forward and grabbed him by the wrist—only to see his beautiful face vanish—replaced by that of Goody Thorpe, who tearfully explained that what with my fevered shakings and ravings, they'd had to close the window. Whereupon I'd scream for it to be opened again.

They gossiped back and forth from opposite sides of the sickbed: my father it seems had taken a 'bachelor's pad' (as several of the tabloids called it) in the midst of the fashionable Mayfair district—he must have squandered the bulk of Delilah's largesse fitting it out in grand style. He only stopped by the townhouse every now and then, for a bite to eat, a change of clothes, or, in his words, to "grab" a quick shower (though how one *grabs* a shower of all things, I've never quite understood).

According to Goody Thorpe and her confederates, his absence helped things considerably. For one thing, the paparazzi stopped hanging about. Pretty soon the servants could come and go without being mobbed by vermin of every size and description. Helen had also been accosted by them every time she tried to visit me. At last the doctors deemed me well enough to receive my best friend.

"Oh, Sylvia," she bent over and kissed me on the cheek, her nearsighted eyes bright with emotion, "I was so worried."

"Leave us," I laconically commanded the servants. Pulling Helen down beside me on the bedspread (as soon as we were alone), I grabbed hold of her with my claws and vehemently whispered, "I'm in love—with *Marcus Agrippa*."

I doggedly stared into space.

"You've really gone off the deep end," she whistled. "I mean, this whole thing could end badly. It's not just your normal, everyday case of calf love, or at the worst, teenage hormones—"

"You don't have to state the obvious."

"How did it happen?"

"I haven't the slightest idea. Anyway I'm sure *he* doesn't love *me*."

"But this is *awful*," she sure wasn't being very comforting. "It's exactly what the tabloids reported—"

"It is not—"

"And here I've been telling everyone I know that you were falsely accused—that the whole thing was a smear job—"

"It *was*," I jerked bolt upright, staring her in the face, my eyes probably bloodshot and livid.

"Well, how do you make that out? I mean—"

"Those articles in *The Daily Carcass* allege that I bribed him to get it on with me—that I plied him with cash, expensive gifts—even hard drugs—in exchange," I blushed, "for his sexual favours, as they phrased it. That's a sickening lie right there. I never once asked him for anything—much less sex—not even a single kopeck—"

"So what about the allegations that you wouldn't leave him alone? That you shadowed his every step—did you really try to follow him into the boys' restroom—"

"For Bast's sake, Helen—"

"Never mind then," she frowned. "It's just, if he really didn't love you, but you were obsessed with him and kept drooling over him every minute of the day—that still gives all those stories, well—a kernel of truth, no?"

"It does not."

"It does if you wanted him, but he flat out didn't

198

want you."

"Even if I never so much as gave him the time of day?"

"I thought you followed him into that empty lounge the day of the assembly, remember?"

"How could I forget? No one shuts up about it for even five seconds—"

"And nothing happened," she uttered the words as a statement (but we both knew they were in fact meant as a question).

"*Nothing happened*," I gritted my teeth. "I thought *The Carcass* even alleged that DNA swabs were taken—that both of us were subjected to, how did they phrase it, 'humiliatingly invasive' examinations with a fine-tooth comb—"

"And to cover themselves, they went on to say that the findings were *sealed* by the Privy Council, to avoid a scandal. That kind of twisted reasoning makes perfect sense to all the lowlifes out there on the street."

"And to you, too, evidently."

"So!" she practically shouted (making me flinch), "Nothing happened in the lounge. Did you *want* it to happen?"

"I guess so—I don't really know," I stared into space. "He was constantly seeking me out, accosting me, handing me notes in class—I guess I got carried away."

"He never once acted like he had any interest?"

"Things never got that far—he *lied* to me, Helen, about having sex."

"What?" she exploded, "What's this about sex?"

"I asked him if he were still," I gulped, "you know, inexperienced—untainted—sexually untouched, so to speak."

"A virgin, in other words."

"I hate that term so much," my voice dropped an octave, "because the tabloids have ruined it with their perversions and insinuations—"

"So what did he say?" she seemed not to be listening.

"He lied to me. Said he'd done it once, with a chambermaid—acted like it was some one-time aberration, like

199

he simply couldn't, that one single time, exercise the necessary self-control to put a lid on his adolescent urges, or drives."

"And you said?"

"I honestly can't remember. I think I passed out."

"From embarrassment? Lust?"

"Probably a mixture of the two—look, Helen," I grabbed her by the wrist, "I hope you appreciate how honest I'm being."

"I do, believe me," disengaging my claws from her sleeve, she began pacing distractedly. "So that was the last time the two of you spoke?"

"I sometimes wish it had been," I took a deep breath, "Delilah got into the picture—this is Top Secret, okay? It could get both of us killed—"

"Oh please," she rolled her nearsighted eyes (which the thick spectacles magnified). "On the one hand you've read too many cheap thrillers. On the other hand, this would *normally* constitute just a simple case of a Cat and a Lion who obviously feel something for each other. The fact that some of the people involved in this happen to be situated at the summit of Supreme Power, above the mere 'government'—"

"Exactly," I motioned for her to lower her voice, "and that means we damn well need to be discreet about this whole thing."

"It wasn't very discreet to follow the Prince Imperial into some dark alcove, without any witnesses."

"Just help me unravel this whole tangled skein—I really need someone objective to help me separate the wishful thinking from the identifiable truth."

"So there *was* another meeting," she prompted. (That's one of the things I like about Helen: she isn't puffed up with a lot of *hot air*.)

"Delilah Capulet had me *arrested*, by the Secret Police."

"Nipples of Bast!" she made as if to cross herself.

"They brought me to the Louvre through the highly restricted Borovitsky Gate (that's the end closer to Whitehall)—at first, it was just Delilah, acting alone. She stage-managed a confrontation between us."

200

I was so pathetically flattered to see Helen leaning forward on the edge of her seat.

"An unimpeachable source told me—and Delilah confirmed—that he avails himself (isn't that a wonderful phrase)—*avails himself* of all these call-girls, and Palace concubines—only the bonded ones, checked over and thoroughly vetted by the Secret Police."

"Slow down and breathe; you look like you're about to pass out."

"I'm sick of lying here, wasting time," I raised my voice. "I'm just lying here atrophying—it feels like I'm starting to break into pieces."

"So what happened next?"

"Who cares?" I flopped over on my side. "He's a complete degenerate. He wasted my time—"

"You mean *you* wasted it," she insisted, "assuming he's really as un-interested as you keep making out."

"Why do you find that so hard to believe?"

"And as for his being a so called degenerate—"

"Maybe I exaggerated—"

"He's a teenaged *boy* for Bast's sake! They'd all go to prostitutes, if they could afford it."

"That doesn't mean we have to admire the ones who actually do."

"I think you're still in love with him."

"Well of course I am."

The words were spoken before I really even knew what had happened, like an ice-cold spring spilling out from some sequestred cleft in the mountainside—bubbling up out of the traitor subconscious.

"It's fascinating, you know," she took off her spectacles, "the way lies can promiscuously drive, and half shape, the truth. Repeat something enough and the lie takes on a life—a shadowy 'truth'—of its own."

"I don't think that necessarily follows—"

"Listen, Sylvia," she intoned, sitting down on the edge of the bed. "I can *understand*. You don't have to be so ashamed. Because I happen to be in the exact same boat, so there." Her eyes glinted almost triumphantly. "Surprised?"

I mechanically nodded.

"I know you don't think very much of my Mother—but Sylvia, she controls my whole life," her eyes filled with tears, "She's got her tentacles crisscrossing everything I've ever wanted, or secretly dreamed that I might someday grow up to experience—away from *her*—but it's like she *follows* me—she's woven a magic spell to keep me small and powerless—and under her thumb."

A single tear broke forth, and made its escape down the side of Helen's angular face. I certainly knew how much she chafed under her mother's overbearing and tightfisted stranglehold, but even so, her little speech took my breath away.

"And now," she choked before regaining the power of speech, "She's found out about me and—Muldoon."

She burst into tears, clutching me for support. On the sly, I tasted two or three of her tears. They were saltier than mine. Even my *tears*, I reflected, were completely tasteless and bland.

"Maybe things'll work out," I cringed at how paltry and fake my voice sounded (this was an alien role for me—trying to be a Pillar of Strength, and a Bringer of Comfort), "And besides—what's his name again," I gulped, "and for that matter, who is he, again?"

"Muldoon," she sobbed, "our driver. He was the family Chauffeur—until," she teetered, hanging in space, "until—my Mother had him discharged."

Muldoon—of course. The Black Labrador.

"She's threatened to have him arrested if he so much as shews his beautiful floppy ears and lolling tongue within half a kilometre of where we live, and—and the thing is," she gasped for breath, "Oh Sylvia, the thing is—he *hasn't*!"

A fresh flood of sobbing and tears wracked her slender white frame.

"I'm so sorry, Helen," I managed, absentmindedly stroking her fur.

It was almost three o'clock, so for the first time in days I'd rung for some tea (much to the servants' resentment—I'm very sensitive; I can always feel their resentment). We sat around sipping from the porcelain teacups in silence. Every so often, one of us would lift a pastry or morsel of cake to lips leached of all feeling—by the tragedy of Love Unrequited (mine) or Love Ripped Untimely from the Womb (Helen's); every now and then we stole glances at each other.

Helen left after shewing me the homework she'd brought, explaining it briefly, then pissing off home to brood and weep over a big grinning, buck-toothed Labrador of distinctly working-class origin—I felt like slapping myself for even noticing the poor creature's bloody *class* origin.

Instead, I rang for the tea things to be cleared away, and wrapping myself in a bathrobe, sat down at my desk (for the first time in Bast knows how long). At first, the intellectual strain of having to conjugate verbs, decline cases and diagram parts of speech caused my temples to throb. Massaging them, I zealously re-applied myself to the drills and grammar problems assigned at the end of chapter 14. Gradually the old thrill came back—the thrill of pure intellectual self-application—without form or physicality—timeless—a thing of pure *Spirit*.

When the buzzing began, I thought it must be an insect, trapped somewhere, perhaps in my coat (which was carelessly draped across the back of the chair). Only after the third buzz did I sit bolt upright, galvanised with the sudden stabbing realisation that this was the cellphone my father had given me last year for my fourteenth birthday (and which I hadn't had the slightest occasion to make use of—even once—until now). The shimmering if ridiculous hope that perhaps Marc was the one trying to get in touch with me made me weak in the knees.

"Mother of Bast," I yanked open the drawers of my writing desk, then rifled through my coat-pockets (they were crammed with all sorts of forgotten notepads, slide-rules, erasers, that sort of thing), "Shite!"

The cursed thing was still going off. I finally found it—in the first pocket (which I thought I'd already checked). But now, which button was I supposed to hit? Gritting my teeth, I pressed one of the two most prominent-looking ones—it was still lit up, but had stopped buzzing—and shoved the thing to my ear—

"Yes?" I squawked, "Is someone actually on the other end of this thing?"

"I'm afraid it's not the voice you were perhaps hoping to hear."

Delilah. I didn't know whether to feel relieved, or devastated.

"But that can be remedied: Marc wants to see you again. He asked me to have you brought back to the Louvre, same drill as last time—"

"*Never*," I gasped.

I heard her saying, "She doesn't want to, Love. Just like I predicted. Girls get tired of having to do everything. Sometimes it *can* be nice to kick one's shoes off, and let the other sex do at least some of the work."

The instant I heard that *other* voice, however (the timbre and intonation of the few syllables laconically mumbled in response to her carping), my resolve of course began breaking down.

Whatever he'd said, it was sulky and petulant. A silvery spray of fountain-like laughter drowned out anything else he might have added (which probably, under the circumstances, wouldn't have been that substantive—I pictured him, biting his nails—my memory of what he looked like was, indeed, a *paltry* substitute. Every time I clapped eyes on the Lion, he took my breath away—it was like seeing him for the first time all over again. So perhaps the inexact, misconstrued *memory* was safer— less sharp-edged—for bandying about in my mind).

"Poor Cousin Marc..."

I wondered whether he liked *her* pronunciation of *Marc*.

"You've finally met your match, I'm afraid," she continued. "This is a complicated, cerebral *Individualist*. She's not impressed by your Looks—"

I almost believed her, and puffed up like a Toad.

"And she's certainly not impressed by your Lineage."

(Now that much *was* true.)

His indolent, hesitant voice that went right through me like a galloping fever asked her something.

"*Serenade* her, you great overgrown Cub! Woo her, seduce her—the way any lad seduces the girl of his dreams."

His muffled voice must have asked her how, exactly, one went about seducing someone.

"By improvising," she seemed beside herself, "trial and error—what else?"

I couldn't hear any more of their conversation; she must have covered the mouthpiece, or switched something off. I began fingering one of the pawns from a chess set on the corner of my writing desk; I could beat everyone in the family except for Philip—a familiar prickling of guilt began to creep up my spine. I really *must* look in on my poor invalid brother.

"Oh, Sylvia," Delilah's voice made me jump. "I thought you probably got tired of waiting, and rang off. *I* should have done so."

"I wish I *had*."

"Well better luck next time," she deliciously projected her voice. "Here's the thing. Marc isn't quite sure of his feelings—"

"Tell him to go shag one of his prostitutes," I rang off by punching several of the buttons (which made the whole thing go dark), tossed the bloody device in the trash, changed my mind and fished it back out again—but to keep some shred of self-respect, kicked it under my bed, and angrily stomped out of the room.

The next morning *The Daily Carcass* screamed the news on Page One: *Helen Bronte, 15-year-old heiress to the Tutworthy Fortune, eloped last night with the family chauffeur, a chocolate Lab named Muldon.* (I felt like ringing them up to point out that they'd misspelled the Lab's name.)

In place of my normally calm, synthesising intellect, there seethed an adder's-nest of conflicting reactions. On the one hand, I was certainly full of compassion for Helen. At the same time I couldn't help feeling a trifle shocked (perhaps even scandalised) at her having fallen in love with a *servant*. Regarding her actually having had the guts to translate her secret dreams into that unknown hothouse known as irreversible *action*, I still couldn't wrap my mind around the sheer enormity of what she'd done, both socially and culturally speaking.

Perhaps what I needed was a gigantic *Press Conference.* The thought had sent ripples back and forth across the enclosed, stagnant surface of my mind more than once. The ripples eventually subsided. But then, fresh pebbles—in the form of this same fixed obsessive idea—kept getting thrown in, and creating fresh ripples.

Almost against my will, I found myself thinking of Tosk. Logic dictated that he was my best (perhaps only) hope for blowing Helen out of the water—with an even bigger, more garishly lurid story for the tabloids to push.

Having *lost* his goddam number (I'd looked everywhere), I decided I'd have to go for a walk—and hope that he just happened to be lurking outside. I know it sounds egotistical, but the brindled Plague Rat kept magically appearing from out of nowhere practically every time I stuck my nose out the door. The only difference this time, as I dashed out through the gate, was that I actually wanted him to intercept me—I needed his advice regarding a number of pressing personal questions. The sort of questions one can only ask face to face.

Hurrying along, dodging drunks and accelerating round the heavier, slower species, I kept my eyes peeled for that souped-up "Galaxy" or "Infinity" or whatever kind of car it was that he drove.

"To have realised my lifelong destiny," I muttered under my breath, "An unsightly, but hopefully deep-rooted, weed."

"Why do you hope the weed has deep roots?" a Rat, having sidled up to me, squeaked in my ear.

For an instant I thought it was Tosk. All rats, however, do *not* look the same. This one for instance had brown fur that was coarse, even matted, in need of a brushing. His lackluster beady eyes were far less brilliant than Tosk's.

"Sizing me up, ay? I'm sure as Ratatosk makes a far handsomer Rodent."

"Who are you?" I brusquely demanded.

"Passport has it printed out as Fiorello Macaulay. But you can call me Fever. My mates do. And though we're not exactly intimate," he suggestively winked, "might as well start the acquaintance off on a friendly, intimate footing."

"I need to find Tosk. Do you know where he is?"

"*Tosk* happens to be the endearment he reserves for his…sweethearts."

"Well I'm hardly *that*," I tried to shake off the parasite, cringing as he pattered along beside me refusing to *be* shaken off.

"Come on, Sil-vyahh!" he shouted in a mortifyingly obstreperous voice, "I thought we were friends. I thought you were the patron saint of Rodentia."

I quickened my pace. The dense throng of pedestrians blanketing Shaftesbury Avenue seemed, if anything, to encourage the wretch. And certainly none of them came to my rescue; most averted their undistinguished, overworked-looking faces and pretended not to see what apparently was an all too common occurrence: the disgraceful spectacle of a young girl being publicly insulted and harried. A few gathered round to watch, no doubt regarding it as a form of free entertainment.

The sharp, almost staccato, toot from a motorcar that had pulled over to the kerb caused me to make for it with the last reserves of my strength. And sure enough, the distinctive skull of a rat—a black rat at that—just visible through the tinted glass gave me the necessary shot of adrenaline to pry myself loose from my adversary's finger-like claws and propel myself into the passenger seat, taking good care to slam and lock the cardoor behind me.

"I know, I know," I panted expecting a lecture, "but I *have* to talk with you—"

My voice dried up. Sitting across from me was a Black Rat I'd never seen before in my life: a complete and total stranger.

"Oh no ya don't," he caught hold of me by the ankle.

"*Please* trip the switch so I can open the cardoor," I tearfully begged, "I promise not to press charges."

"Hoot hoot hoot," Fever giggled from the backseat—he must have slid in behind me, along with a wretched little Weasel and a gibbering Ferret (they both were doubtless 'plants' in the crowd)—and then we took off, accelerating with such a sickening swerve that I would've lost my breakfast had I had any that morning.

"Publicity of this sort, my chuck," the Weasel chortled, "is the last thing your Daddy wants, or quite frankly, needs. He'll not press any charges—"

"*I* can press charges," I shouted, my eyes blazing (at least, they felt like they must have been blazing).

"I'm afraid the pigheaded Courts would wrongly classify you as, technically speaking, a minor without any rights."

"Then I think my Press Conference had better be about the formation of a Children's Rights Party."

That little remark caught them off guard.

"Press conference? *What* press conference," Fever sharply demanded.

"*My* press conference," I tried to return the probing fixity of his insolent black eyes but without much success, "It's going down either this afternoon or to-morrow, venue to be decided, the Haymarket probably."

All four of them burst out laughing.

"Let's go ahead and have the Press Conference *now*," the little Weasel insufferably smirked.

"First question," the Ferret licked his thin lips—

"*If* I decide to hold a press conference," I tried to conceal the fear in my voice, "It'll be for everyone—all your colleagues, as well—"

"You'll stand there, in the middle of the Haymarket, or on the steps of the Seti monument," the Driver piped up (his long black face making me realise how much better-looking Tosk was), "And you'll be covered with cobwebs—"

"It happened over *two weeks ago*," the Ferret chimed in, "Besides, that particular story never caught fire. The Ratings never took off. We just ran it 'cause there was nothing else happening."

"And don't forget the Sex angle," Fever salaciously jabbed him in the ribs, "The *Sex* angle just might've piqued some interest—lots of fucked up repressed virgins out there. One of the Editors thought it was worth gambling that some of 'em might, you know, hook into the story…"

"But they're such a small slice of the market—"

"A money'd slice, all the same."

"Yeah, don't forget that survey—virgins are three times as likely to have started up their own business—start-up capital, and sublimated just-in-time ventures, have practically been founded by virgins—just as many *blokes* with cobwebs festooning their you-know-what, pardon my French—"

I was furiously, but noiselessly, working the door. If only I knew which button controlled the lock.

"Sylvia's trying to give us the slip," the Weasel, who was right behind me, craned his neck round the back of the front seat.

"Of course I'm trying to give you the slip," I spluttered, "You're keeping me here against my will, and minor or no, I have basic rights. Which are being *violated*. Now let me out, or I *will* press charges."

I hoped they knew I was serious. Maybe I didn't know exactly how to 'press charges,' but all the same…

To my surprise, the vehicle slowly pulled over to the side of the Holborn Viaduct. Fever leaned towards me from the middle of the backseat (to my surprise, his breath was completely odourless, as though wafted from some machine in a clinic): "We'll go our separate ways just as soon as you've answered one question. *Two* questions, actually. Here's Question Number One: what's Annie up to these days?"

"She's busy writing a book about her own exploits," I threw my head back defiantly. It felt damn good to answer a journalist's question. Simple. Satisfying. "It's called *Up Yours! Confessions of a Teenage Obstetrician*…"

To my amazement, they began furiously scribbling on notepads (which I guess they'd had up their sleeves—literally).

"She's just *awfully* paranoid about the two other exposés being cranked out," I couldn't help myself, "hot off the presses, or will be soon: *Little Laughin' Annie, Pregnant At Last*— "

Pandemonium broke loose. I could feel the adrenaline firing up our complementary lusts: mine to dish out the crap, theirs to slurp it up, digest it a bit, and urp it back out for public consumption, but rearranged slightly, altered here and there—by the amino acids and enzymes peculiar to professional muckrakers, paparazzi and whores.

"Knocked up!"

"Who's the sperm donor, Stephen?"

"Can you give us any sort of confirmation or proof?"

I'd already painted myself into a corner—that's the worst of their filthy business: once you say something, it can't be *unsaid*. So I licked my lips and cut loose (why do things by halves?): "I didn't say it; Brandenburg Tisch said it. You'll have to go to the horse's mouth—or in this case, the Meme's mouth—for your confirmation; I'm sorry."

"Did Annie run off with Stephen cause her hormones ran off with her better judgement, or was the whole thing a cheap stunt to paste over the fact that, according to you, she's screwing around with a *Meme*?"

"Are you joking?" I heard my voice skipping along on its own, "You saw them both in the Danceteria. She was ready to tear Yvette's head off. If she was in any deeper, she'd have turn'd herself inside out."

"Quick," he savagely whispered to the Weasel, "That's a great headline. Fax it back to HQ."

"So you'd say she didn't seem to care about anything but—"

"Fucking," I calmly, collectedly, turned his question into its own answer.

"Is she, in your opinion, a Nymphomaniac—in need of being instituionalised?"

"I wouldn't know about that," I shuddered (a mild case of the shakes had been creeping up on me for some time now), "I'm not qualified to make that kind of—"

"Bullshit!" he thrust a little recording device (which I noticed for the first time) even closer, "You—of all people—happen to be—*uniquely* qualified. You lived with her, watched her, observed—and tracked—the formation of your older sister's maladjusted character."

"I don't know that I'd go so far as to call it maladjusted," I tried to backpedal—

"Don't let's forget some of the things she's said about *you*—and in this very same paper—"

"Like what, for instance?" I bristled.

"Oh, well, I could easily—"

"What's the paper—to whom am I giving this interview?"

"*The Daily Carcass*," he proudly trotted it forth, "We're all *Carcass* lads."

212

"I want out of this car right now," the shakes were getting worse; I knew I was about to start crying.

"Just one last question—"

"Unlock the door!"

"Do you think Helen's gone all the way with Mr Heraclitus Muldoon?"

"I *know* she hasn't," I said.

"How do you quote-unquote *know*?" his true insidiousness and inherently small-minded malice (which he'd been at pains to keep under wraps, until now) practically bowled me over.

"Because she *told* me so," I spoke as to a very young child—till the composure with which I'd attempted to gird my sagging countenance deserted me, in the face of their loud scornful laughter.

I suddenly felt sick to my stomach. Never in my life had I heard what sounded like genuine laughter *shouted* so deafeningly that the echoes had begun to make things spin round. I wished I could 'go out' like a light-switch being flipped, but they just kept laughing. It somehow made me nostalgic for Tosk.

I dreaded seeing my lies come back to haunt me as headlines. By the third morning I began to hope the immediate danger was past. My father of course would have been livid with hypocritical outrage; he was already furious concerning my so-called *tryst* with Marcus that night at the Louvre—for fear of its potentially upstaging his own little shenanigans?

How much better I could understand my father these days.

"Get in," Tosk flung open the door of an automobile that had seen better days; the paint was scoured away in big splotches as though the underlying frame were afflicted with a bad case of the mange.

I awkwardly deposited myself in the passenger seat, my stomach lurching as he accelerated across three lanes of traffic.

"I know you like playing with fire," he began—

"Where the hell d'you think you're taking me?"

"Somewhere safe, and quiet," he squeaked.

"To do what, ravish me?"

"To protect you from yourself. And don't joke about my feelings that way."

"Your feelings?"

"Stop pretending not to know what I'm talking about," he exploded. "I've *always* liked you, from the very first moment— from the first night in that disco, when you were there with your sister."

"I remember," I mumbled, not knowing what else to say.

"You've used me this whole time, to get what you wanted."

"And you think I want Marcus Agrippa."

He winced.

"Oh Tosk, I didn't mean it like that—"

"You *want* to be tracked down, surrounded, torn to pieces by an army of rats…"

A weird light must have been emanating from my half-open eyes, because his own staring into mine like black opals had now begun to flicker and shine.

"Speaking of being tracked down," I tried to smile, "I was rather surprised not to see any of your lot waiting outside—"

"That surprised you?" he pounced. "Or maybe disappointed you?"

I took a deep breath.

"Believe it or not, I just want to be left alone."

"By everyone, or just certain people?"

"By everyone in the world. Just as soon as I—somehow—set the record straight—except, I don't know how.
I don't know how to *use* the paparazzi. They frighten me. They also," I gulped, "fascinate me. And I don't understand why. I really don't, Tosk—I'm not a complete pathological liar like my father, just a run-of-the-mill, garden variety, every-now-and-then twister of the truth—where are we going?"

We'd been threading our way through a labyrinth of sidestreets and back-alleys. I was totally lost—this was a part of London I'd never seen before; I didn't even know what species predominated (there were several Iguanadon playing tag on one of the corners, but the towering, densely concentrated tenements all around us looked far too well maintained to accommodate Dinosaurs)—suddenly he jerked the steering-wheel, and we veered unexpectedly into some sort of park or extensive nature preserve. The winding road was just large enough for a single automobile. The densely crammed tenements nestled like some cliff along the edge of the park were rapidly being obscured by waxy convolvulus blossoms and masses of tangled vines and creepers festooned with beards of hanging Spanish moss, which gave the whole place a disheveled, closed-in, almost secretive flavour.

"Is this—"

"The Bois de Boulogne."

We coasted off the road, and into a particularly dense thicket of foliage.

"Isn't this a notorious trysting place?" I demanded, "where lovers—of all sexual persuasions—"

"But that makes it nice and private," he grinned like a skull. "Not for canoodling—is that what you thought I was after?" he threw his head back to laugh, but no sound came from his tightly stretched, naked lips.

I couldn't think of anything to say.

"Regarding the exasperating absence of paparazzi from your front doorstep," the Rat said, "you can blame it on me."

I quickly, involuntarily, glanced out the window, at the mass of green leaves and pale blossoms.

"I planted a hot tip to the effect that you'd been sighted, heavily disguised, lurking outside the Louvre."

"You're such a *bastard*," I practically screamed, "Always the most squalid, humiliating scenario. Is that why you 'like' me so much? Because it's easy to degrade me? You seem addicted to spattering me with filth!"

"Let's not get off the subject again."

"What *is* the subject?" I got my emotions under control. "I'm sometimes rather slow at these things."

"The headlines you've generated, and the effect they could have on your life," he in turn was becoming impassioned, "So you don't like me back, fine (and by the way, I like you because you're an extraordinarily attractive, unusual animal in a world full of predictability and humdrum little pinpricks of petty, second-rate sadism)—but now *I'm* getting off the subject—I swore never again to discuss with you, nor even entertain in the secret reticulated crevices of my cunning rat's brain what you mean to me—besides, I'll never mean anything special to you— to my dying day—so let's get back to the subject: the only reason I dared cross the threshold of your selectively defended personal space—spiriting you off to a secluded park—was to shew you the articles resulting from a little conversation you had with some colleagues of mine."

I could feel myself turning pale.

"Any memory of that little transaction?"

"I remember enough, that I feel sick to my stomach."

"I suppose you wanted to make the First Page," he sneered. "Well it only made page 17C—partly because our Fact-checking department ascertained that your sister Annie *doesn't* happen to be pregnant. You shouldn't lie to the paparazzi, dear—it guts whatever credibility you may once have had."

"They—beguiled me," my voice repulsively quavered, "put words in my mouth."

"Save it. For your next Exclusive."

"Oh, Tosk," I moaned, "Why are you being so hateful? I told you I can't control myself—I don't know what's wrong with me. I feel this—"

"Fascination?"

"This *need*," I became self-possessed once again. "Just like my brother Philip, like any other Junkie in the gutter."

"Such melodrama."

"If you find my company melodramatic, then please take me home."

"You'll be gratified to know that Delilah finally leaked the fact of your being at the Louvre last Saturday night, including—"

"Oh, Tosk—"

"Including the unchaperoned encounter with a Certain Someone."

"But I saw the headlines this morning—"

"It hits the stands to-morrow—all the Dailies—I can shew you the layout for the *Carcass*—happen to have an advance copy right here."

"Is it a *Front Page* layout?" my heart skipped a beat.

"Of course."

I realised the tabloids would be playing it for all it was worth, milking it for every last drop—raw sex, red-hot underage fucking (preferably with lots of explicit snapshots that the editors can blur and 'clean up,' driving the mass-prurience of their readership to a phrensy)—even by itself, utterly reduced to its base components, smut sells faster than hotcakes. But exponentially aggravated by all the prior coverage with its simmering buildup, the political fall-out, the scandal interlinking several principals of the Royal Family itself—it wasn't just Marcus, I reminded myself—it was also at least a miniscule ingredient or component that *I* brought to the story—even if just my ugliness, my untouchable Yuck-factor rubbing everyone's collective fur the wrong way—but damn it to hell—nothing on earth could change the fact that our 'love' (or at least *something* between us) had at last somehow been *documented*. Never mind that it was for all the wrong reasons, twisted, reconfigured for the lowest common denominator.

I could picture the screaming headline:

DID SYLVIA FINALLY GET WHAT SHE WAS AFTER (AND WAS IT WHAT SHE DESERVED)?

I gave a languid, sly sort of secret half-smile.

"You appear to be counting your chickens before they've, properly speaking, quite hatched—"

The Rat pulled something out from under the driver's seat. I recognised that familiar banner with its insultingly simplistic format: *The Daily Carcass*. Little flicks and bursts of moisture were beginning to prick and tingle up and down my taut limbs. He shook his head, and began to stuff it back under the seat.

"Give it me," I shouted, and lunged.

And there—palpitating, throbbing, changing size and shape so that I could barely make it out:

SALIVATING SYL MAKES HER MOVE
(AND MARC CAN'T HOLD IT DOWN)!

You can coax a Lion to your bed, but you can't keep him from urping. So the teenaged psychopath and nymphomaniac, Syl, Ferd's pathetic little bookworm, discovered last Saturday night; perhaps she resorted to a nice long wank session, to ease the sexed up frustration of losing the mouthwatering catch for which she's been angling, using every trick in the book—

He tore the galley or proof or whatever it was clean out of my clenched paws, leaving the pads smudged with newsprint (apparently they use a cheap sort of ink that smears, and winds up being hard to wash off).

"I'm sorry," Tosk was trying to comfort me. I pushed him away. He tried to caress my lank, repellent white fur. Perhaps if it had been a sexual come-on, degraded and slimed as I felt at that moment, I should've responded. Instead, I twisted free, and tried to open the door.

"Wait, I've got it locked," he wheezed squeakingly, "At least wait till you've regained control of yourself."

"Control," I managed, "The one thing we've all imbibed far too much of," my voice closed on a sob.

"At least listen to an inside account of how they came up with that muck."

"You probably wrote it," I sobbed.

"I tried to get it suppressed," his voice shook. "Delilah dismissed me from her service. My career's effectively ended."

That brought me up short for a moment. I didn't quite know what to make of, or how to handle, such an unexpected confession.

"You mean she irrevocably—"

"I was meddling in Family politics. But never mind—"

"For awhile," I gulped, "I actually kind of admired her. I think I was even close to viewing what I *thought* she was, as a role model of sorts. She's complete trash. I'm so sorry, Tosk."

"Don't ever say something like that aloud," he grabbed me by the wrist. "There's a power struggle going on. I can't go into the particulars, but please, Sylvia—promise me you'll be more discreet."

"You mean—"

"I mean criticising members of the fucking Royal Family. You could find yourself banged up in gaol—or dumped in some anonymous grave—stop laughing, it's not funny."

"I was smiling, not laughing," I pouted. "I'll never laugh again—after what you shewed me just now."

"Stupid, coarse bit of copy. The whole spread stinks of being thrown together and cranked out way too fast. Even tabloid journalism should adhere to certain standards—"

"You said you could give me an *inside* account?"

"To make a long story short, a rat was spying on you and Marc, recording everything as he hid behind one of the tapestries—"

"And you, I take it, were this hypothetical rat."

"Since I've chucked my own career and livelihood out the window, indeed probably signed my own death warrant, trying to limit the press coverage you keep willfully generating, I leave it to you to try and figure out that little conundrum."

"I'm sorry," I began—

"Pfaugh!" he erupted, "Yeah, right. I'm *always* The Rat…"

"I said I was sorry. Sweet Bast, I'm not exactly at my most lucid this morning."

"Question: do all rats look the same? Can you tell us apart?"

"If you really think I'm capable of harbouring that sort of racial animosity—"

"I'm sorry," he lifted a membranous, bat-like claw, cunningly jointed, the shiny black fur starting only past the crinkly, membranous knuckles (or whatever they were)—involuntarily I flinched, shrinking away from his touch. I couldn't look at him. My shame was too great. Just because I didn't want to do with Tosk that which, to be brutally honest, I'd fantasised and dreamed nonstop of doing with Marc—just because I didn't want to take the Rat as my lover, did I really have to treat him this way—like the lowest scum of the earth?

"That's okay," he sounded choked up.

I reached across and squeezed his bony wrist with my paw. I leaned over and kissed him (the whiskers, not the mouth—as if it made any difference).

He might've flinched or then again he might've hungrily lapped it up. I was seeing myself on some cinema screen of the mind's eye, leaning across and placing my sensitive lips against a rat's twitching whiskers—if *Marc* were watching from amongst the convolvulus blossoms (which would look so beautiful woven into his thick, silky Mane), would it make him jealous, or turned on, perhaps?

Tosk was saying something in that dry, economical voice of his (Marc's voice was so different—even now, looking back, I can't seem to resist making stupid, pointless little comparisons)—

"Could you start again? I'm sorry. I think something must be wrong with me: I'm fucked up in the head."

"I'm taking you home."

"Just tell me what the Rat took down in his little stenographer's notebook, or tape-recorded, or filmed—I'm listening now."

"He claims you *threw yourself* at the shrinking violet of a high-minded young Vestal Virgin, who literally *begged* you to cease and desist—"

"Fine. You can take me home now."

"Several of the servants in Marcus Agrippa's employ swore out affidavits, duly notarised (the tabloids have to protect themselves from litigation, same as everyone else), that you threatened suicide to force the Lioncub, at the risk of compromising his position at Court, even his line-up in the Imperial Succession, to come rushing over to Delilah's antechamber (Delilah gave the paparazzi to understand that you'd totally tricked and manipulated her, biding your time, playing the Alone and Friendless card so skillfully that she was thoroughly hoodwinked, and as soon as she had to leave her apartments on vital State business, *wham!*)—according to the unnamed servants, you basically 'ambushed' the Prince Imperial, threatening suicide—unless he submit to your animalistic advances. You wanted to be serviced—"

"I said, take me home."

"But here's the icing on the cake: when you assaulted him, he was so turned off by your ungainliness, by the low-bred, coarse texture of your transparent manipulations, that not only was he completely unable to perform (as would be the case with any young lad of quality, the paper editorialised) but, nauseated to the very core of his being, he promptly threw up."

"I suppose the story contains a sort of aesthetic uniformity."

I couldn't let the Rat see how much his words were destroying me. I knew he couldn't help it. We both were driven by forces we could only half understand.

"They said he used the vomit as a shield of sorts, or a 'smokescreen'—the way a Squid puts forth ink. He promptly, as you groped for a washcloth, pressed a hidden latch in the paneling and made his escape through a secret passageway originally constructed to foil assassination attempts—"

"I really don't need to hear anymore—I get the idea."

"Our Managing Editor (a lying lard-lipped Hyena, name of Morozov) pulled all the stops to give it *saturation* priority. Which brings us to my own little personal tragedy, above and beyond my insane love for a certain someone who both disdains, and encourages—"

"You know that's not true."

"I've toyed with the notion of offing myself. Because this is my profession. It's the one thing I'm good at. Do you know what it means to be *good at* something, to be *Someone* (or at least to feel like you *might* be Someone, *some* of the time)?"

Yes, I inwardly mouthed the syllable. *I know what it means*.

"You act like you're doing all this to protect me," I listlessly mumbled, glancing out the window (or pretending to do so), "because you like me so much—"

"Rats are incapable of telling the truth, or indeed, experiencing the slightest twinge of the emotion called love—to us it's just an empty word, right? Everyone knows that, right?"

I'd never seen a rat crying—his tears were pretty much like my own: transparent, easily wiped away with a supple flick of the wrist.

"At least this goddam pack of lies about you and some twit of a Lion are gonna be eclipsed pretty damn soon by the contagious fever bubbling at the prospect of the Princess Delilah's wedding festivities."

"Delilah," I spat. "She's not that far above us voiceless, faceless, insect-like nothings teeming and swarming as we get crushed underfoot. Some of us have stings—"

"You should be careful," he warned, "A statement like that can so easily be taken out of context."

"You know what I meant."

"Hidden spies might not be so understanding."

"If the world's that repulsive, I don't want to stay in it, taking up space."

"The ravings of a starry-eyed romantic," he squeaked grinning mirthlessly.

"You know something?" I forced myself to look into the Rat's black beady eyes, "You're the strangest creature I believe I've ever known in my life."

"I was trying to get you to love me."

"Poor Tosk," I forced myself to reply. "I suppose I could give myself to you, if it would make things less awful."

"You'd only be doing it," he squeaked, "because you see me as the personification of filth."

"That's not true—*I'm* the degraded one, or at least Marcus—"

"How dare you talk to me about *Marcus*."

"I didn't mean to make it sound like—"

"Just shut up—not another word—"

"Can we please go back to some street corner within walking distance of my father's townhouse—speaking of which, I think it's secretly mortgaged—I've seen real-estate flunkeys carrying clipboards and doing appraisals room by room—I grew up in that house—"

"Stop playing for sympathy," he turned the ignition and we lurched forward, rapidly accelerating, "All you care about is a

feckless princeling twit of an addlepated nothing—an insect—
can't a rat at least trump an insect?"

"It's not that I don't like you, Tosk—"

"Shove it up yer arse!" he squeaked, his despairing voice
so shrill, it almost made him sound like a bat—I broke into a fit
of pretended coughing, to abort a scream of insane laughter.

We exited the park in total silence, making for the centre
of town in all its pulsating emptiness.

It was time to have it out with my father. I found him in his office.

"Are you selling this house?"

He opened his mouth—

"Just answer the question."

His debauched, bloodshot eyes were shifty-looking, like those of a rat. Tosk's were infinitely more catlike and sensitive.

"Had a letter from Annie," he coughed. "Don't worry; she doesn't (yet) know about the *calumnies* originating from a member of her very own family."

"It could've been *much* worse," I tried to defend myself, "I think they used, not Truth Serum but one of those so-called 'date rape' decoctions—everything was going dim—I don't even remember half the nonsense I babbled—"

"Is *that* what happened?" he helped himself to some brandy. (I recognised the crystal decanter he was using as the very one that had been handed down to my Mother as a family heirloom long before they were married.)

"She's moved to Paris," his voice became warm and confiding, "Broke up with that big dumb lug, what's his name—"

"Stephen," I gritted my teeth.

"Steev'n," he contemptuously mangled the name.

"Frankly, I'm surprised. She seemed to be really in love with him—I mean, as close to love as someone like Annie—"

"Take a look at these clippings."

He pushed them towards me.

They were contained snapshots of Annie. That overbright gleam to the crazed eyes boring relentlessly into the lens of the camera—I could instantly tell that she was on the cusp of one of her demonic eruptions; it amazed me that the Camera had made it so palpable. I slid the stack of clippings back across the desktop.

"You've barely glanced at the first article," he whiningly prodded.

"So that's the smokescreen you're hiding behind: these *newspaper clippings?*"

"They're just the tip of the iceberg," he chuckled. "I've sometimes thought you and I got off on the wrong foot, never properly understanding one another."

"Each other," I primly corrected.

"Look at this: arrested for shoplifting. Or this: beating the shite out of a Weasel—here she is ripping open a camera and yanking out all the film—"

"Clearly she didn't get *every* camera," I sneered, "else where did *these* pictures come from?"

"Some second-stringers were lurking in the background—got themselves a real scoop. Here she is being handcuffed, and fighting—like a Cat."

He swelled with fatherly pride, puffing up like a Toad.

"Typical," I raised my voice a notch, "Annie fucks her life up even more egregiously, and you're pleased—because the spectacle she's making of herself has people buzzing—like hornets—which can coat a much larger animal, and sting it to death."

"These metaphors of yours—"

"If you really cared about her—"

"How *dare* you try and stick your snout in the relationship I happen to enjoy with my daughter."

"One of your daughters," I reminded him.

"We'll get to *that* particular relationship (between you and me) in a sec—"

"The servants are gossiping that you're about to sell this house out from under us."

There, I'd said it.

"Well?" I quickly pressed my advantage, "Do you deny it?"

"Of course I deny it," he squirmed.

"So we'll not be made to vacate this property, in any way, shape, or form?"

I couldn't tell whether the look he flashed me was one of dislike, or sadistic glee bubbling like a broth that was about to boil over.

"Well…" he coughed, "the fact of the matter is…I'm *renting* the house—"

"Excuse me?"

"To a rock band," he flashed me a sheepish grin that made me want to bludgeon his furry skull with a club. "I'm afraid you wouldn't know anything about them (though their fame *is* beginning to crisscross the civilised world). Schoolkids are having their lyrics tattooed on parts of their bodies they can conceal from their parents—"

"You're boring me!" I raised my voice loud enough to interrupt his insufferable yammering, "All I care about is the reason why you're doing this—crucifying your five children. This is the house we grew up in—"

"Sylvia, Sylvia, Sylvia."

He threw his head back and laughed.

"You make everything so melodramatic (*crucifying*, no less!)—it's only for the next several months—they're cutting a new record, with Giorgio McGroder—remember him?

"That lascivious goggled-eyed Elk?"

"Lascivious maybe, but more to the point—"

"More to the *point*?" an upsurge of magma-like rage buffeted me: "He propositioned both me and Helen, separately, when we couldn't have been more than eleven at the oldest—"

"This obsession with the Past, with not letting go," he leaned forward propping his elbows on the polished desktop, "frankly speaking, troubles me."

"Oh yeah?" my flickering anger was becoming white-hot.

"I mean, I can see where you're coming from," he cleared his throat, "He *did* take inappropriate liberties, abusing my openhanded hospitality, driving a wedge between us—between you and me—that beastly disgusting proposition was just the

227

icing on the cake. I deal with painful situations by making light of them, turning them into a joke—I know I'm mentally ill," he gasped for breath, "but I was even more so, back then. Not that it means much, after all the neglect, but I *am* sorry, Sylvia—my poor little Dearheart."

He used to call me *Dearheart* when I was just a small, still impressionable, kitten. My eyes filled with tears.

"Lots of things happened—ugly things—right under my nose, so to speak. I was too busy chasing the next thrill, the next high, the next climax—"

I winced.

"Just because I never knew about some of those things doesn't excuse me. I'm sorry. I never *wanted* to hurt anyone else (unlike most people—yourself included, perhaps)—"

"What's that supposed to mean?" I bristled, "So now *I'm* the villain?"

"Of course not," he assumed an air of wounded petulance, "But I *have* had you checked out pretty thoroughly."

"Excuse me?" I blinked.

"I hear that muckraker, Yaff Bat, happens to be cranking out some potboiler on Annie. This'll blow *his* hatchet-job out of the water."

"What exactly are you talking about?"

"Except it's top secret," he waved a claw in my face. "No one knows about it. I'm only telling you about it because—"

"I don't need your pathetic secrets," I snarled, "Half of which are completely made up, the product of drunken fantasy."

"Oh, *this* isn't one of the fantasies or false carrots on a stick to bait one of my terribly ingenious traps—it's completely straightforward: I'm finally composing a sort of autobiography I guess you'd call it. A red-hot sensationalistic little kiss-and-tell number. I shan't spare anyone, including, regrettably but necessarily, my own children—"

"You bastard."

"Otherwise, it might conceivably lack that special ring of *authenticity*—without which its sales would refrain from shooting where I want them to shoot—which is straight through the roof."

"Oh, please," I managed somehow not to throw up.

"As a matter of fact, I'm going to a sanatorium on the Black Sea, near Sochi. I need complete peace and quiet for this undertaking—the bloke who's ghostwriting the text itself has had to rearrange certain factlets here and there, to make the essence of my life play better."

"You're having it ghostwritten?" I shook my head.

"Don't be such a little prig," he grinned, "This'll pull not only me but all my dependents," flashing me a glance, "from the state of parlous debt to which my profligate addictions have unfairly reduced us."

"Unfairly?" I spat. "Is this a sneak preview of how you'll be 'reconfiguring' the way things actually happened? There's a simpler term: pathological *liar*."

"That's as may be," he gave one of those unassailable chuckles, "but sometimes a repressed little twit's 'lies' turn out to be another bloke's treasure. I know what sells—you obviously don't."

"No one's going to read your filth," I tried to keep my voice steady.

"We'll just see about that," licking his lips—

"Father dear," I beat him to the punch, "I have a secret of my own—I'm spending the Jubilee, this year, in a place of *my* choosing. Don't try to dissuade me—you can't. And if you try to prevent me—"

He raised a coal-black paw, earnestly shaking his whiskers:

"You have my permission—indeed, my encouragement—to do as you please."

"Oh. Well. That's very interesting—"

"Within limits of course."

"I knew there had to be a catch."

"It's very simple. Don't compromise me; I shan't compromise you."

229

"That *is* simple," I sneered. "And so are my plans for spending the Jubilee in London—I'm finally gonna get to see what makes the Dark People tick."

It was just a shot in the dark, but I somehow intuitively picked up on the extreme degree to which the Dark People wigged out my father.

"I wouldn't advise doing that—"

I opened my mouth but he lifted the same paw (black as midnight) again:

"You're free, of course, to do as you think best, but this exciting taste of the Festival may not turn out to be the juicy treat you'd envisioned."

"I haven't envisioned any 'juicy treat'—I don't happen to think that way—"

"Suit yourself. But don't come back to the townhouse; it'll be padlocked till Teenage Lust moves in."

"Excuse me?"

"The world-famous rock band," he baited me. "Surely you've heard of them?"

"Nope. Can't say that I have."

"Shews your level of ignorance. Anyway," he shrugged, "don't come whining to my hideaway on the Black Sea—I'm afraid the Security lads might just shoot first, an' ask questions too late…"

My mind was reeling, as I tried to take everything in.

"It's a *joke* for Bastsake," he guffawed. "Annie's right: you don't have the slightest sense of humour—I thought she was pulling my leg."

"I'm going now," fighting for all I was worth to maintain an external façade of composure.

"Right," he chuckled, "Have we finished our annual father-daughter, no-holds-barred, heart-to-heart manure-slinging session?"

"Not quite," I roused myself—

"Exactamente," he meowed in a sort of singsong cadence, "I almost forgot to give you your stipend. Or allowance, I believe Jane used to call it."

He unlocked one of the desk drawers, opened a metal box with another of his keys, and doled forth a surprisingly large sum of hard cash.

"That should see you through nicely. Don't want you sleeping on the streets, after all. But Sylvia," he unexpectedly fixed me with his bloodshot blue eyes, "I know you think me a selfish bastard, and I suppose that's an accurate enough assessment…"

Draining his tumbler of brandy (liberally tarted up with a cup of blush wine), he unsteadily reached for my Mother's crystal decanter.

"You really ought to give that back to Jane—it's technically hers. She could sell it; she desperately needs money—thanks to your getting the Divorce *rigged*," my throat closed on itself.

"They call themselves *The Faithful*," he seemed almost unaware of my presence, "Pouring into London from every cesspool and housing project, every Shtetl and pissing place between here and the Carpathians. The other side of those mountains, and *their* fanatics converge on The Vatican. But ours," he shook his head, "*Our* lot engage in some truly heartwarming antics: slash themselves, pour hot ash on their heads, chant themselves into a sort of mass frenzy, shouting their fucking *gibberish* over and over again—the Secret Police stay out of sight; it's like the whole city goes apeshit for a couple of days—their goddam Rabbis preach: *To the Faithful, during Makhurrum, all is permitted…*"

"Sounds intriguing."

My voice must have startled him; he spilt his drink all over the desk.

"Didja hear what I just said: *All is permitted.*"

"I wish more people had the cultural sensitivity—"

231

"That's what gets me," he steamrolled right over me, "The way they chant—that gibberish—over and over again. I mean, they leave us alone the rest of the year. So why do they have to swarm all over the place like cockroaches for just that one week? Their ghettos are self-contained little theocracies where girls can be stoned to death for wearing eyeliner. Are *these* the sort of people you want to fraternise with?"

"Just because I don't agree with some of their beliefs doesn't mean I shouldn't try to *understand* them, establish a dialogue—"

"You pretend to be *so* high-minded," he shouted. "And here you're jealous of your own sister, for getting more Front-page spreads in the bloody tabloids like the bloody *Carcass*—the servants have brought me copies of the *Daily Carcass* they found squirreled away under your bed—"

"My private apartments are off-limits to your disgusting tale-bearers and snoops," I exploded. "How dare you transgress and defile a schoolgirl's *only* remaining safe haven—"

"Speaking of which, the paparazzi are clearing out of London in droves."

All my rage and hurt came tumbling against the brick wall of his towering, impregnable selfishness.

"Most, of course, have already decamped to the Riviera, Vienna, Capri—it's only natural for them to follow the Beautiful People, the celebs and aristos and such—the Duchess de Valentinois left just this morning, and caused quite a sensation."

"I'm leaving now," my voice sounded raspy and thin. "Thanks for the allowance."

"Wait a minute—"

The bastard liked to keep endless tricks up his sleeve.

"Nothing on earth could induce me to spend an instant longer than necessary in your drunken, debauched, sickening presence—"

"Not even *Marcus*?"

We both froze, regarding each other from across an unbridgeable gulf.

232

"What about Marcus?" I forced myself to sit down again, balancing on the edge of the chair, muscles tensed, for instant, unstoppable flight.

"He refused to accompany not just the Imperial Court (even I might have done the same, considering the circumstances), but also," he gulped, "He *refused* a *direct* Invitation from His Celestial Majesty—to participate in His Imperial Progress through Bruges, Antwerp and Ghent. Everybody's talking about it—this Invitation *could've* catapulted your little Marcus above the heads of the Crown Prince and the Grand Duke Dmitri, but no! The strain of madness afflicting the Royal Family has obviously claimed its next victim—none of this is in the tabloids of course (there are limits to everything) but you, Miss Priss, I know you like to maintain your own—personal—sources. Like that rat who destroyed his own career for your sake. Quite a little Femme Fatale, aren't we? Which prompts me to ask: your own stubborn determination to stay in London during the Festival—that wouldn't have anything to do with young Marcus Agrippa, now would it?"

"Everything you've just said means absolutely *nothing* to me," I tonelessly strung together the words, "including the fortunes of the Emperor's latest little protégé and plaything, Marcus Agrippa."

The scary thing is, I no longer even knew whether I was lying or telling the truth.

"Listen Sylvia," his voice became all warm and confiding again, "You shouldn't take the paparazzi's lies and distortions to heart. Enough intelligent people are able to read between the lines and venture their own—far more accurate—conjectures as to what really happened."

"What do *you* think 'really happened'?" I challenged him.

He threw his head back and laughed.

"I'm afraid anything I could come up with would just incite you to fly at me with those sharp claws and arched back—not that you could muster even one-tenth of the daemonic fury that Annie uncorks on occasion. Of course, she'll never quite reach the heights that *I've* scaled."

I took a deep breath:

"You're the only person I've ever known who embodies the quintessential meaning of pure selfishness. You *hope* I'll fall flat on my face. You *want* me to be a flop."

"Sorry, dearheart, but I happen to be *far* more newsworthy than you—"

"No you're not."

"I was famous before you were born—"

"That was then, this is now—"

"I can fill a fair-sized reception Annex with 40 to 50 reporters, like *that!*"

He snapped his claws. We were both panting for breath, leaning out over the No-man's land of the polished desktop till our quivering whiskers were practically touching.

"Do it then."

"Maybe I will."

"Go ahead—I'll convene my *own* Press Conference."

"You'll be staring at an *empty* auditorium."

My eyes filled with tears.

"*Don't you think I know that,*" I whispered.

Like a spinning top being launched I somehow zigzagged across the room, made it to the door, and finally scampered off down the corridor, sobbing.

Like a bat out of hell I went straight to see Philip. (He hadn't lasted long in the specially adapted wing of the townhouse; almost as soon as he moved in, he and my father had been at each other's throats—he was now subsisting on a fixed income in a government-funded 'assisted-living' community.) I had to wait for one of the mandatory group-therapy sessions to break up before they'd let me speak with him.

As always, he concealed his true feelings, receiving me with an air of calculated indifference. Maybe he really *didn't* care (except I watched him frantically combing his fur and trying to make himself presentable through the one-way trick mirror the staff shamelessly made use of, to spy on their charges).

I asked him, among other things, if he could recommend any flophouses that were safe (for a single girl) and at least reasonably clean. He wanted to know what had happened so of course I told him. His indignation (so unexpected) brought tears to my eyes. The mood was lost irretrievably however when he asked about Annie. I could tell that his seeming solicitude for me was little more than a viaduct, a shallow artery connecting him to the heart of everything in his life—well she wasn't the heart of *my* life.

He did at least tell me about some cheap but safe rooms over on Liteiny Prospect. They rented them on a weekly basis, and the bathroom stalls, though down the corridor, could be securely latched shut.

I quickly plunked down enough cash to rent not only my room but the other six on my floor (so I shouldn't have to fret about sharing the bloody bathroom).

Involving as few servants as possible, and taking a bare minimum of clothes and necessities (the place was 'furnished'), I tried to keep the whole thing top-secret. But someone obviously blabbed, because on the very day I moved in, returning from a trip to the nearest bookstore (five poetry anthologies and a frozen dinner weighing me down), I was literally *ambushed*—by a ferret hiding under the staircase.

He popped up like a Jack-in-the-box, causing me to spill everything all over the landing. Too startled to scream, I could only gape stupidly as a clicking, whirring sound accompanied the string of 'candids' he was voraciously snapping, filling frame after frame.

So it *wasn't* a rapist or thief... And yet, what else are the paparazzi but precisely rapists, and thieves?

"Could you try to look a little more devastated, heartbroken, at the end of your rope?" the creature cynically wheedled, "C'mon, please? I have a wife and three youngsters to feed."

I looked away. He lurched sideways, trying to get me to mug for the camera.

"They pay us by the picture—*only* those that actually wind up getting published."

He paused for a moment to wind the film in his camera.

"And that's just a *tiny* percentage—as I'm sure you can imagine. You should see the heaps and mountains of film, every morning at daybreak, getting tossed in the shredder..."

"Are you telling me this to try and let me down gently—so when I don't find any pictures of myself to-morrow morning I can somehow resist the urge to slit my throat with a razour?"

"I'm trying to *motivate* you to give me *one* decent shot."

"Just one?" I could feel myself getting red in the face, "Why not five or six?"

"This is hopeless—total waste of friggin' film—"

"Because it's *me*?" I bristled. "Could that be the reason? Because as Judd my dad's right-hand pimp never gets tired of telling me—"

"Wait," he brandished a tape-recorder so small I hadn't noticed it, "I've gotta check to see whether this is working or not. If the fucking batteries—"

"I've got some inside," I volunteered, "My room's just up this flight of steps. Surely you could try just a few more shots against the backdrop of a lonely squalid bedsit." I forced my lips to assume the semblance of a twisted smile. "A tapestry of working-class squalour—I've toppled from heights you'd quite literally need to see to believe…"

I was hoping this was the sort of 'hook' they liked to use in their copy (or whatever they called it); glancing over my shoulder at the bedraggled, famished-looking creature, I unlocked my door.

"Why not," he shrugged, "I reckon there's always time for a quick…"

Something in his intonation, perhaps even his body language, tipped me off that we were, in fact, completely out of sync with each other.

"Wait a minute," I blocked his way. "Just what did you think I was suggesting?"

"I suppose I do technically have a wife," he grinned, "but like most blokes you're likely to, eh, do the business with—"

"Of all the *filth*," I erupted, "You thought I was—was *propositioning* you?"

"As a matter of fact," his voice was dripping with sarcasm, "I hadn't the foggiest notion as to what the fuck you were blathering on about."

"My *interview*, of course," I wanted to smack him. "You were checking your damn tape-recorder to see if the stupid batteries had run out of juice."

"That's because I have twelve more assignments after this one," he shrilled, "several of which include my trying to get a brief statement."

"Well you can take *my* statement out here on the landing," I priggishly sniffed, "*I* wouldn't let you come inside if you paid me."

"I don't need a statement from *you*," he sounded impatient, "Only the names with a star beside them."

237

"So I don't get a *star*?" I could feel myself beginning to lose it.

His expression, surprisingly enough, softened.

"You *want* me to try and get a statement?" he shook his head in surprise.

"Don't you know who I am?"

"Course I know," his face took on a half patronising, half pitying look, "Yer Sylvia, Ferd's daughter, the nympho that keeps making that basket-case of a fucked up Lion puke his guts out, all over the place."

"That's right," I motioned him to step inside though I left the door standing wide open, "I reportedly (if you believe what you read) made a member of the Royal Family barf. I reportedly keep trying to interfere with him, even going so far as to lace the contents of his school lunchbox with a fast-acting aphrodesiac (to quote one of the sleazier rags)—I've drugged him, stalked him, lain in wait for him—best of all (get this!) I've even purloined a teaspoonful of his 'stuff'—to try and get myself, if you can believe it, *knocked up*," I ran out of breath. "If you watch the news, you must've seen all the coverage," I could feel myself blushing, "So, yeah. I kind of know what it's like to be hunted by the paparazzi." I took a deep breath. "As a matter of fact, I love it. I've built a new life around it. I'm a celebrity of sorts—my person as the more priggish porn purveyors like to phrase it, is now public property."

"And you *liked* all that?" he was shaking his head, "The things they wrote and said about you? You didn't *do* any of that stuff—we all know it, on Fleet Street—the way I hear it, he's off his rocker, he wants you so bad."

"He?" my voice crumpled.

"That poor Lion, the Prince Imperial—they've sure put him through the meatgrinder, that's for sure. And looks like they didn't exactly handle *you* with kid gloves."

"I love being handled by them," I sobbingly giggled (or gigglingly sobbed).

"Then why are you crying?"

"Who says he's off his rocker?" I demanded partly to change the subject, but also, at least partly, because I really wanted to know.

"I dunno," he shrugged. "No one ever knows who starts the rumour-mill cranking."

"And with all this," I wiped my face, "you're trying to tell me there's not a star by my name?"

"I gotta go," he snapped shut the lens of his camera. "Twelve more fucking assignments."

"Tell me what it's like, being one of the paparazzi," I switched gears blocking the door. "I bet it's exciting."

"Get it through your thick skull: I'm *not* one of the paparazzi," he whined, "Fucking *rats* have it locked up, tight as a drum."

"Couldn't the weasels and ferrets band together somehow?"

"Divide n' conquer," his eyes flashed, "Simple as one-two-three: they keep us *divided*."

"So the ferrets—"

"Get saddled with all the fucking grunt work n' crap!" his voice went off like a string of caps being smashed with a hammer, "I haven't had a lousy day off in almost three fucking months."

"That's awful," I continued blocking the door. "I could give you a statement deploring the way the rats have turned your whole profession into one giant concentration camp subsisting on the slave labour of exploited troglodytes like yourself—"

"There isn't gonna *be* any statement—I'm sorry," he squared his spindly shoulders, "You're wasting my time; I'm wasting yours—my Editor sent me over for a few shots, just in case. It's nice to have back-up shots, with lurid captions (yours was gonna be: *Syl tossed out as Dad cries last straw*)—they never know how much space they're gonna need till the Layout Meeting, which happens around 1 or 2 in the morning. That's for the Early Edition. The Extras get cranked out by another department—g-d, I wish I could transfer—you should see how much more they make per story, and the perks—Sweet Mithras! Cocaine-snorting parties, plum assignments all over the world— they *would* leave me in London, for this fucking Festival crap."

"Can we at least take some more *pictures?*" I tearfully begged, latching onto him as he tried to push me away.

"Sorry," he sullenly shrugged, "The film's too expensive. Like I said, I've got twelve more assignments to stake out before the next layout meeting. Shite!" checking his watch, "I'd better get going—"

"Who's the next assignment?" my voice rose to a shriek, "Admit it: they're sending you to do a story on Annie!"

As I screamed the word *Annie*, I realised just how close I'd come to the lip of the precipice: gazing down into the volcano of Madness. A strong updraught made the beads of sweat stand out on my face; it was a terrifying mixture of all the best, and worst, smells on earth.

"Annie *Romanoff?*" he was either astonished, or a very good actor.

"Who else d'you think we're both obsessing about," I just couldn't hold back, "but for different reasons, and with differing levels of abso-fucking-lutely muck-spattered dishonesty—"

"You need to calm down and breathe."

"Admit it," it felt like I was starting to foam at the mouth, "She's got a star by *her* name—"

"Annie Romanoff wouldn't even be on one of *these* lists (they're just the small fry)—besides, she's in Paris. Besides," it was his turn to start unraveling, "*I'd* never get a plum assignment like *that*—only the fucking *rats* get to stalk the Big Game—I mean, the Big Names—I mean, the *Beautiful* People."

"Shut the fuck up," I screamed, "She's *ugly*—everything about her—repulsive—but not as repulsive as *I* happen to be!"

"You should see yourself at this exact second," he grabbed the camera and began snapping away.

"I thought you said the film was—"

"Don't talk, it makes your mouth move."

But I had to talk, to keep from fidgeting:

"I used to know someone in your line of work."

"You mean *Ratatosk?*" his face crinkled with a mixture of envy and loathing. "That slimy rat got exactly what he had coming to 'im—*exactly* what he deserved."

"What happened to him?"

"Killed himself."

For a moment, the world—

"Just kidding," he chortled. "*Tried* to off himself but they found him in time."

"They…found him."

"*That's* the look I want—hold it!"

I tried to oblige as the shutter clicked and whirred, making scads of fresh Candids. The film was expensive, he said. That was some consolation.

The first tabloid I bought the next morning was of course *The Daily Carcass*. And of course there wasn't a single reference to my ever having existed.

My *father* was mentioned several times. *Annie* had an article on page 9, regarding whether or not her scratching one of the paparazzi last week—about the face and neck—constituted an actionable, felonious breach of the law. There was speculation that perhaps she'd dipped her claws in a sort of odourless poison before going out on the town. There were two big pictures, in colour. One of them I recognised from the cache my father had been crowing about. The other shewed a bunch of French police trying (unsuccessfully) to handcuff her, as she laid into them with nothing but her teeth and her claws.

Marcus was featured in five different articles: his favourite colour being red (with lots of fashion shots), an analysis of his eating habits, a nostalgia piece on what he'd said and done the day he turned six, an interview with his chief wet nurse concerning what he was like as a squalling Cub, and finally, *Marc Turns 16 Next Month: What Kind of Girl Do YOU Think He'll Wind Up With?*

Delilah was splashed, larger than life, on the Cover. Flipping through the rag—at random, page after page—you just couldn't avoid the Imperial carnivore. I quickly lost count of the pictures alone, not to mention the verbal references, which teemed and seethed on every page like maggots covering slabs of nose-wrinkling carrion.

I hurled the putrid bit of so-called journalism into the nearest rubbish-bin—and proceeded to buy, one at a time: *Lion Beat, Raunchy Bits, Sex, Lust*, Terminal *Hedonism, Clap Chronicles, The Audubon Celebwatching Forum, Premature Jack, Sweaty Palms, Fear and Trembling* (with its sister publication, *The Sickness Unto Death* which printed all the rumours, however dubious, concerning who had picked up what STD, with all the sordid, graphic details of how they'd managed to do so, what plagues were brewing, and who had most recently found out, under conditions of doctor-patient confidentiality, that they were dying of cancer)—and finally even *Spyglass*, *Megaphone*, *Cap Gun*—*still* no mention—the lying bastard of a ferret had toyed with my feelings, pulled the wool over my red-rimmed eyes which had practically swollen themselves shut in trying, and failing, not to cry.

My paparazzi summer was waning. I schlepped over to the nearest bookstore, and bought the first paperback I could find on the subject of the Dark People—*A Matter of Belief: The Unshakable Foundation*, by the Honourable Elijah Divine. When I got back to that squalid little bedsit, I curled up with my purchase, and a notepad, and stylus.

It was strange (almost sinister) that we'd never studied this major religion in school. I supposed the school authorities had their instructions. Here I was, learning for the first time that the Dark People (as opposed to the easily bored upper classes) are monotheistic. They don't believe in images, icons, incense, or candles. They don't even believe in names (which was a tough nut to swallow—until I began to realise that a name, after all, is the ultimate symbol). Their g-d, for instance, doesn't have a name (or a species, or even a sex). It's this abstract entity, or concept, without graspable form. In days gone by, when the State's power was less all-encompassing, gigantic mobs of chanting ecstatic Faithful would rise (like a raging river flooding its banks) and overflow into the genteel districts of London, rampaging and rioting in an orgy of purification—smashing all the so-called 'graven images' of Anubis, Krishna, the Holy Virgin of Guadalupe—even images of our own Cat goddess, Bast.

In spite of all my carefully self-ingrained agnosticism, that gave me an ugly little jolt, or lurch. (I imagined them, wearing their shroud-like chadors, dancing on my grave as they smashed the 'idol' of my headstone to bits. The Personal subjugated to the Oceanic, the Infinite.)

They don't believe in the mediation of a corrupt (and corrupting) priesthood. Nor do they practise the sacrament of confession, abominating the notion of mere flesh-bound, corruptible 'priest' trafficking in souls—only their nameless, fleshless deity can grant the awesome thing known as Absolution—and only after death. Theirs, it would seem, is a gloomy but steadfast religion. Thieves wind up having their hooves and paws amputated. A male (of whatever species) who lies with another male (of whatever other species) is stoned to death by the Faithful. I could understand why: the Tribe had to survive.

No wonder my father hated them. And I was his daughter in one respect: the harshness and seeming primitivism of animals being stoned to death, for various transgressions which didn't seem that shocking or abominable, to my jaded, cosmopolitan sensibilities, troubled me. I found it hard to condone. But that was just it. I *was* jaded, corrupted—by modern relativism. I needed my layers of diseased sophistication to be scoured and scourged by the flail of an almost tribal purity—a return to *values*, in place of relativistic accommodations, facades, hypocrisies—the surface glitz of nail polish, eye-liner, sensationalistic spin, tinsel-plated sham (both double-jointed and inwardly hollow). When the outward gets emphasised, the inner begins to repine.

A swishing sound made me jump.

Someone had slid something under the door.

The neighbourhood was full of massage-parlours, peepshews, and various other playgrounds for the sick at heart; to my surprise however the folded slip of paper was without the usual gimmicky XXX advertising. The stationery itself was strangely pregnant with signification.

Flying down the rickety staircase three steps at a time I heard the bell jingling as the front door swung shut behind someone; I was too late to see who it was.

244

Returning to the squalour of my bedsit, heart still racing for some reason, I sat down on the edge of the bed and tearing open the sealed note, recognised *Marcus'* angular, boyish handwriting.

XXXV.

I went for a long walk before reading the letter. I kept going around the block, again and again. And yet there was no getting around it—I *had* to read it, for better or worse, now or five years down the road, whatever its hastily scribbled penmanship might portend:

"*Come <u>alone</u> to the <u>Purple Parrot</u> in <u>Dogtown</u>. It's not that safe so bring plenty in case ripped off. I'll make it up to you whatever happens. Just <u>be careful</u>. And <u>make sure you're not followed</u>. Can't stress that enough.*

    Be sure to come <u>to-morrow evening</u>, whenever it starts to get <u>dark</u>. I planned it for <u>Friday</u>, because they say <u>Friday</u> is sacred to that weird lot with their flipping Festival (or whatever it is) and the gendarmes and snoops and rats won't be about quite so thick everywhere.

    <u>*Please come*</u>.

    If you don't shew up, know that you've <u>shattered</u> the Life of one who, whatever you may believe, does in fact <u>dearly love</u> and <u>cherish</u> the air <u>you</u> breathe, the ground <u>your</u> precious pads caress, in traversing...

    Signed,
    <u>*One Who Would Die for You*</u>
p.s.—Think it gets dark round 8 to find Purp P take Shadwell junction, go Brick Lane, far as someone's coming just ask—
p.p.s.—Don't tell <u>anyone</u> about this, <u>not even Snoopus</u>. If can't find don't ask anyone looks scary or raises hackles. Trust instinct. <u>BE CAREFUL</u>"

And that was it. A mixture of the telegram's melodramatic brevity with the schoolboy's perhaps hackneyed but nonetheless ardent excess of feeling. That bit about loving the ground I

246

walked on and the air I breathed actually brought improbable
tears to my bloodshot, myopic, overstrained eyes. So what if he
was lying—he stated (in writing no less!) that he would die
for me.

I already knew (on some basic level beyond the reach of
self-censorship) that I'd cherish this letter till the day *I* died
(for *him*).

The excessive underlining caused me to smile (through
my tears). I don't remember how many times I reread it. I could
recite the thing—right now—from memory, backwards and
forwards. But I can never seem to remember which words and
phrases my poor little Prince Imperial underlined, so I've got it
right here, in front of me (surprisingly the Bedlam staff didn't
confiscate it—perhaps they didn't dare—perhaps it was too hot
to handle, to log and inventory and make part of that double-
edged sword known as the Official Record of things—I suppose
they didn't burn it from superstitious reverence: a member of the
Royal Family physically scrawled these loops and squiggles
of ink).

At length, of course, something had to be done. Or rather,
decided. Recognising that my leg was still in the bear-trap (and
always would be, so long as I lived)—that I loved him
hopelessly, unreasoningly—didn't unfortunately give me the
Answer. All it did was highlight the Question. As in: what do we
do about it?

And: does he *really* love *me*?

And worst of all: would my *doing* anything (with this
Love of mine) injure, or compromise, the Object of all this
churning, transfiguring love?

Well of course it would *compromise* him. It already had,
badly. My very *existence*, at this stage, compromised the poor
muddle-headed adolescent in love with the idea of being In Love.

I had to be careful. This whole Annie 'trip'—this
desperate attempt to thrash out in a different direction (and thus
escape the cloying fetters of my own personality's quicksandlike,
stultifying stagnation)—this hopeless attempt to *become* my

247

sister—for the first time I saw just how sick and self-destructive it was.

If you can't stand your basic personality, then putting on a mask—disguising yourself—simply compounds the problem. Because you aren't getting at the root of the problem: yourself.

Annie could smash as many cameras in Paris as she liked—and wind up on the Front Page again and again—till the worm turned, and people decided they wanted to read something new (perhaps more intellectually challenging, perhaps just as meaningless). I fantasised that perhaps they'd want to read about a lonely wallflower—who superseded her beginnings—her very wellsprings of character—by—

My train of thought faltered.

By getting it on with someone who wasn't a wallflower? By feeding on the crumbs of Someone Else's overflowing self-sufficiency—of the sort that can briefly, cheatingly, seem to fill a gaping, unfillable void?

I was back where I'd started. I kept going in circles.

When I was a small child, the circles were small enough to see (and feel) how they curved—even as I was treading the curvature with small, unfaltering steps.

Now, as an adolescent, my steps faltered, but at least I thought I was getting somewhere. Till I wound up back where I'd started, and saw that the latest circle had been a vast thing indeed—miles and miles across.

The pointlessness of my life had merely increased in diameter.

xxxvi.

It was Friday morning. I had to decide what to do. Did I give in
to temptation, and possibly drag him down with me? Or embrace
the hard thing, the pure thing? Except…I didn't know *which*
decision would constitute the hard-thing-the-pure-thing. I didn't
even know what my options were. Perhaps I was overlooking
something. Perhaps the hard-thing-the-pure-thing (the HTPT)
was right there, staring me in the face the whole time.

An almost vibrant buoyancy was in the air, or at least I
imagined it as being in the air, and throbbing up through the
vibrating pavement. Weird-looking, shrouded figures were
drifting past in little knots and, occasionally, larger groups—
which made me clench my teeth in a sort of barely contained
exultation that bordered on panic.

The Dark People. At last.

A weird keening, lilting noise was gradually getting
louder, seeping into my bloodstream through a sort of primal
osmosis that turned me into a unicellular component—reasserting
my individuality with a panicked intake of breath, I realised that I
was hearing tens of thousands—perhaps hundreds of thousands—
of trilling, echoing, percussive, ululating voices in unison.

I had to rush back indoors—I couldn't concentrate—on
my own personal problems.

"Told-ja-ya-shouldn't—"

I hurried past the smirking concierge—

"Go out there," his voice followed me as I pounded up the
half-rotten steps.

Back in my room with its creaking floorboards and
cheesecloth walls, I resumed pacing—but this time forced myself
to concentrate on the problem at hand.

Should I go? Was it just another trick, another snare of
the sort my life, increasingly, had come to be filled with? Did I

even *want* to see him again (never mind the fact that I 'loved' him—whatever that meant)?

I must have spent the rest of the afternoon drifting round London. I somehow found myself on the tube, waiting to transfer to the Shadwell junction line.

I was hoping to find the place on my own. I've always had a good sense of direction. On the other hand, I'd never really explored Dogtown or any other of the bad slums before. I'd wanted to, but Helen had been a wet blanket—that's a lie—why do lies come so easy, and the truth almost never? Helen had dared me to go with her into the Slums, and then we'd both chickened out.

I hoped I could find this place, the *Purple Parrot*, without having to ask. If I got conked over the head, I hoped the five roubles in my pocket would keep them from slitting my throat.

The map of the Underground (which every compartment is mandated by the Transit Authority to have on display) was defaced by switchblades and markers; this cancer-like graffiti covering the walls and ceiling—even some of the seat-cushions—appeared to be quite ubiquitous—I wondered where the hoodlums and streetkids got their inexhaustible fount of nervous energy from—or perhaps it wasn't nervous; perhaps it was g-dbearing; perhaps if I studied it long enough, I'd start meowing in tongues.

Almost no one was on the tube; I began to get nervous. Flitting from car to car at every stop, I finally found a legible map, and determined that I'd overshot my transfer point by one station—two by the time I disembarked. Hurrying across the flyover (eerily deserted of a single person), I duly boarded an inbound train and was soon heading back towards the City centre. Getting off at Whitechapel (picturesque name!) I found the Shadwell line without too much trouble (talk about decrepitude—it desperately needed a thorough washing over and sweeping). The battered old train felt like it could barely limp along, from station to run-down, graffiti-covered station. At least this train had some people in it—mainly harmless old pensioners, but

250

screaming want and neglect from every unpatched rip in their faded clothing, every cripple forced to hobble along on an unsound-looking stick—there were no walkers of gleaming steel, no Sedan Chairs or Litters.

I began to feel terribly ashamed, sitting there in what I'd thought were my own pauper's weeds—compared to these poor folk, I resembled what I suppose I really was: an ill-disguised Aristo addicted to the cheap thrill of slumming.

Across from me, an old Beaver was trying to read the Evening edition. His spectacles were not only taped together—one of the lenses was about to come out; someone had ineptly tried to tape it along the rim, but obviously the cheap, worn-out tape was losing whatever little virtue it may once have possessed.

Try to concentrate, I forced myself to look out the window. *Did the Note say when to get off this Line?* Producing it as inconspicuously as I could (though the crinkling sound, combined perhaps with my furtive manner, made several heads turn), I quickly ascertained that in fact it didn't—just Brick Lane, that was all it mentioned.

Please come.

My eyes, rescanning those childishly underlined words, filled with tears.

"You'n any sort o' trooble, Mees? Los' yer wye praps?"

The poor Beaver had spoken. My gratitude at that moment was so all-encompassing, I couldn't reply. My mouth worked (like that of a fish?). Several onlookers muttered disapprovingly. I heard someone whisper something about leaving "well enuff aloon…"

"I have to find Brick Lane," I tried to whisper.

"Speak oop, Loov," he cupped a withered ear with a dessicated, gnarled-looking paw.

I dasn't speak my Destination to a carload of strangers—even I knew that much. Somehow I crept across to the slashed seatcushion on which he was hunched.

"Brick Lane" I tried to whisper, breathing through my mouth so I shouldn't have to *smell* someone that had both done

251

me an incredible kindness, but also, to look at him, not had a bathe in Bast knows how long.

"Take i' all th wye t' the ehnd," he wheezed, "Go oop Cable… No, go 'way froom th' River; to Ratcliff 'ighway—it crosses Breeck Lyne, or ask a copper. Wha'ever trooble yer in, Loov, I 'ope it cooms out in the wash, as we say roond these parts."

As the train clankingly crept its way into the next station, the poor old creature tried to stand up.

Help him.

I sat helpless, immobilised. I hadn't even asked him his name—but in a Slum, you don't ask folk their names. Yeah, but you can *help* the *infirm*—those disapproving glances and whispers can go to the devil.

I stared fixedly down at the unripped, quality corduroy of my trousers, till the doors slid shut, and we started moving again. Sure enough, the old codger was gone. I'd sat like a bump on a log, repaying kindess with callousness. Marc deserved better than the stuff I was made of—absolute *shite*. I think I detested myself, at that instant, more fiercely than ever before—but then, I've detested myself on and off for most of my life, and that's probably just another exaggeration.

There's no *substance*, no Centre, to my being. (Like there is for the Faithful.)

I thought Marc said this was one of their Holy Days. Perhaps the taking of transport were somehow, on such a Day as this, proscribed for some reason. If that were the case, then I was committing sacrilege—in the eyeless but all-seeing omnipresent sight of their invisible intangible Deity.

With a shudder, the train came to a halt. The doors complainingly screeched open. We must have reached the end of the Line. Sure enough, all the remaining passengers were listlessly processing out onto the shadowy platform. This particular station seemed to be out of doors—a fine mist of summer precipitation was drizzling down, turning everything clammy. Clouds obscured the moon and stars. It looked like the night was about to turn foggy. That was all I needed—fog.

Cursing softly to myself I began trudging up the first street I could find. I realised, however, that I had no idea whether I were heading towards, or away from, the River. With a grim set to my shoulders, I began following a group of pedestrians up ahead.

They were shrouded, I quickly realised—shrouded just as the night was becoming shrouded, with fog. Shivering in my thin summer clothes, I cursed everything and everyone—even Marc—but most of all myself, for listening to Marc. For being such a silly little thing as to fall head over heels for the first 'pretty' boy I should happen to meet.

There's more to Marc than just his Good Looks, I reproachfully told myself in the faintest of whispers. But it seemed some street urchins had heard me. They began giggling, calling me things I shan't repeat, describing sexual practices so abhorrent that even I had never imagined such abominations, staring at the ceiling late at night, in despair.

The shrouded figures in front of me were being joined by others—I took this for a good sign, and continued along the way I was going. Streetlamps, looking weird and ghostly in the mist, beckoned me to the intersection where I could read the street names: Ratcliff Highway the placard said; little drops of condensation made the lettering glisten.

Thank g-d, I fervently, inwardly, shivered.

But which way do we go now?

Surely the Faithful wouldn't conk me over the head. Besides, maybe they could give me directions. Three of the ghostly figures were toiling their way towards me.

"Excuse me," I began—

"That lot don't speak, love—were yeh born yesterday?" a drunk chortled, lurching out of the obscurity—tottering his way unmistakably towards me.

"Help," I gasped, shaking, "There's someone following, and—and I need to find Brick Lane—please—"

253

"They're liable to cut yer up bad," he chortled. "Their lot get contaminated when normal hilthy folk like you and me try to talk to 'em—before *fucking*!" he burst into a repulsive leering guffaw, spit flying every which way (contaminating the purity of the fog's condensation).

I swayed on my feet. A talon caught me by the shoulder—a shrouded talon—I was too shaken to scream. Then I understood that he or she had kept me from falling. Another of the weird beings pointed in the opposite direction. Meanwhile several others had interposed themselves between me and the drunk. I heard him pleading in a slurred voice as they herded him towards one of the darkened sidestreets. Hurrying along fast as I could, I tried to feel grateful, but could only spur myself to go faster, trembling in every joint, my tongue cleaving to the roof of my mouth.

Why did I come here? Will I ever get home? Marc can take me home. I've got to find Marc. He said Brick Lane—

And sure enough, the next intersection, by the flickering glow of the gas-lamps, bore the rain-spattered inscription: BRICK LANE.

A loud obstreperous burst of laughter made my heart leap in my chest and then throb painfully. The revelers were emerging from a one-story tavern. It took my numbed brain a few seconds to decipher the garish neon marquee.

It said: urple arrot.

The Ps must have been shorted out by the misting precipitation—or more likely, had been smashed by rock-throwing hoodlums.

Sticking to the shadows, I worked my way round to the windows, which of course were fogged over. Grimacing, I gingerly placed my shrinking pawpads against that scummy, freezing surface, and tried to wipe a tiny aperture without making any noise, but of course a squeaking sound ensued—to my ears it went off like a cannon, echoing across the whole intersection.

I couldn't see anything anyway—engulfed by unreasoning panic, I pelted round the corner and in through the

254

swinging doors—a foetid warmth, stinking of beer and vomit, assailed my delicate nostrils. I could tell that everyone had turned to stare. You could hear a pin drop.

Staring at the floor, I edged backwards till bumping against the rough grainy surface of the structure's wall I had to figure out whether to edge to my right, or my left. The door was to my left. I simultaneously both yearned towards, and feared, the door. The hum of whispered conversation was starting up again, along with laughter—I tried not to hear what they must be saying—mercifully it was just a jumble of voices.

I almost screamed when a warm hoof worked itself round my waist—a Warthog was trying to lead me off somewhere, to fornicate, I supposed. Would he succeed in his design? I'd either have to fight him, to the death, or live with whatever it was he intended doing to me—I just hoped it wouldn't be painful. Or if I fought him—

"Yer a rum li'uhl psychopath," he whispered.

The fact that his breath stank decided me. Fight, or flight. Perhaps I could break free of him—

"Don't," he whispered, "You'll se' off a riot, see. *I'm* not inh'rested—Horns of Hathor—gimme some credi'…"

"What do you want?" I managed.

"*He* sent me—over there, see?"

Sure enough, a Lion was sitting at the corner table. One of my own kind—he could help me—

The way you helped the Old Beaver?

"It was beyond my control," I bitterly intoned under my breath.

"Just a few more steps," he whickered, as if to a child.

"We're certainly taking the long way round," I pointed out, hoping to convince him that I was just as 'sane' as everyone else in this scabrous dive of a place.

As the creature eased me into an uncomfortable wooden chair (with no arms, but plenty of splinters) I suddenly realised that the Lion right beside me was *Marc*. Everything came into focus.

255

"Feeling more ourselves now?" the Warthong snorted. "Can I bring you a pint, there, Lassie?"

"Do you have any tea, with half-and-half, or even some plain milch?" I enquired.

As usual, I'd said the wrong thing, but for once I didn't care. My relief flooding over everything was simply too great.

"Bring us some more grog," Marcus bestirred himself, his huge golden-green eyes flickering in the gloom as they devoured me, never leaving my person. His *voice* (on top of the Eyes) had me ready to go into orbit—I'd forgotten how irresistible his half-boyish, half adolescent baritone was, resonating like some sexually precocious *viola*.

The proprietor shambled off to get us our grog. I pretended to study the large pewter mug on the filthy table in front of him. It was chipped in places.

"I'm sorry for bringing you to a place like this—you don't have to drink it of course—were you followed? You didn't take a Taxi, I hope?"

Grinning foolishly, I shook my head, No.

"Listen, we don't have much time."

I tried to concentrate on the words floating effortlessly from his sensuous lips.

"Are you," the words having hit a snag seemed less fluid, "Forgive me, but," he blinked, gulping, and nervously scanned the crowded tables (sure enough, almost everyone was watching us, most of them quite brazenly)—

The Warthog slammed two more of frothing mugs on the table, making us both jump.

"*Na zdorovye*," he cackled.

Marcus shoved his index claw down on a lever protruding from a complicated-looking money-belt which the velvet lapel of his jacket, in lifting, disclosed.

"Here. Keep the change."

Whatever he gave the creature must've been astronomical. The squiggly squinting eyes lit up, looking almost beautiful in their greed-stoked nakedness.

Turning back to me, buttoning his jacket, he leaned closer.

"Are you—I'm sorry to ask this—but are you 'on' something?"

I almost lost control and giggled out loud. (It certainly would've confirmed his suspicions.)

"It was quite an experience, getting over to this part of town. A lecher tried to interfere with me—right there, on the street."

"Look, I'm sorry about all that, but we don't have time for it. Can you pull yourself together?"

He glanced at a timepiece before stuffing it back into one of his pockets.

"Why does everything you own look so expensive?"

"Look, *Sylvia*," we both blushed (but probably for quite different reasons), "This won't work unless we get going—now—but I have to explain or you won't understand."

"Sounds plausible. I'm not a mind-reader," I giggled.

A frown distorted his beautiful features. A frown of exasperation, or annoyance.

"You look even *more* handsome when you're furious," I couldn't help making the vapid remark, almost playing it up—like I really *was* on something.

"I do?" he sounded idiotically pleased. "You think I'm goodlooking? Really?"

"I thought you said we didn't have much time."

"Well you brought it up," he seemed to retreat into himself, "And like you, I'm not exactly a mind-reader."

"Can you get to the point and tell me what I'm doing here—what we're both doing here?"

"I've got a Taxi waiting outside. Okay, now listen: I've been planning this ever since that wretched night at the Louvre when Delilah set us both up—remember?"

"Of course I remember."

"You must realise how sorry—how ashamed—I am—"

"I'm also sorry, and ashamed."

Impulsively I reached across and took hold of his golden, indescribably beautiful, paw. I'd read somewhere that when two people have the hots for each other but happen to be, for whatever reason, emotionally fucked up—physical touch can work miracles.

The effect surpassed my wildest hopes: it was instant, electric, going right through my vitals. I felt a warm surge down 'below.' Whether or not he felt the same thing, judging by his outward reaction, I think it fairly safe to conjecture that probably he *did*.

"Sylvia—"

I inwardly shuddered, not just from the warm panting breath, but also his vibrant strength; I could feel the tendons in his angular wrist as he gripped my own delicate white little paw (which was dwarfed by his own).

"I want to make up for that awful farce—"

"You *can*," I stammered (my face felt like a furnace), "*We* can—I mean, if you want, we can go back to my flat."

I sat there breathless.

"We can't! We have to hurry!" he brought his fist down, spilling some of the grog. The room went totally quiet.

"Great," he whispered, "That's all we needed."

Well it wasn't my fault I almost said, but caught myself just in time.

"Listen. We don't have much time—we should already be out of here—maybe I should explain in the car—damn! We need to ditch the driver; I can't if we sit out there, yakking."

"Will you please tell me what's going on?"

His gleaming opal-like eyes turned my guts to jelly; looking him in the eye was like being consumed by the sun's golden splendour.

"I've been planning this for a long time now. Ever since that terrible night. You're the only one I can even think of doing this with—listen—stop smiling—I gave 'em the slip at the Trocadero, on Piccadilly. Pretended to have the trots—tricked

258

'em," he stammered, "into thinking I'd gobbled a huge platter of gooseberries."

The blank look on my face seemed to vex him.

"*Gooseberries*," he intoned as if a light were supposed to go on, in my head, "I always get sick whenever I eat them—"

"Well I didn't know that."

"The tabloids go on and on about it," he sounded almost insulted.

"Must be nice—"

"Actually it was humiliating—I think one of my enemies at Court—"

"Must be nice to have all the details of your life known to everyone—I mean—to someone lonely like me—an insignificant nothing, like me—it seems nice, from where I'm standing—or in this case, sitting."

He took out the timepiece again.

"Sod it!" his voice almost squeaked reminding me, for an instant, of Tosk. "Okay, no more digression—we've *both got* to stay on track."

"I'm listening."

Anyway you're the one keeps digressing, not me.

"Pretended to wolf down this huge plate of gooseberries. Actually I flushed 'em down the loo, but ran the water, so they wouldn't hear. They were like, Your Grace, how could you *eat* those—you *know* the effect they have on your Royal digestion..."

(The infectious grin he flashed me was hard to resist.)

"I pretended to get the trots pretty soon—had to kill time in there, pretending, for over 45 minutes, burning matches—they know how fastidious I am; they knew better than to prowl round the door—you should have seen the look on their faces when I announced that I was going to the Trocadero, that instant! My Chamberlain urged me to lie down instead. I snarled that I was sick of having abdominal cramps, and sitting hunched on the loo. I wanted to have some fun for a change. But Your Grace, they remonstrated—I petulantly brushed aside their misgivings,

259

ordered them to have the bulletproof, armour-plated Jag down below, at the South entrance, and quickly had my gentlemen dress me as befits a Prince of the Blood—breeches of crushed silk, clogs with silver buckles, the blue velvet cloak with the tassels and wide flaring collar, and the diamond-studded Cross of Saint George surmounting the emblazoned Star of the East, each squiggly, flickering point representing one of the Eight Great Houses on which our dynastic sovereignty rests."

"What does all this have to do with—"

"I'm getting there," his eyes flashed. "So anyway, I was dressed to the nines, a strutting little popinjay aglitter with Imperial privilege—don't cha see, they wouldn't have thought I could get very far in weeds like those—unbeknownst to them," he grinned, "I had a travel case packed and waiting—for just such a moment. Literally crammed with travelers cheques, golden Guineas, pieces of silver—as well as the toned down, functional outfit I'm wearing now—plus a number of other ingenious accessories and gadgets—all for the road—for being on the run, so to speak."

"Since when have *you* ever been—"

"Please let me finish," he demanded in a tone of voice that instead of cutting me to the quick simply 'pissed me off' as they say. "This is frightfully clever (in *my* opinion at least)—"

He risked a sidelong glance. I managed a borderline smile.

"At the Trocadero," he continued his little yarn, "I told them they needed to find me a loo—"

"Does it ever bother you, to be so utterly helpless—to let them practically choreograph your every step, anticipating your slightest—"

"Don't you see that that was a *rôle* I was playing, to beguile them into relaxing their vigilance—and above all, to write me off as a complete Basket Case?"

But I noticed he'd turned a bright red—under the golden fur—and his tail had started to twitch, probably from a mixture of shame and anger. I do have a particular talent for sniffing out people's weak spots.

"So they cleared the entire facility, checking every stall—making the attendant wait outside along with everyone else."

"What if someone else had also had the trots?"

"But I didn't have the trots—I was only pretending!" he gesticulated, "The whole thing was a ruse—to buy time."

"I understand that," I gritted my teeth—

"Several weeks before that, when I really did have to use their loo, I was checking the casement with its translucent, fogged glass—I'm always casing, wherever I go, checking windows and security systems—a prisoner always keeps on the lookout for that one camouflaged chance at escape."

"Let's not be melodramatic."

I suddenly realised that I sounded just like my father.

"You don't know what it's like," his eyes (brimming with tears) went right through me, to the very depths of my soul.

"But I do, though, believe it or not," I squeezed his huge paw, "I just get hung up sometimes on my own stupid little trips—please don't pay any attention—so you found your camouflaged chance at escape?"

My own lackluster, nondescript eyes locked with his, begging, *compelling* him to continue:

"Yeah, but listen to how I did it," he squeezed my paw so hard that the pain became a thing of delicious enjoyment, "The casement latch was broken; it looked like it was latched, but it wasn't, see?"

"So what happened then?"

I somehow couldn't imagine him summoning the initiative to hoist himself out through a window.

"Is it that boring?" he exploded, "Is that why you keep trying to get me to fast-forward to the end of the story?"

"But I—I haven't been doing any such thing," I managed, my eyes filling with tears as my throat closed on itself.

"I'm sorry," he gulped. "I guess I was doing what my shrink calls projecting. We don't really have time for me to try

261

and dazzle you with a long, drawn-out anecdote of how clever I was in giving 'em the slip—"

"*I* think you're indescribably clever, and brilliant," I found my voice again. "And goodlooking as hell."

He didn't say anything, but the millions of capillaries veining his exquisite skin fairly thrilled and thrummed with an infusion of warmth. His euphoria reached out with invisible tendrils, enfolding me—catapulting me to the stars, and beyond.

"I guess they've raised the alarm by now," he brought me back down to earth, nervously licking his lips, "But how could they ever find us *here*—that's part of what makes me so proud of—of, you know, my plan."

"You have every right to be proud," I took a deep breath, "I never could've—"

"I know we didn't have time for me to go off on this tedious little recitation of just how cleverly the whole thing—my little escapade—was contrived and executed—by someone who never *executed* anything else in his life—but I just couldn't stand it any longer—the secrecy of the thing—holding it all inside—I had to tell *someone*, or burst."

"So you didn't really care *who* you confided in," I tried not to raise my voice, "It could've just as easily been that smirking Warthog."

"I didn't mean it like that."

Everything about him suddenly seemed to enrage me.

"Bookworms and wallflowers, or is it bookflowers and wallworms, make the most perfect sounding-boards—we listen like no one else can listen but then at the same time since our opinions don't really count—"

"Shut up," he tried to speak forcefully but his voice spluttered, "I can't stand it when you talk like that, devaluing yourself—"

"If I don't do it, who else is going to?"

He didn't smile. (But then, neither did I.)

"Don't you understand that I wanted to share this with *you*—with you *specifically*—"

262

I began to melt, like a big block of sugar. But he had a bad habit of shooting himself in the foot, groping for words and blurring the beautiful sketch on the canvas:

"I mean, why d'you think I'm wasting—I mean taking—precious time to divulge all this—"

"Because you want me—me specifically—to share in this brilliant deception, this carefully contrived stratagem—which proves to both me and the world that you *are* a self-starter, that you *do* possess initiative, gumption, and cunning?"

My outburst didn't go over very well; the corners of his trembling mouth tightened.

"Why the fuck do I even try to impress you?" the bitterness in his voice for some reason surprised me, "You've thought it all out in advance, understanding people even better than they understand themselves (or think they do)—"

"Marc," I whispered.

I took him by the paw, squeezing it. If I expected another surge of hormonal fireworks going off in my head, I was disappointed, but all the same, a twinge of warmth crept through my innards.

He must have felt it as well; he shifted in his chair, blushing slightly, his eyes like flickering greenish-gold bits of flame.

"So I'm here," he sounded even more boyish, more hoarse, than usual. "And you're here. The Security bastards 'll be on our trail. We're the Hunted, now, you know."

I nodded, praying they wouldn't find us any time soon.

"So. Here's my proposal," he gulped: "We really should stop mucking about and get married. Please? I want—want it—want you—so very badly—please say yes! It has to be right now—this very night—we've *got* to get going."

He clumsily got up, came round the table and tugged at my wrist.

I felt paralysed. My head was swimming. The tabletop seemed to be turning to liquid.

"I was afraid you might not want to," he sounded on the verge of crying. "You can always divorce me after the first—"

The word *divorce* did something to me.

"Are you crazy?" I gasped, "Of course I'd marry you in a heartbeat!" I had to take a deep breath, as several of them (heartbeats) felt like they were pounding my ribcage to bits—

"C'mon, c'mon," he began jumping up and down, like a small child on his birthday, impatient for the cake and candles and gifts.

"Wait a minute," I was still short of breath and slurred the words, "Please...let's sit again; we have to think this through..."

"What's to think about?" he sounded exasperated, "I've spent my entire life impotently *thinking*—locked in *mazes* of thinking."

"I know," I tried not to sound dismissive, "So have I. But sometimes, like right now, we have to sit down and think. Or plan, maybe that's a better word. Please sit down, just for a minute?"

He pulled the chair round till it was right beside mine. His haunch was practically brushing against my own, sending sparks tingling up and down my spine, inflaming my bloodstream. I realised that he was waiting for *me* to do the thinking, the planning.

I chose my words carefully:

"The Privy Council would never permit you to sully your bloodline—"

"Sod the Privy Council—I'm sick to death of the Privy Council—they rubber-stamp my Uncle's decisions—they play 'bad cop' to the Emperor's 'good cop'—"

"Same problem: the *Emperor* would never—"

"Sod the bloody Emperor," he predictably growled, and in far too loud a voice, "I'm taking you right now—there's a Registry Office just ten blocks over. We can get there before the Security detachments track me down—it'll be a *done* deal—dead as a doornail for all *they* can do about it!"

"Oh, Marc," tears came to my eyes, for several different reasons. "Nothing in life ever works out that simple—it's never 'done'—till *you're* dead as a duck."

"I prefer my Doornail to your Duck."

"I was thinking of that awful creature, my Stepmother—"

"She was for about thirty seconds, till your father married my cousin, Delilah."

"And she played him for all he was worth."

"Wasn't that justice—for his divorcing your Mum?"

"I used to think so. I don't know. Probably."

"Look, the Registry Office 'll do a blood test, give us a ream of papers to sign, a Magistrate gets roused out of bed, mumbles a few legal phrases, bangs a gavel, and presto! Signed, sealed and delivered. We have a *notarised* Marriage certificate."

"But Marc—"

"They can't keep us apart, don't you see?"

Not even by ripping your precious Marriage document into a thousand pieces, having it quietly annulled by daybreak, committing me to some out-of-the-way Bedlam?

"Oh, Marc—"

I didn't know what to do.

"Just picture the look on their faces. Interfering bastards! I'd be kissing you, my Bride, all the paperwork validated and stamped—we could pose for the bloody tabloids even—so the bastards couldn't try and destroy the records (not that I'm gonna be letting them out of my tightfisted grasp for even a split-second)—and don't forget, to the gendarmes and secret service types, my Royal Person is sacred, inviolable; for them there's no getting around it."

"They won't care about—"

"Listen!" his eyes gleamed emitting invisible moonbeams which slipped and slid against each other (reminding me of slippery stepping-stones—that could take me to paradise), "As I *kiss* you: deep, thirst-slaking kisses the way I've never kissed anyone, you'd feel how much I couldn't wait—*can't* wait—you can feel me, right now, under the table. Our marriage night can

265

be consummated anywhere you want it to be: the flat I keep in Mayfair, that cozy little bedsit you've rented (I fantasised so many times about simply going there, and throwing you down on the bed), the Ritz Carlton—or a field under the stars."

He grabbed me by the wrist; I resisted, but to my surprise he was genuinely stronger than I was. At the same time the charnel flesh, the stupid clay of my own body, knocked sideways with an answering need, was cranking open the sluices (of my bloodstream) to a sort of chemical lust, a desire of such intensity, I could hardly breathe, devouring his 'Royal Person' with my bloodshot but smoldering eyes, my paw (under the table) making him groan softly, as—

"Get yeself a bloody room, mate."

"No 'andjobs under the bloody table—this is a respeckable stablishment," the Warthog slatheringly, licking his porcine chops, bellowed sanctimoniously, heaving himself ponderously upright, and lurching towards us.

"Make sure she ain't got any diseases," someone shouted, "An' don' give 'er the mooney till after."

A coarse burst of laughter sent us scrambling for the door. I was buffeted by groping talons and hooves. I heard Marc cursing and snarling; his sharp claws and fangs were enough, it seemed, to hold the largely herbivorous assemblage of drunks and degenerates at bay long enough for us to scurry through the tattered remnants of fog (a breeze had sprung up; it must have been blowing from the River—a stench of dead fish and mildew wrinkled my quivering nostrils) and round the corner.

"Shite!" he exploded.

"What's wrong?"

"The bloody car—the Taxi!" he shook me, "It's gone! Wha' do we do now! I hate life—I HATE LIFE!"

"C'mon," I grabbed him by his broad shoulders, digging my claws in, "We can't just stand here blubbing like my kid brother Dougie," I wanted to slap some sense into him. "Buck up! We've got to formulate a contingency plan."

The stricken look on his face really did for an instant make him look just like Douglas. Impulsively I kissed him on the cheek. The transformation was truly astounding: I could feel him pulling himself together, rallying his flagging emotions.

Like the crack of a bullwhip, he was bounding into the street, making me run hard as I could to keep up—till a pain in my side, and tearing ragged gasps of breath caused me to fall back, which brought him up short.

"I can't do this," I gasped, "Go on, without me."

"Nothing doing," he snarled, "Ratcliff highway *has* to have some traffic—c'mon."

Sure enough, I could hear the rumble of automobiles and see pedestrians just up ahead. Marcus took off at a lolloping canter and was soon out of sight. When I reached the streetcorner, a dented rattletrap that had certainly seen better days veered over to where I was holding onto a streetlamp (for support). The door opened, and to my surprise Marc sprang forth as though shot out of a cannon.

"Hurry! I was able to get this one by offering him an astronomical tip. We can go now."

The pavement felt like it was slanting under my feet, like some giant was tilting it to make me keel over—Marc clumsily tossed me onto a ripped seatcushion (I was lucky the protruding springs didn't put an eye out), scrambled in behind me and slammed the cardoor. We lurched into motion.

"How far from here to Shoreditch?" he demanded in the breathless voice of a youngster trying to sound tough, but in fact scared out of his wits.

"Not far, but this is the Festival, kiddos—it's shut down the entire frickin' East End."

"So take us there—what are you waiting for?"

"Tryin' to work out the best way to get there, Laddie— you want to drive?"

"I think *so*," he drawled the words perhaps to distract attention from his chattering teeth.

"Marcus," I laid a hand on his shoulder.

267

"Praps you lot should get out of this machine—"

"Perhaps *you* should," he thrust a wad of crinkly rainbow-coloured ten- and twenty-rouble notes at the Driver, who turned on the overhead light. It was a Wolfhound of some sort—clearly *not* to be trifled with.

"D'you know how much this is?" he sounded suspicious.

"About five times the value of this pitiful wreck when it was brand spanking new. So it's mine now. Out you go then."

"Is this some sort of a joke, Laddie?"

"Do you want the money or not?" my young Lion was visibly trembling.

(He's got a fever, I remember thinking to myself, he's not responsible—just like me, when I visit my mother.)

"I've got to make sure this is real—and I'll need some sort of identification, and then we'll have to go back for the ownership papers—"

I couldn't believe it. The creature sounded like he was actually taking the crazy proposition halfway seriously.

"We don't have time for that shite!" Marc fumbled in his jacket, and brought out something that glinted. The claw located at the end of his thumb primed it with a loud, ominous click—next thing I knew he was jabbing a gun of some sort in the poor creature's face.

"Put it down—now!" the Dog barked, "Else I press charges!"

"Do you have any idea who I am?" he projected such an overbearing, supercilious intonation into his voice that the mangy Canine actually hesitated.

"Take the money, which is more than you've ever seen in your life, and back off. They'd never prosecute even if I did pull the trigger—don't make me!"

This was like a nightmare—everything was happening at the speed of light.

"Marc, don't," my voice quavered, "They wouldn't prosecute, but Anubis would see what you did—so would Bast, and Sekhmet—remember Sekhmet—you don't want blood on

268

your paws, please—not when you approach those terrible Scales, on the Day of Judgement."

He started to shake—with suppressed laughter. Here I was with tears in my eyes, and the beast was laughing.

"Look," he gasped, "Look at him—running from the Scales of Anubis."

The Dog really *was* pelting off down the street.

"Your little speech about the Gods," he sniggered, "and that quaver in your voice—convinced him I was off my bloody rocker—without you," he leaned over and kissed me (a bit too perfunctorily), "I never could've pulled it off—you're a brick, Sylvia—a real brick."

He vaulted into the frontseat, turned the ignition, and we lurched forward, cruising along at a snail's pace.

"D'you want me to climb up there, into the passenger seat?" I somewhat resentfully asked him.

"If you can manage it without distracting me; I told them I wanted to learn how to drive a car—pretended it was just a whim—they gave me a few lessons, but I wish I had more experience."

"Why did you perform a *carjacking*?" I demanded, plopping down into the front passenger seat.

"Look at them," he pointed.

A steady trickle of shrouded figures was snaking its way down the street, parallel to us, and going at about the same speed.

"I'm gonna risk shifting gears; here goes nothing—"

"Wait," I took hold of him by the wrist, "You haven't told me why you commandeered this vehicle—illegally, for all the money you gave him."

"I didn't trust him, that's why," he grinned as if pleased with himself, "The first one screwed me over—who's to say this one might not be do the same—or even worse, work for the Secret police?"

"That's balderdash."

"I never would've thought I could actually pull something like that off—wasn't it a rush—I'm still shaking, see?"

269

"I could think of some other descriptive terms—we were just damn lucky, that's all."

"What is it about you," he gritted his teeth, and we veered over toward the column of silently trudging robot-like figures—I grabbed the steering-wheel in the nick of time, "drives you to shoot me down *all the time*?"

"I didn't mean to shoot anyone down—"

"Here I am, driving my bride to the Registry office—"

"Marcus look out!" I screamed—

He slammed his foot on the brake, just in time. In front of us, spanning the entire boulevard from one side to the other, swarming in what looked like tens of thousands, the Dark People—all of them shrouded, silent—were drifting and shuffling and surging past, innumerable bare hooves and talons and paws slapping and rasping on the pavement to create a dull, subsonic rustling that wormed its way between the joints of your bones, between the stacked vertebrae of your backbone—it was a raging, inexorable river—of Faith.

I could feel myself breaking out in gooseflesh. At the same instant my fiancé (such a strange, almost surreal, state of affairs) burst into tears. He must've finally reached the breaking point. I leaned over, to comfort him.

"What the fuck is this!" he sobbed.

"Isn't it obvious?"

"I can't just plough through this many people—"

"They'd tear us apart," I licked my lips, "And no one could save us—not the police, not the Security organs, not even the Emperor Himself."

"So what the fuck are we s'posed to do!" he pounded the steering wheel as snot dripped from his nostrils.

"Wait for them to finish marching past, like army ants without end—this is Infinity, Marcus—we're looking at Infinity…"

"This could take hours—we've got to find another way to get there—what street is this anyway?"

"Looks like it says…Via Dolorosa."

"There's no such street in London!" he exploded—his rage almost frightened me.

"I was joking," I tried to caress him by the shoulder, "It's Holborn Viaduct... I'm sorry—I really am—"

"You don't want me," all the fight, and tension, went out of him.

Instantly, the balance (of power) had shifted.

"But I do, Marc!" once again tears welled up in my eyes. "Can't we find another Registry office? There's got to be hundreds—this is the largest city in the world—"

"I only researched the one fucking place—that's the only one I know about—it's on Shoreditch, and now this fucking tidal wave of living flotsam—"

"Don't call them that," my eyes blazed, "You'll bring a Curse down, on both of us."

"Then tell me what to do Sylvia," he let out a deep breath. "I keep trying—"

"I know. I'm sorry. But don't let's talk about the Faithful that way. Can't you feel it?"

"Is there an underpass or a bridge we could find?"

"I don't know," I bit my lip, fighting back tears.

"This fucking street bisects the entire fucking East End!"

"I know—please calm down."

Every time he pounded the steering wheel, his feet stomped the floor, within a hairsbreadth of the gas-pedal.

"Let's turn off the ignition; we can concentrate that way."

"I wish we had some of those outfits they're wearing."

"What, chadors?"

"Whatever they're called. We could melt right into that heaving mass of Dervishes, or whatever they are—work our way clean over to the other side—I can see it; it's just a stone's throw—and the fucking Office is just a few blocks farther down."

"Why don't you *bribe* your way across?" I tried to keep the sneer out of my voice.

"Don't be daft," he frowned. "They're fanatics. They don't care about money."

271

"Must be nice."

"If we could just get across somehow—"

"I love the idea of donning shrouds and sneaking across. On the other side we could just divest ourselves of the disguises and calmly walk down the street. In plain view of all those hundreds of thousands of devout folk whose Faith we'd just desecrated."

"I bet that street turns, has some dark alleyways—we could *do* it."

"Well I wouldn't, even if we could pull it off."

"Oh?" the sneer in his voice annihilated me. "Why's that? Thinking of converting, all of a sudden?"

"No," I looked away, biting my tongue, "But it *would* be Sacrilege, and—I'm sorry if you don't feel the same way…"

It was my turn to burst into tears.

To my surprise he was all over me, wiping away the tears, whispering words I could no longer, in my suddenly raging, hormonal desire, understand—he began kissing me, and I remembered his description of what our 'wedding night' would be like.

"Do you have a blanket, or something to cover us?" I gasped, mindful of the implacable River filing past, just yards from our fumbling limbs as we ripped off our clothes. Somehow, a sort of filthy tarpaulin had been left on the floor of the backseat. We clambered down under it, and then, our hot breath filling the car and fogging the windows, a river of a different sort uprooted everything—and it was both the way I'd imagined, and *not* the way I'd imagined.

xxxvii.

"If *I'd* been there, I would've punched his face in."

I was telling him about the 'masher' that'd followed me down the street, in the fog. We were lying there, under that filthy canvas matt, my skull cradled against the beautiful golden fur of his shoulder. I'd never felt this way—peaceful, relaxed, able to let go and watch the world drifting past from some secret, safe, unassailable hideaway. It almost scared me, to feel so wonderful (like a price-tag was crouched in ambush, on the other side of the balance sheet). But for now, all such thoughts were at a safe remove, and we could idly converse about this and that, enveloped in each other's protection.

"You followed my instructions, right? And took the Shadwell Junction line?"

"Of course," I played with his whiskers.

"Wasn't that Shadwell line something else? The train was practically falling apart."

"I know."

"If I ever become Emperor," he yawned, "I'm gonna renovate the whole system."

"And the Faithful?" I wanted to know. "Would you sign a general Edict of across-the-board religious tolerance, lift the restrictions, sweep aside the centuries of discrimination hanging over them like a black cloud?"

"I suppose so," he shrugged. "I don't know very much about them. Why do you keep harping about them?"

"I'm not harping," I gave a sleepy smile of contentment, snuggling against him and wishing that I could always feel so warm and self-satisfied. For once there were no rough edges; I wasn't prickly or ready to fly off the handle. His obtuseness regarding the Faithful registered intellectually, but it was only skin-deep. There was no need to take things to heart.

"If I ever ascended the Throne," he murmured, causing us both to giggle, "I'd appoint you my Chief Minister, and take all your advice. Even if you told *me* to put on a shroud."

"I'd rather see you without anything—you're far too beautiful to have your good looks concealed."

"Except," his eager grin vanished, "I never will…"

"Never will, what? Take your clothes off again?"

"Get my claws on Supreme power."

My mouth almost dropped open.

"Delilah would have me assassinated. My friend Diocletian tells me things."

"What sort of things?" the unexpectedly serious turn our banter had taken left a sour taste in my mouth.

"He's a Reformer, like you and me."

His face became furtive, almost Rat-like as he whispered, "I shouldn't have said that."

"You don't trust me, all of a sudden?"

"Of course I do," he kissed me. "Knowledge like that, though, can be a burden. It's like the kiss of death, destroying everyone to whom it gets told."

"I prefer your kisses to those of Death," I smiled, determined to put things back on a carefree, light footing.

"He doesn't love her," he whispered. "I mean, he loves fucking her," he blushed, "but that's about all. He's in an awful position. I feel sorry for him. He wants to make a difference, take up where the Great Cleopatra left off. If Delilah claws her way to the top, eliminates Nero, and drags Diocletian right up there with her, to the summit of power—"

"She'd never let him enact any reforms," I shuddered, remembering her cold, brilliant green eyes.

"For his sake, I hope you're wrong."

"So do I."

"Let's," he blushed, "you know, do it again."

"I'm surprised the Security organs haven't caught up with us yet."

274

"Everyone's afraid of these Dark People, as you call them. This was the smartest thing we could have done."

"How long do you think we'll have to wait here?" I asked.

"Maybe till the sun comes up?" he scratched himself, yawning.

I began combing his beautiful hair with my claws, running them through its silky fragrance, parting his hair, and then kissing him between the large sapphire-like eyes. I could tell that rejoicing in our sexual *perfectness* (for each other) he was raring to go at it. But something held me back. Some sixth sense of warning.

"You think we can still get to the Registry office?" I asked him.

"It's supposed to be open round the clock. I can force them to summon a Magistrate—I'm a frigging Prince of the Blood, after all."

"Why does Nero come before you, in terms of the Imperial Succession?" I asked (mainly just to make conversation).

"He doesn't. Delilah does. But none of us would put anything past him. He murdered Philip, you know. The greatest assassination of them all. I'm so glad I hadn't been born yet."

"Marcus," I forced myself to try and sound calm, "I think someone's coming; we better get dressed."

"What makes you say that?" he sounded both childishly annoyed, and—terrified.

"Hear those motorcycles?"

"The *paparazzi*," he snarled, "The goddam fucking paparazzi—why did we waste all this time!"

"Hurry—hand me my shift."

"Where are my drawers?"

"Here, under my foot."

"Hurry," he grabbed them knocking me sideways.

I knew it'd been too good to last.

He was pulling his clothes on—frantically—impeding my own efforts to get dressed, in his selfishness.

Speaking of the paparazzi, a hidden voice whispered somewhere deep in my being, *perhaps you'll finally get that Press Conference—you deserve it. No one else does, certainly not your Beloved Protector—in his eyes it's every Lion for himself.*

"Stop it. That's not fair."

"What's not fair?"

Before I could say anything, the unmistakable whine of motorcycles zooming up the street behind us caused him to fumble with his trousers, and curse tearfully. I was still only in my shift, begging him to hand me my clothes from the front-seat.

"Listen; they've backed off again," he whispered, crouching down in the backseat, refusing to lift his haunches to let me pull on an undershirt.

Peering out through the window, I saw that indeed he was telling the truth; they'd turned tail, and retreated about halfway down the street. More and more of their kind were zooming up from every direction. In the distance we could hear a police siren, presently joined by several others, getting closer with each pattering heartbeat.

"They're scared of *that* lot," he gestured towards the slow-moving tide that still blanketed the entire boulevard, in both directions, as far as the eye could see, never speeding up or slowing down—certainly never *stopping*, for any power on earth.

"What did you think," I lost my temper, "that they were scared of *us*?"

"There's no need to be an absolute beast," his mouth quivered.

"I'm sorry, Marc, I just—please hand me my trousers—"

"Shall we try and disappear into the midst of all those shrouded Hottentots or whatever they are? Tell 'em the circumstances—they must know what it's like to be in love—"

"Don't you see they've pinned us down?" I tried to speak as one speaks to a child, "They know where we are—we'd never make it to the Registry office."

276

"You're a fucking liar," he burst into tears, "You just don't want—you can't stand me—"

"That's not true," I exploded, "And stop playing mindgames! They'll incarcerate me—you know that, I hope. But I don't even care—having been loved by a Lion who loves like it's the last minute of his life—because he's the truest, gentlest, most beautiful beast ever whelped. I mean that—I hope you believe me."

He began quietly weeping. (He was almost as good at weeping as lovemaking.) My mind was on overload. Images had started piling up on top of one another—his beautiful tear-stained face bathed in revolving flashing bursts of blue light—police vans and automobiles ringing us round—cutting off all hope of escape—but hanging back for some reason—it suddenly hit me that even the dreaded Secret police were undeniably afraid to get too close to the Faithful.

But then, Marcus was also a member of the Royal Family. I could see them calling for reinforcements, for Riot control, with truncheons and water cannon and plastic bullets and teargas. It was time we put this whole shameful intrusion, this voyeuristic blot on the Holy Festival of Makhurram, to rest.

"Marc," I whispered, "Let's go back, now. You can *make* them allow you to be with me, if you're strong enough."

"How do we know if I'm strong enough?" he sniveled.

"We'll find out. It's time to find out."

At that instant, both the doors were yanked open disclosing shadowy figures reaching in to grab us by the arms and legs. Marcus threw himself into my arms like a small sobbing child seeking its mother, instinctively trying to burrow under her skirts (except I wasn't wearing any). Several police (for what else could they be?) tried to pull me out through one door, whilst another lot tried to take Marcus. It seemed he was holding onto me with such a death-grip, they couldn't pry him loose; he was screaming some sort of toneless gibberish. The detectives on his side of the car suddenly had a brainwave, and started pushing

277

him—as my lot pulled. Both of us came tumbling out onto the pavement.

So there we were: flagrantly nabbed in a state of undress bordering on the salacious. Marc continued clinging to me (as the deflowered youth to his seductress—or should I say *prostitute*, for so the tabloids would brand me). At first I couldn't figure out why the Secret police were still hanging back—from here on out it should have been relatively straightforward: separate us, arrest one of us, convey the other with kid gloves back to the Gilded Cage in which (I feared or perhaps hoped) he'd never again sweetly sing for his supper. As the stag must feel when surrounded by hounds, I half prayed for a miracle, half wished they'd simply get it over with. Then I realised that the River of Faith had stopped flowing—tens of thousands of shrouded folk were silently watching us.

Perhaps another twenty seconds dragged past. Then the hunters began to move in on their prey. Marc began keening and whimpering, burying his face in my armpit (thank goodness I'd given myself a 'whore's bath' at the outset of this grim Final Day). To their dismay he was holding onto me with a vise-like, practically unbreakable grip; clearly they were loath to use force (on *him* at least).

"You bastards," he was sobbing, "How dare you! I'll have the lot of you executed for this—I command you to unhand us this instant!" he gulped. "Please let us go—I'm begging you— don't you see how much I *need* her—I'll never forget this! You just better hope I never inherit the Sceptre!"

His ravings, it seemed, were having some marginal effect, after all. Several of the operatives exchanged nervous glances, and one of them actually let go of me and knelt down on the pavement. I wished the paparazzi would start taking pictures, letting me go out in a blaze of glory at least. Then I remembered: photographs constitute a 'graven image' to the Faithful. There could be no camera-play against such a backdrop as all the Dark People of the East End: ominous, unmoving, unwinking (like a Graven Image, themselves).

"Sylvia," my Beloved continued to moan.

"I'll be in some place of detention," I sniveled (surprising myself). "You can find me, Marc! Please find me! Please don't let me rot there for the rest of—oh, no—please," I screamed.

They were prying him loose from me, claw by claw, as gently as they could, but irresistibly, without the slightest hint of compassion.

"You bastards," he sobbed (almost as if he couldn't believe this was happening).

They were down to the last claw. All that connected us was one trembling, hooked claw. As it came loose he stubbornly dug the others back in.

My first reaction was more of panic than relief—would this agony of humiliation, of being physically subdued in public, never come to an end? I felt like a traitor for even thinking it. In expiation I wetted my lips and shouted, "Good for you, Marc! Hang on! For Bastsake hang on!"

But the 'bastards' as he insisted on calling them were getting impatient; it was time to bring out the heavy artillery. We both yowled, our fur zapping out in every direction as some sort of rod charged with electricity came between—and bisected—us.

For an instant there was nothing in the universe but white light, and pain. The first thing I became concretely aware of was the fact that I was being handcuffed—and none too gently. A big lug lifted me by the scruff of my neck. Marc was still fighting and twisting and biting. They had to threaten him with the stun gun, singeing and zapping his whiskers. I saw the fight go out of him; he suddenly just gave up, and his body went limp (like a jar of milk smashing on the pavement, its white liquid spreading in every direction). Several retainers bearing the Imperial coat of arms hurried forward, solicitously swathing him in an ermine-trimmed cloak. At the same time a Rolls Royce with tinted glass, its engine purring, sidled over to where they were guarding him.

Meanwhile to my surprise (I'd expected a Black Maria) they hustled me into an idling van of sorts (it looked like a four-wheel-drive Land-Rover). As they radioed ahead, obstreperously

279

announcing my capture, the motorcycles like a screaming swarm of hornets took off after the accelerating Rolls Royce, which, flanked fore and aft by armoured cars, had vainly tried to give them the slip and was now making for a warren of dimly lit side-streets. I could've told them they were wasting their time—already their hornet-like pursuers were hemming them in, getting ahead of them, driving them the way a pack of rabid scavengers drives a gigantic—but terrified—bullock.

My own situation was far less dramatic. It looked like not a single one of the paparazzi had stayed behind to photograph or witness my own particular martyrdom. Just as well, perhaps. The tawdry scene of a scared young Cat chucked into the back of a van that'd seen better days—what excitement or 'glamour' could be got from something like *that*?

"Try to stop crying," a decent-enough-looking Saint-Bernard wearing officer's shoulder-boards leaned across and barked in an undertone, "You'll not be mistreated, dear. Now try to calm down."

I hadn't realised that I was crying.

"We've notified a Juvenile caseworker—she can contact your family."

"That's a laugh," I tried to sneer—and started crying all over again.

"You'll feel better once you've had a nice cup of tea."

"Listen to this," one of his underlings shouted: "Headquarters."

A radio was shoved in his face. He swung the door shut. It slammed with a muffled thump slightly rocking the vehicle. The big lug didn't know his own strength. The radio glued to his ear, he was barking orders right and left. His squad were piling into the jeeps and vans, revving them up, their revolving blue lights winking hypnotically. Wheezing from the exertion he scrambled up onto the running board, and slid in beside me. We idled for a moment before shifting gears and lurching forward through the wet London night.

"What're they going to do with me?"

I wondered if I were still crying; I couldn't tell from my voice.

"I already said none of my lads—"

"I don't mean *you*," I tried to breathe slowly, to keep from hyperventilating, "I mean—you know—*His* Family…"

"That's the question, isn't it?"

His jowls were almost as flabby as those of a Bulldog.

"*I* didn't try to seduce *him*," I somehow sounded like a pathological liar. "It was," I swallowed, "the whole thing was such a mess—it wasn't *his* fault—I'm not trying to assign blame—it was nobody's fault."

"Something tells me *They're* not going to see it like that."

"I know." (My voice betrayed me with a vengeance; I was definitely crying.) "So what do you think They'll do—to someone like *me*?"

"Oh, probably lop that pretty little head off, for a start. Spike it on London Bridge for the crows and ravens—hey!"

He turned to face me.

"It was just a joke, Love. Here I was trying to be of comfort, and just making things worse."

"No, please. I need someone to talk with," I gulped, "Or I think I'll go mad."

"There, there," he patted me, "Intelligent young girl like y'self… Your whole life…"

His kindly face became thoughtful.

"My whole life ahead of me—that's what you were going to say, or something very much like it," I gazed down at my furry wrists (which were handcuffed), "Except that it's been irredeemably poisoned. Stunted. And not by this. This is just the outward expression of the intrinsic decay, deep inside."

"I'm too uneducated—stupid, really—to follow what you just said."

"No you're not. It's just sham and tinsel. Window-dressing."

"Don't keep pickin' yerself to pieces that way," he frowned. "Plenty of others around to do that."

"I know. But I can't help it."

"If you don't mind my asking, dear—"

"Ask me anything. The more questions—"

"Why'd ya do it?"

I gulped (in slow motion).

"You mean, agree to the rendez-vous? You did know, I hope, that this whole thing was *his* idea—still," I gulped, "as my father likes to say: It takes two to tango…"

"He's *Royalty*!" the Dog woofed. "As far above you as you are above me."

"Now you're picking yourself to pieces," I manufactured a smile. "None of us is better than anyone else. Snoopus taught me that."

I should've stopped. I could see that he didn't like what I was saying.

"I did it because he's desperately unhappy, and lonely. I felt sorry for him. And that's the truth. Or part of the truth. There's more which I *have* to confess: because he's goodlooking, because, as the tabloids like to phrase it, he *turns me on*—"

"Shut up," he almost clamped his big rubbery pawpads across my small, trembling mouth. "Don't ya know this car could be bugged?"

"Well then in that case you haven't exactly been the model of discretion, yourself."

"I talk too much."

"So do I."

"Let's both shut the hell up."

He hunched his bulk towards the window.

Instantly a mixture of panic and despair caused me to start crying again.

"Don't, please?" he twisted uncomfortably. "This'll sound strange, but you remind me of Alice."

"Alice," I held onto the name for dear life.

"She'll turn seven, Thursday after next."

"You must be getting her lots of nice presents."

Isn't that the kind of small talk you're supposed to make, when confronted with a doting parent? I of course wouldn't know, never having had any, myself.

"Not as many as I'd like, on *my* salary."

His eyes became moist. I could tell because they began reflecting the passing streetlamps.

"My precious, beautiful Angel."

His voice was almost painful in its doglike nakedness.

"Course, *you* were someone's precious, beautiful Angel."

It was on the tip of my tongue to say something sarcastic—he obviously didn't know anything about my 'loving' family—but suddenly I imagined Goody Thorpe sitting there in his place, trying not to cry, staring out the window to keep me from seeing her face.

I couldn't bear to think of her reading the tabloids first thing to-morrow morning.

"I keep thinking," he mumbled almost under his breath, "What if she decides to flush *her* life down the toilet?"

"The way I have, you mean."

"Shite!" he ejaculated as the car suddenly swerved, to the screech of brakes, "They followed us after all. Gather your things and be ready to *move*—"

"I'm in manacles," I reminded him, "And all my 'things' including most of my clothes are still presumably—"

"You can lean on me, going in—here, lean forward— we'll put this round your shoulders—"

"What about my things?" I obstinately demanded like the insufferable little brat that I was. The thought, however trivial, gave me something to which I could cling.

We screeched to a halt opposite a sort of command-post or bunker. It was a low, squat building of reinforced steel and concrete, with a jutting roof or balcony that gave its physiognomy a brooding, sinister aspect.

"Now. Let's go."

The cardoor was flung open. I heard motorcycles screeching up behind us, to the inevitable serenade of catcalls and taunts.

"They came after all, they came for *me*, they came, after all," I heard myself yammering in a sort of singsong ecstasy.

"Shut up. Great Anubis, this is a fine kettle of fish."

"You can't escape the paparazzi," I tonelessly gibbered with all the syllables strung, or mashed, together, "They inform all our yesterdays and all our to-morrows, giving substance to the emptiness of our petty routines, manipulating us but at the same time uplifting us—even me—even such a squashable insect as their lenses and cameras can turn *anyone* into—even Delilah (it'll happen someday)—reducing, distorting our Bast-given individuality to the lowest common denominator—"

"I said, shut up," he was barking for all he was worth, "They'll hear you—"

"I want them to hear me."

"I'll slap this industrial-strength tape across that prating little smart mouth of yours—"

"Do it," something possessed me to bait him.

"Please don't make me—"

"Alright then. I can afford to be gracious."

He lifted me bodily down to the ground, supporting me with an unexpected tenderness as, buffeted by the melee of cameras and shouted questions, I teetered precariously (kept from crumpling only by my faithful protector), as scuffles broke out all around us and the Vermin surged forward closing in on us from all sides.

The sheer concentrated intensity of the flashbulbs going off momentarily blinded my guards. Several snarling animals collided against us and we all went down in a nightmare of snapping teeth, slashing claws.

I think I must have blacked out for a moment.

The next thing I knew, someone was lifting me up off the pavement and wrapping a blanket round my aching shoulders. Who else but my big lug of a Saint-Bernard could've exhibited that kind of rock-solid kindness? Not that I deserved it—the only thing in the world I cared about at that instant was the fact that for once *I* appeared to be the bloody centre of all the bloody attention. It felt…even now I don't quite know how it felt. The rapid-fire click of Nikons and instamatics going off all over the place—the solid 'wall' of lenses—of flashbulbs exploding like crazy—made me wonder if this was what a sexual climax felt like? I think I'd almost had one in the car with Marc—I'd never felt so peaceful or satisfied afterwards, but this—I was quaking, sagging, swaying on my feet like a speed-freak—this was even better—was the best of all possible feelings.

POSTSCRIPT——

"Exercise interval," the Doberman barked.

"But it's almost time for my poke," I tried to keep my voice steady. "Besides, I already took my walk round the courtyard—"

"Stand up, toes against the wall," he barked. "Eyes straight ahead. Any wrong moves and you get a stun-gun, mixed with plenty of pepper spray, right in the face."

I'd never seen this particular turnkey before. Something about him gave me the creeps. When he pulled a black hood down over my face, and drew the string so tight I could barely breathe, my heart began hammering.

"If you make a sound, or move, we'll ram this fucking taser where the sun doesn't shine—you dig, Pussycat?"

Coarse laughter receded. A door must've opened from behind me (I intuited the sensation of air being displaced). Someone was creeping towards me. The word *Lobotomy* kept trying to coalesce—I was fighting it, trying not to make a sound, trembling as I tried not to move.

"That *can't* be Sylvia—"

My eyes flew open from inside the hood.

"I could've used duct tape instead of the hood," the Doberman condescendingly barked.

"*Get the FUCK out of this room*," my sister screamed in that ringing, demonic voice I remembered so well.

"Five minutes—I've just clicked down on the stopwatch…"

I must be dreaming, I reasoned—*they've already given me my bloody poke for the night. I'll have to ask what they shot me with (so I can avoid it next time).*

"Sylvia," she yanked off the hood and began shaking me till my teeth rattled, "Snap out of it"—she gently slapped me—

"Stop it," I sniveled, but the act of physically *speaking* had somehow flipped a cognitive switch: this wasn't a dream, it really *was* Annie—

"What have they done to you," she broke down, to my amazement, and began softly crying.

"I think that hood was suffocating me."

"I promised I wasn't gonna do this," she clenched and retracted, her claws. "We don't have much time—"

"So what the Hell are you doing in a quote-unquote state facility for the incarceration of the criminally insane—"

"Shut up and listen—I bribed the Commandant—we only have five minutes—"

"They won't let me read the newspapers, not even the tabloids—"

"You haven't had any visitors because they're holding you in the Isolation wing as a political prisoner—"

"Has Marcus tried to visit me?"

My lip began quivering.

"I don't have time to put things gently, so listen to this for your own good—"

"He hasn't even left the goddam Winter Palace, right?" I could feel tears welling up in my eyes. "Well? Has he? Has he even made the slightest fucking effort to see me?"

"He's in Sorrento, at one of the secret summer retreats the Emperor keeps there, along with *Delilah*," I shuddered (her voice had become so corrosive), "and that pretty little fiancé of hers—"

"Marc's a Hell of a lot handsomer than Diocletian—"

"Oh for fuck's sake—come off it," she stomped the floor, "We don't have time for this—look, Sylvia," she slipped a slender but wiry arm round my slouching shoulders, bringing her velvety black cheek against the anemic-looking white fur of my own, "I know Marcus turned your head; he probably would've turned my head—I guess I was even a little bit jealous—I couldn't believe someone that *Goodlooking*—"

"I know," I forced a lopsided smile, "But it happened. That's the amazing part. It actually happened."

"A fat lot of good that does *you*," she exploded, "Bang'd up in this fucking shithole—listen, forget about Marc—he's not worth it—he never was—take it from a slut who knows all about boys—"

"I *refuse* to forget," I pulled away from her, baring my incisors the way Big Cats flash their fangs, "But I know it's over—maybe he was just toying with me; maybe he really *did* try, in his own pathetic little way, to make things work out—he isn't strong enough: to defy the Royal Family, to go against the grain, to think for himself—I'm sure he'll take some Grand Duchess to wife and forget all about me—but I *won't forget* about him," I flashed what felt like a glinting crazy-edged smile, "The whole world saw what happened—every Network must have devoted—"

"But Sylvia," she uncharacteristically gulped (and something about that little gulp of hers, so unexpected, so out of place, bothered me to the extent that I actually caught myself reflexively gulping, myself), "There was no coverage—I'm sorry—it must have been too explosive—the government Censors—"

"That's a lie," I whispered, "You're just jealous—"

"Do you want me to waste precious seconds and run down to the staff lounge to bring you back a fucking fistful of tabloids?"

Everything felt surpisingly razour-sharp and in focus. Even my heart was no longer painfully knocking against the cage of my sternum.

"How could hundreds and hundreds of swarming photographers—all of them taking pictures, shooting Super-8 footage and rolling videotapes—microphones, Annie—fucking *microphones*…" my voice had dried up.

"The Emperor must have sent out a secret Decree," she soothed. "It happens. It happened when Cleopatra got poisoned, when Alexis—your Marcus' dad—was assassinated—some things are simply too hot to handle, too explosive to let out of the bag."

"You're saying there wasn't a single *headline*?" I whispered, "A single *feature* in one of the *Columns*?"

"I'm sorry," she tried to squeeze my shoulder but quick as greased lightning I wrenched free.

"So how's Philip?" I tried to sound jaunty, "He'd probably like this stuff they're shooting me with."

"We don't have time—"

"How much did you have to pay the Commandant for this clandestine—"

"Enough that this is the only one—I can't afford any more."

"Dad must've hit the ceiling, having to cough up that kind of bread."

"*Ferdinand* didn't pay for this," her voice sharpened, making me flinch. "Your poor little friend Tosk gave me his life's savings—he's totally cleaned out—he had permission to come here himself; I tried to get him to come along with me—"

"Time's up," the Doberman barked barging into the room.

"No, please," she begged him, "Sylvia, listen—I've got a solicitor—we're fighting to get you a Court hearing—it was a goddam Sealed Letter—that bastard Nero signed it, but I know Delilah's behind him—we can beat this thing—you've got to keep fighting and not go under—let go of me!" she screamed as a crew of odious little sidekicks and henchmen began dragging her towards the exit, "We can help each other," she sobbed knocking them down like ninepins, right and left—paralysed, I could only stand there, taking it in.

"I'm so sorry for everything," she tearfully bellowed.

With a buzzing sound and a flicker of blue light, a stun-gun zapped her—her fur stood up in every direction, and she slumped forward—I was trying not to throw up—before they dragged her half-prostrate form out the door, she revived enough to mew the words which zapped me like a different kind of stun-gun: "I love you Sylvia—remember, I love you—I promise—"

Another zipzapping sledgehammer of fucking blue-white electricity filled my nostrils with the hideous stench of singed fur. The last thing I did before the door slammed shut and electronically locked was to scream, "*I love you Annie come back*," as loud as I could.

*   *   *   *   *   *   *

Did it really happen, or was it just another of those loopy hallucinations the Magic Pills they shove down your throat in this place all too often have the tendency to make you believe, till you stop believing in anything?

I've created so many different guises for myself: Mummy's favourite, Bookworm, Introvert, Flash-in-the-Pan— could it be that what was underneath all the masks actually amounted to something, possessed a kernel of substance?

It really doesn't make any difference. Either way my task is the same: I'm going to strike out on my own across the landscape known as survival. Or, quite simply, die trying.